The Smell of Rain

By the Author

By the Dark of Her Eyes

The Smell of Rain

The Smell of Rain

by

Cameron MacElvee

2018

THE SMELL OF RAIN

ISBN 13: 978-1-63555-166-2

This Trade Paperback Original Is Published By
Bold Strokes Books, Inc.
P.O. Box 249
Valley Falls, NY 12185

First Edition: May 2018

Credits
Editor: Ruth Sternglantz
Production Design: Stacia Seaman
Cover Design by Melody Pond

Acknowledgments

My thanks to Bold Strokes Books and Len Barot for giving me a place to tell my stories and reach a wider audience. I also owe a huge amount of gratitude to Sandy Lowe for believing in this story and supporting me in my quest to see it in print. Further, this novel wouldn't have come to fruition without the guidance and counsel of my editor, Ruth Sternglantz. Thanks, Ruth, for once again guiding me through the potholes and plot holes.

I was blessed to have a number of consultants on this book, and each of them contributed to this story in important and significant ways. To each of you I owe a debt too enormous to ever pay back: to Major Stacy Miller, USAF (Ret.) for providing me insight into military life and the battles our returning veterans face daily; to Dr. Lori Deibler and the staff at USA Physical Therapy for helping me understand the struggles of amputees; to Dr. Karla Hauersperger for expanding my understanding of the medical issues many of our service men and women face; to Professor Stavroula Popovich for patiently giving me encouragement and insight into the lives of Greek Americans and the power of the Yiayia; to my former student Cassandra Safis, who inspired me as a teacher and writer; to Dr. Nalan Babür, who long ago told me tales of Turkish life and encouraged me to see beyond the labels of race and religion; to the journalist Ama Tierney, who first opened my eyes to the bravery of Kurdish women and their continued commitment to the lives of women everywhere; to Professor John Liffiton, Director of the Genocide Conference at Scottsdale Community College, who tirelessly works to bring awareness of the Armenian Genocide along with the many other atrocities man has committed; and to Dr. Rhonda McDonnell for aiding me in uncluttering my prose, adding beauty to my static phrases, and pointing out the necessity of the story's message.

I was fortunate to have the loyal readership as well as friendship of a number of individuals who have not only helped me reason through my story but who have also served as my own cheerleading squad. Thanks to Nadine Ausbie for that last-minute grammar check and our long discussions about the state of the world; to Deanna Banks and

Barbara Christman for reading my drafts and encouraging me to stick with it when I was ready to give up; and to Jacky Abromitis and all the readers at LesFan who were willing to read the first sketchy draft of the story and give me feedback.

In addition, I am once again deeply grateful to Lodeerca, who often encouraged me with a bit of music, a taste of literature, a touch of art, or simply a dash of her wisdom and wit, which got me through a number of long, dark nights of self-doubt and despair.

And finally, without my partner, Taime, and our daughter, Eleanor Rose, my will to write and complete this story would not have been realized. The two of you have saved me from my nihilistic tendencies and encourage me to smell the flowers and dance in the rain. For this, you have my heart and my love.

For Dora, who continues to hope when all is hopeless

Chapter One

London, England

Wiring a bomb to the ignition was labor intensive. And, since he had no way of knowing when she'd return to her vehicle, he opted instead for a tilt fuse with mercury. He looked around the parking structure, waited until a car passed before he placed the device on the undercarriage beneath the driver's seat. The intel he'd received indicated his target employed a driver who also functioned as her personal secretary and interpreter. That one would die instantly, probably not feel a thing. But he'd been sure to equip his device with the smallest amount of explosives he could manage. This way his target would be incapacitated by the blast and burn slowly. That fact would bring his employers a great deal of joy.

He pulled out his phone and took a selfie with the doomed vehicle behind him. He sent the image with a message, then looked around once more as he scratched at his neck beard and laughed. By the time he landed in Dammam, a celebration would be waiting for him, and another apostate would be in hell.

❖

The loosely draped scarf covering her head accented her tunic and brought out the gold highlights of her mahogany hair. The men around the table watched her, mesmerized by her beauty, by her voice rising and falling like a cello solo. For the last two hours in Lord Hadron's parliamentary office, hers was the voice saturating the air, dominating the men's. She'd captivated each of them, three members of parliament and two members of Britain's military intelligence. When the meeting concluded, she stood and took each man's hand, then motioned for her personal secretary to come along.

"Mrs. Arslan," Hadron said leading her to the door, "dear lady, your courage shines as brightly, if not more so than your late husband's."

Reyha Arslan inclined her head. "You honor me with your words, Lord Hadron." Her perceptive eyes rested on the others, who were apparently envious of Hadron that he should be the one to escort her from the office. "Gentlemen, I assure you, I will not rest until Emin's goals are realized. His legacy is now mine." She took her leave, turning toward the hallway with her secretary following alongside.

Hadron caught up with her. "Let me walk with you." He glanced at her profile, which was partly obscured by her head covering. "May I say, you're looking quite well. I'm happy to hear doctors are optimistic. Indeed, America's Mayo Clinic has a remarkable reputation. It was good of your doctors to make those arrangements."

Reyha paused at the exit and watched the rain. Not looking at Hadron, she said, "Doctors are always optimistic." She turned to her secretary. "Ophelia, have you our umbrella?"

Ophelia pulled one from her bag. "Yes, but please, I know your hip has been giving you trouble. Allow me to bring the car around."

"I can send a boy," Hadron said.

"No need," Reyha said. Then to Ophelia, "I'm feeling much better today. I would not have you drenched bringing it around."

"No trouble at all, ma'am." Ophelia pushed past Reyha and Hadron. "It's just there at Abingdon."

"Let me accompany you partway," Hadron said, having retrieved his umbrella from his assistant.

They exited and walked along St. Margaret Street with him holding the umbrella and helping her step around puddles.

Reyha held out her hand to the rain. "I have never gotten used to your country's weather even after all these years in exile from my beautiful Konya plains and my busy markets of Istanbul." She watched Ophelia dodge ahead.

"It's a loss for Turkey, but a gain for the United Kingdom."

They paused on the corner of Abingdon and Great College just as Ophelia made her descent into the parking structure.

"I hope my work will be a gain for many countries, Lord Hadron, including my own." She stepped from under the cover of the umbrella. "See here, the rain has stopped and I am just meters from my automobile." She smiled. "And you are being so gallant to walk with me."

"I don't object to your company. I think you know that."

She laughed, knowing men desired her, yet she had no intention of being possessed by any man ever again. However, her amusement vanished when a blast punctured the wet air and rattled the ground. A plume of black smoke billowed from the parking structure's entrance, and car alarms screamed in discord. People began running, yelling, pointing.

"Ophelia!" Reyha ran toward the entrance.

"No, Reyha, you mustn't." Hadron attempted to catch her arm.

But she broke away and pushed against the horde of people scrambling out of the garage. She collided with many of them, and her head covering fell to her shoulders. She pulled its end to her mouth and coughed with each breath of toxic smoke as she lurched forward with twisted steps.

"Ophelia!" she cried out again.

As debris from the damaged structure began to settle and the smoke wafted in waves toward the open air, she caught a glimpse of flames and struggled toward it. By now the sirens of first responders mixed with the mayhem of car alarms. A man barked at her to get out. She ignored him and took a few steps more. She halted when she recognized her car's number plate, blackened and twisted, dangling from the vehicle's remains. She dropped to her knees and screamed, twisting her mouth with each desperate plea.

Hadron reached her and fell next to her. He tried to bring her into an embrace, but she would not have him touch her. She pushed away and collapsed prostrate to the ground, shrieking and pulling her hair.

"It was meant for me! For me!"

Emergency personnel clustered around them. Security pulled Hadron to his feet and assisted Reyha to hers, but she continued to push them away while tearing at her hair and cursing at them in Turkish, crying out Ophelia's name. Finally, a female officer approached her, put a blanket around her, and began leading her away.

"She should not have died." Reyha staggered as she took limping steps. "She was my friend. My dear and faithful friend."

The officer nodded as she led her from the destruction, back out onto the streets where emergency vehicles waited, and the sky released another surge of rain.

CHAPTER TWO

Washington, DC

The steady hiss of hot water, almost too hot for comfort, drenched Chrys's downturned head while her dark hair formed a curtain over her eyes. She held her face in both hands and wept.

"We do not break, Chrysanthi," her grandmother said as she placed the phyllo dough in a baking pan. "We rise. We always rise. It is in our blood, our character."

Chrys sobbed harder. "I can't, Yiayia. There's nothing left."

She teetered on the shower stool when her right foot slipped, and her grandmother's image dissolved. She was left with the sight of her severed leg below the left knee where the mottled skin glowed pink. She covered the stump with her washcloth and closed her eyes. The trace aroma of her grandmother's avgolemono simmering on the stove careened her into another memory, one nearly as calming—the beauty of the desert, the smell of black tea and honey, and the whiff of flatbread cooking in a cast-iron skillet. But there was one scent she longed for the most, the smell of rain as it fell to earth, a rich fragrance tinged with the scents of damp reed grasses and fir trees.

The bathroom door opened, and her crutches clattered to the floor. She jerked with memories of exploding earth and red smoke carrying with it the stench of burning flesh.

"Mary?" Chrys gripped her chest.

"Sorry," Mary said. She pulled back the shower curtain. "Are you okay?"

"Why wouldn't I be?"

Mary's eyes dropped to Chrys's hand on the washcloth before she looked away and pulled the curtain shut. "I've been home almost thirty minutes. I was getting worried—you've been in here a long time."

"I like long showers." But she knew what Mary feared.

"Right." Mary's shape bent to retrieve the crutches. "PT go okay?"

"Yes."

"It won't be long until they fit you for the definitive prosthesis."

"Not long."

"Sorry I bothered you." Mary stepped out and shut the door.

Chrys slapped off the faucet and leaned against the tile wall. After clearing away her anger at the interruption, she began the process of getting out of the shower. With care, she held the safety bar the apartment manager had agreed to have installed and pulled herself out. She cursed when she saw Mary had set her crutches out of reach. Now she had no choice but to lean against the wall and hop toward them. Once she reached them, she snatched a towel and covered herself. Thankfully, the hot shower had steamed up the bathroom mirror, and she was spared the sight of her body. Within minutes, she'd dried and wrapped the towel around her hips and dropped it low enough to shield the remains of her left leg. She opened the bathroom door. Mary wasn't in the bedroom. She lurched with her crutches to the side of the bed where she'd left her prosthesis hidden beneath sweatpants and a T-shirt. She cringed as she pulled on her underwear, then slipped on her shirt before looking back at the bedroom door. Then she set to work on getting her leg attached.

She dried the scar tissue again. Moisture was her enemy, hot spots and pressure ulcers a constant threat. Once she was sure the skin was dry, she pulled on a fresh protective sock, and over that, the nylon sheath. With the discolored skin covered, she relaxed and took more time securing her limb in place. It was only the preparatory prosthesis, one designed to fit the knob of her leg where doctors had removed the shattered bone and burnt flesh. It'd been refitted a few times as the swelling had receded, and now that she'd become adjusted to walking with it, in another week or two, she'd be fitted for her definitive unit consisting of a more elaborate socket, shank, and foot. And if she was lucky, one of those nonprofits might fund her running blade.

To run again, that was something to work toward.

She fell back on the bed and imagined the ground beneath her, falling away with each rhythmic slap of her feet. Those Nebraska back roads where she'd trained in high school, all those meets with the cute girls in running shorts. Even on deployment, she'd found a way to run. That'd been her only addiction. The one thing to keep her centered and whole.

She shot up when Mary knocked on the door and entered. "You got off early," she said as she fluffed her hair, already turning to loose curls as it dried.

Mary sat on the corner of the bed. She hadn't changed out of her scrubs, but she'd let her red hair out of its ponytail. "I texted you all morning, but you didn't answer."

"Sorry. I think my battery's dead." Chrys snatched her phone from the nightstand. "Forgot to charge it last night—it died this morning."

"Long wait?"

"Only three hours today. Maybe the new admin is getting things turned around." Chrys checked her phone, then glanced at Mary, who stared at the meds and empty beer bottles cluttered on the nightstand. "Anyway, I didn't mean to worry you." She bent down to plug in her charger, but her unsteady hands made it difficult. She gave up and sat back on the bed with her fists under her butt. The narcotic was wearing off, and her body cried out with anticipation of the pain prowling beneath the surface of her skin.

"I got two days off," Mary said.

"That's nice."

"Michelle and Kathy asked if we wanted to come over Saturday. They're having a Memorial Day barbecue. I'll be on call, but it'd be nice if we could spend a few hours with them. They've been asking about you."

"Not up for it."

Mary's eyes focused on the nightstand once more.

Chrys followed her gaze. "Maybe we can go to dinner or something. Catch a show instead."

"I wish you wouldn't drink on those meds."

Chrys flared her nostrils, hardened her mouth.

"You're not going to get any better if you—"

"Stop." Chrys fell back on the bed again. "Just stop." Staring up at the ceiling fan, she tried to follow one blade. Around and around and… When Mary touched her arm, she sat up and pulled away. "I saw my squadron commander today after therapy."

"About?"

Chrys snatched an envelope from the nightstand, which caused some of the prescription bottles to topple.

"What's that?" Mary asked.

"A response to my petition." Chrys set the envelope on the bed. "The Physical Evaluation Board turned me down. I'm done."

Mary drew a deep breath through her nose. "I know you're disappointed."

"*Disappointed* isn't the word for it."

"You gave your country ten years of your life." Mary laid her hand on Chrys's leg. "You served honorably. You have no reason to be ashamed."

Chrys examined Mary's hand. It was inches from where the socket met the remains of her knee joint. She lifted the hand and set it aside. "I'm not ashamed. I'm pissed off." She planted her feet and pushed off the bed. "My leg doesn't affect my ability to interpret and translate. I can still carry a weapon and fight. I'm still useful."

She returned to the bathroom and pulled a comb through her hair, all the while being careful not to rake the teeth over the sensitive spot where Army doctors had pulled out shrapnel and stitched a gash. After seven months, most of her hair had grown back from being shaved to the skin. But that one spot still resisted, and the scar, like a fat pink worm, was still visible even if she tried to make her curls cover it.

Mary came up behind her and leaned on the bathroom door.

Chrys made eye contact with her reflection. "I was supposed to pin on captain."

"I know."

"And how many military interpreters speak fluent Turkish, Kurdish, Armenian, and two dialects of Arabic as well as I do? Not to mention Farsi, Greek, and a smattering of Russian." She threw her towel to the floor. "You know what he suggested I do?"

Mary shrugged.

"He said I should apply to the DLI in Monterey as a civilian instructor. Said I could train the next generation of interpreters. Said my experience and aptitude made me a valuable asset to my country. Yeah, right."

"That's not a bad gig, is it?" Mary asked. "The West Coast is beautiful, and I'm sure my mom would love it if we moved to that side of the country."

"But it isn't the work I was doing." Chrys retrieved her towel and hung it up, taking her time to make the corners even and the edges smooth. "There's so much more that needs to be done." She studied the perfect crease in her towel. "For every woman we freed, two more were taken captive and hundreds more suffered. They're still suffering. It just never ends."

She turned toward the mirror and examined her reflection. There was a time she considered her smoldering black eyes and boyish youthfulness attractive. She could charm anyone, male or female. Yet now her eyes were always bloodshot, her youthfulness replaced by hardness, and she doubted anyone, Mary included, found her appealing, not with this mutilated body. She touched the left side of her face. It still showed signs of swelling, and the scars from the lacerations along her chin and forehead pulsed red. She touched an older scar cut into her right eyebrow. It had faded over the years and now glowed white against her dark complexion.

"Fell right on my damn face," she muttered. "Didn't even have time to catch myself."

"Catch yourself?" Mary cocked her head.

But Chrys didn't respond. Instead the sounds of others running and panting flooded around her. She passed a runner from an opposing team, a girl she liked. She turned to smile back at her, and her feet slipped on the wet gravel. Down she went face-first. Commotion gathered about her, parents rushed to her aid, but she pushed them away and sprinted ahead, determined to place in the top three. She came in second and laughed at the spectators who gasped at the blood gushing down her face and school jersey.

"So much blood for such a tiny cut," she said, gazing at the dissolving images playing out in the mirror.

Mary stepped closer. "I know, but the scars will fade."

"I meant this one." Chrys pointed to her eyebrow and smiled, causing dimples to blossom in her cheeks. "Did I ever tell you when I went to the hospital to get this stitched up how Yiayia got so worked up with worry that when they wheeled me out into the waiting room she started cursing at me in Greek and swatting me with her purse? You should've seen the looks on the nurses' faces."

"You've told me that story."

Chrys traced one of the new scars along her chin. "Imagine what she'd think of me now."

"She'd be proud of you." Mary touched her shoulder. "Just like I am."

Chrys stepped away. "Yes, Monterey's nice. Hell of a lot cooler than DC, I guess."

"If that'll make you happy."

"I didn't say it would make me happy. I said that's what he suggested."

Mary bowed her head. "I'm only trying to support whatever decision you make. It shouldn't be hard for me to get a position there. Trauma nurses are always in demand." She turned to leave.

"You can stay in DC. I know how much you like the people at George Washington."

Mary paused. "What I want is to be with you."

"But I don't expect you to give up a job you love and follow me to the other side of the country. It wouldn't be fair."

Mary spun around. "What is wrong with you?"

"Sorry." Chrys looked away.

"Do you even love me anymore?"

Chrys rubbed her face. "Of course I do. It's just…I don't know. I'm sorry." She forced herself to pull Mary close, but every point on her body making contact screamed with pain.

Mary leaned in. "I miss you."

"But I'm right here."

"No, I want the old you back, the loud and silly you. The obnoxious shithead who yells at waiters for messing up her order, the sweet woman who always gives up her seat on the Metro, the one who makes me laugh at stupid stuff."

"You really want that woman back? She sounds like a handful."

"I do, and I want your joy back, your smile, your confidence."

"I seem to recall you accusing me once of being overly confident. Arrogant, I think you called me." Chrys forced a comical expression. The diversion didn't work.

"Even after Mosul you came back smiling. When you buried your father and then your grandmother, you grieved for a month and got right back up. But this time"—Mary touched Chrys's face—"this time I feel like I'm losing you."

"Let's go get some dinner," Chrys said, pulling away.

"I need you to talk to me."

But she wouldn't burden Mary, couldn't let her see the truth. "I haven't eaten since this morning. I'm starved."

"Please, I need you to—"

"How about Zenobia's? Come on, I know you like their food."

Mary frowned. "I'd rather have a plain old American cheeseburger and fries."

"Why, Nurse Grady, that shit'll give you a heart attack." Chrys managed a weak giggle, but it did little to ease the tension. "Burgers and fries it is. Come on, let's spring for an Uber. I can't handle the Metro this time of night. Too many people."

At the bedroom door, Mary pulled her to a stop. "I was wondering, if I sleep on your right side, can I stay with you in our bed tonight?"

Chrys studied the tips of her running shoes. Her left toe was turned out. She readjusted it.

"Please?" Mary asked.

"I don't know."

Mary patted her arm. "It's okay. I'm sorry I asked." She left the bedroom and from the hallway called back, "You know, I'm not that hungry after all. Go ahead and order in a pizza if you want. I think I'll turn in early." She disappeared behind the door of the second bedroom where she'd been sleeping for the last six months.

Chrys wanted to run after her, to beg her to understand, but it would do no good. Instead she returned to her bedroom and dosed her pain before grabbing a cold beer from the refrigerator. She drank it in front of the television with news reports of suicide bombers, school shootings, and missing children. There wasn't one damn place in the whole world free of terror. Not one. And by her fifth beer, the television was nothing but background noise as she descended into darkness and passed out on the sofa.

That's where she woke up the next afternoon.

CHAPTER THREE

The meeting room stank of disinfectant and burnt coffee, and the overhead lights blinked sporadically—the fluorescent kind that hummed at a frequency only a few unfortunate souls could hear. Chrys was one such soul. She slouched forward with her elbows on her thighs and her head supported in her hands. The hum of the lights, the smell of the room, and the uncomfortable metal chairs made these sessions difficult.

Dr. Woodley took notes and congratulated each participant for his or her progress that week. Chrys wasn't sure what progress actually looked like. None of them were ever going to grow limbs back or walk again.

"It's like this," said Ramos, a former Marine who'd lost his left hand and right arm up to the shoulder, "a man shouldn't have to ask his lady to hold his pecker to take a leak. But what the fuck can I do? I'm afraid I'll lop it off with these bitches." He held up his prosthetic hooks.

"At least you still got your pecker," said another man, Dworsky, a former Marine as well.

"You still got your dick, Dworsky," Ramos said. "You just don't feel it. Poor bastard. At least my lady can give me one hell of a blow—"

"Yo, Ramos," interrupted former Army Specialist Torres. He was missing both legs above the knees. "We got women in the room. No one wants to hear about your lady sucking you off."

The men in the room, sans Ramos, gave Chrys and the other woman, Morrison, apologetic looks. Ramos sneered.

Former Petty Officer Cherae Morrison, who'd lost her arm just below the right elbow, glanced at Chrys. They had an unspoken bond between them, and this wasn't the first time Ramos had gone off about his penis and his girlfriend's ability to get him off.

Woodley cleared his throat. "Torres is correct. This isn't the place to discuss your intimate affairs, Ramos."

Horrigan, a former Air Force pilot and now a quadriplegic, said, "You did tell us, Dr. Woodley, the purpose of this group is to allow us to speak about those things we can't discuss with our families and friends. If Ramos is having a hard time with sex, I think we should talk about it."

"But there's a way to discuss these matters without debasing ourselves." Woodley glanced at Chrys and Morrison. "Or making others uncomfortable."

"Wait, wait," Ramos said, waving his hooks. "I never said I was having *difficulty* with sex. I was talking about taking a damn leak." He leered. "Besides, I'm sure you two aren't having any issues. Am I right?"

"Give it a rest, Ramos," Morrison said.

"And how are things with you, Safis?" Woodley asked Chrys. "Last week you told us you were thinking of applying to the Defense Language Institute in Monterey. Any progress with that?"

Chrys shrugged. She'd filled out the paperwork, had promised Mary she'd sent it in, but instead it lay hidden in her dresser under a stack of neatly folded T-shirts.

"Any word about funding for your running blade?" Woodley asked.

She shook her head.

"Some of us still waiting on hands." Ramos clanked his hooks together. "Least you got your fake leg. Not like you need that enhancement."

Chrys scowled. "I was a distance runner. Planned on doing an ultramarathon by thirty."

Ramos slouched in his chair. "Whatever."

Chrys turned to Woodley. "I've applied to two different nonprofits, but I know other guys need stuff, too. Lots of stuff." She glanced at Horrigan and the other men in wheelchairs. "Special chairs and vans to carry them. I'm sure there's a waiting period." She rubbed her left knee, traced along the edge of the socket. "I just need to be patient, I guess, because there's no way I'll be able to foot the bill myself."

Ramos snorted. "*Foot* the bill? Funny, Safis, real damn funny."

"Shut up already," Morrison said. "You think you're funny, but you're nothing but an overbearing asshole."

Ramos rose to his feet. "Listen, bitch."

Chrys instinctively came between them. "Go on, try me," she said in a low voice while the scars on her forehead and chin throbbed.

Woodley rushed in and held out his arms. "Settle down. No need for this. Sit down, Ramos. Safis, sit."

The group fell silent except for the angry mutterings of Ramos, who kept sneering Chrys's way. Woodley went on to the next person, but not before writing down something in his notes.

When the hour ended, Chrys hung back out of respect to those in wheelchairs. She noticed only she and Morrison ever hung back. The others, the mobile ones, always ducked out quickly as if they couldn't wait to get away from the sight of mangled bodies, as if somehow they could rid themselves of their own mutilations.

"Ramos is an ass," Morrison said.

Chrys lifted her bag to her shoulder. "Yes, he is." She started toward the door when Morrison touched her shoulder. She recoiled and turned around to apologize.

"So you think you'll get that job?" Morrison asked. "At least it's something."

"I'm not excited about being a teacher, but I guess it'll keep me from losing it."

"Losing it?"

"My language abilities."

"I thought you meant…" Morrison made a corkscrew motion about her head with her good hand.

Chrys smiled. "I'm certain I've lost it up there, too. But no, I need to speak the languages on a regular basis, or my fluency starts to drop off."

"Right, I got it." Morrison's forehead creased. "I'm still trying to find something. Tried working at a supermarket, but"—she flapped her half arm, and the sleeve flipped in the air—"bagging groceries and stocking shelves takes me longer than most."

"Something will come up." Chrys checked the time on her phone. "I was going to grab some lunch before I get in line for my med check. You wanna come along?"

Morrison hesitated.

"My treat?" Chrys said.

"Sure. Thanks."

❖

They settled in at a table at a corner diner on Fourteenth and H Streets NW. Chrys positioned her back to the wall and faced the door. "Kind of warm for soup."

Morrison held up her spoon. "It's a lot easier with one hand."

Chrys looked away. "Sorry."

She didn't know Morrison well, didn't have much in common with her as she'd served in a different branch of the military. But she was a woman, wounded, and aware of the brutality of the world. For that reason, she felt a sense of loyalty toward her.

"Can I ask you something?" Morrison said.

"Okay." Chrys pushed her sandwich away. The food tasted bland, and she really wanted a cold beer instead.

"Earlier when you said you were afraid of losing it…"

"Right, my languages." She studied the sweat beading on Morrison's forehead.

"I know." Morrison wiped her mouth. "But have you ever thought about, you know"—her face twisted—"finishing yourself?"

"Have you?"

"Maybe."

Chrys glanced around the diner. No one was close enough to hear them, but she leaned forward anyway. "You need to talk to your doctor about this."

"I don't want to be put on watch."

"Doesn't matter. It's irresponsible for you to keep those thoughts to yourself."

Morrison's mouth tightened.

"You got a kid, don't you?" Chrys asked. "A son? Think of him."

"I have."

"Shit, Morrison." She dropped her head into her hands and raked fingers through her sweat-damp hair.

"So have you?"

Chrys squeezed her eyes tight against the one memory always lurking in the background, prowling in her mind without end, with blasting shells and exploding earth, everyone scrambling for cover, leaping into truck beds, Diren holding the line, firing shot after shot while yelling for retreat, a truck bursting into flames, shit and brains and flesh spraying skyward, red smoke, the taste of blood.

She jerked when the waitress refilled their water. After the woman departed, she gazed into Morrison's tormented face and admitted her secret. "Every day. I think about it every day."

Morrison licked her lips. "Have you talked to your doctor?"

"No."

"Why not?"

"I don't have a son. I don't have a family."

"I thought you had a girlfriend. Weren't you guys getting married?"

Chrys sputtered. "It's not the same. And besides, she's…I can't…" She sank into her chair. "It's not the same."

Morrison leaned on her good elbow and cast her eyes on the table. "My mom raised my brother and me after our dad ditched us. Now she's raising my son. He's still afraid of me, won't come close to me. When she's at work, he stays in his room and plays video games. When school starts back up in the fall, it won't matter if I'm there or not."

"Stop it. You're his goddamn mother."

"And like I said, my own mother is raising him just fine. Better than I could. Plus taking care of me and all the bills. Besides, I'm never gonna find a man who'll want me, not now, not like this." She touched her wounded arm. "I'm a burden. A fucking burden to my mom and son." She scoffed and her shoulders collapsed forward. "I'm tired, too. So tired. I can't get any relief, and the drugs don't do anything. They just keep me from shitting regularly."

Chrys folded her hands in her lap and stared at her plate. Mary did the cooking and cleaning and laundry. Everything, including shouldering the added burden of worry, the constant unspoken threat. Twenty-two vets a day dead by their own hands. But worse, the desire Mary once had in her eyes had been replaced with pity. Yet even Mary's pity would turn to revulsion if she glimpsed the magnitude of the scars.

"Thing is," Morrison said, her voice shaking, "I don't want either my mom or son to live with the shame, and I want them to get my benefits when I'm gone."

"That won't happen if you kill yourself."

Morrison fiddled with her glass. "But if it looked like an accident."

Chrys winced. "Stop."

"No, listen, I've thought about it." She leaned in and lowered her voice. "I take the Metro all the time. Sometimes I stare at that warning sign, you know, the high voltage one along the track? And I think, I could step close, lean like I'm looking for a train, look at my phone, drop it just as a train pulls in, and if I time it right, the electrical shock will stop my heart before the train hits me." She shuddered. "I won't feel a thing that way."

Chrys downed the remainder of her ice water and signaled for the check before responding. "I should report this."

"But you won't."

A tour group of school children wearing matching T-shirts flooded into the restaurant, their loud voices and sweaty prepubescent bodies depleting the last of the oxygen. Chrys hurried to pull a pen from her bag, to scribble on a napkin.

"Here, take my number and promise me when you get these feelings, you'll call me. Day or night, anytime, I don't care, you call me." She pushed the napkin into Morrison's hand and closed it into a fist. "Promise, Cherae, promise me now or I'll have to say something."

"Does it matter one way or the other?"

Chrys sat back and stared past the swarming kids, out the window at the tourists strolling the sidewalks. They were oblivious to anything beyond their small world protected in a fragile bubble of security.

"No, it doesn't matter. But for the sake of your son, let's pretend that it does."

Chapter Four

The bedroom reeked of sweat-soaked sheets, and the buzz of a television from an adjoining unit filtered through the thin walls. Chrys sprawled on top of the blankets with pillows covering her face. The bed moved, and she rolled to her side and sniffed. Some pleasant scent cut through the rank air. Coffee. She sat up, but recoiled when she saw Mary sitting on the bed next to her.

"What are you doing?"

"I brought you coffee." Mary pointed to the nightstand where she'd placed the cup among the prescriptions and empty beer bottles.

Chrys wiped her face. "What time is it? You leaving for work?" She propped up on pillows and reached for the coffee, but her hands shook so much she was forced to set it back down.

"It's just after six."

"Why'd you wake me, then?"

"Six at night."

Chrys blinked, looked around the dim room, down at her shirt, sweatpants. "I slept all day?"

"Looks like it."

"Damn, missed PT. So much for being compliant." She stretched her arms and arched her back, winced, and rubbed down her thighs.

"Drinking while on those meds isn't compliant either."

She avoided Mary's eyes. "It's only a few. Besides, it helps me sleep through the night."

"Not last night."

"No, not last night." Chrys smoothed the wrinkles on her T-shirt. "Did I wake you? I'm sorry."

"I was already awake. But, yes, I heard you. I heard you calling for Diren and Sirvan and Asmin. You seem to call out for them every time you have a nightmare."

"I miss them." She swallowed in an attempt to stop the onset of tears.

Mary touched her arm. "It's okay, baby, you can cry."

Chrys pushed Mary's hand away and reached for her painkillers. But Mary intercepted her, grabbed the bottle, and studied the label. She shook it, rattling a few pills.

"You just had a med check last week. Where's the rest of this?"

Chrys shrugged. "I'm in pain."

"I know." Mary placed the pill in Chrys's hand, helped her hold the coffee cup steady as she sipped.

"I'm not sure I need coffee this late in the evening," Chrys said. "But thanks." She studied Mary's expression. Pity and disgust, it was all there.

"Have you heard from the DLI?" Mary asked.

Chrys shifted on the bed and repositioned her left leg. "Thing is, I was reading up on some NGOs in Syria and Iraq. Lots of humanitarian organizations who could use interpreters." She managed to bring the coffee cup to her lap, the liquid inside vibrating with her trembling hands. "There's a few good ones, some like Doctors Without Borders." She smiled. "Remember when you told your mom you were going to join up with them so you could be in the same part of the world as me? She almost killed you." She chuckled and sipped her coffee.

Mary didn't laugh.

"I also looked into another possibility. It's just something to consider. You know how important that work is to me."

Mary looked away.

"I told you about the foreign mercenaries, remember? That one gal, Kimberley something? And there're others, too, from Germany, Spain, Japan." Chrys smiled again. "It reminds me of what my uncle Manolis told me about the civil wars in Europe, how all these expats got caught up in the fight and joined revolutions."

Mary's jaw tightened. "Are you serious?"

"Why not? I have combat training. I understand the cultures, the languages. I know some of the other YPJ commanders, friends of Diren's, that'd be happy to have me join them." Chrys stopped when Mary started to cry, waited a few moments. "You know how important this is to me. I would think you'd understand that. These women are making a stand, fighting for their lives."

"There's nothing glamorous about fighting, no matter who's doing it," Mary said. "You've gone native that's all, romanticized them."

Chrys rose up, sloshing coffee from the cup. "Romanticized them? They aren't some hippy-dippy social justice warriors whining about rape culture. They're stopping rape. Killing the rapists. They're fighting not just for themselves but for women all over the world."

Mary scoffed. "And since when are you a feminist?"

Chrys sucked her teeth. "You think wearing stupid little pink hats and T-shirts with obnoxious slogans does any good? You want feminism? Let me see you join up with one of those NGOs over there and get a taste of what most women in this world face."

Mary slapped the bed. "Do you hear how judgmental you sound? You have no idea what everyday life is like in this country. You've been so cocooned in your little imperialistic world, cheerleading and waving your flag."

Chrys scowled. "I served my country proudly, did my job, followed orders."

"And you're done now. No more orders, no more deployments. You're home safe. You don't have to go back there and prove anything to anyone."

Chrys gripped the coffee cup tighter. "The world's abandoned them. I won't. They need me."

Mary slouched. "And I need you. Alive." She stood and began pacing the room. "I don't understand this. If you want to help them, take the position in Monterey, train more interpreters."

"I don't want to teach. I want to fight."

Mary stopped pacing and glared at her.

Chrys drew back. She could see the conflicting emotions on Mary's face—anger, pity, resentment, love, worry.

Mary took a deep breath. "I need you to listen. Yesterday, I got a call from Natividad Medical Center in Salinas. It's about forty minutes east of Monterey. My mom found an apartment in Seaside. The VA clinic is there, too."

"Wait, what?"

"The apartment's a little pricey," Mary continued, "but with your pay at the DLI, we should be okay. Unless of course they offer you housing. Either way, I figure the drive for either of us won't be too bad."

Chrys frowned. "I don't understand what you're saying."

"I got offered a position at Natividad."

"In California?" Chrys pressed the scar along her temple. "But when did you apply?"

"A month ago, after you told me about Monterey. I start in two weeks."

"Two weeks? But I haven't even sent in the DLI paperwork yet, and I—"

"You lied to me?"

Chrys held up her hand. "No, not lied. I was waiting. I'm not ready. You keep pushing me, and I'm not ready."

"You may never be ready, but I can't risk waiting until you are." Mary scrutinized the nightstand, the bottles of pills and beer. "This hanging in limbo is killing me, and I'm scared it's literally killing you."

Chrys pounded the bed causing the coffee in her other hand to slosh over the rim again. "I said I need more time."

"You've had time. Weeks, months. And nothing's changed."

"You think this is easy for me?" Chrys set the coffee aside and pointed toward the door. "You know how hard it is to see you go to work every day, come home and clean up after me? You think I don't see the way you look at me?"

"I love you. I'm worried about you."

"You're repulsed by me, and I don't blame you. I can't stand to look at myself either."

Mary sat on the bed. "I don't care about the scars. You're still gorgeous to me."

Chrys put out her hands to keep Mary back. "Stop it. I don't want your damn pity."

"For God's sake, you won't even let me touch you." Mary reached for her.

Chrys slapped her away. "Don't. Don't touch me. It burns." She drew her legs up, struggled with her left, and cowered against the headboard.

Mary sank back. "You think this is hard for you? Do you know how hard it is to come home and find you drunk and passed out every night? Wondering if I'm going to find you breathing or not? You never leave this damn apartment unless you're going to PT or group. You won't see our friends. You won't talk to me. All you do is drink and watch the damn news." She tossed her hands in the air. "And I'm done. I'm done waiting for you to get your shit together."

Chrys shivered and hugged her knees. Across the room, Diren leaned against the wall and watched.

"There was another way," Chrys said in Kurdish. "We could've held them off."

Diren shook her head. "No, heval," she said using the Kurdish word for friend. "There was no other way. If only there had been."

Mary turned her head. "Who are you talking to?"

"I needed more time." Chrys looked past Mary and spotted her grandmother frying ladopsomo in a pan.

"Time is expensive," her grandmother said.

"But I need more," Chrys said in Greek.

Mary turned and looked to where Chrys was staring. "What are you…Who…?" She pivoted slowly and her chin began to quiver. "I'm gonna be straight with you, baby. I don't know how much longer I can take this." She stood and walked backward toward the door. "So a fresh start in California, for both of us, it'll be best. You'll see."

Chrys rubbed her eyes and blinked. Diren was gone, and so was her grandmother.

Mary continued toward the door. "Gabby's son will help me pack a truck and drive with us. I've talked to a few gals at work who'll sublet our apartment until the lease runs out. All you need to do is sober up and decide to join me."

Chrys finally focused on Mary, shook her head. "I can't leave yet. I won't leave. I need more time to figure things out."

"You have two weeks. And if I'm really that important to you, you'll be on that truck with me."

Chrys ground her teeth. "You do not make decisions for me," she said, her voice a deep growl.

"Be mad at me all you want. Yell and scream and have your tantrum, but we're going, so get your paperwork in, okay?" Mary pulled the door shut behind her.

Chrys tossed her legs over the edge of the bed, but having slept the entire day in her prosthesis, she was too stiff to stand. "Don't you walk out on me. Goddamn it, come back here."

But the door remained shut. She tore at her face and hair and yelled a host of multilingual expletives, then heaved the coffee cup across the room. It shattered, spraying brown liquid against the white wall. She stared as an image of intestines uncoiling from a body materialized. She clasped her chest with one hand while the other snatched a prescription bottle, threw it, grabbed another, struggled with the cap. Finally, she popped a pill in her mouth, chewed it, and washed it down with stale beer. In moments, her breathing evened out, and she fell back on the bed where, like a trapped and wounded animal, she whimpered with the sounds of explosions surging in her head.

People eddied around the crowded Metro platform, the air heavy with the humidity of the summer day. Chrys leaned against a pillar and watched the movement of people while her eyes darted left and right, patrolling her surroundings. She adjusted the strap of her satchel draped across her shoulder causing her shirt to cling to her sweaty back. Her head hurt, and she was sick to her stomach. She kept swallowing, trying to keep the queasiness from climbing up her throat. If only she had a bottle of water to dilute the beer she'd consumed over the last two hours at one of her favorite pubs. But she deserved that small pleasure after her morning at the VA with the long wait to see a doctor followed by an hour of group and more of Ramos's obnoxiousness. She checked the time on her phone. Her train was running behind, and the platform was growing more congested as people got off work. She needed to sober up, to get home before Mary and finish packing. In two days they'd be leaving, yet her paperwork for the DLI still lay hidden in her dresser drawer.

A couple crowded next to her. The woman hung off the man and played with his neck. He patted her ass, kissed her temple. Chrys looked away. It wasn't out of disgust, but shame for her own failings. No one deserved to be forced into celibacy. Mary hadn't signed up for that, for any of this. She deserved better, a whole and unblemished woman.

She stumbled when a man bumped into her, and she cursed him under her breath. Too many people, so much noise. The rattle of an arriving train caught her attention. It zipped along the track and came to a halt in front of her. But it wasn't the one she needed. She slid down the pillar in defeat. Nothing was going right. No word about her running blade, not even an email. On top of that, her new definitive prosthesis hadn't been fitted properly, and she'd developed pressure ulcers, so now every step brought pain. She'd have to wait until her file was transferred to the VA in Seaside to see about getting any relief. She was losing muscle mass, too, unable to keep up with the rigorous workout her therapist at the VA had designed for her. She had to stay strong if she planned on fighting again. But first she needed money to afford a plane ticket to Germany and a connecting flight to Syria where she could join up with other mercenaries. Maybe she should teach a semester, maybe two if she could tolerate it. Just enough to earn her fare. Then she'd tell Mary, set her free, set them both free.

Someone tripped over her and cussed her out, triggering her rage. She yelled at him while struggling to her feet ready to beat his ass. But the jerk disappeared into the throngs of people while others turned and looked at her with contempt. Pain crawled up her leg to her hip and back, and she spat on the ground and winced. She tried to distract herself by counting backward from a hundred in one language after another, but her eyes kept finding the high voltage warning signs down along the track. She turned away and faced the platform wall where her grandmother sat on one of the benches, her big purse on her lap.

"If it were not for hope, the heart would break," her grandmother said.

Chrys lifted her hands and let them fall. "But my hope's broken."

A woman standing near watched her with wary eyes and stepped away.

When Chrys looked again, she saw her grandmother shake her head before dissolving into the pattern of the wall.

She pressed her fists to her eyes and swayed. "*Shitshitshit.*"

A group of teenagers bumped into her. Two mocked her, one barking at her as he pushed her away. She fell back against one of the pillars and covered her face. The sound of an approaching train rumbled in the distance. She opened her eyes and found the track again. Morrison had said the key was to time it just right. No pain, just a quick death. She pushed off the pillar and glanced at the oncoming train. It wasn't hers, but it would do. She pulled her phone from her pocket, began to lean forward, reaching her arm outward. Across the track behind the barricade, Diren made the peace sign, Sirvan opened his little arms to her, and Asmin and the others watched.

"Young woman!" Someone grabbed her arm.

Chrys stumbled back while the train screeched past her in a streak.

"You have to be careful. Don't get so close," the stranger said.

Chrys staggered to a bench. Right then her phone vibrated in her hand. She focused on the incoming number, but it wasn't one she knew.

She answered gulping. "This is Safis."

"Lieutenant Chrysanthi Safis?"

"Former lieutenant, yes." She held her heart, panted for air.

"This is Sean Gordon, Secretary of State Collins's chief of staff. Am I calling at an inconvenient time?"

"No." She plugged her other ear to mute the crowd.

"Glad to hear that." He paused, and she heard him speaking to someone while papers shuffled in the background among muffled voices. "I apologize. We're in the middle of a situation, and I'm juggling too many things."

"Situation?"

"How's your Turkish?"

"My Turkish? Fine. What's this—"

"Are you free tomorrow morning? Secretary Collins would like to speak with you to discuss an important diplomatic assignment."

"He wants to speak to me?" She focused intently. "Yes, I'm free, but what assignment—"

"I have here," Gordon interrupted, "you're at the Riverview Terrace Apartments in Huntington."

"Yes, but what—"

"I'll send a team for you at ten hundred hours. Thank you, ma'am. We'll see you in the morning."

"Wait, Gordon." She groaned. He'd already disconnected.

Right then her train barreled to a stop, and she pushed her way inside to a corner seat where she fell against the window. She began shaking, almost convulsing with the realization of what she'd come close to doing, and despite her best efforts to hold it in, she threw her head between her legs and vomited.

Chapter Five

It had taken an entire pot of coffee and a long, cold shower for Chrys to make herself presentable the next morning. No drugs, no beer. She couldn't risk any indiscretion. It was the Secretary of State, after all. And now two agents escorted her through security and proceeded to guide her through the Harry S. Truman building. She was pleased to see hardly anyone bothered to give her a second glance. To an outsider, she figured she probably looked like another agent in her dark tailored suit. And although her civilian attire lacked the inherent nobility of her service dress uniform, she knew she wore it well. For even that morning, she'd stood in front of the bathroom mirror and admired the cut of her suit. Somewhere under those sharp lines and fitted trousers was a hint of the Air Force officer she'd once been.

She paused with the agents as one of them spoke to the receptionist. A moment later, a man rounded the corner and came toward them.

"Ms. Safis, Sean Gordon. Thank you for agreeing to meet this morning." He extended his hand.

"Yes, sir, I'm happy to be here." She shook his hand. "However, I'm uncertain for what purpose."

"That'll be explained shortly. And please, no formalities between us. Call me Sean."

Gordon dismissed the two agents. "I can tell you, for the past week we've been trying to find the right person for this assignment with absolutely no luck. Our guest has very particular needs."

"And who would that be?"

Gordon paused at the doors. "She'll be joining us in a bit. Commander Banks, head of her security team, is bringing her over from the Hay-Adams."

"Security team?" Chrys glanced back at the two men who'd

picked her up that morning. They stood guard at the end of the hallway. "Diplomat?"

"Turkey, but she's been living in the UK for the last five years." Gordon started to open the doors, stopped. "Just so you know, she chose you out of all our suggestions. She said she thought you had honest eyes."

"Excuse me?"

"Your head shot." He grinned. "And I have my brother to thank for recommending you. Captain Kyle Gordon? You served as his unit's interpreter six years ago in Mosul."

"Gordon's your brother? How about that." Chrys studied him, the expensive tie, the silk shirt. "Good man, your brother."

"The best. And by the way, he wanted me to tell you congrats on finishing up your degree and receiving your commission."

Chrys shifted on her feet. "Yeah, he was always rooting for me." She leaned toward the doors but noticed Gordon continued to linger, a smile on his face.

"Also, I just wanted to say I was happy to learn of your engagement."

She stiffened.

He continued, "You realize we had to fully vet you, even with your security clearance."

"Sure, I get it." Sweat gathered at her temples.

Gordon put a hand on her shoulder. "It always makes me proud to see one of us take full advantage of the new laws, especially our servicemen and women. So congratulations. You'll have to let me know the date so I can send a gift."

She suddenly wanted to bolt and regretted not taking at least one tranquilizer before leaving the apartment. "We're not…I mean, we've postponed it for the time being." She patted her leg. "I'm still on the mend."

Gordon cleared his throat. "Yes, I was sorry to hear about your injuries. I'm glad to see you're up on your feet again. I mean, well, you're looking great. Shall we go in? We have a couple of senators who're eager to meet you."

Her stomach flipped-flopped. "Senators?"

Inside the door, Chrys stood at attention as a distinguished gentleman approached her. Two others, a man and woman, sat around a low table but stood when she entered.

"Chrysanthi Safis, thank you for coming. I'm Secretary Robert Collins."

She took his hand. "Yes, sir, I know. It's a pleasure to meet you."

He pulled her over to the others. "You may know the senior senator from New York, Lillian Granger, USAID's coordinator for gender equality and women's empowerment."

"Ma'am."

"My pleasure, Ms. Safis," Granger said. "I was just reviewing your file. Excellent work with the Syrian Kurds. You're to be commended for your heroism."

"Thank you, Senator. However, I was a simple interpreter helping coordinate Kurdish and US forces. The men and women of the YPG and YPJ are the true heroes." Heat radiated from her scalp. One beer chaser with coffee wouldn't have been such a bad idea.

"Best damn allies we got in that region." A barrel-chested man stuck out his hand. "Bill Zobava. I worked my tail off for enough votes to get those people weapons and supplies."

"And Senator William Zobava of Alaska," Collins interjected. "One of your most enthusiastic supporters and chair of the Senate Committee on Foreign Relations."

Chrys smiled, but her lips trembled. "Thank you, and yes, sir, the Kurds have proven themselves again and again. And believe me, they're grateful for every bit the US does for them."

"Better us than the Russians," he said, patting her back. "Am I right?"

She frowned. "I suppose so, sir. I'm not really—"

"Won't you have a seat," Granger said. She indicated the sofa, poured a cup of coffee, and thrust it into Chrys's hand.

"Thank you, ma'am." The china cup rattled against the saucer as Chrys tried to steady it. Finally, she placed it on the low table in front of her.

"You're wondering what this is about," Collins said.

"Yes, sir." She smoothed her hands down her trousers. Her leg throbbed. Bad idea to go without pain meds this long.

"Let me begin by saying our discussion this morning is confidential. You're not to discuss anything we speak of today outside this room."

"Of course." She made a quick side-to-side glance at the others. "May I ask, is this concerning my last mission in Syria, my report?"

"I've read your report," Zobava said. "You have my sympathies for the loss of your friends. I'm not sure how those Daesh devils escaped our satellite surveillance and got the jump on you."

Chrys ground her teeth. Her wild conjectures probably shouldn't be aired in this distinguished company, but the pain in her leg weakened her self-control. "As I suggested in my report, sir, the Turkish military most likely helped them go undetected. There's no other explanation."

The piercing stares she received indicated she'd said too much.

"Hang on there." Zobava lifted his hand. "We walk a fine line of diplomacy here, Safis. Turkey's our NATO ally, and our airbase in Izmir is critical to our fight against terrorism. Those sorts of speculations are unwarranted."

"Yes, sir." She seethed now, struggling to keep her temper in check. She knew better, was trained better.

"It's a delicate situation," Collins said. "That business with their president's visit last year and his bodyguards assaulting those protestors in front of their embassy strained our relationship significantly."

"The Turks are no friends to the Kurds," Chrys said, working to keep her voice calm. "Not to those in their own country or anyplace else." Her head pounded, and she pressed her finger against her temple. Across the room, she saw Diren sitting in the window.

"No friends but the mountains," Diren said, grinning.

Chrys blinked and Diren's image melted into the curtain, transformed into mountains, a campfire, a glass of black tea. Asmin sang, other women danced. They skipped and stepped around and around with their arms linked together while the rhythm of the goatskin drum mixed with their voices.

"Do you need cream?" Granger asked.

Chrys twitched. "Pardon me?"

"Cream?" Granger held out the silver dispenser.

Chrys nodded.

"That may be so," Zobava said. "But there are exceptions."

"I'm sorry, sir, I didn't catch that." Chrys doused her coffee, her hands shaking.

"You can't paint every Turk with a broad brush," Zobava said. "They have, after all, taken in the lion's share of refugees since this damn civil war broke out."

She shrank back. "I didn't mean to imply—"

"And there're a number of activists, some in their own parliament, who work to address the abuses against their ethnic minorities," Zobava added.

Chrys studied his posture, the aggressive expression on his face. "Of course." She retrieved her coffee, her hands still trembling, but the echo of the drum, the smell of the campfire had soothed her some.

"And we digress," Collins said. "Let me get to the point before our guest arrives." He brought a file into his lap. "As Bill says, there are exceptions. Are you familiar with Emin Arslan, the Turkish MP, and his work with the Kurds in Cizre?"

"I am," Chrys said. "He served as the head of their pro-Kurdish party, the HDP, for a number of years and was considered something of a hero among the Syrian Kurds as well." She searched her memory. "If I remember, he was killed about five, six years ago along with his sons. Car bomb, correct?"

Collins nodded. "Are you also aware before his assignation, he'd been planning on speaking to the UN to make a formal acknowledgment of the Armenian Genocide?"

Chrys choked on a sip of coffee and wiped her chin. "I was not."

"It was central to his political platform," Collins said. "His goal was to bring his country face-to-face with its past sins and hopefully heal the rift among the various ethnic groups, particularly the Armenians, and of course, the Kurds and Greeks as well."

Chrys took a long breath, and her eyes focused on the window once more where a wall from her childhood home materialized. Centered on that wall among religious icons and other family pictures hung old photographs of her grandparents as young children, their faces gaunt and eyes mournful.

"Are you feeling all right, Ms. Safis?" Granger said, touching her leg.

Chrys nearly leapt off the sofa. "I'm fine." She attempted a smile but seized up at the strange way the others looked at her. "Sorry, I'm not following you, Mr. Secretary. Am I here to translate for you? Interpret for someone?"

Collins chuckled. "Mrs. Arslan's English is impeccable, as you'll soon see."

"Emin's wife? I mean, widow? Is she in need of my services?" Chrys asked.

"Yes," Collins said. "She arrived last week from London. It took some coordination with British intelligence and our agencies, but we've got her here, have her secured at the Hay-Adams." He chuckled. "Commandeered an entire floor, and at quite the expense, I might add."

"And how am I to be of service?"

"Four primary functions," Collins said. "First, she's requested a personal secretary of sorts to help her with some correspondence and other personal matters."

"I'm to be a secretary?" Right then Monterey and the DLI sounded exciting.

"That's not all. She's also interested in perusing our museums and monuments, seeing the sights like any tourist, and sampling our music venues and theaters."

"She's never been to the United States," Granger said. "And she taught American and British literature at Istanbul University for nearly twenty years. She has quite the interest in our culture."

"A tour guide?" Chrys stifled a groan and rubbed her knee. Crowded museums, rude tourists, not to mention all the walking.

"You might want to keep her out of the throngs of school groups coming through the Air and Space Museum," Zobava said. "Although I suspect that's your favorite."

"Yes, sir. My favorite." She stopped herself from rolling her eyes.

"And then there's the matter of accompanying her to the Virginia Hospital Center in Arlington," Collins said. "She's expressed some trepidation about this experimental treatment her doctors in London have arranged for. She's asked to have someone escort her, someone who can explain things in her native tongue."

"Is she ill?" Great, and a nursemaid, too.

"Doctors are hopeful," Granger said, but her expression indicated otherwise.

"And perhaps most important," Collins said, "she's requested someone to accompany her to the UN in late November. Given the nature of her statement, she wants to deliver it in Turkish and have her own interpreter stand with her on the platform."

Chrys cringed. "You want me to..." She swallowed. "I've never translated in front of that many people. I'm not sure I..."

She saw Collins's shoulders droop, his expression turn grave. Granger frowned and shifted in her seat. Yet Zobava glared at her as if to reprimand her for challenging the request of a government official. She looked down into her coffee, remembered the mess she'd made in her bedroom a few weeks ago. Whatever dignity she'd had as a young officer had been stripped from her. Clearly, they'd picked the wrong person for this job. She wasn't a diplomatic liaison, an escort for political VIPs, someone to interact with the muckety-mucks of the UN.

"Forgive me, Mr. Secretary," Chrys said, "but are you certain I'm the individual you want for this mission? I've only been home since December, and I'm still having issues with my prosthesis."

"Let me be honest with you," he said. "Mrs. Arslan has refused every other recommendation we've offered. At this point, you're our best bet. You not only have the language skills we need, but also the security clearance required for this assignment."

Chrys bit her tongue to suppress a sneer. Second string, not even first choice. But she was damaged goods these days. What else could she expect? She straightened her shoulders. "But of course, sir. Whatever I can do to help. And may I ask, what is the topic of her UN statement?"

She saw Zobava twitch, uncross then cross his legs again.

"Two parts, really," Collins said. "First, she'll be beseeching member nations to contribute to the establishment of more settlements for refugees."

Granger leaned forward. "Her foundation, of which I serve as a member of the board of directors, has done some magnificent work. Do you recall the village established two years ago for women in northern Syria?"

"I do. That resulted from her work?" Chrys asked.

"Yes, through the foundation she and Emin started seven years ago."

"It's some good work, too," Collins added. "With the president denying so many of them asylum, and the European states overflowing with refugee sites that resemble prison camps more than anything, these settlements may be the only safe havens left to these people, particularly the women and children."

Granger nodded enthusiastically. "She's done a remarkable job of engaging other NGOs who supply medicine, food, and school supplies. It's ingenious really, and if UN member nations agree to supply the defensive forces to protect them, we may never have to see another refugee child drowned and washed up on the beach."

"Admirable work," Chrys said. She shivered as Sirvan's laughing face pressed around her, his little fingers poking at her dimples.

Collins exchanged a look with Granger, and Chrys detected there was something else, a part of this mission they were saving for last.

"And the second part of her statement?" Chrys asked.

Collins tapped his pen on the file in his lap. "At the end of her statement, she'll speak her late husband's words and acknowledge the 1915 genocide of the Armenian people."

"She have a death wish?" Chrys flinched when the words left her mouth.

Zobava harrumphed and shook his head.

But Collins's face darkened. "I think Mrs. Arslan is aware of the gravity of her statement. Two months ago, her assistant was killed in a car bomb not far from Parliament."

Chrys's insides coiled tight. "And is the United States prepared to stand behind her when the fallout happens?"

"Right behind her," Collins said. "Senators Zobava and Granger have already prepared their press statements, and the president will take the podium as soon as it hits the airwaves and the internet."

"It'll be a media frenzy, to say the least," Zobava said. "And I can tell you right now, we're going to get a load of blowback." He shook his head. "I'm still not convinced the subject of the Armenians belongs in her statement."

"It's a small thing really," Granger said more to Zobava than Chrys, "but carries with it so much importance. Her words may help reshape our relationship with Turkey as well as their relationship with the rest of the world. You can understand that, can't you?"

Zobava shrugged.

Chrys watched all three of them, but her attention zeroed in on Zobava's posture again. "Well, I'm not sure what she hopes to accomplish or what will change as a result, but I admire her courage. Any Turkish citizen who has attempted to speak about the genocide has been imprisoned or…" She lowered her eyes. "Like I said, I admire her courage."

"Then you'll accept the assignment?" Collins asked. He opened the folder in his lap and laid it on the table. "You'll be compensated for your time and talent, of course."

Chrys blinked at the numbers before her, at all those zeros before the decimal. There was a running blade in that sum, a plane ticket to Germany and on to Syria, and a savings account she could open for Mary. She continued to stare at the document as she thought of Mary and of the boxes stacked in their living room ready to be loaded on a truck. They were scheduled to leave for California tomorrow.

"Would you like to negotiate a different amount?" Collins asked.

"No, sir," Chrys said. "The amount is more than acceptable, and I'll be happy to assist Mrs. Arslan with her mission. But may I ask, did you say she's already here in DC, yet her UN appearance isn't until November?"

"Correct. You'll be staying with her at the Hay-Adams for the next five months helping her prepare her statement, showing her around town, accompanying her to the hospital, and later to New York."

"I'm to live at the hotel with her? For five months?" Chrys asked.

"The last two weeks in New York, but yes. Will that be an issue?"

Chrys looked at the promised payout again. "No, sir, I guess not."

"Good. Glad to hear that. And thank you." He glanced over her shoulder and stood. "And here she is, our guest of honor."

Chrys detected the scent first, the heavy aroma of cloves. She got to her feet and turned but had to suppress her surprise. She'd expected a much older woman, one in her seventies, similar in age to her late husband, Emin. But this woman couldn't be more than forty or forty-five tops with cinnamon eyes and rich brown hair coifed in a colorful scarf. Her dress was a combination of modern and traditional, the style provoking sophistication, and from her poise, it was clear she came from money. As Chrys watched the woman take Collins's hand, she couldn't help but recall stories from her childhood of classical beauties like Cleopatra and Helen of Troy. She was so captivated with her, in fact, she didn't immediately register the other woman, a security agent, who'd escorted Arslan in and who now stood at attention by the office door.

"A pleasure to see you again, Mr. Secretary." Reyha addressed him, but she was watching Chrys.

"Mrs. Arslan, I'm happy to introduce you to former United States Air Force Lieutenant Chrysanthi Safis."

Chrys marched toward Reyha, hand extended. "It is a great pleasure to make your acquaintance. Welcome to the United States," she said in Turkish.

Reyha gripped Chrys's hand and responded in her own language as well. "You do me a great service, Ms. Safis. Thank you for your warm welcome. Peace be upon you."

Chrys inclined her head. Reyha's rich voice reminded her of honey oozing over hot flatbread pulled right from the fire, and it stirred within her a wave of reverence.

"I am happy your Secretary of State Mr. Collins has managed to employ your services," Reyha said, but this time in Kurdish.

Chrys didn't miss a beat and responded in the same. "It is an honor to offer them to you, ma'am."

Then in Armenian, Reyha remarked, "From your service record I have observed you have had many notable accomplishments, many commendations and medals, and you who are so young."

Chrys answered in Armenian as well. "Thank you. It has been a privilege to serve my country."

"Your country is fortunate to have one so talented," Reyha said, but this time in a dialect of Arabic.

It occurred to Chrys that Reyha Arslan was testing her language ability. She met the challenge and responded in another dialect of Arabic. "I've been fortunate to have my talents required and so used for the betterment of my country and our allies."

Reyha chuckled and continued to grip Chrys's hand. "Your pronunciation and accent are by far some of the best I have heard from an American," she said, speaking Greek.

"Your praise honors me, ma'am."

"It is well deserved," Reyha said, this time in French.

For a moment, Chrys struggled to comprehend. She stuttered as she answered. "I'm afraid I haven't had much practice with French, not since high school."

Again Reyha laughed. "Nor have I."

She released Chrys's hand and turned to Granger, whom she welcomed with a hug and kisses on both cheeks. The two women began chatting, apparently old friends, and Chrys returned to the sitting area and remained standing until Reyha and Granger took their seats.

"Well, yes," Collins said. He gave Chrys a look of respect laced with surprise. "Ms. Safis is one of the Defense Language Institute's most qualified graduates."

"I should say she is," Reyha said. She sat next to Chrys on the sofa, so close the hem of her tunic brushed against her. She began speaking with Granger, taking the coffee offered.

Chrys didn't bother to listen to the conversation. Instead she studied Reyha from the tip of her shoes to the details of her tunic to the visible strands of her hair lying along her shoulder. As the conversation continued, she sensed Gordon's eyes on her, and when she looked up, he grinned and raised an eyebrow. His expression probably meant something, but she was too distracted to decipher it. She returned her focus on Reyha once more, on the folds of her scarf draped and wrapped around her shoulders, on her profile and mouth, on the way she spoke with her hands.

"…and I've already warned her," Zobava said.

Everyone turned to look at her, but Reyha's smile blurred the rest of the room.

"I am sure I would not mind," Reyha said to Chrys.

"Mind? I'm sorry, mind what?" Chrys blinked rapidly, trying to focus.

"The Air and Space Museum. But promise me, we will have a good long day at the National Art Gallery and the Library of Congress," Reyha said.

"Of course, whatever you want, Mrs. Arslan. I'm happy to do what I can to make your stay in the US memorable."

Reyha tilted her head. "I would like you to address me by my first name. And may I call you Chrysanthi? A beautiful name."

"Yes, or Chrys, either will do."

Without warning, Reyha turned on the sofa and brought both of Chrys's hands into her own. "I think you and I will be very good friends, yes?"

Chrys waited for the impulse to pull away, but it never came. Instead, the tension in her shoulders eased, the trembling in her body stilled, and her skin cooled.

"Yes," Chrys said, and her smile broadened. "I believe we will be friends, very good friends, as you say."

And the dollar amount, the compensation she'd been offered, was eclipsed at the moment, forgotten, as she gazed into Reyha's welcoming eyes.

CHAPTER SIX

Moving boxes, labeled and taped shut, filled the apartment's living room, some stacked on top of each other forming unsteady columns. Chrys separated out those boxes she knew contained her belongings, items from her past which no longer meant anything. Afterward, she went through her closet and found all the best clothes she owned—trousers and fine shirts, jackets and dress boots. Without the benefit of her uniform, these would have to do for the five months she was assigned to be Reyha Arslan's liaison. She packed her nice clothes in garment bags and stowed the rest of her gear in large duffels, then dragged them out to the living room and plopped them by the sofa. For the rest of the evening, she sipped on beer and scrounged for food, most of which had been gone through in preparation for the move. She finally ordered a pizza and settled back to wait for Mary. While she waited, she rehearsed what she would say and hoped it would be enough.

Mary arrived home from her last shift close to midnight. She peeked around a column of boxes as she set gift bags and a potted plant by the door. "Hey, you, why you still up? Can you believe Gabby and the rest of them? I wish you could've stopped by. They had a cake for us. For you and me, wishing us good luck in California." She gave Chrys a tired smile and began to remove the clip from her hair. "I'm going to miss that crew."

Chrys drew a long sip from her beer.

Mary shook her hair free and stretched. "God, I'm beat. You wouldn't believe the mess that came in, and on my last day, too. A huge pile up on sixty-six. Five vehicles, two fatalities, and one open fracture with an arterial injury. Sheesh, what a night." She plopped down on the sofa, and her eyes focused on the beer in Chrys's hand. "You finish packing your room?" Then she noticed the garment bags and duffels. "Good, you cleared out your closet."

"Mary, I need to tell you something." Chrys searched her face. It was a face she'd come to love years ago. There was history in that face, stories in those eyes. So much tenderness, loyalty, and friendship. She dropped her gaze. "I want you to know these last seven years have been some of the best in my life. You're the only woman who actually liked me for me, not for my rank and status or my looks." She scoffed. "Not that I have that to rely on anymore. Anyway, I wanted to say thank you for being my friend. My best friend, actually." She raised her eyes to find Mary had gone pale, her lips set tight in a line.

"I knew you would do this," Mary said. "I knew it. You're not coming with me." She stood and punched one of the boxes and headed toward the hallway.

"But I got a job," Chrys said standing.

Mary spun around, angry tears already cascading down her face. "Fuck you, Chrys. I just quit a job I love and spent most of our savings to move us across the country, all for you."

Chrys bristled with rising anger. "No, that was for you. You came up with the plan, not me. I told you I didn't want to go."

Mary stormed toward her, got up in her face. "I did it for you because you can't make one goddamn decision anymore. All you do is hide in this apartment and drink and drug yourself into unconsciousness."

Chrys pressed back, spitting her words. "I got my fucking leg blown off and half my head. What the hell am I supposed to do?"

"You're supposed to pull your shit together and move on from your little pity party."

Chrys blinked with shock, stuttered. "What the fuck?"

Mary hugged herself. "No, you won't make me feel guilty for that. I'm done trying to cater to you and protect your damn ego. For years I've done just that, postponing everything in my life so your life could be perfect, so you could have a stable home, someone and someplace to come home to, so you could prance around with me on your arm like some sort of ornament. But I'm done, and I'm done crying myself to sleep because you're repulsed by me."

Chrys stepped back, her anger dropping to a simmer. "I'm not repulsed by you. I love you."

"You say that, but you can't stand for me to touch you. I've only kissed you...*really* kissed you...once, when I met you at the airport. You may love me, but you don't want me." Mary flung herself down on the sofa and buried her face in her hands. "I just don't know what you want anymore."

Chrys started to touch Mary's bent head, but stopped. "I want you to be happy. But don't you see, I'm draining you. Just look at us. Since I've been back you've been working double shifts, doing everything at home, and taking care of me. And what do I give you? Worry, hurt. You have to believe me—I don't want to hurt you."

Mary looked up. "Then why do you pull away from me every time I try to touch you?"

Chrys shrank back even farther. "Come on, you don't have to pretend." She lifted her arms and let them fall. "Look at me. Look at my face. And this. Look at this." She lifted her shirt and touched the sickly pink and mottled white scars down her left side. She let her shirt fall and motioned to her leg. "This isn't what you want, and I don't want you to pretend because you pity me."

"You think I'm that shallow?"

"No, I think you're a good person, but I know you'd force yourself out of obligation." Chrys fidgeted with her hands, not knowing what to do with them. "Besides, I don't even have a drive anymore. I just don't want it."

"That's normal after what you've been through."

Chrys grimaced, pulled her hair as her frustration mounted. "This isn't about sex. It's about me. Who I was. What I believed. I'm trying to tell you it's not just my outside, it's the insides, too." She pointed to her head. "Up here, something's not right. I keep seeing..." She squeezed her eyes tight. "Shit, I can't tell you what I see."

"If you'd talk to me, I could help you work through it."

"I can't." Chrys teetered and caught hold of one of the boxes. "She didn't give me time. I needed more time. We could've made it out. All of us."

Mary stood and came closer. "Who are you talking about? Time for what?"

Chrys mumbled and pressed the bridge of her nose.

"Your hands are shaking, baby. Are you in pain?" Mary asked.

"I'm always in pain."

Mary tried to pull her down on the sofa, but Chrys resisted.

"Stop. Don't. I just need to explain this to you."

"Okay." Mary stifled a sob.

"Yesterday, I got a call from the State Department, from the chief of staff for the Secretary of State. They've offered me an assignment. It's only for five months, but the pay's good."

Mary tilted her head. "You got offered a job with the State Department?"

Chrys nodded.

"For what?"

"I'm not allowed to say."

"Why?"

"Because it's a sensitive situation involving one of our allies."

Mary's eyes narrowed. "A five-month situation? Are you making this up?"

Chrys clenched her fists. "I'm being completely honest with you."

"Which ally?"

"I'm not at liberty to tell you."

Mary folded her arms across her chest. "How convenient for you."

"What does that mean?"

Mary slapped one of the boxes, and it slid off its column and toppled to the ground. "Don't insult me with some made-up bullshit. If you want to break up, just say it."

Chrys stretched her neck taut, her temper close to spilling over again. "I'm telling you the truth."

"Really? So I'm expected to believe you're all of sudden on a secret mission with the government? What are you now, a spy? Did they give you a decoder ring, too?"

Chrys jabbed a finger in Mary's face. "Knock it off. You're not being funny. I'm completely serious. I've been asked to serve as an interpreter for an international dignitary. I can't tell you anything more."

"For five months?"

"Yes."

"Who is it? Who's the dignitary?"

Chrys rolled her eyes. "For fuck's sake."

"A woman?"

"I can't say."

Mary stiffened. "So it is a woman. One of your Kurdish rebels you grew to love so much?"

Chrys spoke through clenched teeth. "I never had that sort of relationship with any of them, and you know that."

Mary pointed toward the bedrooms. "You call out their names in your sleep almost every night. That Diren woman, the one you kept writing me about. Are you going to deny you were in love with her?"

Chrys's chest heaved as she yelled. "I saw her blown apart, goddamn it!"

An empty beer bottle clinked over on the coffee table from the vibration of Chrys's outburst. They glared at each other until finally Mary bent and set the bottle upright.

"And when these five months are over, what then?" Mary asked.

Chrys pushed hair back from her eyes. She was suddenly exhausted, spent from her outburst. "I'll use my pay to get passage to Syria. I'll send you what's left."

"I don't want your fucking money."

Chrys's shoulders sagged. "I want you to have it. You deserve something."

Mary scoffed and shook her head repeatedly. "All my friends warned me. Don't date someone in the military, you'll only end up lonely. And don't date that one, she's full of herself. Look at the way she struts around. She'll break your heart—you'll see."

"I know I've hurt you. I'm sorry." The exhaustion pressed against her, a deep tiredness accompanied by defeat.

Mary's face reddened, and her lips hardened into a straight line. "Oh, I'm sure you are. You're always sorry."

Chrys held her palms up and tried to soften her voice. "That's why I think it's best for you to go on with your plans. You'll get a fresh start, be close to your mom, be back in California where you're happiest." She dropped her hands to her sides. "And it'll give me time to try to figure out my shit."

"And what shit is that exactly?"

Chrys pressed against her eyes with her fists and sighed. "You know I can't sleep. I can't concentrate. I can't even run anymore to get relief. And I don't want to teach and live some nine-to-five job like everything in the world is just fine. It isn't. The world's on fire. Everywhere, not just over there. I turn on the news and some school's been shot up, some poor kid's been raped and tortured, some dog beaten to death. It's everywhere I turn. I can't get away from it." She sniffed and wiped her nose. "And people are clueless. They walk around bitching about stupid shit, arguing about idiot celebrities and politicians while the rest of the world goes to hell."

Mary's posture relaxed. "And how is going back to Syria going to solve anything other than getting yourself killed? It won't bring Diren back. It won't bring any of them back."

"But I can save others."

"And who will save you, Chrys?"

Chrys blinked, stepped back. "I'm not asking to be saved."

Mary's back stiffened again as she sneered. "My God, you think you're the only one who's ever suffered?" She stabbed her own chest with a finger. "You think I haven't seen terrible things? You think I don't see how brutal the world is? Nearly every week mutilated bodies and innocent people suffering, scared little kids, parents destroyed."

"It's not the same."

"You don't own a license on grief," Mary said, nearly yelling the words. "I suffer, too, goddamn it. But I'm not so self-absorbed that I can't pull myself together and get out of bed every day and try to make the world a little better." She hitched one hand on her hip and pointed to the door. "You think taking your drunk ass back over to Syria and blowing away a few more ISIS freaks will absolve you of your pain? It won't. No matter how many of them you kill, you won't feel any better about what happened to you, about the friends you lost. And you can lie to yourself all you want and say you're doing it for those women. But the truth is, you're doing it because for once in your otherwise perfect life, you were defeated, and you can't handle it. So now you'd rather die a martyr than face the fact sometimes life sucks and you lose." She yanked something from her hand and threw it. "And take your grandmother's ring. I don't give a damn what you do anymore." She marched down the hall and slammed the door.

Chrys picked up the ring, held it in the palm of her hand, and stared at it. Movement in the kitchen caught her attention, and she glanced up to see her grandmother at the stove, her apron tied about her while she stirred a pot.

"An uphill road is followed by a downhill road, Chrysanthi," her grandmother said. "You will rise again."

"And fall again."

"Oh yes." She stopped stirring and pierced Chrys with her gaze. "But you are my granddaughter. You will not remain on your knees."

Chrys kissed the ring. When she looked again, her grandmother was gone.

❖

The next morning, Chrys and Mary moved around each other in stony silence. The young man who'd agreed to help them showed up before ten and started hauling boxes to the truck. Chrys helped out, too, despite Mary's objections. In a few hours, the apartment was nearly stripped clean.

Chrys pointed to her pile of boxes that remained. "Those are mine, but I don't know what to do with them. You can toss them out if you want."

"I could ship them to your brother," Mary said.

"I guess, but let me know how much that costs."

"I told you, I don't want your money." Mary grabbed some table lamps and went out.

Chrys headed toward the bathroom. She had to be ready in another hour to be picked up and moved to the Hay-Adams. As she got into the shower, she winced with pain. She'd forgone her usual dose of pain medication because she wanted to be alert, but now she wondered if she should take something after climbing the stairs and hauling boxes all morning. When she finished with her shower, she reattached her leg, pulled on a pair of thin wool trousers and a dress shirt, then allowed herself a half dose of pain meds. She squirreled away the other half in her pocket along with a few tranquilizers.

Out in the living room again, she found that Mary and her helper had cleared the apartment completely, minus her bags.

"You're limping," Mary said to her as she rested against the wall drinking a soda. "You take something?"

"Half." Chrys set her crutches next to her bags.

Mary handed keys to the young man. "I'll meet you downstairs," she said to him. When he'd left, she turned to Chrys. "You went up and down those steps a lot this morning. Don't let the pain get ahead of you."

"You're the one always nagging me not to take so much."

Mary rolled her eyes. "Forgive me for being such a nag, but I was worried you'd OD by accident." She looked away. "Or on purpose."

Someone knocked on the door.

"I told him I'd be right there," Mary said. She opened the door and the two agents from the day before stood in the doorway.

The taller one with pale hair and the build of a NFL linebacker removed his sunglasses. "Excuse me, miss, I'm here to retrieve Ms. Safis."

Mary turned back to Chrys. "You were telling the truth?"

Chrys stepped forward. "Quinn, right? Yes, this is my…This is Mary."

Quinn tipped his head.

"And this is…" Chrys pointed to the other agent, a thin man with nondescript features. "Agent Smith?"

Smith nodded.

"Anyway"—Chrys indicated her things—"if you guys wouldn't mind getting that stuff, I'll meet you downstairs in a moment."

The two men took her belongings and left Chrys and Mary alone in the empty apartment.

"Secret Service, wow, this must be important," Mary said.

"Technically protective services for the State Department."

"Were they wearing guns under their jackets?"

"That's the protective part."

Mary closed her eyes a moment and exhaled. "I'm sorry I didn't believe you."

"I'm sorry I messed up your life."

Mary shrugged. "I know you didn't mean to." Her eyes dropped to Chrys's feet, then she lifted her gaze up her body and rested on her face. "You look really nice. I haven't seen you look so good since the last time I saw you in uniform."

Chrys smoothed the front of her shirt, one Mary had given her for her birthday a few years back. "Thanks. I'm trying to clean up my act, you know?"

"You'll manage to stay sober, won't you? I don't want to hear about you in the news creating some international incident."

Chrys chuckled. "Yeah, that would be bad." She looked at Mary's mouth, her hair, her eyes. "I'll come see you before I head overseas."

"Don't. I don't need you to tear my heart out twice."

Chrys hung her head. "Will you let me know when you make it to your mom's at least?"

"You don't get that privilege any longer."

"Right." Chrys kicked at a spot on the carpet. "So I guess this is good-bye."

"I guess it is."

Suddenly, Mary was against her with her hands around her neck and her mouth pressed to hers. There was no mistaking it for anything other than a farewell kiss. When Mary broke away, she turned and left without another word.

Chrys willed herself to breathe, to shove the grief deep into her stomach, but she couldn't halt the few tears determined to escape. She looked at the bare walls and empty kitchen. Then she walked through the rest of the vacant apartment one more time. She paused in the entryway before pulling the door shut. She was certain that like all the previous doors shut in her face, this one would never open again.

Downstairs, the moving truck pulled toward the parking lot's exit, and Quinn and Smith waited for her by the SUV. Quinn opened the back door.

"Are you all right, ma'am? Is there anything I can do for you?" Quinn asked.

"I could use a beer, but since I'm expected at the Hay-Adams, it'll have to wait," Chrys said.

She climbed into the back seat, adjusted her left leg, and watched the moving truck turn toward the highway, in the opposite direction the SUV was getting ready to head.

Chapter Seven

Smith pulled the SUV under the canopy at the front entrance of the hotel. Staff approached the vehicle, but Quinn waved them off and helped Chrys from the back seat.

"The commander has asked we take you to the dining room where Mrs. Arslan is having tea."

Chrys reached for her bags. "I can get those now."

But Quinn insisted he and Smith take them.

She followed them through the doorway, where another agent waited just inside. She gaped with amazement at the luxurious expanse before her, all plush carpet, arches, dark wood, and extravagantly crafted furniture. Quinn motioned for the other agent and Smith to gather her bags, then signaled for her to follow him. They went through the lobby to the dining room where tables were covered in white linen, the walls illuminated by numerous chandeliers. Immediately, Chrys detected the dulcet tones of Reyha's voice. There in one corner, in a private area, she spied the commander of the detail, Barbara Banks, standing at attention with an impenetrable stoic expression and her blond hair pulled back in an austere ponytail. She stood next to Reyha, who chatted with a little man, his head a mane of gray hair brushed back in a dramatic sweep. When Reyha saw her, she rose.

"And here you are, my friend, welcome to my temporary home." She embraced Chrys by the shoulders and planted a kiss on each cheek. "A palace fit for royalty, yet I am only a humble teacher."

The man stood as well. "Nonsense, Mrs. Arslan, if you're anything, you are a queen among queens."

Reyha laughed. "Ah, Mr. Carmichael, your hyperbole is well intentioned, I am sure."

Carmichael turned to Chrys and bowed so low she thought he might fall over. When he stood, he took her hand, kissed the back of it, and held it between velvet palms.

"Sterling Carmichael at your service, Lieutenant Safis. My staff is at your disposal. However, if you need anything, anything at all, you'll be sure to call my number directly."

"Thank you, sir, but it's former lieutenant actually." Chrys tried to pull her hand away.

He held it firm. "I daresay, once an officer, always an officer." He giggled and pulsed his eyes. "And aren't you the handsome military officer, so formal, so rugged." He studied her shoulders, her hips. "Mrs. Arslan has been telling me about your service. A Purple Heart, no less." He released her and tapped his chest. "Be still my own heart."

Chrys raised her eyebrows. "Thank you. I guess." She noticed Banks and Quinn suppress smiles.

Reyha watched this strange exchange, a grin on her face. "You will find our Mr. Carmichael a most gracious host."

He clicked his heels and bowed once more.

Reyha linked her arm through Chrys's. "Shall I show you to your room? Dinner will not be for some time, and I am sure you will want to settle in."

"Yes, please," Chrys said, walking stiffly as Reyha led her.

Carmichael followed them to the elevators. "As you've requested, Mrs. Arslan, dinner will be delivered to your suite. I've taken it upon myself to choose an appropriate wine to pair with your entree."

"Thank you, Mr. Carmichael."

Reyha entered the elevator, and Chrys followed with Banks, Quinn, and Smith crowding around them.

"I've had your luggage put in your suite, Ms. Safis," Smith said.

Reyha glanced at her. "You will find you cannot venture far without our loyal bodyguards." She laughed. "Such trouble I have caused. I feel I am an inconvenience for your Mr. Collins."

"I'm sure he doesn't find you an inconvenience," Chrys said.

The elevator's doors opened, and an additional agent met them and fell in line as they proceeded to the door of a suite. Chrys glanced down the hallway where another door stood ajar, revealing computer screens and three other agents talking.

"You guys have the entire floor?" she asked Banks.

"Yes, ma'am. I'll introduce you to the rest of the team later."

Banks activated the key to the suite and swung open the door. Chrys spotted her bags inside the entryway.

"And here we are," Reyha said. "I think you will find this most acceptable."

Chrys stepped inside. "But I don't need this much room to myself."

Reyha and Banks exchanged glances.

"You misunderstand. We will share this together," Reyha said. "You have your own master bedroom and private bath on one end, and I on the other." She entered and removed her heels and replaced them with slippers.

"We've stocked the refrigerator this morning with the items you requested yesterday," Banks said to Reyha. "Anything else, let me know."

"Thank you, Commander." Reyha took a step toward Chrys. "Is there something you have forgotten?"

Chrys looked down at her bags. "I'm to reside with you in the same suite?"

Reyha stepped closer. "I apologize. I thought I had made it clear to Mr. Gordon and Secretary Collins I prefer you to stay within my apartment."

The other agents had by then taken up their posts down the hallway, but Banks remained. Chrys gave her a look that begged help to resolve this misunderstanding, but her expression conceded nothing.

"That's gracious of you," Chrys said. "But I wouldn't want to be any trouble. I'm sure you'll want your privacy."

"This suite will comfortably accommodate us both. My privacy is not in question," Reyha said.

Chrys stepped side to side. "Actually, I'm restless when I sleep and, well..." She stole another glance at Banks, who apparently wasn't going to help her get out of this. She cleared her throat and pulled at her shirt collar. "You see, I often wake up at night, and sometimes I cry out when I'm dreaming. I don't want to disturb you."

Reyha made a momentary frown. "You cry out in your dreams?"

"Nightmares actually." Chrys curled her hands into fists.

"I see." Reyha studied her, nodded. "I do not intend to make you uncomfortable. You are already giving your time and care to me. However, I would ask one favor."

"Of course."

"Would you agree to spend one night here? Perhaps you will find your room acceptable after all." Reyha took a step back. "As you can see, the suite is quite spacious, and your room is on the other side of the living area and kitchen from mine. I doubt if you do cry out in the night I will hear you."

Chrys looked from one woman to the other and down at her bags again. She leaned in to inspect the kitchen, living, and dining areas, the French doors that opened to the balcony. Through the sheer curtains pulled against the afternoon sun, she spotted the Washington Monument in the distance.

It was a big area for sure, a finely furnished living space, much bigger than the two-bedroom apartment she'd shared with Mary. She swayed as pain shot through her hip and her chest tightened with worry and grief over Mary. But then she felt Reyha lift one of her fists and uncurl her fingers.

"I see I have put you in an awkward position," Reyha said. "My apologies. Let me call down to Mr. Carmichael and have him prepare a private room for you."

Chrys tugged her hand free. "That won't be necessary. As you say, I can try it for one night at least. It's a lovely accommodation. Thank you."

"And thank you." Reyha pulled the scarf from her head, revealing the true splendor of her hair. "If you will not mind, I would like to lie down until our meal arrives." She inclined her head and glided to one side of the suite where she disappeared behind a shut door.

Chrys let out an audible sigh.

"Let me know if there's something you need, Ms. Safis," Banks said. "It won't be any trouble for me to arrange it."

"Thank you."

"May I take your bags to your room?"

"I'm fine."

Banks turned to depart.

"North or South Carolina?" Chrys asked.

Banks smiled, revealing an agreeable face, with hawklike eyes accented with long lashes. "South. I haven't been home for years, but no matter how hard I work, I can't completely suppress this accent."

"Actually, I just noticed it." Chrys considered her build, her rigid posture. "Former military, I'd guess. Marines?"

Banks smiled again. "Coast Guard. Eight years. Then on to the FBI for three, and now protective services. This is my fifth year with the State Department."

"A coastie, huh?" Chrys grinned at Banks's expression. "Nothing wrong with that."

"More of a duck scrubber, I'm afraid. Spent most of my service in the Gulf cleaning up oil spills."

They studied each other, smiling, as if they'd just discovered some familial relationship between them.

"Is there anything else?" Banks asked.

Chrys shifted on her feet. The pain was accelerating. "Actually, if you wouldn't mind, could you pick up a case of beer for me?"

"Any particular brand?"

"An IPA will do."

"Let me see what they have downstairs first, but I'll send someone to get a case for you to have on hand."

"Thank you."

"Not at all, Ms. Safis."

"You can call me Chrys, you know."

Banks hesitated, gave her a long look up and down. "Protocol, ma'am. You understand."

"As a matter of fact, I do."

After Banks left, Chrys dug the other half of her pain pill out of her pocket. She needed relief fast, so she chewed it and made a face until she found the bottles of water in the refrigerator. As she drained a bottle, she explored the interior of her new home. She went about the living area, touching tables and lamps and admiring the artwork. She stopped at the desk in the corner where a laptop and a number of files sat. She fingered through the papers. Many of them contained handwritten information, an elegant script with the cedilla and the diaeresis of the Turkish alphabet.

She picked up the remote for the television, but not wanting the sound to disturb Reyha, she tossed it back on the coffee table. She considered the closed bedroom door and wondered what Reyha might look like at that moment. Perhaps she'd changed into nightclothes for her nap, her hair flowing over the pillow, her perfectly shaped mouth open slightly. The image drew an unexpected sharp breath from Chrys's chest, and she fanned herself and went to the balcony. There she found a pleasing view overlooking Lafayette Square with the White House in the distance. Below on the street, she spotted two agents in position on the corners. She turned to leave but stopped when she spotted an ashtray on the little table. It overflowed with cigarette butts of dark brown paper, circumvented with an embossed gold line.

Out of curiosity, she picked one up and sniffed. Cloves, perhaps mixed with fine Turkish tobacco, but cloves to be sure.

Back inside, she carried her bags to her room and tossed them on the king-sized bed, then turned a full circle. The room was like a palace room. Large pillows garnished the bed, covered with a thick comforter. Off to one side was a sitting area with a table that bore an enormous bouquet of fresh flowers and a bowl of fruit. The wooden wardrobe opened to a cavernous inside where a fluffy bathrobe waited, and to the other side of the wardrobe was a paneled bookshelf and television. She turned on the news, muted the sound, and unpacked her belongings.

She was in for another pleasant surprise when she entered the bathroom. It was as big as her whole bedroom back in her apartment in Huntington. She gazed at the sunken tub, inspected the stone-lined walk-in shower, and touched the curve of the faucet handles. When she'd finished stowing her gear and standing her crutches against the wall, she slipped off her dress boots, swung her legs across the duvet, and kicked back on the bed. With the television humming and her pain medication kicking in, she soon found herself sinking into the pillows.

❖

Chrys startled awake when her phone vibrated on the nightstand. "This is Safis."

"Commander Banks, ma'am. I'm coming up with your beer if you could meet me at the door."

"Beer?" Chrys looked around the unfamiliar room and tried to process who the heck Banks was.

"As you requested?"

She wiped her sweaty forehead. "Right."

She got up, a little too quickly, and shifted at an uncomfortable angle and cursed as she limped to the door. When she opened it, she found Banks there holding a case of beer.

"No IPA at the bar," Banks said, "but here's a case of cold ones I had Smith pick up for you."

Chrys took the bundle. "Thanks."

"Dinner will be delivered within the hour."

"That's fine."

Banks stepped away, paused as she scrutinized her. "Are you feeling all right, ma'am?"

"I fell asleep, woke up a little disoriented, that's all."

Chrys thanked her again and brought the beer into the kitchen, popped one open, and chugged it down. Instantly, her body cooled. She glanced at Reyha's door. Would she find her a philistine for preferring beer over wine? And just what would they talk about at dinner that night, or for the next five months?

With a second beer in hand, she returned to her room and plopped back on the bed. The news station was running a story about a missile strike in Afghanistan. She turned up the volume and listened. Footage of broken concrete barriers, rebar, and smoldering plaster flashed across the screen. Men with bloody faces, civilians crying, trying to speak to the reporter, but their voices muted by the news announcer's summary. The scene cut away to bodies covered with blankets, women wailing and shaking their hands skyward. She got up for another beer and found Reyha sitting at the desk.

"Dinner will arrive soon," she said as Chrys came within view.

"That'll be fine." Chrys sat on the sofa.

Reyha looked up from her notes, removed her reading glasses, and watched Chrys with a curious expression.

"I hope you don't mind," Chrys said holding up her bottle. "I had Commander Banks bring me some beer. I'm not much for wine."

"I do not mind in the least."

Chrys took a sip and shifted her leg. Reyha seemed to be waiting for something. Finally, in Turkish she asked, "Did your rest strengthen you?"

"It did." Reyha joined her on the sofa. As she sat, she put one arm along the back, turned, and faced Chrys. "I seem less able to recover from traveling than I could when I was a younger woman. Getting older has its drawbacks, but many advantages as well. You will see." She patted Chrys's thigh.

"You look in wonderful health."

"I feel in wonderful health."

"Then your treatments, are they…" Chrys looked away. "Forgive me, I didn't mean to pry."

"There is no need to apologize. You will be accompanying me to the clinic for the ten days I undergo this experimental treatment. I am not uncomfortable discussing it with you."

"Experimental? In what way?"

Reyha played with the hem of her tunic. "It is a drug that will with some hope slow the growth of the cancerous cells." She tugged a strand of her hair. "And they have told me they have a new technology, an ice cap I will wear upon my head to prevent hair loss. This is something that pleases me. It took me nearly four years to grow it back from my last bout."

Chrys studied the strand of hair in Reyha's hand. Her fingers itched to touch it. "Four years. You've been in remission that long?"

Reyha nodded.

"And now, if I may ask, what is your prognosis?"

Reyha inclined her head, let her hand fall on Chrys's thigh once more. "You must not concern yourself, my friend. I have lived a long and good life."

"You can't be more than—"

"Fifty-one."

"You don't look it."

Reyha smiled. "My mother was a true beauty, and I have been blessed with her remarkable skin. For this I am grateful." She brushed Chrys's cheek. "And you, I saw in your file you turned twenty-nine this past May, yet I see in your eyes you are an old soul."

Chrys blinked, amazed at the way Reyha's hand had felt on her cheek, and even more amazed she hadn't recoiled from the touch. "The nineteenth, yes."

"And such a portentous day."

"In what way?"

Reyha reached her hand once again and stroked the line of Chrys's jaw, traced one of the scars. "It is one of the many days of remembrance in your homeland, is it not? A day to remember the atrocities committed by my people against yours."

Chrys's shoulders tensed. "Yes, May nineteenth is one of the days of remembrance for us, for the Pontic Greek communities along the Black Sea." She turned her face away as she thought about a more significant date, the day engraved into her childhood memory and of the stories her grandmother told her of the carnage and suffering heaped upon innocent people, her people. Before her, photographs of her grandparents materialized, still young children, yet aged in their souls. The scents of spanakopita baking in the oven filled the air, and she could see herself leaning against her grandmother's shoulder while she listened to the deep rattle in the old woman's chest as she spoke.

"We do not hate," her grandmother said, "but neither do we forget."

Chrys shook herself, and the remembered sights, sounds, and scents evaporated. She pushed her finger against her pulsing temple.

"I have no animosity against the Turkish people. I learned from my grandmother—the crimes of one nation against another don't damn an entire people."

"Your grandmother was a wise woman."

"The wisest."

A knock on the door brought them to their feet. Reyha excused herself and welcomed in the hotel staff, who began setting out dinner.

While the staff worked, Chrys used the restroom, where she washed her hands and face and ran her fingers through her hair. She studied her reflection and stroked the very scar Reyha had just traced while wondering what Reyha had meant when she said she could see an old soul.

❖

"Do you like the flowers in your room?" Reyha asked, pouring a glass of wine.

"Yes, they're lovely," Chrys said as she returned and sat at the table.

"I picked them out for you."

"Thank you. That was a nice gesture. I thought the hotel had put them there."

"It is custom to bring a gift of flowers or wine." Reyha toasted her glass. "I am a visitor in your country, your home. I wish to honor you."

"But I'm staying in your suite. I should've been the one to bring you flowers."

Reyha patted Chrys's hand. "You are giving yourself. That is a gift unlike any other." She tucked her napkin in her lap. "But yellow roses are my favorite."

"I'll keep that in mind." Chrys began to eat the rich food set before her. She was too embarrassed to ask what she was eating and could only guess it was French cuisine because the portions were small and arranged geometrically about her plate. After a few bites she said, "Secretary Collins informed me about your assistant's death a few months back. You have my condolences."

Reyha placed her fork on the edge of her plate, lowered her gaze, and took a sip of wine. "Ophelia was dear to me. A good friend. I cannot tell you the regret in my heart for losing her, my sorrow for her husband and children."

"I've lost friends, too. I know it's hard."

Reyha raised her eyes. "And it never becomes easier, does it?"

"No, never." Chrys focused on her plate, tried to appear busy with her knife and fork. "I also wanted to say, you have my sympathies for your husband and sons. I remember reading the news when it happened." She glanced up to find Reyha frowning.

"Thank you, however, neither Kerem nor Cinar were my sons. They were Emin's sons by his first wife, Leyla."

Chrys put down her utensils, took a sip of beer. "I didn't realize." She scanned her memory for the images of the newspaper accounts and broadcasts concerning Emin's assassination. Of course the two younger men couldn't have been Reyha's sons. They'd been Reyha's age at the time of their deaths. She cleared her throat. "I wasn't aware your husband had been previously married."

Reyha returned to her food, took a while to chew a bite before saying, "Yes, Leyla was his first wife. His true love, I would add." She bowed her head, seemed to contemplate something. "Leyla was Kurdish, you know, and such a beautiful woman."

Chrys put her hands in her lap. She detected some painful memory behind Reyha's words.

"She and my mother were best friends," Reyha continued. "Perhaps you are not aware, but my mother and Leyla were executed in the aftermath of the coup in the early seventies."

"I didn't know, I'm sorry." Chrys leaned on her elbow and held her chin with one hand as she continued to watch Reyha pick at her food. She wanted to ask how she'd come to marry Emin, a man old enough to be her father, but figured it had something to do with a political alliance, an arranged marriage of the sort that wasn't uncommon in that part of the world. And perhaps not that uncommon after all, for her own father had been fifteen years older than her mother. Clearly, age differences didn't matter much between men and women.

Then, as quickly as the moment had turned somber, it vanished as Reyha flipped at the air with her fingers. "We should not discuss such sadness while we eat. Please, tell me about your childhood, your family, why you joined the United States Air Force, how you came to be so gifted with languages."

"My life hasn't been that interesting, really."

"I will not accept that. Now please, let us open our hearts and talk. We have such a short time together, and I want us to be very good friends." Reyha finished her request with a sip of wine and a wink.

Chrys stopped partway to her mouth with her fork. Reyha's wink, a seemingly innocent gesture, seized her for a moment. She resumed her bite, chewed, and swallowed. "I'm going to have another beer. Can I get you something while I'm up?" She fanned herself as she went to the kitchen and back.

"Just you and your company. That is all I ask." Reyha waited until Chrys sat again. "So, tell me, what generation did your family immigrate to America?"

Chrys took a long pull from her beer. "My mother's family came over from Greece and first settled in Canada at the turn of the century. Her grandparents moved to the American Midwest when they were first married. However, my father was first generation. His parents immigrated to the US after spending a few years as kids in a refugee camp in Mexico. They eventually settled in the same town as my mom's family. That's where my parents met." She grinned. "But I consider myself practically first generation, too, because my yiayia, my dad's mom, lived with us and raised me and my brother, so sometimes I feel I grew up in another world altogether."

"Refugee camp?" Reyha frowned. "From which conflict did they escape?"

Chrys hesitated, shifted her body weight. "Smyrna, the great fires of Smyrna. Yiayia was eight, Pappou fifteen."

Reyha covered her mouth.

"They escaped the Ottoman assault on the Greeks and Armenians. Yiayia lost her parents and her two sisters. Pappou's family took her in, escaped with her as their own." Chrys diverted her eyes, unsure how much more she should share. But these were the stories she'd been raised on, the deep roots of her identity shaped by tragic memories. She cleared her throat and continued. "I grew up hearing about people stampeding while trying to flee the fire, some jumping into the harbor and trying to swim to ships only to drown, of burning bodies, bloated corpses floating off the pier. Of women and girls who were…" She lowered her eyes. "Well, my grandmother spared no detail."

Reyha turned her face away.

"Despite that," Chrys hurried to add, "despite everything my grandparents witnessed, for all they suffered, they never had hate in their hearts for the Turks. For anyone, really. And believe me, we weren't always the most warmly accepted group in Omaha, Nebraska, either, yet I'd like to think we were good neighbors all around."

Reyha turned back and wiped her eyes. “This is where you grew up?”

“A whole lot of us,” Chrys said. “Cousins and second cousins and a whole host of aunts and uncles on my mother’s side. We had our own part of town in south Omaha the locals call Greek Town. It really was like growing up in another part of the world.”

“You were bilingual even as a child?”

“Oh yes, and I attended Greek school after my regular school day, was brought up in the Orthodox Church, St. John’s, where my little brother Giorgos is now a priest, and I spent every Saturday morning at my father’s bakery, helping set out the loukoumades and melomakarona.” She patted her stomach and smiled. “But I think I ate more than I put on display.”

The sadness dissipated from Reyha’s eyes. “You had a good childhood? A warm family?”

“The best.” Memories flooded Chrys’s mind all at once—the taste of her grandmother’s cooking, the scent of her father’s bakery. She’d been a happy child, a loved child. She’d forgotten just how good it’d been.

“We Turks are your brothers and sisters,” Reyha said. “Still, we fight among ourselves as to who was firstborn.”

“And who gets credit for the world’s great inventions, am I right?” Chrys chuckled at Reyha’s feigned offense. “I’m aware you’d like to take credit for inventing yogurt, but that’s all ours. That and democracy and the Olympics and a whole lot more.”

“I will give you democracy and the Olympics, but yogurt I will have to fight for.” Reyha winked again as she laughed.

Chrys tilted her head and gazed at her face.

“Is something the matter?” Reyha asked.

Chrys shook her head since her mouth refused to work.

“Then please, carry on,” Reyha said. “Tell me more about your childhood, your wise grandmother, your time in the Air Force.”

Chrys forgot about her fresh beer as she began her dull biopic. But through it all, Reyha asked lots of questions. At moments, she would slip into Turkish, and Chrys would answer in Armenian. Then enthusiastically, Reyha would continue in Kurdish, and Chrys would counter in Greek. Reyha smiled always, seeming to enjoy the playfulness of the languages and the confidence Chrys had in speaking them. There was only one long pause, a respectful silence when Chrys told how her mother and youngest brother Nikolaos had perished when their car had rolled off the road during a Nebraska snowstorm. Chrys had been eight, her brother Giorgos six. Her father had lost his mind, and it was her grandmother, her yiayia, who had held the family together.

"My grandmother was my best friend," Chrys said. "And my teacher and confidant. She passed six years ago at the age of ninety-seven, just before my second deployment to Iraq." She swallowed to halt her tears. "I miss her a lot."

"She sounds to have been a wonderful woman."

Chrys studied the pattern in the fine china before her. She'd not had such expensive items growing up. She'd always filled her life with practical things, useful things, never luxuries. It went against her nature, her grandmother's ethic of living frugally.

"It was interesting to me," Chrys went on, "tragic in some ways, I guess. You see, my dad had a heart attack and died six months before her death. I always thought she died of a broken heart. Strange, isn't it? She'd been so strong as a little girl living through everything, stronger still when my pappou passed, but with my dad's death she just couldn't recover." She took a sip of beer, now warm, and wiped her mouth. "I know it was more than him being her firstborn child. He was extra special because she and Pappou had tried and tried to have children and had almost given up hope." She thought a long moment, considered what her grandmother had lived through, how she'd never backed down or given up in the face of the many hardships she'd endured.

"I have heard the loss of a child is perhaps the most devastating of all losses," Reyha said, interrupting Chrys's thoughts.

Chrys refocused her eyes. "Yes, I witnessed that in Iraq and among the villages we liberated in Syria." For an instant, she smelled smoke, tasted blood, and she gripped the edge of the table to ground herself.

Reyha pushed back from her plate. "Join me on the balcony while I enjoy a cigarette?"

Chrys stood on quivering legs. She brought her beer with her and leaned against the railing while looking out at the lights of DC, at the monuments lit up like cathedrals.

"Perhaps when we are more acquainted you will tell me about your time in Syria," Reyha said.

Chrys turned. The city lights illuminated Reyha as she reclined in the chair with her head back and her chin lifted as she brought her cigarette to her lips.

"I hope I'm able to help you accomplish your goals while you're here in the States," Chrys said.

"And perhaps beyond my stay."

"I don't understand." Chrys pulled up a chair.

But Reyha waved her off. "For another time."

Chrys watched Reyha bring the cigarette to her lips once more. "Can I ask you something?"

"You may ask me anything."

"Do your doctors know you smoke?"

Reyha chuckled. "There are few pleasures left to me. Good food, good wine, and a good cigarette." She held Chrys in a lengthy gaze. "And of course, good company."

"But doesn't it hinder your recovery?"

Reyha peered through the smoke. "I do not expect to live forever, nor should I want to."

Chrys looked away and forced herself to focus on the Washington Monument and not on the images of Diren and Morrison attempting to invade her mind at that moment.

"What are you thinking?" Reyha's voice cut through her thoughts.

Chrys lifted her beer. "May you live long," she replied in a traditional Turkish blessing. "May your illness be in the past."

Reyha hoisted her wineglass. "And may these blessings fall to you as well, my friend." She clinked her glass to Chrys's bottle, then lit another cigarette.

When they finally bid good night, Reyha clasped Chrys around the shoulders and kissed her cheeks. "I feel I have chosen a most suitable companion for this adventure."

"I hope I won't disappoint you," Chrys said, standing rigid in Reyha's embrace.

"I do not think that possible."

Chrys watched her retire to her end of the suite before she went to her own. She changed for bed but paced the room for a bit trying to dispel her tension. Still she couldn't relax. She tried watching television and flipped channels until finally she settled on a twenty-four-hour news station. She programmed the sleep timer on the TV, lined up her prescription bottles, and estimated how much of the sleep aid she'd need to fall off, but not so much she'd oversleep or sleep for the whole day as she'd gotten into the habit of doing these past months. After settling on a reduced amount of medicine and swallowing it down with the rest of her warm beer, she removed her prosthetic leg and placed it on the chair next to the bed.

But even with the hum of the television and her sleep aid in her system, she stared up at the ceiling as she thought about Mary and her grandmother, Diren and her other companions, Banks and her team, and that silly little man, Carmichael. She replayed her conversation with Reyha, considered her playful wink, her affectionate nature. It wasn't unusual for someone from that region of the world to be so affectionate. Her own family had been so, and there had been a time in her life when she'd liked the physical closeness, a time not so long ago before missiles rained down on her and her friends. She rolled to her side and tried to make her mind stop spinning, tried to block the sounds and smells rattling at the cage of her memory. Finally, focusing on one of her childhood memories, one aroused by her conversation with Reyha, she relaxed and found comfort in the oblivion of sleep where her mind might rest until the trauma coded into her every cell broke free once more and ravaged her.

She warms her hands by campfire, her weapon slung behind her, the scarf Diren gave her wound about her neck. She laughs at a joke, watches the faces of the women who circle the fire with her. She takes a whiff of their meal cooking in the pots, tastes the hot black tea laced with honey. Small hands touch her shoulders. Sirvan climbs into her lap and pokes her dimples and says he loves her. Will she marry him when he is older, when he owns an automobile and an apartment? Will she give him many sons? She hugs him. She will marry no other man. Diren watches from across the fire. Smoke obscures her vision, encases the camp. She shouts, but none answer. Missiles scream through the blue sky, the earth explodes around her. Diren yells for retreat as fighters dressed in black crest the horizon, their banners fluttering. They swarm, hundreds of them raging in the name of their angry God. Asmin races with Sirvan in her arms. She follows behind, turns for Diren, sees her strap on the explosives. Stop, wait, no, no, no, no. She runs back for her, tries to run faster. Diren smiles, flashes the peace sign, tosses a grenade, and charges headlong into the horde. Blood and shit and flesh rocket skyward, in every direction, and before she can scream again, she's lifted in the air as a truck explodes into a fireball.

She flailed with her arms, cried out in Kurdish, screaming for

Diren to stop. But someone grabbed her wrists and held her. She struggled, her eyes not comprehending anything but the images burned into her memory.

"You are safe." Reyha's voice sliced through the fog of the nightmare. "Be calm."

Chrys cringed in the glare of the bedside lamp.

"You are safe," Reyha repeated and eased up on her hold.

Chrys gasped, looked around wildly, pushed against Reyha's hands.

"Be still," Reyha said. "There is no danger."

Chrys heaved for air. "Shit, I woke you. Oh God, I'm sorry."

"You must not apologize. I had gone to the kitchen for some water. That is the only reason I heard you cry out." Reyha's hair was tousled about her shoulders, and her robe was untied, revealing a sheer nightgown underneath. "Let me get you water." She left the room.

Chrys glanced at her prosthesis on the chair, right there in plain sight. She groaned and pounded her forehead with her fist.

"Here, sip." Reyha resumed her spot on the bed while handing Chrys a glass of water. She watched her take a few gulps, then got up and went into the bathroom and returned with a damp washcloth. "Let me." She began to draw the cloth over Chrys's face and along her neck. As she did so, she gazed into Chrys's eyes as tenderly as any lover might. "Better?"

Chrys held her breath, so unaccustomed to being touched this way and amazed at how she had no impulse to recoil. "Better, thank you." She drained the rest of the water and set the glass on the bedside table while knocking over a few prescriptions.

"You have these dreams often?" Reyha asked, setting the bottles upright.

"Yes."

"I am sorry for you. Secretary Collins gave only a brief account of the events you suffered during your time in Syria. I understand there were many casualties."

"Yes. Many."

Reyha focused on some inconspicuous spot on the bedspread. Finally, she regained eye contact and placed her hand against Chrys's cheek. "You are reliving the attack?"

Chrys nodded, soothed by Reyha's cool hand.

"I wish I could take the memory from you. To ease your suffering mind and troubled heart."

Chrys lifted her hand and covered Reyha's. "Thank you."

"Sleep now." Reyha leaned forward, strands of her hair falling into Chrys's face as she pressed her lips to her forehead. She sat back. "Think of something that calms you, something beautiful and pure." She stood and took the glass, paused at the door where her eyes touched on the prosthetic leg. Her brows furled then straightened as she smiled. She turned and was gone.

Chrys shivered and gulped for air while she stared at the door. Reyha's face, her smile. For an instant, she'd seen the face of her dear friend Diren looking back at her. She held her head, pounding with the blasts of rockets and gunfire, and touched the place Reyha had kissed her. She could still detect the aroma of her cigarettes and perfume, and soon it overpowered the putrid smells hanging in her memory while the reverberation of Reyha's deep voice drowned out the explosions in her mind.

She wiped her face on her blanket and looked around the room. Thankfully, no apparition appeared, no hallucination brought on by stress. She switched off her lamp and sank down into her damp pillows where she cried until she fell back to sleep.

CHAPTER EIGHT

When Chrys became aware of the cool sheets on her skin, the smell of coffee seeping around her, and the sound of music reaching her ears, she rolled over and checked the time on her phone. She shot up and cursed. She'd slept too long.

She hurried to attach her leg and pull sweatpants on over her boxers. Out in the living room, she found Reyha sitting at the desk. Classical music, a cello piece, played on the sound system. At the table, a carafe of coffee sat among plates of muffins and croissants, cut fruit, and bowls of yogurt and granola.

"I'm sorry," Chrys said going over to the coffee. "I didn't mean to oversleep."

Reyha lowered the volume on the sound system. "Not at all. We have nothing particular scheduled for today. You should sleep as much as you need." She approached Chrys. "Were you able to fall back to sleep?"

"Yes, thank you." Chrys busied herself preparing her coffee, yet she was aware how close Reyha stood. "You haven't waited on me, have you?"

"Of course, I waited. Well…" Reyha pointed to a partially eaten muffin and chuckled. "I did take a bite. Now sit. Have something to eat."

Chrys did so and pulled her napkin onto her lap. She glanced over at the sound system on the wall. "Nice music."

"Bach's Cello Suite number Two in D Minor. One of my favorites. It helps me think, think and feel. And I am happy to say, your Mr. Gordon acquired tickets for us to see an accomplished cellist at the Kennedy Center. I am sure we shall hear some Bach, perhaps some Elgar or Dvořák."

Chrys paused with her cup midway to her mouth. "Sounds great."

Reyha laughed outright and patted Chrys's leg. "You do not sound so enthusiastic. Am I to understand you are not a fan of classical music, or only of the cello?"

"Actually, I was thinking I'm going to need to get something to wear. Without my dress uniform, I don't have anything formal enough."

"I am sure Mr. Carmichael can direct you to an appropriate tailor. I learned he has his own suits custom-made."

"I'm sure he does." Chrys studied Reyha's hands, counted five rings, two on one hand and three on the other, one ring crested with a large diamond. "Would you be okay if I have a tux altered to fit me?"

"Why would I not?"

"I wasn't sure if you felt it would be inappropriate." Right then, Chrys realized how she was dressed and looked down at her sweats, her wrinkled tank top. "I should've changed out of my pajamas. I hope I haven't insulted you." She started to get up.

"Sit. Eat. This is your home for the time being. As I told you the first morning we met, there should be no formalities between us. And yes, I believe you will be quite stunning in a tuxedo fitted for your frame."

"You're very kind." Chrys pushed one of her curls out of her eyes and returned to her food. She looked up to find Reyha scrutinizing her shoulders.

"You seem to be quite fit, very muscular," Reyha said.

"I'm actually out of shape. I'm hoping to use the facilities downstairs to get back to the level I was at before my injuries." Chrys narrowed her eyes. Reyha's cheeks had just flushed pink. "Are you okay?"

"I am fine. Perfectly fine." Reyha poured another cup of coffee. "If it is not too personal, I wonder, might you tell me what injuries you sustained?"

Chrys tapped her head. "Concussion and a bit of shrapnel lodged in the side of my head. Doctors were able to remove it, but to be honest, it's nothing less than a miracle I didn't have brain damage." She swept down her left side. "Also a lot of shrapnel in my side here, some burns." Under the table she tapped her leg. "And I lost my left leg just below the knee joint. That's pretty much it."

"To look at you, I would not suspect you had endured such injuries."

Chrys scoffed and pointed to her face. "Really? The whole left side of my face is slashed up."

"Yet your beautiful black hair obscures much of it, and you must know, when one looks at you, it is your eyes and smile that draw the most attention."

Chrys tilted her head. Reyha's face had flushed again.

"Now tell me," Reyha said, focusing on her coffee, "I understand you are currently being treated at the Veterans Hospital. What schedule must you keep?"

"I'm down to once a week for physical therapy, plus a group session. I also go in for a med check every four weeks. Other than that, I'm open, free to do anything you want." She repositioned her leg and winced. "In fact, I'm due in a few days to see my doctors and my therapist to get an adjustment on this new prosthesis."

"You are in discomfort?"

"There's always some pain."

Reyha chewed a bite of food and examined her plate. "I noticed a number of medications by your bedside last night. They are for your pain?"

Chrys buttered her croissant. "Pain and sleep mostly."

"Yet still you dream of your time in Syria."

"Yes." Chrys reached for the jam, noticed her hand shaking.

"Your group meetings, do they help you?"

"Not really, but I go because I should, because it's the responsible thing to do, because there's another woman, a former petty officer who I've become acquainted with. I'm worried about her, and I think if I don't show up, she'll be on her own with all those guys, with no one to talk to."

"Thinking of others. I would expect this of you."

"Why?" Chrys watched as Reyha's gaze traveled over her face.

"It is in the nature of your people," Reyha said. "This love of doing the right thing, no matter how difficult. The sense of honor which is the bedrock of your character."

Chrys relaxed and grinned. "*Philotimo*." She said the Greek word with reverence.

"Indeed."

Chrys continued to smile and ran fingers through her hair. "You know, Yiayia would say philotimo is something we Greeks carry in our bones, the very essence of our being, and something that can't be imposed by law. It demands free will to choose the right path, and it's the only reason why we shouldn't, for all our flaws—and we have many—why we shouldn't be destroyed by the anger of the gods."

"As I said, your grandmother was a very wise woman."

Chrys lifted her coffee cup in a toast. "I'm glad you understand. I've never been able to really define philotimo for my non-Greek friends. Especially Mary."

"And who is this Mary?"

"A friend, just a friend." Chrys piled fruit on her plate and inwardly cursed herself for the slipup. "What would you like to do today? I'm up for anything."

"Yes, these next weeks shall be for pleasure. As many museums and monuments as we can visit before I must undergo my treatment."

"I'm sorry you have to endure that."

"I am afraid the tiller man must be paid."

"The tiller man?" Chrys raised an eyebrow.

"Charon, if you please, but that seems morbid, does it not?"

Chrys's heart skipped. "The ferryman to Hades? You're not that ill, are you?"

Reyha laughed, her face brightening. "It is only an expression. I have no doubt I will regain my health quickly. I am in fine fettle otherwise."

"That's an expression I haven't heard before."

"Old-fashioned English. I picked it up from a dear friend while I was at university in London. She taught me English idioms, and I gave her Turkish wisdom. It was a fair exchange, I believe." Reyha seemed to grow pensive, but after a pause, she shook off her melancholy. "So shall we be tourists and embark on our journey this afternoon with you as my own personal tour guide?"

"Your very own personal tour guide."

"I enjoy the sound of that." Reyha patted Chrys's hand and winked as she'd done the night before.

Chrys only realized she was staring at Reyha's flirtatious…no, playful…face when a blueberry dropped from her suspended spoon and plopped in her lap. She put it on her plate and made an offhand remark. "A closed mouth gathers no feet and apparently no blueberries either." She covered her embarrassment with a chuckle.

"Explain, please."

Chrys thought about it. "Well, you've heard the phrase *put your foot in your mouth* when you say something inappropriate?"

"Yes, that one I know."

"So, *a closed mouth gathers no feet* means you can't say something inappropriate if you don't talk." Chrys shrugged. "I just added to it when

I was younger. I was always missing my mouth when I ate, distracted by my dad and uncles arguing at the table."

Reyha frowned, tilted her head.

"I like to play with languages," Chrys explained further. "I think that's why I've always like learning them."

"You made up your own idiomatic phrase, or rather altered one to suit you?"

"Yes."

"And here again I see I have chosen a talented polyglot who not only speaks my language exquisitely but is also a companion who has the love of words as I do." Reyha glanced up from the muffin she buttered. "But tell me something."

"Yes?"

"Were you just now distracted?"

Chrys's cheeks burned. "Maybe. A little."

"Hmm." Reyha winked again and chuckled.

For the next several days, Chrys kept a rein on her prescription drug use and on the amount of beer she allowed herself at lunch and dinner, and in the evenings. But the symptoms of her partial withdrawal were troublesome and not easily concealed. She was sure Reyha could see the intensified quiver in her hands and the heavier sheen of sweat on her skin. Even Banks seemed to watch her more closely, her hawk-like expression questioning, almost judgmental. But one thing Chrys began to notice was how easy it was to ignore her pounding head and queasy stomach any time Reyha engaged her in conversation. She found herself so spellbound by Reyha's voice and her animated way of speaking, she'd forget her physical symptoms, even many of the thoughts that troubled her regularly.

She also found herself mildly entertained as they toured the museums while Reyha offered a running commentary of all the artifacts they saw. Often she found herself laughing at Reyha's naive understanding of some American idiomatic saying along with her comical interpretations. As each day progressed and they examined new galleries and sights, Chrys also began to notice the occasional looks from other tourists. Even if Reyha hadn't been surrounded by bodyguards, a sure indicator she was someone of importance, Chrys was sure she'd still draw attention. It wasn't just the fact she covered her hair when out in public. There were plenty of observant Muslim women enjoying the sights among the other visitors. No, it was something more, and all Chrys could determine was the way Reyha carried herself, so confident, so in charge; she couldn't help but draw appreciative stares. And when Reyha spoke, whether in English or in one of the other languages she knew, her soothing voice permeated the quiet spaces within the buildings, often causing people to turn and listen.

For Chrys, those first several days and evenings presented a stark contrast to the months she'd languished in her tiny apartment. Here she had the most amazing food, with evenings punctuated by stimulating conversations on the hotel balcony while she leaned against the railing and Reyha smoked. And to her surprise, she found her large bed seemed to ease her into a deeper sleep, one less hampered by nightmares. Concentrating on Reyha served as an effective diversion, one that kept her mind off Mary, off those persistent memories of Syria and the friends she'd lost. It promised to be a good five months, and by the end of the fourth day, Chrys committed herself to resuming her rigorous physical training in the hotel's fitness center. Before long, she'd be strong and healthy and ready to return to Syria, to her Kurdish sisters and their cause.

But on the fifth day, Chrys felt herself faltering, struggling with some of the images they'd seen, the sad history of brutality lurking under a veil of patriotism. By the sixth morning, the growing disquiet twisted inside her brain. Finally, on the seventh morning, she gained some relief when they visited the National Museum of American History. Despite the ache in her leg and hips from all the walking they'd been doing, she started to enjoy herself again, having a wonderful time watching Reyha swing from childlike amazement at the sight of Elvis Presley's leather jacket to exuberance at Judy Garland's ruby slippers from the motion picture *The Wizard of Oz*.

"Do you think when we go to New York that we might get tickets to *Wicked*?" Reyha asked as they moved through the *American Presidency* exhibit. "I would so like to see it. I have a great fondness for your Mr. Baum and his courageous Dorothy."

"The musical is more about the witches actually, good and evil, that sort of thing," Chrys said.

"I understood the theme to be how good and evil reside in each of us."

"Something like that. I don't know. I'm terrible at interpreting movies and plays. But sure, there might be tickets. I'll have Banks call Gordon and see what he can turn up. It's a great production, by the way. I took Mary to see it a few years back." Chrys pinched the bridge of her nose and grunted softly once she realized what she'd said.

Reyha pulled her to a stop in front of the Andrew Jackson display. "I would like to know more about this Mary."

"A friend, as I said."

"And where is she now?"

Chrys rubbed the back of her neck. Banks stood within earshot and turned her head as if she was waiting to hear the reply as well. "California. She moved there the same day I came to the Hay-Adams."

"You lived with her?"

"When I wasn't deployed." Chrys tried to step away, but Reyha touched her arm.

"For how long did you live with her?"

Chrys studied Jackson's famous sword from the War of 1812. How many heads had he severed? Limbs? She teetered with memories of the videos she'd been forced to see, of men and women, some young children, on their knees as masked men made proclamations and slowly severed their victims' jugulars as they thrashed and pleaded with suffocating cries. She wiped a drop of sweat from her temple.

"Seven years," she said. "We were together for seven years." She pointed to another display. "Hey, there's Harrison. You know, he only served a month as president. Got pneumonia standing out in the cold giving his inaugural speech." She fanned herself. "Wow, it's warm in here. Do you mind if we move along?"

Reyha came up alongside her. "I do not care for what these men have done. History is bloated with their stories. Let us see something women have contributed to your country."

In the *First Ladies* exhibit, Reyha paused in front of the inaugural dresses and took time to read the information for each set of White House china on display. Her brows remained bunched the entire time. After examining the display, she returned to the china set that had once graced the tables during Franklin Roosevelt's term in office, the set his wife Eleanor had chosen.

"Interesting," she muttered in Turkish.

Chrys leaned in. "Yes?"

Then in English, Reyha said, "Your Eleanor Roosevelt worked on the Universal Declaration of Human Rights, and she was one of the most influential members of the United Nations Human Rights Commission."

"That's right."

"Yet she is represented here only by her inaugural gown"—Reyha pointed behind her—"and her choice in chinaware."

Chrys shrugged. "All the First Ladies are represented by their dresses and dishes."

"Exactly." Reyha turned to her. "It is insulting. These women, not just your Mrs. Roosevelt, but the others as well, contributed so much more to your country and its culture. Why relegate them to this small exhibit of dresses and dishes? Are women no more than side notes to your history?"

Chrys opened her mouth to speak, but only managed a stutter.

"We are fifty percent of the human population," Reyha said. "The only half to bring life into the world, to nurture it to fruition, yet we have such little say in how the world works."

"But that's how it is, the way things naturally progress."

"There is nothing natural about it."

"I don't understand why you're so upset. It's just a museum exhibit."

Reyha's beautiful face hardened. "Is that all it is?" She held up her hand. "No. Do not answer." She motioned for Banks. "Please, I wish to eat something."

Banks signaled for the two agents in the distance while speaking into her radio. She took point while Quinn and Smith flanked them as they headed toward the exit. Once inside the SUV, Reyha leaned against her window, and Chrys watched out her own and wondered what had upset her. Still, she was thankful the topic of Mary had been dropped.

❖

At the restaurant, Chrys scooted her chair close. "Can you tell me why you're upset about the *First Ladies* exhibit? I'm really curious to understand."

The waiter brought their drinks, and Reyha approved the wine and waited until he left.

"The world is not a kind place to be female." Reyha sipped from her glass.

"The world isn't a kind place in most respects," Chrys said. "It doesn't matter much whether you're male or female."

"You think not? Have you not been involved in the liberation of both Kurdish and Yazidi villages? Seen the enslavement of girls as young as nine?"

"But they killed the men, too, sometimes brutally."

"Yet their target was the women and girls, to enslave and abuse them."

Chrys sighed. "I'm well aware of that fact." She drank her beer and looked past Reyha to the other customers. She was tired, hurting, and struggling to keep focused. "Yes, the world's a shit hole no matter who you are, and I agree, it can be doubly so if you're born a girl in many cases." Once she realized what she'd said, she covered her mouth. "My apologies for the vulgarity."

Reyha giggled. "Although not an elegant way to describe the current state of affairs, I do agree with you."

"When I get tired, my mouth just spews stuff out. Really, I'm sorry."

"I am sure your restless sleep contributes to your exhaustion."

"It hasn't been so bad these last few nights." Chrys played with her linen napkin.

"No more bad dreams?"

"I haven't had any lately, but they're always there, always lurking."

"As I said, if I could take those memories from you I would." Reyha touched Chrys's leg under the tablecloth. "Perhaps these long walking excursions are helping you sleep more soundly."

Chrys signaled the waiter for another beer. "Maybe so."

The food arrived, and Reyha remarked on the quality, told a story about a restaurant in London she frequented, then asked, "So tell me, how do we fix it?"

"Fix what?" Chrys set down her fork.

"The world, this shit hole as you call it."

Chrys laughed. In Reyha's mouth, the words sounded absurd. "I don't think we can."

"No? Then why do we struggle to do so?"

"I ask myself that every day." Chrys pushed her plate away as the images from the last two days bombarded her—slave shackles, cavalry massacres, internment camps. She was beginning to sweat through her shirt, and her hands were starting to shake. With urgency, she looked for the waiter.

"Why did you join the Air Force?"

Chrys caught the waiter's attention and pointed to her beer. "I told you, to pay for my education. There was no way for my dad to afford college from the profits of the bakery. He gave away more food than he sold."

"But why did you fight?"

Chrys smiled. "That's how the military works. They give orders, you follow."

"No, you did so because you believed in doing good because you are good, and doing the right thing comes naturally to you."

The waiter set a bottle in front of Chrys, but she ignored it and kept her focus on Reyha, on those perceptive eyes. "Truthfully, after the last two days of looking at the long history of conflict and war in the US, the genocide of the American Indian, the holocaust against African slaves, I'm not sure doing the right thing makes any difference in the world. We certainly haven't evolved as a species, and I'm not sure we deserve to survive much longer."

Reyha's eyes widened. "Do not say that. You must never say that."

Chrys set her jaw. "My apologies." She slipped her fingers into her pocket and drew out a tranquilizer and inconspicuously put it under her tongue. The bitter taste flooded her mouth and she swallowed a mouthful of beer to wash it down.

"You must not become a nihilist," Reyha said. "The world sits precariously on the edge of extinction. If people like you and I give up fighting, we are certainly doomed."

Chrys's fingers buzzed and the busy restaurant seemed to mute around her. Right then something in her gut began to ache. "But it doesn't matter how much good I do, anyone does," she said. "Love doesn't conquer hate. I don't care how many times people say it, how many signs they carry at rallies. Nothing ever changes. History bears it out. Can't you see that? We're doomed no matter what we do. Sometimes I think the merciful thing for all of us would be for an asteroid to pummel the earth and put every living thing out of its misery."

Reyha held her hand to her throat. "Why are you saying these things?"

Chrys groaned. No one ever understood this, not her friends, not Mary, no one but the men and women who'd seen the truth of what the world was like.

"There was this village we liberated," she said keeping her eyes on Reyha. "The children rushed out singing to us, the women hugged us, kissed our cheeks as they wept. Old men sat down in the middle of the road and cried like babies, and we knelt down and kissed them on their heads, gave them water and cigarettes. Then the women…" Her voice began to quiver. "All those women began stripping off their niqabs, tossing them to the ground. Woman after woman until the road was full of black cloths, like corpses laid out for the vultures. They were finally free." She broke eye contact and rubbed her forehead. "You should've seen the celebration that night. The campfire, the singing and dancing. They made a feast for us with what little they had. Blessed us over and over. The joy on their faces was…" She shook her head and sniffed.

"And this is why you fight," Reyha said, touching her hand.

"We marched on two days later. The next week we heard the village had been hit by drones. Fifty dead." Chrys pulled her hand away and took a deep swallow of beer. "And another dozen villages lay before us. And after that a dozen more. It never stops. Never, never stops." She stood. "Excuse me. I need to use the restroom."

Alone in a stall, she shivered as she fished another pill from her pocket. She swallowed it dry, then sat on the toilet and squeezed her eyes tight against the bombardment in her mind. The sounds. The smells. The taste of blood. There had been so much blood.

"Chrysanthi, you must not give in to despair." It was her grandmother's voice.

"I can't do it, Yiayia. There's nothing left of me."

"Let me in. I will strengthen you."

She swung open the stall door, and found Quinn standing there.

"What the hell, Quinn. This is the women's restroom." Chrys pushed past him to the sink and began washing her hands.

"The commander asked me to check on you. You've been in here for over twenty minutes." He blushed when the door opened and a woman squeaked with surprise.

"He's leaving," Chrys told the stranger and pulled Quinn out by his arm. "Seriously, I'm not the one who needs protection."

Quinn brought her to a stop. "Ma'am, you're aware of what happened to Mrs. Arslan's last assistant."

"Fine. Come on, I want to finish my lunch."

When Chrys sat again at the table, Reyha and Banks looked at her with faces full of worry.

"I'm sorry. I got overheated. Just needed to cool off," Chrys said.

"We should return to the hotel for you to rest," Reyha said.

"Nonsense. I'm fine. It's still early, and I thought we could see some of the National Gallery."

"I would like an entire day for that. Perhaps we could stroll in the Sculpture Garden instead."

Chrys fanned her napkin around her face. "I guess. It'll be warm, but there's plenty of shade if I remember." She smiled and took a bite, but she could see the look of concern on Reyha's face as well as the look of misgiving on Banks's.

❖

She held up her hand and shielded her face from the late afternoon sun, but once they entered the garden, Chrys was relieved to find most of the paths were indeed shaded by large trees, and the great round fountain in the center sprayed forcefully enough that a cool mist fell upon them.

Reyha strolled along a path. She seemed contemplative although her eyes took in the geometrically designed hedges and flower beds as well as the modern art of steel, marble, and wire. Finally, she motioned toward a bench by a tree and patted the seat next to her. Chrys sat while the agents took strategic positions around them.

"I would like to ask you something personal," Reyha said.

"Okay."

"Do you believe the world to be getting better or worse?"

Chrys gazed off at the crowd of visitors moving on the paths. A man held up his phone, apparently taking pictures, a lot of pictures in their direction.

"To be honest, worse."

"Have you always believed that?"

Chrys wiped her eyes. "There was a time in my life I thought I could make the world a better place, that good would triumph over evil, love would trump hate."

"But no longer."

"Not after what I've witnessed." Chrys strained her eyes. The man she'd noticed a second ago now hid in the shadow of an enormous abstract sculpture resembling decapitated red horses. He was taking a selfie and scratching the beard along his neck.

"I remember being so devastated after my mom and brother died," she continued. "I just couldn't see life without them. But then Yiayia would tell me I had to be strong, to grow up and be a good example in society. That was what my mother would want, she'd say." She shook her head. "But I can't change anything. I can only put a bandage on a festering wound and watch as the world goes septic."

"Perhaps you cannot change the world alone, but together we can…" Reyha followed her gaze. "What are you looking at?"

Chrys leaned forward, her body coiled for an attack. The man taking pictures lowered his phone and met her gaze. His lips curled into a snarl, and he jutted his chin at her as he scratched under his beard once more. Chrys bolted up, spun on her good foot to shield Reyha.

"Commander Banks, two o'clock, over my right shoulder by the red horses. Full beard, white shirt."

Reyha tried to stand. But Chrys held her down until Banks pulled her up and Quinn corralled and moved them while two other agents went into action. She tried to turn back to get a better look at the man, but she was pushed forward, and before she could protest, she was shoved into the back of the SUV with Reyha and Banks sliding in next to her.

Banks began shouting into her radio as Quinn sped the SUV out into the streets.

"What's happening?" Reyha asked.

Chrys scooted close and held her around the shoulders. "Everything's okay. Some guy was taking your picture. A lot of pictures."

"But they are tourists. Of course he is taking pictures."

"No, there was something about him. Something off."

In moments, they rendezvoused with the other SUV, and Smith approached Quinn's driver's side window and leaned in. "We lost him, Commander."

Banks glared at him. "Did you see what direction he went?"

"No, ma'am, but in truth we never actually caught sight of him."

Chrys leaned between the seats, kept her voice low. "Dark complected, full beard, midforties. He had on a white shirt and a vest of some sort, like part of a suit."

Smith shook his head. "We didn't see anyone with that description."

Banks waved him off and told Quinn to drive on.

Chrys turned to her. "I saw him. Something was off about him. He gave me this look."

"It was probably nothing, Ms. Safis," Banks said.

Chrys started to say something else, but Reyha cut her off as she addressed Banks. "What is happening? Explain."

"It's fine, ma'am. False alarm probably." Banks met Quinn's eyes as he glanced back. He shook his head.

"But I saw him," Chrys said again, trying to control her growing frustration. She looked down when she felt Reyha's hand in hers.

"Thank you for your concern, but I am certain the commander has things under control."

Chrys's anger dissipated some, but the looks Banks continued to give her kept it simmering at a low heat.

❖

While Reyha rested before dinner, Chrys went down the hall to the suite being used as the control room. Inside, she found Banks with Agent Christman, a dark-eyed woman with short cropped hair and a pretty smile. They huddled together and studied a four-panel feed of CCTV.

"It was closer to sixteen hundred, go forward," Banks said.

Christman fast forwarded the videos.

Chrys looked over their shoulders and watched the multiple screens showing the area she'd seen the man, but the red horse sculpture he'd hidden behind was just out of frame in every shot.

"I don't see him," she said more to herself.

Banks turned. "We've been over the feed from this afternoon, and neither I nor Agent Christman has spotted the individual you describe."

"He was there—I swear it," Chrys said.

Banks took Chrys by her arm and led her to the door. "I'm sure you saw someone, but I'm wondering maybe you misinterpreted what you saw."

Chrys scoffed. "I didn't imagine it if that's what you're saying."

Banks nodded to her team, and they all went back to their duties. In a hushed voice she continued, "Ma'am, I'm not judging you, please understand, but I did observe you consumed three alcoholic beverages at lunch, and by your own admission, you felt overheated and had to collect yourself in the restroom."

Chrys's temper flared and she pushed Banks's hand from her arm. "He was glaring at me, at her, taking pictures."

Banks sighed. "Yet I've found no one of the description you gave, and none of my men spotted him when they surveilled the area."

Chrys pointed to the monitors. "He was by those damn mutilated horses. You can't see it clear enough. Get another angle."

Her raised voice caused the others to turn and look. Banks pulled her from the room, and the agent sitting in the hallway stood.

"Thomas, take ten," Banks told him. Alone in the hallway, she faced Chrys. "While I appreciate your diligence, Ms. Safis, I'll remind you I'm in charge of Mrs. Arslan's security, and I and my team are doing everything we can to protect her. You also need to remember you were brought on as her assistant, not her bodyguard."

Chrys pulled herself up to her full height and stepped right into Banks's face. "He was there, and he was a threat. I've seen that look before—I should know." She refused to give ground and realized neither would Banks.

The suite door opened and Reyha came toward them. "What is happening?" She turned to Chrys. "Why are you yelling?"

Chrys twitched but held her stance and stared down Banks who looked away to reassure Reyha.

"It's nothing, ma'am. We were just discussing the individual Ms. Safis saw this afternoon."

"And? Have you identified him?" Reyha asked.

"No, but I'm confident he was no more than a tourist." Banks shot Chrys a disparaging look, bowed out of the way. "I'll check on your evening meal. Excuse me." She disappeared down the hall toward the elevator, and the agent she'd excused returned and took up his post.

Reyha scrutinized Chrys. "Your posture and face indicate you are upset." She took her hand and pulled her inside. "Were you just now arguing with Commander Banks?"

Chrys ground her teeth and marched to the kitchen where she pulled a cold beer from the refrigerator. "It was nothing." She swallowed a mouthful and leaned against the countertop while she trembled.

"I do not understand what has happened," Reyha said, moving toward her.

"I saw him. It wasn't a hallucination this time. He was there." Chrys caught a glimpse of suspicion in Reyha's eyes, the same doubt Mary always had. "I'm not crazy."

"I never indicated you were." Reyha reached out to touch her arm.

Chrys pulled away. "Don't. It hurts to be touched." She grunted with embarrassment and covered her face.

The awkward silence grew thick around them as a sudden aroma filled the kitchen. Chrys sniffed and peeked between her fingers to find her grandmother layering moussaka in a baking dish.

"Show me you are my granddaughter," her grandmother said. "Show me you have the strength to do your duty."

Chrys inhaled sharply and looked at Reyha. "Do you see her?"

"See who?"

Chrys glared at the beer in her hand, over to her grandmother. "She deserves better than me, Yiayia. I'm not as strong as you."

Reyha tilted her head. "Why do you speak to the dead?"

Chrys rubbed her eyes and her grandmother's image faded. She set aside her beer and held her hands up to keep Reyha at bay. "You need to call Gordon. Tell him you need a new interpreter, secretary, tour guide, whatever the fuck I am. Get someone else." She grabbed her bottle and drained it, then pushed off the counter and opened the refrigerator for another.

Reyha stopped her hand. "I want no one else. I want only to know why you are in such distress."

Chrys bit back her rage, yanked her hand from Reyha's grip. "I should've never taken this assignment. It's too soon."

Reyha stepped toward her. "Let me help you, my friend." She reached out once more.

Chrys recoiled and fell against the counter. "Don't. Please." She covered her face again and slid down to her butt where she pulled her left leg under her. Her whole body shivered, and her heart beat faster and faster while she gulped for air and held her chest.

"You are having a panic attack." Reyha knelt down but kept her distance. "Tell me what I can do. Do you need the medicines by your bed?"

Chrys stuttered and tried to speak while perspiration beaded along her lip, dripped down the sides of her face.

Reyha held her palms toward her. "Shh, do not try to speak. Let me get them." She went to Chrys's room and returned with all the prescriptions and laid them on the floor. "Which one do you need?"

Chrys snatched up the tranquilizers and fumbled with the lid. Reyha took the bottle from her, opened it, and held it out. Chrys shook out the pills and chewed a double dose while she gagged and choked.

Reyha retrieved a bottle of water and handed it to her. "Here. Drink."

Chrys guzzled the water and coughed, then held the cool plastic to her forehead and counted, focusing on her breathing until it began to even out. Finally, once she had regained some composure, she said, "You have no idea how humiliated I am right now."

"You should not be ashamed."

"But I am." She finished the water and rested her head against the cabinet door. "I'm serious. You need to call Gordon. I've disrespected you and let you down. You need someone else."

"But I chose you."

Chrys wiped her eyes. "Gordon and Collins should've read my medical records more carefully. I'm not in any condition to serve as a liaison for the State Department."

"Your injuries are not healed?"

"Maybe on the outside."

Reyha scooted closer. "You have the post-traumatic stress?"

"That's what they tell me."

"And it is the cause of your nightmares and panic attacks?"

"Among other things."

Reyha settled against the cabinet. "And do you have thoughts of self-harm as well?"

Chrys cringed. "I don't want to have those thoughts. I swear."

"I would think not."

Chrys released the top button of her shirt, held her head. "You're a wonderful person, Reyha, and I admire all you've done and intend to do for the women of Syria. And I think you're brave to go before the UN and speak about the atrocities against the Armenians. I really look up to you. I do." She stole a glance at Reyha's face and was seized momentarily by its exquisite beauty, blended, at that moment, with sincere concern. "But I'm a mess. Surely you see that. You need someone who's got her act together."

Reyha smoothed the length of her tunic with her graceful hands. "Mr. Gordon provided me with many suggestions, many files of qualified individuals. Yet it was your file, your photo that drew my attention."

"Why me?"

Reyha smiled. "To start, your beautiful black eyes and your disarming smile arrested my attention immediately."

Chrys hung her head. She was hardly the handsome woman she'd once been.

"Yet it was more than your attractiveness," Reyha continued. "I saw you have firsthand experience with the population of women I wish to serve. And you have proven yourself on the battlefield, have risen in rank. This tells me you know how to face danger and how to lead."

"Those things have nothing to do with showing you around DC and standing with you at the UN."

"No, but they are qualities I am seeking nevertheless."

"Why? For what?"

Reyha studied Chrys's head, shoulders, the hands gripping her knees. "For another time. What I want to know now are your plans when our time together is done."

Chrys shrugged. "I'll go back to Syria and be a mercenary, join the ranks of another YPJ unit, and fight Daesh."

"I see."

"I figure I'll use these months to get myself back in shape and off the meds. Use my compensation to buy a blade and start running again, get airfare to Germany, transport to Syria. Maybe put the rest in the bank for Mary."

"Your friend Mary."

Chrys lowered her eyes. "She was my fiancée, but not anymore." She glanced up. The revelation hadn't seemed to faze Reyha.

"And tell me, what happened between you that you are no longer betrothed?"

Chrys shrugged again. "She left me. Or maybe I left her first. I don't know." She shook her head with regret. "She's my best friend, or was. I love her. Probably not the way she wanted me to, but I do love her." She sighed and struggled to her feet and held herself against the counter. "Don't worry about me, though. I'll find some crap job here in DC, maybe hole up with some old friends until I have enough to get back to Syria. My running blade will have to wait, but I'll figure it out. I always seem to figure it out eventually."

Reyha held up her hands. "Will you please help me stand?"

Chrys lifted her up, but when she attempted to release her, Reyha drew her close.

"I do not wish for another companion," Reyha said. "I want you to stay, for you to let me help you."

Chrys lowered her eyes. "How can you still want me around after all this?"

"I have a good sense of people, and in you, I sense deep compassion, true greatness."

Chrys shook her head and continued to look away, but Reyha gripped her chin and pulled her gaze toward her.

"I want you to rest now in your room," Reyha said. "We will discuss more after our evening meal."

"But I—"

"Do as I say." Reyha released her and moved toward her room. "And do not ask me again to replace you. Fate has brought us together, my friend, and we should not refuse her gift."

CHAPTER NINE

"Did your rest strengthen you?" Reyha asked as Chrys came out of her room.

"I do feel better, thank you." Chrys surveyed the food on the table. "I didn't even hear them knock. Was this just delivered?"

"Only a moment ago."

She sat down and watched Reyha begin to fill her plate. She wasn't particularly hungry at the moment, but she was thirsty. She tapped her water glass with a finger and debated about getting up for a beer.

"Would you like to try the wine?" Reyha asked holding the bottle toward her.

"No, thank you. I'll stick with water." Chrys spooned small amounts of food on her plate and began to eat, aware her fork quivered in her hand.

"I would like you to tell me something."

"I can tell you many things."

Reyha smiled. "Why do I suspect you were somewhat insolent as a child?"

"I could be a handful, I won't deny it, but it only took my grandmother giving me her look and warning me not to dishonor myself or my family, and I'd shape right back up."

"You did not wish to disappoint her?"

Chrys shook her head. "That was the worst."

Reyha took a sip of wine and nodded. "She was a great influence on your life, perhaps more so than your own parents. Would you agree?"

"Yes."

"And does she appear to you often?"

Chrys froze.

Reyha set down her glass. "Does she not manifest herself to you?"

Chrys pushed back from the table and wiped her mouth. "Ever since that day"—she touched the side of her head—"ever since I woke up in that hospital in Germany, I keep seeing her."

"As you did earlier this afternoon?"

Chrys rested her elbows on her knees and held her face. "I told you—it's okay if you want someone else." She looked up when she felt Reyha's hand on her arm.

"And I indicated I do not wish to discuss that matter again." Reyha pointed to the table. "Now, eat. You need your strength."

"I'm not really hungry."

"That matters not. You will nourish your body with good food. You ate very little of your lunch today and filled yourself instead with alcohol. If you wish to regain your health, you will need to be more responsible."

Chrys pulled back ready to object to being treated like a child, but Reyha's severe expression dissolved with her smile. "You sound like my grandmother," she said, scooting back to the table.

Reyha chortled.

"I'm serious. She was always telling me and my brother to eat. Always in the kitchen cooking up something." Chrys grinned. "This one time, we had this big cross-country meet coming up, like a state championship or something, and she overheard me telling one of my friends about carb-loading. Later, she told me to invite the team over the night before the race, and then she spent the entire morning cooking. You should have seen the looks on my friends' faces. There were only eight of us, but she'd made enough food to feed an army." She shook her head and laughed.

Reyha chuckled along with her. "I have heard the legend of the Greek grandmother. You were blessed to have her. I never knew my grandparents from either my mother or father. Instead, after my mother's death, I had a series of governesses, and let me tell you, there was little warmth in their hearts for me."

"I'm sorry you were denied grandparents. That's sad." Chrys glanced at Reyha's rings. There was a world of differences between them, she realized. Not just age and religion, but culture and wealth as well.

Reyha set her food away, leaned back in her chair with her wineglass balanced in one hand, and watched Chrys with her perceptive eyes.

Chrys squirmed under her gaze. "So, yeah, I see my grandmother sometimes. But not just her. Sometimes I see Diren or Asmin or Sirvan. Sometimes the others."

"Your Kurdish friends?"

Chrys nodded. "Diren was the commander of the YPJ unit I'd been embedded with. Before she'd joined up, she'd been taken captive by Daesh during the siege of Kobani. She lost her entire family in that assault."

"I remember the terrible news. Turkey had a flood of refugees from the attack."

Chrys moved the food around on her plate with her fork, which began to vibrate even more as her hand shook harder. "Those monsters did terrible things to her. Some of the most brutal…" She choked and took a gulp of water. "I won't even tell you what they did, what scars they left on her body." She bowed her head and took deep breaths as she tried to keep her voice calm. "When she escaped, she vowed to fight to the death to see every one of those bastards in their grave. She wasn't just fighting to avenge herself, but every woman and girl they'd taken. She even fought in northwest Iraq, near the village of Sinjar, to avenge the Yazidi women who'd been enslaved."

"I'm afraid the world still does not acknowledge the depths of the genocide against the Yazidi."

Chrys looked up. "Like I said, the horrors never stop."

Reyha nodded, but did not speak.

Chrys wiped her nose and continued. "That morning, the morning we got hit, Diren…she…she sacrificed herself." Chrys felt her body gear down, the muscles along her shoulders contracting with the expectation of the remembered assault. "We'd gotten cut off from the YPG unit we'd been fighting alongside, got cornered against a ridge. Diren gave the command for us to retreat. Asmin, her second, grabbed Sirvan and started racing for one of the trucks. I was right on their tail, just feet behind them, when I realized Diren wasn't with us. When I looked back, she'd grabbed a munitions vest and was strapping on explosives, and I started yelling at her, but she just gave me the peace sign and smiled." She squeezed her eyes shut and her mouth twisted as the words came painfully. "Then she started running right at them, screaming at them to come get her, firing at them and tossing grenades to draw their attention. And I…" She clutched the table as her body began to shake harder and sweat dripped along her neck.

Reyha touched her hand. "Go on. Say what you must."

Chrys shook her head back and forth. "I started running toward her, screaming for her to stop, that we could all get out, but she…oh God." She dropped her head to the table as the agonizing words tore at her throat. "I saw her go everywhere."

She heard Reyha groan, felt her hand on her shoulder.

"I don't know what happened next," she continued. She pressed her forehead against the linen tablecloth and shuddered. "But somehow the truck Asmin had jumped into had circled back around to me, and then"—she lifted her head—"and then I was flying through the air."

"The truck was destroyed?"

Chrys nodded, wiped her eyes.

"And this is how you were injured?"

Chrys nodded again, swallowed over and over before speaking. "I found out later the rest got away, thanks to Diren. But I cost the lives of Asmin and Sirvan and the others in the truck. They shouldn't have come back for me. But they did. And now…" She stared off with vacant eyes, red and wet.

"And now that awful memory plagues you each night when you try to sleep."

"Yes."

"And is there no happy memory of your friends, of Diren, that you might focus on instead?"

Chrys shrugged. "Sure, lots of good memories. She was a remarkable woman. Smart, fearless, funny. And when I learned the full extent of the abuse she'd faced, I just couldn't believe how she kept going, how she always managed a smile and a laugh. Even right up until the end, she was smiling."

"Like your grandmother?"

Chrys's eyes widened. "Yes, like Yiayia." She touched her chest. "Whatever quality she and Diren had, that ability to be happy while the world is falling apart, I don't have it, not anymore."

"You are speaking of resilience and perseverance. Qualities of the soul quite rare these days."

"Very rare." Chrys rubbed her eyes and looked down at her food. She'd lost her appetite recounting that terrible morning, but realized it was the first time she'd been able to voice it. She'd never shared it in group, never told Mary, and had only given the sparse facts in her report.

"What are you thinking? You look so contemplative," Reyha said.

"I was thinking I haven't been able to talk about this until now." Chrys glanced up at her. "Maybe it'll help with the hallucinations.

Maybe not. Either way, I don't plan on mentioning them to my doctors. I'm afraid to."

"What do you fear?"

"That they'll put me on antipsychotics or worse." She rubbed her head, the place where the thick scar lay hidden under her curly hair. "I know I should probably say something, but none of my recent scans shows anything unusual. My best guess is they're a stress response. I really only notice them when I'm having flashbacks or a panic attack."

"Or when you are drinking alcohol?"

Chrys lowered her eyes in shame. "Maybe. I guess."

"And you are certain they are hallucinations?"

Chrys scoffed. "I don't believe in ghosts. Besides, I can taste and smell things when it happens. I read somewhere that's not uncommon with PTSD." She diverted her eyes again. "I hope I'm not losing my mind. That's about all I have left."

Reyha rose and gathered her cigarette case. "Sit with me."

Chrys followed her to the balcony and leaned against the railing and sipped her water. She took a deep inhale and gazed up at the moon, its refreshing cool light bathing her face. "It's a nice night, pretty moon. I miss being outdoors."

She turned to watch Reyha, who reclined in her chair and blew smoke rings.

"We never camped when I was a kid," Chrys continued. "My dad had to work all the time. But I loved being outdoors, to train for my long runs out on those Nebraska back roads. Especially when the corn harvest came due, right about the time the fall weather hit and there'd be these early morning rain showers." She held the side of the railing and closed her eyes. "I'd get up early and have my uncle Manolis drive me outside of town so I could run home by breakfast. There's nothing like an early morning run right after the rain with the smell of the wet earth and warm asphalt all around you." She released the rail, folded her hands behind her head, and lifted her face to the sky. "I could run and run and run and never get tired. It didn't matter what was going on in the world. I could lose myself on those back roads with the red grass and tall corn to keep me company. What I wouldn't give to run again in the rain. Just one more time." She dropped her arms and looked at Reyha. "You have anything like that? Something that gives you peace of mind, makes you grateful to be alive?"

"I do. Art, music, literature, these things have sustained me through troubling times."

"Those are nice, too." Chrys sat down next to her.

"Your injury prevents you from running?"

"If I ever want to get anywhere near the capacity I was before, I'll need a running blade, but they're expensive, so I'll have to wait until I save enough. And who knows, maybe one of those nonprofit organizations I wrote to will come through for me."

"May I make an observation?"

Chrys turned her head. "I enjoy your observations. You're such a smart lady. I guess you get that from being a teacher all those years." She grinned. "I think I would've liked being one of your students."

"You would have found me a taskmaster."

"Really? I think I could've handled it. I'm pretty tough."

Reyha laughed. "Of this I am certain." She blew another smoke ring and smiled. "However, my observation is this—when you speak of your grandmother, of your time growing up among your friends and family, of your running in the rain, your face brightens, your shoulders lift, and your voice is like music. You have had so many wonderful things in your life, so many blessings even among the hardships. Do you not see when you despair for the state of the world that there are reasons to be grateful as well? Do not these things give you hope?"

"But my grandmother's gone, and I can't run like I used to. Everything good always ends. The bad stuff goes on forever."

Reyha put out her cigarette. "My dear brave friend, do you not understand it is the impermanence of such things that makes them so beautiful? Even the art and music and literature I love are fleeting, for they too can be destroyed." She gestured with her hand to emphasize her words. "You must remember this always, just as I suspect your grandmother did and your friend Diren as well. You will see. You have not lost your resilience and perseverance. You have only misplaced them."

"Will I get them back?"

"Do you want them back?"

Chrys looked up at the sky again, followed a line of stars. She used to know the constellations when she was little, had been able to spot her own, the Taurus.

"I think I do," she said to the sky.

From her peripheral vision, she glimpsed Reyha's smile.

❖

With her late afternoon nap and beer-free evening, Chrys found herself wide awake at bedtime. Reyha had retired an hour ago, but she continued to fidget in bed while flipping through channels on her television. Finally, she reattached her leg and pulled on some sweats. As she shut the suite door, she turned to find the agent who'd witnessed her confrontation with Banks earlier.

"Good evening, Ms. Safis," he said, standing and greeting her with a nod. "Is everything all right?"

"I need to speak with Mr. Carmichael. I'll just head downstairs to see if he's still in his office."

The agent brought up his radio.

"No need to notify anyone," she said. "I'm sure Quinn's sleeping, Smith, too. I'll be back in an hour or so. Carmichael and I have some business."

"Yes, ma'am." He sat again and resumed his mannequin-like pose.

She found Carmichael in his office bent over files on his desk. When he saw her, he stood and giggled.

"Ms. Safis, my dear, it's late. Is everything all right?"

"I'm good." She hesitated and looked around at the bizarre artwork, some of which depicted bare-chested men. "Listen, I'm sorry it's so late, but I couldn't sleep, and I remembered a few days ago Mrs. Arslan informed me that she had tickets for a performance at the Kennedy coming up."

"Splendid."

"The thing is, I don't really have anything appropriate to wear for something like that, and she suggested I speak to you."

He clapped his hands. "I am to be your dresser? How fabulous."

"Okay, wait a second." She took a step back and held up one of her hands. "I don't want a gown and heels and all that. I'm looking to be fitted for a tux. Nothing too expensive either."

He came around the desk with his arms held out toward her. "A tuxedo, of course. I would envision you in nothing less." He placed his hands on her shoulders and studied her head to toe. "It must be of the right hue to bring out the richness of your olive complexion. And simple lines, nothing garish." He dropped his hands and held his chin while he turned his head side to side. "And a silk shirt, a warm color, something earthy." He flitted his hand as if waving away a fly. "I would say a traditional tie, not the bow. But the color of your waistcoat…I'll have to consider this."

"Okay, whatever you think's best."

He held up a finger. "I will call Gustav first thing in the morning and request a private consultation. The man works marvels. You'll see."

"Thanks. Let me know, and I'll have Quinn take me."

"And may I come as well? Would you allow me that courtesy?"

She shrugged. "Sure, why not."

He almost danced in place. "Thank you, my dear. You will not regret this." He flourished his hands in the air as if to frame her. "I can already envision you and Mrs. Arslan arm in arm, such a stunning couple."

She wrinkled her nose. "What?"

He led her by the elbow to the door. "I'll be sure to speak with her, to let her know our plans." He bowed. "Thank you again for this privilege."

"But what does…? Okay, whatever. Listen, one more thing. I know the fitness center closes at ten, but do you think I could use it tonight? I need to work out some of the knots in my legs from all the walking."

"Certainly, come with me." He took her to the front desk and programmed a special keycard. "I've had these made for Commander Banks and her team so they may make use of the facility at odd hours and not compete with the rest of the guests." He handed her the card. "Enjoy your workout."

"Thanks." She could feel him watching her all the way to the elevator.

❖

When she stepped off on the second floor, she was relieved to find no agent waiting to monitor her every move. But when she used the key to activate the fitness facility's door, she caught the sound of soft giggles and women's voices. She walked past the dressing rooms and locker area and peered around the corner. Sitting on a bench, Banks and Christman huddled close together. Both wore tight fitting T-shirts and shorts, revealing their toned arms and legs. Chrys found them fascinating, especially Banks, who seemed relaxed, not all rigid and formal as usual. Christman moved a piece of Banks's hair, which had come out of its ponytail. Then Banks put her hand on Christman's thigh and leaned over and kissed her.

Chrys backed up into the shadows and covered her mouth. After she got control of her surprise, she went back to the door of the fitness center and swung it open and let it close with a crash. She began to whistle as she rounded the corner. As she suspected, by the time she came in sight, Banks was on her back at the bench doing presses while Christman handled free weights and did curls.

"Sorry," she said, trying to appear startled to see them. "I can come back if you'd like."

"No problem, Ms. Safis." Christman set down her weights. "The commander and I were just finishing our routine. We'll be out of your way in a moment." She picked up a towel and spoke to Banks. "I'll see you up in the control room, ma'am. I'm going to hit the showers."

"Carry on, Christman," Banks said as she sat up from the bench. "Good workout," she added. She looked at Chrys with her usual stoic expression. "I thought mornings were your preferred time. Quinn's recorded twice this last week after breakfast."

"I couldn't sleep. Thought I'd work off some energy." Chrys stretched and tried not to stare at Banks's legs. "I guess you guys all need to stay in shape, too, even while you're on assignment."

"True." Banks set the weight for the leg press. "Most assignments aren't this plush, though. We're seldom housed in luxury like this."

"A perk for protecting an international diplomat?"

Banks grinned. "International diplomats comprise most of our missions, but few are as dignified and cultured as Mrs. Arslan, and Collins was insistent she be given only the best accommodations. I can't say any of us is complaining much."

"Yes, dignified and cultured." Chrys bent to tighten her shoelace. "And beautiful."

"She's that, too."

Chrys watched Banks position herself into the leg press and begin the movement. "I wanted to apologize about earlier for being an ass. I shouldn't have gotten up in your face like that."

Banks brought her set to an end. "I get it. You were worried for her safety."

"But like you said, I'm not her bodyguard." She peeked at the setting on the leg press. "I'm impressed."

"I do all right," Banks said.

Chrys got up to load plates onto the barbell and noticed the amount Banks had been pressing was twenty pounds more than she could currently press. That along with the amount on the leg press caused her competitive spirit to kick in. She wiped down the bench with her towel and got into position.

"You need a spotter?" Banks asked.

"I probably got it."

"Maybe I'll stand here just in case."

Chrys settled into position and looked up between Banks's breasts and into her downturned face. She sucked in a breath, tightened her grip, exhaled, and lifted. As she lowered, she sucked in another deep breath, and then thrust up as she exhaled once more.

"Extraordinary," Banks said, her hands ready to rescue the bar from Chrys's grip. "You're in some good shape yourself."

"I…try." Chrys pushed up on her third repetition, but as she lowered the bar a fourth time, her elbows protested. "Nope."

"Got it." Banks lifted the bar into its cradle.

Chrys panted for breath. "Damn, I have to say I'm impressed with myself. That's twenty pounds more than I'm used to."

"And at three reps," Banks said. "Looks like the Air Force isn't a bunch of sissies after all."

"Hey, now." Chrys stood up laughing. "That's an undeserved stereotype."

"Not any worse than what we coasties get."

"Yeah, cuddling little ducks. That's a side of you I can't imagine."

Banks raised an eyebrow. "I have my sensitive side. Just like you."

Chrys scoffed. "Sensitive has never been a word used to describe me."

"Really?" Banks shrugged. "You seem very sensitive to Mrs. Arslan. Very attentive, too." She began curling dumbbells, but her razor-sharp eyes remained glued to Chrys.

Chrys set her weight on the leg press, but it was only half of what Banks had pressed. "It's hard not to be captivated by her. She's one of the most interesting women I've ever known." She hooked her feet into place before glancing over at Banks taking a break between sets of curls. "And I've known a lot of women in my life." She let her gaze linger and watched the proverbial wheels spin in Banks's head.

"Is that right?" Banks sat down on the bench and watched Chrys do her reps.

Once she'd finished one set, Chrys said, "So tell me something, how long have you been leading this team?"

"Two years."

"And that's how long you've known them all?" Chrys returned to the bench.

"Some a few years more." Banks pointed to the plates. "You sticking with this amount?"

"Let's bring it down twenty. I'll concede to your greater strength." Chrys grinned and removed plates from one side, as Banks did so on the other.

"I don't know. I've reached my limit in the bench press at this point," Banks said. "But you got some solid strength going on there. I think you'll surpass me before long."

Chrys took her place. "Maybe we'll have a rematch when I get myself back in shape."

"Ready?"

"Yep." Chrys dug into it and managed to push out a solid eight reps with the lower weight. Once the bar was in its cradle, she sat up and leaned forward to catch her breath.

"You know," Banks said handing her a towel, "you really are in amazing shape. If you ever get tired of being an interpreter, let me know. I'd love to have you on my team."

"I'm not sure my bum leg would make me the best qualified."

"Wouldn't be an issue."

Chrys blinked, smiled. "Really?"

"Really. I think with your military training along with your language skills, you'd be a real asset to protective services."

"I'll keep that in mind." Chrys got up and readied for another set on the leg press. "So tell me, how's your personal life in this line of work? You able to have one?"

"It depends. It takes a special person to be involved with one of us. We travel a lot and when we're on assignment, we live with our client or reside in close proximity. That doesn't bode well for a long-term relationship or family."

Chrys pressed out her reps and relaxed to catch her breath. "So you're single." She turned her head and watched for a response.

"In a manner of speaking."

"No plans to start a family?" Chrys got up and set up her dumbbells for curls.

"Well..." Banks fidgeted with her water bottle. "Actually, I'm getting married come January."

Chrys began her curls. "I wish you and Agent Christman well."

"Excuse me?"

She counted out her reps before answering. "I came in and sort of caught a peek. Sorry about that."

Banks wiped her face. "No, I'm the one who should apologize. You weren't meant to witness that."

"Hey, it's okay." Chrys went over to the pull-up bar. But before she reached up, she said, "Don't worry. I won't say anything. Your secret's safe with me."

"It's not a secret, actually. And in fact, this is the last assignment Deanna and I will serve on together. The State Department discourages personal relationships between agents on the same team. So once we decided we were going to move forward, she put in for a transfer." Banks frowned slightly. "It'll be tough. She's the best cyber specialist I've worked with."

Chrys grabbed the bar with an overhand grip and hoisted herself up.

Banks watched her a moment, then asked, "Have you always been in this good a shape?"

Chrys dropped down and swung her arms around in wide circles. "Mostly, but since I got injured, I've let it fall off some. I'm trying my best to get some of it back."

"I read in your file you were a distance runner."

Chrys grabbed the bar again, this time with a wide underhand grip, and hung there a moment. "High school mostly, set a few state records I'm proud of, but I kept it up even after joining the Air Force." As she lifted herself, the muscles along her shoulders and upper back strained. When she finished, she dropped down and bent over to hold herself by her knees. "I'll run again. Eventually."

"I'm sure you will." Banks sat again. "You know, Sean Gordon and I are old buddies."

"Is that right?" Chrys fiddled with the setting on the triceps extension.

"He mentioned you were engaged, too."

"I was. We broke up."

Banks sipped her water before responding. "I'm sorry to hear that."

Chrys shrugged. "It's better, better for Mary anyway."

"And for you?"

Chrys scoffed and pointed to her face. "I wasn't going to condemn her to a lifetime of living with this mug."

"But when you love someone, that stuff doesn't matter."

"Believe me, it matters." Chrys yanked on the triceps bar and huffed out her reps before returning to the leg press.

After a long pause, Banks said, "That was out of line. I apologize."

"Forget it." Chrys focused on her quads, on keeping her prosthetic leg lined up as she pressed.

Banks gathered up her belongings. "I'll leave you to it, Ms. Safis. Have a good night."

"Tell me something," Chrys said before Banks got to the door. "You and Christman, after this assignment and you two are married, you said she'll be transferred to another team."

"That's right."

"But that means you'll hardly see each other."

"We'll be sure when we do, we make the most of it."

Chrys wiped her face with her towel. "Don't you think it'll be hard? She could be on assignment in another state or some other place in the world. And there's always the possibility of injury or death. The risks are real. I know for Mary that was the hardest part of me being in the Air Force."

Banks took a step toward her. "That's true, but you see, when we met a few years back and started falling in love, we had to make a decision. Would we decide to ignore our feelings and stay committed to our profession? If that was the case, nothing could've developed between us. Or the other option was to take a chance, embrace our feelings, and face the risk we might be separated or worse."

"That's a big risk."

"Yes, well, love doesn't come around every day," Banks said. "When it does, I say jump on it before you look back and curse yourself for letting it slip through your fingers."

Chrys nodded. "Well then, I hope you two have a long and beautiful life together."

"Thank you. And let me say, I hope whatever you choose to do when this assignment is over, wherever you end up, that you'll find someone to share your life with. Going it alone is hard." Banks stepped away and headed for the exit.

"Commander Banks?" Chrys called after her.

Banks turned.

"I know it isn't protocol or whatever, but thanks for spotting me, for talking."

Banks smiled. "Have a good workout, ma'am."

Chrys watched her leave, then lifted the dumbbells into a curl and counted out her reps. When she'd finished, she walked over to the mirrored wall and examined her face. She pulled back her hair, which by now had grown past her ears. She turned to inspect her profile, particularly the area around her disfigured earlobe where the skin had been shredded and lacerated.

Banks was wrong. Sometimes going it alone was better.

CHAPTER TEN

I have always wanted to view these in person," Reyha said. "Magnificent."

They sat in front of four large oil paintings inside the West Building of the National Gallery of Art. They'd already seen the rest of the gallery that morning and afternoon, and this was the last stop, one Reyha had saved for last.

"They are more beautiful than I could have imagined," she said and turned to Chrys. "Mr. Thomas Cole founded the Hudson River School of Art."

"Oh." Chrys stifled a yawn and rubbed her left knee, which ached, yet she remained sitting at attention next to Reyha, being respectful of her interests. At the moment, Reyha's legs were crossed, and Chrys was looking at the skin along her ankle.

"He gives us a glimpse of the American wilderness much like your Miss Willa Cather. Have you read *My Ántonia* or any of her prairie trilogy novels?" Reyha asked.

"Huh?" Chrys stretched her eyes. "Sorry, no, I'm not much for literature."

"Yet you love languages."

"That's different. Languages and linguistics are mathematical."

"You grew up in Nebraska. I would have thought you had read some Cather. Her descriptions of the Nebraska grasslands are most remarkable."

Chrys offered an apologetic grin. "I mostly stuck to practical things like math and learning languages."

"Practical?"

"As in knowledge you can use."

"I see." Reyha turned her attention back to the paintings. For a moment she simply continued to study them, but then she pointed and leaned close. "Look here at this one. It is called *Childhood*. See how the angel is the tiller man for the boat, the infant a passenger?"

"Yes."

"But look here"—she scooted closer and put her arm behind Chrys, cradled her around the hips—"the one titled *Youth*, the infant is now a young man and must steer his own boat. The angel only points the way."

"Yes, I get it. It's an allegory. The four stages of life. I understand that."

Reyha squeezed her. "Correct." She turned her eyes on Chrys. "Do you see the detail in the third painting, the one called *Manhood*?"

Chrys stiffened. Reyha sat so close that she could feel the wisp of air coming from her nose, the breath from her mouth. She focused on Reyha's lips as she answered. "I guess so."

"Cole shows us the ugly side of living. The storms, the dangers, the hopelessness." Reyha grinned. "Our dirty little depraved world we discussed earlier."

Chrys nodded, snared by the closeness of Reyha's face, the soft hush in her voice, the scent of her hair.

"And what is he doing?" Reyha asked.

"I don't know, what?" Chrys couldn't look away from Reyha's gaze to the painting just feet away.

Reyha cupped her chin and turned her face. "Look. Tell me what you see."

"Looks like he's praying." Chrys's heart thudded, her hands shook.

Reyha released her and stood. "Yes, yes, praying. But look here." She pointed to the canvas. "The angel is nowhere to be seen."

Chrys joined her and indicated the last painting. "And there the old fool is at his journey's end. Frail, sick, and old. Lucky him. He lived through the hell of life only to arrive back to his angel." She glanced at Reyha. "I know this fairy tale. I heard it every week in church growing up. I'm sure you've had a similar fairy tale pushed down your throat growing up in Islam. The details might vary, but the story's still the same."

"And tell me, what story is that?"

"We're born, we struggle, we suffer, and we die." Chrys curled her lip into a sneer. "And the world keeps turning as if we never existed."

Reyha held up a finger. "But while you exist, you have the ability to make an impact on others, perhaps something felt long into the future."

"I suppose."

"Isn't that why you want to return to Syria and fight?" Reyha linked her arm through Chrys's and began a slow stroll toward the main hall.

"I guess."

"You guess? For someone so sure of herself, so confident, you seem rather indecisive."

Chrys pulled them to a stop. "No, I'm not. I know what I want. I want to fight those bastards as long as I'm able and send every one of them to hell."

"Fighting is sometimes necessary, I agree. But have you thought of another path, one where your efforts might make a greater impact?"

Chrys scoffed, looked around the lobby, noticed Banks watching. "I don't want to talk about this. I'm tired. My leg hurts. My back, too."

Reyha leaned toward her. "You have been doing so well these last weeks. I have watched you turn away from your alcohol, seen a glow come over your face since you have been doing your exercises more regularly. And your appetite has returned. But last evening, I heard you crying out in your sleep again. And I worry for you, wanting to return to combat."

"That's months away," Chrys said, stepping back. "I'll have fulfilled my obligation to you by then."

"Am I not allowed to care about you and your welfare?"

"Of course you are but…" Chrys looked for the exit, an escape from Reyha's interrogation.

Reyha took her hand. "Tell me, do you enjoy when someone reads to you?"

"Do I what?" Chrys tried to pull away.

"Is it pleasant when someone reads to you, as in a bedtime story?"

"You want to read me a bedtime story?"

"I do. Did not anyone read to you as a child?"

Chrys shrugged. "Sometimes. Mostly my grandmother told me stories of her own. I was never really sure which ones were supposed to be real and which were made up. But either way, she could spin a tale like no other."

"Well then, I shall be honored to bestow on you your first bedtime story since you were a child." Reyha began to pull her along.

Chrys sighed. "You make my head spin sometimes, you know that?"

"Interesting idiom. I hope you mean that in a good way."

"Not really."

Reyha laughed all the way to the SUV. Once inside, she leaned forward and spoke to Banks. "Is there a bookstore or library nearby? Someplace I might find classics of American literature?"

"I'm sure there's someplace," Banks said, pulling up her phone.

"What are you looking for?" Chrys asked.

Reyha held up her hand as she waited for Banks's response.

"There's a chain bookstore about three and half miles north of here," Banks said.

Reyha removed a notepad from her purse, scribbled down something, and handed it to Banks. "Will you please purchase these titles?"

Banks looked at the note. "Sure thing."

As they drove, Reyha leaned against Chrys's shoulder and smiled.

"What books are you getting?" Chrys asked.

"You will see."

"Why all the mystery?"

"Patience."

"I don't have a lot of that."

Reyha patted her thigh. "I have become well aware of that fact."

They arrived at the bookstore by sunset. After twenty minutes of being inside, Quinn returned and handed Reyha a bag. "Got copies of both just as you requested. I hope paperback is okay."

Reyha took the bag and peeked inside. "They are sufficient. Thank you, Agent Quinn."

"Anything else?" Banks asked.

"That will be all. Let us return to the hotel and have the chef prepare our dinner."

As Quinn merged into traffic, Chrys pointed to the bag in Reyha's lap. "So what do you have there?"

"Your bedtime story." Reyha took out two books, both fairly thick.

Chrys studied the covers in the dim light. She recognized one; it was the title Reyha had spoken about earlier. "*My Ántonia*. Huh." She narrowed her eyes and read the title of the next. "*The Age of Innocence*.

Haven't heard of it." She looked at Reyha. "These aren't romances, are they? I'd rather have action-adventure or spy stories if I have to read something."

"Romance literature has not always meant a story involving an amorous relationship between two people. At one time, it meant a style of heroic prose."

Chrys wrinkled her nose.

Reyha swatted her shoulder and chuckled. "You remind me of my students back in Istanbul. You fear you will be bored, I take it. But you must trust me. Literature, art, and great music can become your friends. They have sustained me in the darkest of times."

"If you say so."

Reyha tapped the books. "Reading Cather will be an enjoyable evening pastime for us and beneficial to you, I believe. Perhaps your dreams will be filled with images of young Jim and Ántonia as they explore the grasslands of Nebraska, endure the winters with their families in their sod houses, and investigate the happenings of their colorful neighbors."

"Sounds interesting." Chrys heard the flatness in her voice and worried Reyha would be insulted. She cleared her throat. "I mean, if I can experience them with you, I'm sure I'll enjoy myself no matter what."

Traffic lights glinted off Reyha's eyes as she gazed at her. "It is always better to share such enjoyments with a companion, particularly one so agreeable."

Something shifted right then for Chrys, something too absurd and fragile to name. At the same moment, she became aware Banks had turned her head to the side and was observing them. She squirmed and pointed to the other book. "This one's awfully thick. Are you going to read this one to me also?"

"I would ask instead that you read it to me," Reyha said.

"You want *me* to read to you? Seriously?"

"Yes, if you would." Reyha took the book and flipped through the pages. "The last time I sat through chemotherapy…" She sighed and stared down at the book. "Well, it was not a pleasant experience. I thought listening to a story I love, read by someone with such a lyrical voice, would soothe me while I undergo treatment."

"I have a lyrical voice?" Chrys laughed at the absurdity of that description.

"You do not think so? I find the manner in which you speak quite emotional and expressive."

"Okay, if you say so, but you'd be the first." Chrys nodded toward the book. "So what's this one about? More stories of the Midwest prairie?"

"No, quite different. It takes place in New York, right after World War I." Reyha bit her lip, a gesture Chrys hadn't seen her do before. "It is rather a sad story, however, one of unrequited love."

"If it's sad, why do you want me to read it to you?"

Reyha didn't answer right away, but instead gazed out the window while she tapped her fingers on the book's cover. Finally, she turned back to Chrys. "I have read it many times, taught it as well. And perhaps I am hoping that somehow the ending will change. I want poor Mr. Archer to embrace his love for the Countess Olenska, for the two of them, as you Americans say, *to live happily ever after*."

"And why don't they?" Chrys's heart constricted at the sight of Reyha's damp eyes, her sudden trembling voice.

"Social barriers, cultural constraints." Reyha bowed her head. "It is a pity for him and for her that he is unable to liberate himself from the artificial limits class and convention put on love. It is the truest of human tragedies that we do not allow ourselves to embrace love and passion when it presents itself into our lives. We have so many man-made rules, so many stifling laws around whom we can love, for how long, to what degree. And yet"—she wiped a tear from her cheek and smiled through her mysterious sadness—"love is the most natural condition. Natural, yet so elusive."

Chrys's muscles grew taut all over her body as Reyha watched her with an expression that unnerved her. It was a pleading look, one full of misery and wretchedness.

"Tell me," Reyha said as she touched Chrys's thigh, "why do people prevent themselves from embracing love when they can? Why deny themselves the one pure thing life offers?"

"I don't…I don't know." Chrys tried to swallow, but her mouth had gone dry.

"Neither do I," Reyha said, and she returned the books to the bag and fell silent for the rest of the journey.

❖

Before dinner, Chrys soaked in her sunken tub and massaged her sore muscles. She'd been working out consistently for the last two weeks, joining Banks and Christman in the evenings. But tonight, she'd first obliged Reyha with her strange request to read to her after they'd completed dinner. She wasn't sure what this would accomplish, but Reyha had seemed so eager, and she couldn't turn her down.

As she lingered in the warm water, her mind kept replaying their exchange in the SUV that evening. *Tell me, why do people prevent themselves from embracing love when they can?* Reyha had asked her despondently. *Why deny themselves the one pure thing life offers?* The age difference between Reyha and her late husband struck Chrys once more, and she wondered if Reyha had denied herself the love of another man, or if one had deprived her. Either way, Chrys felt sorry for her. Reyha obviously still nursed a broken heart for some unrequited love of her own.

Once she got out of the tub, she pulled on her usual workout clothes—sweatpants and a sports bra along with a tank top—in order to be ready for later that evening. Out in the living area, she found Reyha pouring wine at the table.

"I feel a hundred percent better after that." Chrys took her seat. "You don't mind, do you?" She touched her tank top.

Reyha scrutinized her, her eyes trailing along her shoulders and exposed arms. "Not at all."

Chrys began to place the little elegant appetizers on her plate but jumped when she felt Reyha's hand on her forearm. She watched as Reyha's fingers traced along the ridge of her arm, then meander upward and encircle her bicep. She raised her eyes to find Reyha scrutinizing her with an intense gaze.

"You are amazingly strong," Reyha said, "and I see your exercises are making you even stronger." She let her fingers drift down Chrys's bicep once more, then trace a vein from the middle of her forearm to her index finger.

Chrys watched the beat of Reyha's heart at the hollow of her throat, saw Reyha cup her own neck with her other hand while her fingers rubbed the pulse line. As she watched, she felt herself growing light-headed, her mouth turn dry.

"What exercise do you do exactly?" Reyha asked, her voice lower than usual, breathy almost.

Chrys shrugged, tried to speak, but her tongue lay heavy in her mouth.

"Do you lift weights or simply use your own weight to gain such strength?" Reyha asked.

"Yes," Chrys blurted out unable to make any other coherent sound.

Reyha continued to play along her own neck. "Perhaps sometime you will let me observe you exercising. I would like to see what you do which gives you such defined muscles."

Chrys took a quick sip of water and let the words pour from her mouth. "I have to keep my upper body strong to maneuver myself when I'm not wearing my prosthetic leg."

"I see."

"In and out of the shower, that sort of thing." She shoved a bite of food in her mouth to throttle the nervousness in her voice.

"And in bed," Reyha added.

"Pardon me?"

"To get comfortable in bed."

"That, too."

"So tell me." Reyha released Chrys's arm, but continued to play with her own neck as she lifted her wineglass to her lips. "Do you want me to read to you here on the divan, or would you like me to read to you in bed?"

Chrys squeaked.

"Is something wrong?" Reyha asked.

"Divan, couch, sofa, whatever." Chrys fanned herself with her napkin. "Wow, it's really warm in here. Do you mind if I adjust the temperature?"

"By all means. Anything to make you more comfortable."

At the thermostat, Chrys took her time and focused on the little numbers, trying to appear interested in them just long enough to let her body get a grip, for her mind to stop racing, and for her heartbeat to return to normal. None of this made sense—her signals must be crossed, her body and mind misinterpreting once again. She glanced over to the kitchen expecting to see her grandmother, but the kitchen was empty.

"Better?" Reyha asked when Chrys returned to the table.

"Better. Thanks." Chrys sat down again and resumed eating, feeling a little disappointed this latest hallucination hadn't continued for a bit longer.

After their meal and before they began their story, Reyha invited Chrys out on the balcony for her usual evening cigarette. As before,

Reyha relaxed back into her chair and lifted her chin as she blew smoke rings about her head while Chrys stood at the balcony and gazed at the illuminated monuments in the distance.

"What are you watching?" Reyha asked.

Chrys pointed. "Do you know the Washington Monument was built by slaves?"

"Sadly, yes."

"I guess nothing good in life is untarnished."

"If not by men's greed, then by time."

Chrys scooted up a chair and sat down. "I know this is personal, and maybe I'm overstepping, but I was curious about something."

"Yes?"

"Your husband, Emin, you must miss him terribly."

"He was a good man."

"You must have loved him a great deal."

"I respected him." Reyha didn't move her head, but rather narrowed her eyes and shifted them in Chrys's direction. "Why do you ask about Emin?"

"How did you come to marry him? I mean, he was a great deal older than you and the husband of your mother's best friend."

"That is not unusual in my culture, for a woman to marry a much older man, particularly one known to the family."

"I understand. My own dad was fifteen years older than my mother. In fact, he was forty-five when I was born."

She sipped her water and remembered her father's booming voice and strong arms, thick with muscle from his manual tasks at the bakery. He had loved all of them, her and her brothers, had lifted them up each evening in his powerful arms and proclaimed his pride in having such beautiful and well-behaved children. She glanced over at the rings on Reyha's hands.

"So did you want children? I mean, did you and he ever discuss having children of your own?"

"No." Reyha put out her cigarette. "He had two fine sons by the woman he loved. He wanted no others."

"But did you?"

Reyha shook her head. "As we have discussed, this world is an ugly place. Enough children suffer. I did not wish to bring one into the world and see her suffer as well."

"I see your point."

"And you? Did you and your Mary plan on having children someday?"

With the mention of Mary, a wave of melancholy washed over Chrys. "At most we'd talked about adoption sometime in the future."

"Yes, so many children who are desperate for a loving home."

Chrys turned away and began thinking about the children she'd known in Syria.

"Tell me what you are thinking now," Reyha said. "Your face betrays your sadness."

"The YPJ unit I was with, we came across a lot of orphaned children. A boy, Sirvan, he was about eight, I think, but he was so small, his hands so little. He took to me right away. He liked my dimples."

"They are remarkably disarming, I must say."

"Thank you." Chrys touched her cool glass to her cheek.

"Your Sirvan, he is the one that was killed with the others?"

Chrys nodded.

"I am sorry."

Chrys lowered her head while she remembered the joy in Sirvan's eyes when she'd handed him a chocolate bar, how his little hands pressed around her neck as she held him close in the evenings, how he touched her lips and begged for a lullaby. Wrapped up in her thoughts, she began to hum, not realizing she'd started vocalizing the words until she heard Reyha's voice join hers.

"You know that one?" Chrys asked.

"I do."

"It was one of those things I learned when I first started speaking the language. Sirvan asked me to sing it to him all the time. It's a beautiful song, don't you think?"

"And your voice makes it more so."

The echo of the Kurdish lullaby nearly overwhelmed her, and she could've fallen against Reyha right then and wept against her breast as the memory of Sirvan brought another wave of sorrow down on her. But determined not to let her mood take a downward turn, she stood up and shook off the sensation. "I'd like my bedtime story now."

"And you shall have it."

Reyha led her to the sofa, then retrieved the book and her reading glasses and sat down next to her, nuzzling against her.

Hesitant at first, Chrys allowed herself to put her hand along Reyha's leg and lean into her as well. As Reyha began to read,

Chrys couldn't tell if she really liked the story, if she cared for Jim Burden or his Bohemian neighbor, Ántonia Shimerda. But what she did like, adored actually, was the sound of Reyha's soothing voice as she pronounced the English words, her inflection as she delivered the characters' dialogue. She could witness right there the literature professor who savored words as if they were delicacies set before her on a plate, and some part of her truly wished she'd been one of Reyha's students.

As the hour continued, Chrys found the courage finally to acknowledge the fragile and absurd feeling she'd experienced in the SUV, the tingle of hope she'd sensed only a while ago when Reyha had admired her strength. But she knew the differences between them were too great, and even if those differences could be overlooked, Reyha with all her refined beauty would never desire a body scarred and mutilated by war. Yet it was a pleasant fantasy, one which she found no harm indulging.

Reyha closed the book and removed her glasses. "You will dream tonight of Jim and Ántonia, of the red grass of Nebraska."

"I hope so." Chrys covered her mouth as a yawn escaped.

"Shall I tuck you in? Is that the saying?" Reyha asked and smiled.

Chrys giggled. "Yes, that's the saying."

"I could sing to you a lullaby as well. Perhaps you know this one." Reyha began to sing a traditional Turkish lullaby.

Spellbound, Chrys watched Reyha's eyes as big and brown and full of light as Jim Burden had described Ántonia's. And with Reyha's gentle voice singing the sweet tune, she found herself drawing closer. When Reyha concluded the song, Chrys realized just how close she'd brought her face to Reyha's.

"Yes, I know that one," Chrys said in a trance. "And you have a beautiful voice as well."

"Thank you."

Chrys focused on Reyha's lips, on the moist sheen left by the tip of her tongue.

"Are you not well?" Reyha asked. "Your face has paled."

"I'm fine." Chrys extracted herself and pointed to the door. "But actually, I need to get down to the fitness center and get my workout in."

Reyha stood. "Then I will not keep you." She gripped Chrys by her shoulders and planted a kiss, first on her right cheek, and then on her left. "I hope you will sleep more soundly afterward. Good night."

Chrys watched Reyha go to her room and shut the door. In her wake, the scent of her clove cigarettes lingered, as did the feel of her lips against her cheek. Chrys let out a huge sigh and fanned herself. Then she hurried down to the second floor, threw herself into her routine, and enthusiastically embraced another round once Banks and Christman joined her forty minutes later.

CHAPTER ELEVEN

By the middle of the second month, Chrys found herself less reliant on her medication, particularly the tranquilizers and sleep aids. In addition, the remaining bottles of beer in the suite's refrigerator stood untouched. She'd gained traction with her workouts, too, getting stronger and fitter. Kayla, her physical therapist, remarked about the change, and so had her fellow vets in group, as well as Dr. Woodley. But she'd not seen a lot of Morrison, who'd been attending sporadically. Chrys worried about her, tried to get her to talk afterward, but Morrison always had someplace she needed to be. Despite those worries, it was a magical time for her, punctuated by the fact her nightmares had in fact begun to recede.

Still she continued to dream. But these dreams were filled with images of her childhood, of the trees around her home—the ones she liked to climb as a little girl, of her brothers and parents, and of course of her yiayia. She dreamed of Mary as well, their time together on vacations, playing softball with a city league, watching sunsets on the Potomac. The few dreams she did have of her time overseas were filled with the faces and smells that had brought her joy. Diren was there often by the fire, as was Asmin and the other women. And always Sirvan and his little hands on her face. If she woke up from these dreams, she didn't find herself screaming and struggling. Instead she'd discover her eyes damp and her cheeks wet. Yet she had no memory of weeping.

She was changing from within—she could feel it—all as a result of Reyha's companionship and company.

As usual, when she attended a group session at the end of the second month of the mission, she sat uncomfortably in the metal chairs as Woodley and the others talked. She noticed Morrison kept looking at her.

Before group had started, Chrys had asked if she was okay.

"I'm good," Morrison had said, but even now as the group proceeded, she kept looking over at her with questioning eyes.

Ramos held up one of his new artificial hands, presenting them like they were trophies won in some competition. "You would've thought they could've matched my skin tone. Other than that, I think I got the hang of them."

"I'm happy for you," Woodley said. He glanced over at Chrys. "Safis, you're looking well. Your consulting job with the State Department must've been the thing you needed."

"As consulting jobs go, it's not bad," Chrys said. "The little odd jobs keep me occupied." She'd offered the ruse of being hired as a consultant as a way to keep the others from asking too many questions. "And who knows, it might not be long until I'll be able to get fitted for a blade. The pay's pretty good."

"So you're able to work it with that knob of yours?" Ramos asked.

"Excuse me?" Chrys frowned.

"This *consulting* job. I think we all know what that means, those *odd jobs* as you put it," Ramos said. "Guess a girl can always earn a living on her back."

Chrys shot up. "What the hell?"

"Ramos, knock it off," Woodley said. He turned to her. "Safis, sit down."

"He just accused me of prostitution," Chrys said. "Again, always with the sex comments. I'm getting sick of him and his penis obsession."

"I think it's you who's got an obsession with me and my dick," Ramos said. "Don't think I haven't seen you checking it out."

Chrys shoved her chair backward and charged Ramos, who stood just as quickly, sending his chair clattering backward as well. The sound of metal chairs banging to the floor seemed to shock the others out of their numb complacency, and if Horrigan hadn't moved his wheelchair between them, she would've been on Ramos in an instant.

"That's enough," Woodley shouted. "Ramos, outside. Wait for me in the hall." He turned to her. "Safis, pick up those damn chairs and sit down."

Chrys wanted to spit, to punch something as she cussed under her breath and set one of the chairs in place.

"You good?" Morrison asked, setting up the other chair.

"Fine."

"He's an ass," Horrigan said.

The other men all nodded their agreement.

"You got to ignore him," Torres said. "Man's a piece of shit."

"You let him talk that way," Chrys said.

"He's a Marine," Dworsky said. "We all talk like that."

"Not all Marines," Chrys said.

Woodley returned, sat down, and adjusted his notepad. "Having these rages more often, Safis?"

"What are you talking about?" Chrys asked. "That jackass insulted me, and I'm sick of it. And what do you mean *more often*? I've never said a thing about having anger problems."

"We all got 'em," Torres said. "It's part of the mess inside our heads."

"Torres is right," Woodley said.

"Yeah, well, I don't have that issue," Chrys said.

"She has a right to be upset," Horrigan said. "Ramos is way over the top most times, and it isn't fair to her or Morrison."

"Agreed," Woodley said. "I'll see about getting him transferred to another group. But at the moment"—he turned to her—"let's talk about your anger issues."

Chrys rolled her eyes. "I don't have anger issues. Shit, I've been in this group for months and have listened to that asshole week after week. Did it ever occur to you that I've finally had it with him? Besides, I'm doing really well at the moment. The nightmares are getting better. I'm not drinking as…" She stopped, aware that the others watched her, especially Morrison. "Like I said, I'm not angry. I'm just done with him."

As usual when the session was over, Chrys and Morrison hung back so the men in wheelchairs could get out the door first.

"Glad Woodley's gonna get Ramos out of our group," Morrison said.

"Me, too." Chrys held the door. "Hey, how are you really? You look like you don't feel well."

"It's nothing. Just not getting enough sleep."

"Nightmares?"

"Yeah."

Chrys checked the time. Quinn and Smith were waiting across the street in the SUV even though she'd argued with them every time for the last two months she could walk from the Hay-Adams to the VA. "You want to grab lunch? We could talk about it."

"Naw, thanks," Morrison said. "I need to catch the Metro home. My mom's been sick, and I need to help with dishes and laundry."

Chrys walked alongside her toward the lobby and noticed Ramos talking loudly with Torres, who'd stopped, apparently waiting for the wheelchair van to pull up out front.

"Have you tried reading?" Chrys asked.

"Reading? What do you mean?"

"I don't know, just something to take your mind off things. A novel, maybe. Like an adventure novel or science fiction or something?"

"I'm not much of a reader," Morrison said.

They stopped at the exit, and Chrys saw a van pull up, glimpsed at Torres, who waved to Ramos and left through the automated door. At that moment, she became aware Ramos was watching her and Morrison.

"It's just I've been reading, and it's been helping me with the bad dreams."

Morrison scoffed. "Really?"

"Maybe try it?"

"Yeah, maybe."

Chrys touched her shoulder. "You got my number, right? You know you can call me anytime."

Morrison pulled away and pushed through the door. "You're a good person, Safis. Whatever it is you're doing to get yourself together, keep at it. It shows. I don't think I've ever seen you this…I don't know…alive before. You're usually sitting there silent and dazed like the rest of us. So whatever it is, reading books, popping pills, shooting up, the more power to you."

Chrys followed her down the steps. "You'll call me, won't you? I mean, what we talked about last time?"

Morrison was already hoofing it toward the streetlight. "Be careful out there. Streets are full of dangers. All kinds of accidents can happen, don't you know?" She offered a limp wave and crossed the street.

Chrys sighed and spotted Quinn leaning against the side of the SUV across the street. But before she could take a step toward him, she heard Ramos behind her.

"You and your girlfriend have a fight there, Safis?"

She swung around. "Fuck off."

"Is that it then? You got the hots for pussy, and not dick. Is that why you're such a bitch to me?"

He advanced upon her, and she took a step closer to him, not giving him the satisfaction of seeing her retreat.

"I said, fuck off."

He gave her an ugly smile. "So tell me, how's a dyke gonna scissor her bitch with half her leg missing?"

A bolt of rage struck Chrys between the eyes, and without considering the implications of what she was doing, she dove for his midsection.

Her unexpected move and the force of her blow caused him to fall back hard on the concrete steps. She pounced on top of him, pummeled his face with her fist. It wasn't but a second later one of his artificial hands connected with her jaw and then her temple as he kneed her in the groin and kicked at her false leg, landing a foot on her knee joint and sending her crashing back on her ass. She rolled to protect her face from his oncoming silicone fists, but thankfully Quinn and Smith along with two MPs showed up and pulled him off.

"You cunt," he screamed, "you broke my fucking nose."

She coughed on blood and spit it at his feet. Quinn dragged her toward the SUV while Smith pulled one of the MPs aside and flashed his badge. After Quinn dumped her in the back seat of the SUV, he returned to Smith's side. She watched them out the window and cursed, reeling with the pain in her leg. She could see the agents arguing with the police while another MP dragged Ramos back inside the building. Finally, she saw Quinn give the officer a card, and he and Smith returned to the vehicle.

"How bad hurt are you, Ms. Safis? Do you need medical attention?" Quinn asked.

Chrys leaned against the window and wiped blood from her mouth. "Just get me back to the hotel."

❖

Quinn pulled through the hotel's circular drive, and Smith tried to take her arm to escort her up the steps, but she shooed him away.

"I said, I'm fine."

Inside, Carmichael looked up from the front desk and came rushing over.

"Goodness, my dear Ms. Safis, whatever happened?"

"Could you get me some ice?" she asked. "A cold beer, too?"

"Yes, yes, of course." He motioned to one of his assistants.

"And I need to sit here in the lobby for a bit, calm down before going upstairs."

"Over here." Carmichael directed her to a high-backed chair and handed her his handkerchief.

She accepted it and put it to her mouth. "Thank you."

It smelled like expensive cologne and was made of fine silk. She was embarrassed to stain it with blood, but the weird little man was being so cavalier she couldn't bear to turn down his offer.

Soon the assistant arrived with the ice and beer, and she sat back and closed her eyes while she focused on her erratic breathing.

"Is there anything else?" Carmichael asked.

"I just need a moment."

"I understand." Carmichael returned to the front desk but kept looking over at her.

She scooted her chair so her back was to him and the front door. But even shielded by the tall back, she could hear him whispering to his assistant, and Smith and the other agents mumbling. No doubt they were discussing the spectacle she'd made of herself. Right then she heard the front doors opened and assumed it was Quinn returning from parking the SUV, but when she heard Carmichael's nervous voice, she went on alert.

"May I help you, sir?" Carmichael asked.

"I am looking for accommodations," the man said.

Chrys recognized the accent, and the skin on her arms prickled. She peeked around the chair and stifled a cry. It was him, the decapitated red horse man with the camera phone.

"I am sorry to say the Hay-Adams is completely booked for the next several months," Carmichael explained.

"You do not have even a single room? I will be happy to pay an upgrade for a suite."

"I'm afraid not." Carmichael's voice shook as he offered his lie. "The tourist season, you see. And we booked an entire ballet ensemble from…from Bangladesh."

"Bangladesh?" The stranger glanced around the lobby as he scratched the beard under his chin. "Well then, I shall be forced to seek other accommodations." He turned to leave.

"My apologies," Carmichael said.

Then at the door, Chrys saw the man bring his phone to his mouth, heard him speak in a dialect of Arabic and snarl the words, "She is here, I am certain."

Chrys jumped up. "Stop him, he's after Reyha!"

The man made eye contact with her, and his mouth went from surprise to loathing. He spit on the carpeted floor and bolted for the door just as Quinn came in.

"Get him!" Chrys dashed forward, but her leg crumpled from her recent assault.

Quinn spun around as he began shouting into his radio while Smith and the others drew weapons and ran out the door, knocking other guests aside.

"What is it? What's going on?" Carmichael asked, helping her to her feet.

Chrys shoved the bloody handkerchief into his hand and hobbled to the elevators. "They know she's here."

Carmichael whimpered. "Oh dear."

But she had no time to comfort him. She had to get to Reyha.

When the elevator doors opened, Banks had just pulled Reyha into the hall.

"It's him. I saw him. I didn't imagine it," Chrys said.

Reyha rushed toward her. "What has happened to your face? Who has done this?"

Chrys ignored her. "Quinn and the others went after him."

Banks pushed her earpiece to her head and shouted orders into her radio while pulling Reyha toward the control room.

"You are hurt," Reyha said, trying to reach out to Chrys.

"Not now." Chrys brushed her aside.

"You got him?" Banks said to Christman, who sat behind the wall of monitors.

"Got him," Christman said.

Chrys crowded behind and watched the screens with Reyha close by her side. She observed herself standing and pointing, then trying to run and collapsing.

"What were you doing?" Reyha asked taking her hand.

Chrys shushed her, then pointed. "Freeze it. Right there. Can you zoom in?"

Once Christman brought the image into focus, Banks turned to Reyha. "Do you recognize this man, Mrs. Arslan?"

"I do not understand," Reyha said. "Please tell me what is happening."

Chrys pointed. "That's the same guy who was taking pictures of you in the garden." She glanced at Banks. "I told you I didn't imagine him."

Banks clamped her lips tight and pointed once more at the screen. "Mrs. Arslan, please look closely, do you recognize this man?"

Reyha stared at the image, shook her head. "I do not recognize him." She looked at Banks. "But why has his presence caused you alarm?"

Banks held up one hand as she pressed her earpiece with the other. "All right," she said into her radio, "run the plate." She looked at Chrys. "Quinn said you indicated this individual was after Mrs. Arslan. Explain."

Chrys pointed to the screen. "Wind it back, right when he starts to leave." Christman did so, and as the scene played out, Chrys explained. "See right there, when he brings his phone up? I heard him say, *She's here.* It was a dialect of Arabic."

"That is all?" Reyha asked. "That does not seem to warrant alarm. Maybe he is looking for someone else."

"Reyha, for God's sake, listen to me." Chrys held her by the shoulders. "That's the man in the gardens. And as soon as I stood up and shouted just now, he recognized me, spat on the ground. He knows we're on to him."

"Actually, Ms. Safis, your actions only verified for him that she's here," Banks said.

Chrys jerked around. "Are you kidding me? He's probably been tracking her since she landed in the US. And I told you about him almost a month ago, but you decided I was imagining it."

Reyha shook her arm. "Stop this immediately. Do not raise your voice to Commander Banks. She was not implying you have put me in danger. I have been in danger from the start."

"But she *is* implying that." Chrys spat her words as her rage notched up.

Right then Quinn and the others swept in. "Plate traces back to a rental under the name John Anderson. Driver's license and insurance under the same name. Residence in Ohio."

Chrys lurched forward. "You lost him?"

Reyha pulled her back. "I would ask you to control yourself immediately."

Banks held up her hands. "Ms. Safis, please, Mrs. Arslan is right. You need to calm down. We have this. We got a good image of him, and we'll run facial recognition and figure out who he is. I'll alert the State Department and local law enforcement, and we'll track him down. Now please, I think the two of you should return to your suite."

Everyone froze and watched Chrys. She eyed each of them, saw Reyha ready to say something. "If anything happens to her…" she said, seething.

"Not under my watch," Banks said.

Chrys stormed from the room and paced the hall while Banks brought Reyha along.

"Ma'am, I would ask until we've identified this man that you and Ms. Safis limit your activities and remain in the safety of the Hay-Adams." She operated the key to the suite's door.

"I think not," Reyha said. "I will not be a prisoner to your fears. You are not even certain who this individual is."

"With all respect, Mrs. Arslan, you must understand—"

"Thank you, Commander Banks," Reyha said, "but it is you who must understand. I am not easily frightened, and I will not curtail my plans on such flimsy evidence."

"But I'm—"

Reyha held up her hand. "Please. I will not discuss this further. If and when you identify this individual as someone who wishes me harm, I will reconsider your request."

Banks swallowed a few times, glanced at Chrys. "I'm only doing my job."

"And you do it well," Reyha said. "And for the time being, we will remain in our suite. But may I remind you, we have tickets for the Kennedy Center next week. I do not plan on missing the performance. Now will you please have Mr. Carmichael arrange for afternoon tea?" She glanced at Chrys. "And perhaps a first-aid kit for my friend here."

"Right away, ma'am."

Reyha entered the suite and went immediately to her room. Chrys lingered in the hallway and faced Banks. She'd calmed down some, but still shook with adrenaline. "I guess I overstepped. Sorry, but I'm very protective of her."

"I understand, and I'm sorry I didn't believe you the first time," Banks said.

"Right." Chrys touched her throbbing eye. "I'll see if I can talk some sense into her about hanging low until we—rather, *you*—figure this all out."

"Good. She'll listen to you at least."

Chrys scoffed. "She's a strong-willed woman. I'm not sure how much she'll listen to me, but I'll try."

Banks smiled. "I've been watching you two interact. She hangs on every word you say. If anyone can convince her to keep a low profile, it's you."

"Let's hope so." Chrys turned toward the suite.

"Ms. Safis, what exactly did happen to your face?"

Chrys smiled, but flinched with the split in her lip. "Ask Quinn and Smith. They saw it blow by blow."

She shut the door and went to the kitchen sink where she splashed her face with water and then gathered some ice in a towel. She hesitated at the refrigerator and finally grabbed a beer and popped it open. Over in the living room, she settled on the sofa with the ice pack to her eye and waited for Reyha to emerge from her room.

Finally, Reyha opened her bedroom door. "You will tell me this instant what happened to your beautiful face."

"It's nothing really."

Reyha glided over and instead of sitting next to her on the sofa, she knelt down and pulled the beer from Chrys's hand. "You do not need this."

"You're right. I probably don't."

Reyha touched the bruise on her cheek. "You have acted rashly. Your impetuousness has potentially put yourself in danger for my sake."

"Don't worry, I won't let him hurt you."

"It is for you I fear, not myself," Reyha said, gripping Chrys's hands.

To Chrys's surprise, Reyha began crying, causing her mascara to blend with her tears and smear down her cheeks.

"If he is someone dangerous," Reyha said, "do you not realize he saw you point to him, knows you are connected to me."

Chrys stroked her hair. "No one's going to harm me. I promise."

"Yet someone has already hurt you."

She pulled Reyha's head to her and kissed the crown, then hugged her. "Shh, it's okay. I'm not badly hurt."

Reyha fell against her and encircled Chrys's waist with her arms.

"I will not lose you as I lost Ophelia. I cannot bear to have you taken from me."

"You won't lose me," Chrys said, rocking her in her arms.

Not knowing what else to do, she began to sing snippets of a lullaby, the very one she used to sing to Sirvan. And as she sang, Reyha melted deeper into her arms. She looked around the suite, waiting for Diren to appear, for her grandmother to manifest, but her mind remained clear, focused on the woman in her arms.

CHAPTER TWELVE

The hot granite burned through Chrys's slacks as she sat on the stone block. She wondered how it wasn't uncomfortable for Reyha with her elegant pants made of thin material, her flowing tunic of equally lightweight cloth. But Reyha apparently wasn't bothered, for she sat completely still, in a trance almost, as she gazed at the man-made waterfall before her while she held her brightly colored parasol over her head. It was yellow, a blazing yellow the color of the sun. Chrys held one, too, although reluctantly. Hers was a crimson red with dangly tatted lace at the end of each rib's tip. Why Reyha had chosen the plain yellow one and she had ended up with the girly one didn't seem quite right.

The umbrellas were a new addition from just that morning. Reyha had sent Banks on a mission to find the shades as the day was going to be a scorcher, and Reyha insisted they visit the Franklin Delano Roosevelt Memorial, Chrys's favorite. Banks had protested them going out in public, but Reyha said she'd been held captive for an entire week and was determined to carry on with her plans to see DC and enjoy herself. This despite the fact the red horse man, alias Anderson, had not yet been found or identified.

Now under the protective shade of the parasols, they sat together on a rectangular cube of gray granite that bordered one of the waterfalls of the FDR exhibit while the sun did indeed beat down on them mercilessly. The agents stood near, some in the shadow of one of the memorial's walls, others out in the direct sunlight. They had no protective umbrellas and sweated in their dark suits and sunglasses while they watched.

Chrys twirled her girly cover. "We might as well go ahead and draw a bull's-eye with black marker on each one of these. We couldn't be any more conspicuous."

Reyha chuckled. "You predict we are to be assassinated in broad daylight in the middle of your country's capital?"

Chrys tossed her free hand in the air with exasperation. "You know, people do get assassinated in broad daylight even with protection. JFK? King? Malcolm X?"

"Benazir Bhutto?"

Chrys flinched. "She died in Pakistan, and please don't compare yourself to her. It gives me chills."

Reyha shrugged. "I have been told I resemble her."

"No. You're even more beautiful."

Reyha smiled. "Ah, thank you, my friend." Then she wagged her finger. "But I must correct you. Your Dr. King was assassinated in the early evening. Not during the middle of the day."

Chrys rubbed her temple. "You're missing my point. I don't understand you. A week ago you were hysterical and now you're acting like it's no big deal that that freak is still out there somewhere."

"I was weeping out of exhaustion and concern for you."

Chrys grunted. "Talking to you is like talking to one of these granite blocks, you know that?"

"Is that a complimentary comparison?"

"No, it is not."

"You are angry with me."

"Not angry." Chrys shifted. Her ass was really beginning to cook on this hot stone. "I'm worried and scared is all. I've grown to care for you."

Reyha put her hand on Chrys's thigh, leaned toward her, causing their sunshades to overlap. The move provided a sense of privacy, intimacy. "And I feel the same for you."

Chrys watched Reyha's eyes, glanced at her mouth, the beads of perspiration on her upper lip. "If something happened to you, I don't know what I'd do."

"Yet what happens to me is of no consequence to your plans to return and fight in Syria."

"What happens to you is of huge consequence to me."

Reyha moved a curl from Chrys's eyes, brushed against her bruised cheek. "But if something happens to me, you will be strong. You must promise me this."

Chrys pulled away. "Will you please stop talking like that?"

"We cannot deny the possibility." Reyha stood. "Now come. Enough of this. Show me the rest of the exhibit."

They began to meander along the stone walls as Reyha stopped and read the inscriptions. Chrys glanced around them, noting the other tourists, keeping tabs on where each of the security detail stood. At moments, she found herself scanning the distant horizons, looking for anyone who seemed out of place. All the while, she kept wiping her eyes, drawing her arm across her forehead to mop the sweat that dripped down her face.

"And here she is," Reyha said as they came upon the bronze statue of Eleanor Roosevelt. "Such a grand woman. Your country was blessed to have had such a heart and mind."

"She was something," Chrys said. "Do you know this is the only presidential memorial to depict a First Lady? She was that important."

"I would argue each First Lady was important in her own right, but yes, Mrs. Roosevelt was particularly extraordinary." Reyha touched the statue's folded hands. "We are more than our dresses and dishes, are we not, dear woman?"

Chrys chuckled. "That still bothers you, doesn't it?"

"Enrages me, actually." Reyha sputtered a curse in Turkish.

Chrys laughed.

They strolled on as Reyha asked questions, pointed out something interesting, or pondered a quote engraved in the stone. She seemed to be caught up in her thoughts more than ever that afternoon, and Chrys wondered if she was thinking and worrying about that Anderson fellow and the threat he potentially represented.

They came to the still pool where the engraved relief of Roosevelt's funeral procession stood on the stone wall behind it. Reyha sat on the edge of the pool and touched the tranquil water with her fingers.

"I would like to return to this memorial after dark sometime," she said. "It is peaceful even now during the day, but I would like to see it illuminated at night."

"We can do that. It certainly would be a whole lot cooler." Chrys sat at an angle with her left knee touching Reyha's. She became aware of it and scooted away, not wanting Reyha to feel the hard plastic cup that gripped her stump.

Reyha appeared to be studying the ripples in the water as she continued to dip one finger in and out. "May I ask you something personal?"

Chrys stifled a snicker. "I think at this point you don't need permission to ask me something personal."

Reyha lifted her head. "I would never want to assume."

"Assume what?"

"That I am welcome to be intimate with you."

Chrys blinked. "Intimate?" She immediately stomped on the image that flooded her mind. Was she no better than Ramos, always seeing hints of nonexistent flirtation, interpreting everything as a sexual challenge? She smiled, her lips quivering. "Of course you're welcome to ask me anything. We're friends, after all."

Reyha brushed her fingers against Chrys's bruised cheek once more. "Yes, friends. Yet we are so different, you and I. Even still, there is a thread that runs between us, something that binds us."

Chrys swallowed, her tongue thick. "I feel it, too."

"I see myself in you in so many respects. Your compassion, your determination."

Chrys smiled.

"As well as your rage."

The spell broke, and Chrys sat back. "What?"

"I understand your rage—I do," Reyha said. "When I was your age, I was filled with it. But you see, it does no good unless it is channeled toward something constructive."

"What the hell is this? First Woodley, now you?"

"I asked Agent Quinn about your confrontation on the steps of the Veterans Hospital. He informed me it was you who attacked first. That part of the story you did not relate to me."

Chrys ground her teeth. "Ramos was being a jackass. I had every right to beat his ass."

"Yet your blows are visible on your own face."

Chrys side-eyed her. "I didn't realize you were a pacifist."

"You say that like it is an infectious disease."

"You and Mary." Chrys shook her head. "I could never understand why she went out with me in the first place."

"Your Mary is also a pacifist?"

Chrys laughed. "Well, let me put it this way—she was raised in California by a hippie mother and Berkeley professor for a father. When she got out of high school, she joined the Peace Corps before going to nursing school. And"—she tapped her head—"she marched on the Capitol wearing one of those ridiculous pink cat hats."

Reyha tilted her head. "Why do you mock her convictions?"

"I'm not mocking them. I just think she and a whole lot of women in the developed world haven't a clue what's really going on."

"And what is really going on?"

Chrys stood and stretched. She twirled her umbrella and gazed up at the blazing sun. "You probably already know this, but one reason the Kurdish fight in Syria is so important to me is what it represents. This isn't just another proxy war for the US. This is ground zero for the liberation of women, for all women."

"I agree with you on that point." Reyha pointed toward another part of the memorial and began making her way. "The only way the world will transform from the terror you see it to be is for women to transform their roles in society. We know from countless studies that the freedom and autonomy of women is the truest predictor of freedom for all sections of society."

Chrys studied Reyha's profile. "Exactly, and pink pussy hats don't do much but make a laughingstock of all women."

Reyha stopped. "This is where you are wrong, my friend. Each culture must address the issue of women's oppression in their own way. The women of the United States have one avenue, the women of Syria another. You should respect all efforts toward liberation." Reyha laid her hand on Chrys's arm. "And please do not be so judgmental. It does not complement your otherwise generous heart."

Reyha moved on, but Chrys hung back, frowning. She watched Reyha stop in front of the bronze statue of Roosevelt seated in his wheelchair, saw her turn and look at her, held her gaze. The sun penetrated Reyha's yellow shade, illuminating her face. With the scarf she wore on her head, she looked like some biblical saint, some divine goddess. Chrys smoothed her frown and relaxed her lips, but a tight sensation continued to grip her chest as she watched Reyha.

"So, what about this thread that binds us?" Chrys asked as she started toward her. "The personal question you wanted to ask?" She stopped when their parasols collided.

"I wanted to know why you and Mary ended your relationship."

"Oh, yeah, that." Chrys squeezed the bridge of her nose. "She's a really good person. You should know that."

Reyha nodded.

"Anyway, things just changed between us after I came home all smashed to bits."

"Your injuries came between you?"

"Partly, I guess. But it was more than that. She wanted me back the way I was before. But I couldn't."

"What could you not do?"

Chrys looked at the Roosevelt statue, studied the outline of the wheelchair. She could've been injured much worse. She could be like Horrigan or Dworkin and in a chair for life. Then a chill rippled through her. She could be dead. Perhaps she should be, but she'd been spared while others had died. She flashed on Asmin's face, on Sirvan and the others in the bed of the truck, on Diren shouting for retreat as others ran for cover while she threw herself into the fray.

"There was so much blood," she muttered, dropping the umbrella and teetering.

Reyha held her shoulder. "Why do you speak of blood?"

Chrys shook herself, wiped her eyes. "What?"

"Are you feeling well? We were speaking of Mary and then you—"

"Mary." Chrys loosened the top button on her shirt and pressed a finger against her temple. "I didn't want Mary to be my nurse. But she ended up being just that, taking care of me like a cripple, like I was too broken to take care of myself." Feeling dizzy, she held her forehead. "Maybe I was, but that wasn't what I wanted for us. I mean, I loved her, knew she loved me, but she wanted…" She swept her hands down her body. "But I couldn't do that anymore. Besides, I saw the way she looked at me. She felt sorry for me. I want to be wanted, not pitied. But who could want me now?"

She bent to retrieve the umbrella and the ground wobbled beneath her as she stood. She reached out her hand, pitched forward into Reyha's arms. Suddenly Quinn was there, pulling her against his chest.

"Please, ma'am, sit down." He guided her to one of the stone benches.

She heard Banks giving orders, Smith shooing away spectators. A bottle of water was forced into her hand, someone's damp handkerchief placed on her forehead.

"They are bringing the vehicle," Reyha said. "We will get you someplace cool."

"I'm okay," Chrys said as she sipped the water.

"No, you are not," Reyha said. "You have gotten overheated. This is my fault. I insisted on coming out in the middle of the day."

"It's fine. I'm…" Chrys's stomach heaved, and she leaned forward on her knees and held the damp hanky to her face and wondered if she looked up if her grandmother and Diren would be among the crowd.

Soon the SUV arrived along the memorial path, and with Banks on one side and Quinn on the other, Chrys was helped into the back seat. Reyha climbed in next to her, and in moments the SUV's air conditioner filled the dark cabin with cool air.

"Is there something more you need, Ms. Safis?" Banks asked from the front seat.

Chrys shook her head.

"We will be home in moments," Reyha said. "And I will help you into a cool shower and feed you some lunch. You will see. I will take care of you."

Chrys sagged against her window. She'd been doing so well, had made so many gains, but now Reyha, like Mary, would be forced to carry the burden.

Reyha pushed the plate toward her. "You must eat something."

Chrys wiped hair from her eyes, still damp after her cool shower. Luckily, she'd convinced Reyha she didn't need help getting in and out of the shower. That would've been even more humiliating. "I'm sorry for cutting our day short. I know you wanted to see the Martin Luther King Memorial."

"It is of no importance. We will see it another day." Reyha put a fork in Chrys's hand. "But I must insist you try to eat something. I want you fully recovered from your heat sickness so that you may accompany me tomorrow evening to the Kennedy Center."

"You can go without me. Banks would be a good stand-in."

"While I agree she is an attractive woman, she is not the woman I wish to share my evening with." Reyha stabbed a piece of chicken with Chrys's fork and brought it to her mouth. "You are the one I wish to have on my arm."

Chrys giggled at the ridiculousness of Reyha's expression and obediently chewed the bite of chicken.

Seemingly satisfied Chrys would eat, Reyha dug in to her own salad. "And did you not promise to be my date?"

"Your date?" Chrys giggled again.

"Is that not the correct expression, *to go out on a date*?"

"Yes, but that expression implies a romantic courtship."

"Does it?"

"It does."

"Hmm." Reyha focused on the roll she'd just broken open. "I had hoped to share this music with you. It is important to me, and something I think you will enjoy."

Chrys thought of the tux hanging in her closet that Carmichael had delivered a few days ago. She'd seen herself last week in the near-final product at the studio where Carmichael and his friend Gustav had circled her and nodded their approval. She had to admit, she did look good in it. But now with her eye still discolored and her lip still swollen, not to mention this latest setback, she wasn't sure she wanted to risk making a fool of herself again.

"You won't be embarrassed to be seen with me and my black eye?" Chrys asked.

"You could never embarrass me."

Chrys slid her plate close. "If you're sure."

"I am sure."

"Okay, then I'd be happy to be your *date* tomorrow night." Chrys snickered.

"I promise to have you home by curfew." Reyha winked as she took a bite of her roll.

Chrys shivered and looked away; Reyha's wink somehow always made her tingle. After a few bites, she set her fork down. "I appreciate everything you do for me, Reyha. But you need to understand, I was hired to serve you, not the other way around. Besides, I don't want you to feel obligated to look after me."

"I am concerned for your welfare."

"The thing is, being mothered makes me uncomfortable."

Reyha stopped eating. "You think I am mothering you?"

"It sort of feels that way."

"The age difference, I see." Reyha wiped her mouth with her napkin. "My intention has not been to mother you, but to support you as any friend might, as perhaps even your Mary did."

"But Mary did the same thing. I told you. She was like this little mother hen fussing over me all the time."

"I do not think of you as my daughter or I your mother. There is nothing further from my mind." Reyha pointed her fork toward Chrys's plate. "Keep eating. Afterward you will lie down. I want you rested."

Chrys smirked. "Yes, Mother."

Reyha swatted at her. "Now you are wearing big sassy britches."

Chrys gurgled on her water and laughed. "Wearing what? I think you got your idioms mixed up there, lady."

"To wear *big sassy britches* is not a saying?"

Chrys laughed again. "It's *wearing sassy pants* or being *too big for your britches*. Both of which have probably described me on occasion."

"Only on occasion?" Reyha raised her eyebrows.

Chrys blew a raspberry and returned to her meal.

She woke up from her rest feeling unusually refreshed and free of pain. Out in the living area, she found Reyha sitting at the desk and working on her laptop.

"You were right," Chrys said, coming over to the sofa. "I needed that nap."

Reyha continued to focus on her screen. "Mother always knows best, they say." She looked up and smiled.

"Now who's wearing sassy pants?" Chrys asked, making a comical face.

Reyha laughed and came over and sat next to her. "Do you like ice cream?"

"Why are you asking me?"

"It is a simple question, yes or no?"

"Of course, I like ice cream, who doesn't?"

Reyha pulled a magazine off the coffee table. "Look at this. Have you been here?"

Chrys examined the glossy image. "The Capital Wheel at National Harbor? Yes, I've been there. It's right along the Potomac."

"Do you know I have never ridden a Ferris wheel?"

Chrys drew back. "But they have amusement parks in Turkey. I've been to Lunapark in Izmir."

Reyha shrugged. "Yet I have never had the occasion to ride a Ferris wheel."

"That's just sad."

Reyha pushed against Chrys's shoulder with her own. "Will you take me tonight? I would like some ice cream and to ride this wheel."

"You know Banks will have a fit." Chrys pointed to the magazine. "That's a big tourist attraction, especially in the summer. Lots of people."

"But it is in the middle of the week. Perhaps fewer people."

Chrys patted her hand. "If that's what you want, that's what you'll have."

Reyha's face beamed. "Splendid. My first time shall be with you."

"Excuse me?"

"My first time upon a Ferris wheel."

"Right. The Ferris wheel." Chrys fanned her face and stifled a groan as her body tingled all over while she silently chided herself once more for allowing her mind to envision not only the improbable, but also the impossible.

❖

As Chrys had anticipated, Banks objected to the whole idea entirely. But Reyha held firm until Banks conceded. As they loaded into the SUV, Banks pulled Chrys aside.

"I thought you were going to try and discourage her from going out as much. Wasn't this afternoon enough?" Banks asked.

Chrys grinned. "She wants her ice cream and Ferris wheel ride. Did you see her face? Come on, how can you turn down that face?"

"You're not helping," Banks said, unable to hide her aggravation.

Chrys chuckled and climbed in alongside Reyha.

After arriving at National Harbor and finding parking, Banks directed two of her agents to proceed ahead and speak to the ride's operator; she sent two more ahead to scope out the ice cream shop. Now she, Quinn, and Smith fell in alongside Chrys and Reyha as they walked along the marina and perused the little shops. The Capital Wheel loomed in the near distance, already lit up red-white-blue in the darkening sky.

After getting their ice cream cones, they continued inspecting the shops. Reyha wanted the sky darker before they ventured on the ride, and once she was satisfied it was dark enough, the group proceeded to the boardwalk and waited while Banks spoke with the wheel operator. Just as Reyha had noted earlier, there were fewer tourists than usual, so when the operator explained to the waiting guests he was required to board a VIP party first, there were only a few groans. He held the door to one of the gondolas, and Chrys helped Reyha take her seat. Banks started to join them, as each gondola held up to eight, but Reyha intervened.

"Do you mind if I share the ride alone with Ms. Safis? I do not see how I could be in harm's way so far up."

Banks hesitated, glanced over at Quinn and Smith. "As you wish, ma'am." She shut the door and stepped away.

"Our Commander Banks seems to think an assassin waits for me at every turn."

"She's only doing her job," Chrys said. "But you're right. I doubt you're in any danger riding a Ferris wheel."

Reyha scooted closer and laced her fingers in Chrys's hand. "Especially with you by my side. I feel confident you would intervene on my behalf."

"You know I would."

They sat back as the wheel began to turn. It was a slow rotation, allowing those in the gondolas to view the White House and Capitol, the National Mall, Arlington Cemetery, the city of Alexandria, Prince George's County, and the lush parklands throughout the DC, Maryland, and Virginia region in the distance. Chrys pointed out each landmark and smiled at Reyha's oohs and ahs. Before long they halted at the very top, lingering there while the gondolas ahead of them emptied and filled of their passengers.

In the dim light, cut only by the glow of the colorful bulbs outlining the giant wheel, Reyha turned her attention to Chrys. "You know, I have the strangest feeling you and I have ridden a Ferris wheel together before."

"But you told me you'd never ridden one."

"Not in this lifetime." Reyha leaned closer. "Do you not remember the first evening in our suite I told you I could glimpse an old soul in your eyes?"

"I remember." Chrys gazed at Reyha's mouth parted as if inviting a kiss. "But I'm not sure I believe in reincarnation or even an afterlife."

"No? Yet an afterlife is part of your religious upbringing."

"You can't grow up in a Greek American family without being inculcated by the church, but I'm Orthodox in culture only."

Reyha nodded. "As am I."

Chrys cocked her head. "You're not observant?"

"Have you seen me pray?"

Chrys touched the silk scarf along Reyha's head. "But you cover your hair."

Reyha nodded. "You may be aware of the headscarf ban in my country back in the eighties. As a university professor, a public servant, I was told I could not wear one while teaching my classes." She tugged on the end of her scarf. "The ban did not impact me, however. I had never worn covering, for my parents did not require it. But you see, many of my female students were devout in their beliefs. Without the covering, they would not attend their classes and, therefore, were denied their rightful education. So as a way to protest and to stand in solidarity with them, I began wearing a loose scarf."

"But you haven't lived and taught in Turkey for five years. Why wear one now?"

"I can only tell you I became accustomed to wearing one while in public and drew some comfort from doing so particularly after I lost all my hair from my previous chemotherapy."

Chrys squeezed Reyha's hand. "I understand. Army doctors had to shave my head, and I wore a baseball cap for months afterward. I hated the thought of Mary or anyone seeing my big melon with its gnarly gash."

Reyha wound one of Chrys's curls around her finger. "And how I adore your hair. I love the way it curls about your face and along your neck."

Chrys's throat constricted. "I usually wear it short, but I'll keep it long for you if you'd like."

"Would you?"

"You can have anything you want from me. I think you know that."

"Anything?"

Chrys stared at Reyha's lips and imagined the kiss. But as she did, her chest constricted tighter, and she realized even if Reyha was suggesting what she hoped, she couldn't offer her absolutely everything. The wheel lurched forward, and she pulled back. "Anything within reason."

Reyha turned her head toward the scenery passing beyond them. "Within reason. Of course."

When they disembarked, Banks scrutinized them.

"Something wrong?" Chrys asked.

"Are you okay?" Banks asked.

"Sure, why?"

Banks looked at Reyha, back at Chrys. "Nothing, it's just you both seem…" She shook her head. "It's nothing. Are we all done? Can we head back to the Hay-Adams now?"

"Yes, I would like my dinner," Reyha said. She held her hip and walked a few steps ahead of Chrys on their way back to the SUV, but she did not engage Chrys or the others the entire ride back to the hotel.

❖

Once inside the suite, Reyha pulled off her scarf. "Will you call me when dinner arrives?"

"I will." Chrys followed her. "Everything is okay, right? You seem out of sorts."

"My hip is bothering me. It is nothing."

Chrys shrank back when Reyha shut the bedroom door. She flashed on the many times Mary had shut the door in her face. Frustrated and confused, she paced the living room, hung over the balcony, flopped on her bed. Finally, dinner arrived and she knocked on Reyha's door.

"You feeling better?" Chrys asked when Reyha came out of her bedroom.

"I feel wonderful." Reyha seemed her old self now and took her place at the table.

Chrys joined her. "I enjoyed my Ferris wheel ride with you," she said, serving up her plate.

"Thank you for allowing yourself some playfulness."

"Hmm?" Chrys looked up from her food.

"You are too serious too often. I want you to embrace life's joys as I have told you before. I expect you to live up to your namesake. Chrysanthemums, no?"

Chrys wrinkled her nose. "Well, it means golden flower, actually, but yeah, chrysanthemums, more or less. But I hate them—they're an old lady flower."

Reyha laughed long and hard. When she got control, she patted Chrys's hand. "They are beautiful, and they represent joy and optimism, something I believe you need in your life."

"I know. I remember my mother explaining my name to me when I was little."

"And your name day is for the martyr Chrysanthos and his beloved Daria, is that correct?"

"Yes, March nineteenth."

Reyha's eyes lit up. "I share my birthday with your name day."

Chrys put down her fork. "Well then, I think someone's due for a belated birthday present. I'll have to think of something."

"As I told you, yellow roses are my favorite."

Chrys held her heart with mock offense. "I'm hurt. I would've thought by now chrysanthemums would be your favorite."

"A close tie." Reyha winked.

Chrys dropped her hand and stared. Reyha's wink really was like some potent potion, an elixir that made her entire body warm.

"Do you know why I like flowers?" Reyha asked after a long pause.

"They're pretty?" Chrys said still spellbound by Reyha's wink.

"Of course, but that is not the only reason."

Chrys folded her napkin and sat back. "Go on then, teach me the great mystery of flowers."

Reyha wagged a finger. "I detect that mocking tone of yours."

"No, I'm serious. I've enjoyed learning from you these past months. The art, the music, the reading." Chrys gave her a playful glare. "The politics. So go on, tell me about flowers."

"Ah well, you must understand, it is the cornerstone of my life's philosophy."

"Interesting." Chrys smiled at the seriousness on Reyha's face.

"As such, being an apostate, and not having a formal religion as a guidepost, I created my own."

Chrys leaned forward. "Wait, you're an apostate? I only thought you weren't observant."

"My enemies wish me dead for more reason than my support of my Kurdish brothers and sisters."

Chrys shut her open mouth, and for a split second, news images of the faces of men and women cut down by religious fanatics overwhelmed her.

"What is wrong?" Reyha asked.

"This isn't just about your UN speech, your husband's work with the Kurds," Chrys said. "You've pissed off a whole lot of people. The wrong kind of people."

"I will not cower to others' expectations of me."

Chrys gripped Reyha's hand. "This is serious. You need to stop being so nonchalant about it like it's all about people not liking you for your taste in clothes or wine."

"I have excellent taste in my attire and wine."

"Stop joking." She gripped Reyha's hand tighter. "People are trying to kill you. This isn't a game."

"Do you wish to hear my flower philosophy or not?" Reyha asked clearly aggravated. "If you would rather wring your hands like an old woman, then please, do so in the other room. I will focus the time left to me on things of beauty that bring me joy. I will not allow fear to rule me. Not any longer."

Chrys pulled away feeling scolded. "Fine. What's up with the flowers?"

Reyha held her forehead while taking rhythmic breaths. Chrys waited, watched. Apparently, she'd touched a nerve.

"You will recall I said life's impermanence is what gives it meaning," Reyha said finally. "Knowing this, you must make the choice of whether you will fall into the philosopher's torment and bemoan the short brutal existence that is full of so much pain, or if you will accept that this very impermanence is what brings beauty."

"What's this got to do with flowers?"

"Because flowers continue to grow amid the dung heap of this world, the shit hole as you called it."

"That's what I called it."

"As such," Reyha continued, "a single flower pushes its way upward toward the sunlight, unfolds its petals to the bright day, and worships the sky and air with its simple elegance as it sits among the ugliness of existence."

"Okay, as nice as those words are, particularly coming from you, I still don't get your point."

Reyha leaned on her elbow, reached and cupped Chrys's chin. "The flower will exist for only a moment in time before it withers and dies. But in that short time, it brings joy and love and hope to all those mired within the excrement."

Chrys melted against Reyha's hand. "That's a brave little flower."

"Indeed, for the flower knows it will wither, but it struggles to be born, no matter. It knows it will fade, but it courageously unfurls its petals. It knows it will wilt and be consumed back into the darkness." Reyha leaned closer, her eyes full of warmth and spirit, her impatience dissolved. "Yet it chooses to live fully, to be a beacon of hope."

"What kind of flower?" Chrys asked, mesmerized by Reyha's touch and words.

"Any kind you wish."

"Yellow roses?"

"My favorite."

Chrys's heart pounded. "Can I have daisies instead of chrysanthemums?" She placed her hand over Reyha's.

"You may have any flower you choose." Reyha slowly pulled back, taking her hand from Chrys's hold. "But tell me, will you take your turn at being that small flower of hope, that elegant daisy?"

"Is the alternative to roll around in a pile of shit?" Chrys ached for Reyha's touch to return.

Reyha laughed. "That is one way to think of it."

"Then let's go out and plant daisies and roses."

"To grow together?"

Chrys swallowed. "Intertwined?"

Reyha's smile dissolved. She took a sip of wine, wiped her mouth. "While I am flattered, I meant the metaphor to apply to the world at large. But if you are offering your flower to me, how could I not accept such a gift?"

Chrys pulled her eyes away, rubbed her knee. She'd done it again—allowed herself to see a deeper meaning than Reyha meant. And even if Reyha was implying what she hoped, Chrys knew once again she was making an offer she couldn't fulfill, an offer she was certain Reyha would reject anyway. "As you said, you were speaking metaphorically."

Unexpectedly, Reyha pushed away from the table.

"Are you going to smoke?" Chrys asked. The pained expression she'd witnessed earlier on Reyha's face had returned.

"Not this night. I am rather tired. I think the heat has gotten to me as well."

Chrys stood. "Can I get you anything?"

Reyha gazed at her, seemed to be right on the edge of saying something. But she shook her head and instead brought Chrys into an embrace and kissed her cheeks. "I am fine. Thank you, my friend, for a lovely evening."

Against her better judgment, Chrys drew Reyha in closer and held her around the waist. "It was a lot of fun tonight, wasn't it?"

Reyha nodded.

"It's been a long time since I've had fun."

Reyha lowered her gaze.

"I'm sorry I got on you about the religious thing. It's just I don't want anything to happen to you."

Reyha reached behind and disengaged Chrys's arms. She faltered slightly on her feet and hugged her hand to her hip. "Good night, Chrysanthi. Dream well." She limped toward her bedroom and shut the door.

Chrys groaned and pounded her fist against her head, then cursed as she went toward the kitchen. At the refrigerator, she opened the door and stared at the bottles of beer, but finally she turned away empty-handed and went to dress for her evening workout, for another night of working off her heart's frustration as well as the growing tension in her body.

CHAPTER THIRTEEN

Standing in front of the bathroom mirror, Chrys worked to get the silk tie knotted while longing for the simplicity of her Air Force neck tab and dress uniform. After her fifth try, she gave up and let the tie dangle around her neck. She then pulled on the orchid waistcoat and looped her jacket over her arm and went out to find Reyha. As she entered the living room, Reyha's door opened. What she saw made her gasp. Reyha wore a full-length dress, fitted at the waist, cut with a layer of petticoats which revealed layers of silk underneath in various shades of purple and blue and embroidered with white and black leaves and vines. Her headscarf, part of the set, draped loosely over her styled hair. To this ensemble, she'd added dazzling amethyst earrings which dangled from her ears along with a matching necklace hanging low in the vee of the dress's neckline.

"You're beautiful," Chrys said.

Reyha walked toward her, stopped inches from her, and slid her finger down the loose tie. "And you are stunning."

"I don't look ridiculous with my black eye and split lip, do I?"

The touch of Reyha's warm fingers on her lip almost made Chrys jump from her skin.

"Not at all," Reyha said.

"Can you help me with this?" Chrys lifted the ends of the tie. "I never learned to knot one properly."

Reyha took the ends and began to loop them while keeping her eyes pinned on Chrys. "Our Mr. Carmichael has done well."

Chrys snickered. "He's a regular fairy godmother."

Reyha slid the knot into place, smoothed the shirt's collar, and stepped closer. She began to button the waistcoat. "You should not mock him. He is a good man."

Chrys looked down and watched Reyha's fingers work the buttons, watched them climb higher. "I'm only teasing. But I think it's interesting how he flirts with me when he's clearly…" She stopped as Reyha's hands finished their work and rested flat against her chest, just above her breasts.

"He is clearly what?"

Chrys looked up. "Hey, we match."

"Hmm?"

"The purple in your dress and my waistcoat. How'd that happen?"

"I made the request before you and he went to see his tailor. I desired us to be a matched set for our evening out." Reyha touched Chrys's hair, moved a curl behind her ear.

"A matched set? Like a couple?"

"Does that displease you?"

"No, not at all, it's just I'm not used to wearing these sorts of clothes. I mean, this isn't like my Air Force uniform. That fits differently. And, you know, it isn't like I've had lots of opportunities to go places like this, so I'm not sure if…" Chrys stopped talking when she realized she was rambling.

"Yet you carry yourself with such dignity, one would never know you were not born to bear yourself in such a manner and don such exquisite finery."

"It's all that standing at attention and marching and stuff."

Reyha took the jacket from Chrys's arm, held it for her while she slipped into it, then moved behind her with her hands on her shoulders. "Shall we go?"

Chrys turned and held out her arm. "I am greatly honored to accompany you this evening," she said in Turkish.

Reyha inclined her head. "The honor is all mine." She took Chrys's arm and, at the door, slipped off her slippers and pulled on the dress shoes she'd placed there earlier. Right then she suddenly grew three inches taller.

Chrys lifted her head. "Hey, no fair, you're taller than me now."

She froze with anticipation as Reyha pulled her by the waist, inclined her head, and gazed down into her eyes.

"Taller and older. That is not a problem, I hope."

"A problem? No, not a problem." Chrys's voice came out like a squeaky hinge, and she cursed herself silently.

Reyha grinned and opened the door.

They were met by Banks and Quinn, both of whom wore dark, formal suits.

"Ladies," Banks said. She scanned them both while Quinn smiled appreciatively. "We'll be down to three tonight. Agents Quinn and Smith and myself. Mr. Gordon has reserved a private box for four. Quinn and Smith will alternate positions."

"How lovely," Reyha said. "I am delighted you will be allowed to enjoy tonight's performance, Commander."

When they disembarked from the elevator, Carmichael met them in the lobby where he began to buzz about them in such a fit of enthusiasm that Chrys feared he might stroke out.

"My goodness," he said, panting with exuberance. "I feel I am the footman at a Cinderella ball. You ladies will steal the attention away from the stage, I just know it." He presented two corsages. "May I?" He pinned Reyha's on first before moving to Chrys. "My dear Ms. Safis, I see you have no need for my Professor Higgins to your Eliza Doolittle, for you have already transformed yourself into the fairest of ladies."

Chrys frowned. "Huh?"

He gripped her hand and patted it between his pink fingers. "Enjoy your evening."

Since Banks was required to sit in the back with them, Chrys scooted over, dragging her left leg in line to give her room. She was in the middle between Reyha and Banks, and even though she was turned slightly Reyha's way, she was aware of Banks looking at her from her peripheral vision, Quinn stealing glances in the rearview mirror, and Smith glancing back occasionally. She guessed she and Reyha must look pretty impressive. She put her arm through Reyha's and thought how nice it would be if this were an actual date.

Reyha patted her thigh. "Indeed, our Mr. Carmichael is quite taken with you."

"I'm not so sure about that Eliza Doolittle crack," Chrys said. "I speak a lot of languages, but Cockney's not one of them."

Reyha giggled. "He was only complimenting you, comparing you to the Greek myth of Pygmalion and Galatea. It is quite appropriate, I think."

Right then Smith began to hum, and Chrys saw him give Quinn a playful shove to the shoulder.

"Are you humming 'I Could Have Danced All Night' from *My Fair Lady*?" Chrys asked.

"That's one of my favorite musicals," Smith said, and to her shock, he belted out the chorus.

"Agent Smith." Bank's scolding voice cut him off before he began another verse.

Smith sat at attention. "Sorry, Commander."

Chrys cocked her head, and Reyha covered her mouth as she suppressed a laugh.

Quinn caught Chrys's gaze in the rearview mirror. "He only knows that song from *The Birdcage*. He's watched that movie a million times."

"But they stole it from *My Fair Lady*," Smith countered.

"Gentlemen," Banks said.

Quinn and Smith exchanged a look.

"Our apologies, Commander," they said in unison.

Chrys looked to each of the agents, then over at Banks. She leaned against Reyha and whispered, "What the heck is going on?"

Reyha put a finger to Chrys's lips. "Shh." She put her mouth against Chrys's ear and said, "Our dutiful bodyguards are allowing their human side to show. Do not embarrass them."

Chrys pulled back and nodded. She understood the implication now, and she darted her eyes from one man to the next. But right then, she became aware Banks was watching her again, so she nonchalantly sat back and curled close to Reyha and watched out the window as the glowing lights of the DC streets whizzed by.

As they strolled into the lobby of the Kennedy Center heads turned. Men and women alike watched as they made their way with the three agents in close formation. Chrys wondered if it was out of curiosity, just as people had looked at them for the last two months while they'd visited museums and monuments. But as they gathered more and more approving looks, Chrys was sure people were admiring Reyha's beauty. Yet in some way, she hoped it was because the two of them made such a nice pair, a matched set, as Reyha had said.

At intermission, Chrys was sure people were admiring Reyha, for even as they made their way through the crowds to the restrooms, the throng of people parted as if they were aware some regal entity graced their venue. Chrys couldn't help but feel proud to be with her, to be *the woman on her arm*, as Reyha had put it earlier. And while the second half of the performance played out, Chrys allowed her mind to fantasize about them as a couple. It was easy to do with the moving music, soulful and even deeply romantic in some places. At one point, she glanced over to find Reyha watching her with teary eyes and holding her hand to her heart. Chrys smiled and threaded her fingers through Reyha's for the rest of the concert while feeling somehow the cello spoke a language that only the two of them could understand.

By the time they arrived back at the Hay-Adams, it was after midnight. They were greeted by Carmichael as they came through the front doors of the lobby. He looked flustered and red in the face as he approached them.

"Good evening, Mrs. Arslan, Ms. Safis," he said, giving his characteristic bow of deference. "I hope your evening was a pleasant one."

"Most pleasant," Reyha said, looking at Chrys.

Chrys smiled.

Carmichael licked his lips, wrung his hands, and glanced from Banks, back to Reyha, then once more to Banks. "Might I have a word with you, Ms. Banks."

"That's *Commander* Banks."

"Pardon me. I've lost my manners," he said in a bluster.

Chrys watched as the eccentric man pulled Banks off to the side, his hands gesturing erratically. As she and Reyha entered the elevator with Quinn and Smith, she saw Banks's back go rigid, saw her motion two agents over while her forehead wrinkled.

"I wonder what that's about," Chrys said as the elevator doors closed.

At their suite door, Chrys and Reyha said good night to the agents and slipped inside. Reyha pulled off her shoes and returned to her usual height.

"I'm going to get into some sweatpants and a T-shirt," Chrys said.

"Join me on the balcony first, will you?" Reyha asked. "I am afraid it is too late for our reading tonight, but I would like to spend a bit more time admiring you in your tuxedo." She began to unbutton Chrys's jacket. "But I know how hot your body temperature runs. Please, you may remove your jacket."

Chrys watched Reyha's fingers on her jacket's buttons. "How hot I run?"

Reyha put her hand on Chrys's forehead. "I have noticed you perspire a great deal."

Chrys shrank back with embarrassment. "It's the meds. Sorry."

"Do not feel ashamed." Reyha draped the jacket over a chair and went to the kitchen and returned with a bottle of wine, two glasses, and her cigarette case. "You have done so well to refrain from your alcohol. Still, would you allow yourself one taste of this wine? I chose it for tonight especially."

"Why tonight?"

"Our first date."

Chrys chuckled. "You're cute."

"Cute? How do you mean that?"

Chrys tried to open the French doors, fumbled with the knobs. "Adorable actually, not cute. That doesn't really suit you. But also witty. I like how you make jokes." She pushed through the doors and out onto the balcony.

"I was not aware I was making a joke," Reyha said from behind.

Chrys didn't turn around. Instead, she gripped the railing and focused on taking deep breaths to clear her mind of her unreasonable fantasies. As she looked out, she saw agents below on the street; there seemed to be more than usual. She leaned forward to count them, but jumped when she heard the cork from the wine release. She turned to find Reyha pouring, watched her set the bottle down, lift the two glasses, and glide toward her.

"A toast?" Reyha handed her a glass.

Chrys took it, saw how it vibrated in her trembling hand. "And what should we toast to?"

"To friendship. To love."

Chrys squelched the yelp that tried to escape her mouth and lifted her glass, brought it to her lips, and sipped. The wine tasted dry, yet fruity.

Reyha watched her over the rim of her own glass. "Do you like it?"

Chrys nodded.

"Good." Reyha went to her usual chair, sat, and lit a cigarette.

Chrys leaned against the railing and watched the red smolder of the cigarette move from Reyha's mouth and down again. She took another sip of the wine, held it in her mouth, and swallowed. Reyha's cigarette made another slow arc up and down. Then the warble of a nearby siren caught Chrys's attention, and she turned back to examine the street below. She spotted two unmarked SUVs pull across the street with emergency lights flashing on their dashboards and men and women piling out just as a patrol car came alongside.

"I wonder what's up. Banks say anything to you about other high-profile guests staying here?" Chrys set her wine on the railing and began to undo her tie.

"She has said nothing."

"No? Well something's up."

"Indeed."

Chrys turned to see Reyha's eyes travel the length of her body. She paused in her efforts to undo her tie as she was no longer able to breathe evenly with the mixture of confusion and excitement gripping her from the look Reyha was giving her. But the urgency to get the tie loose caused her to yank at it with more resolve. Still the knot would not give. "Would you please untie me? I can't get this to budge."

Reyha's eyes traveled Chrys's body once more. "I should not wish to see you out of your attire quite yet."

Chrys frowned. "I'm sorry?"

"Our Mr. Carmichael is quite right in comparing you to Galatea."

"Are you suggesting I'm cold like marble?"

"Ivory." Reyha clicked her tongue. "You should know this story. It is of your culture."

Chrys wiped sweat from her forehead. "Actually my yiayia didn't spend a great deal of time recounting Greek myths. She stuck to real stories, to history." She walked closer, looked down at Reyha. "Besides, it's sort of a sad story, isn't it? Guy couldn't get a girl on his own, so he carved one out of ivory and prayed to Aphrodite to bring her to life."

Reyha put out her cigarette and stood. "Watching someone you care for return to life when she has been dead inside is not only a story for Greek mythology."

Chrys stiffened. "You're not making any sense."

Reyha stepped closer, brushed hair from Chrys's eyes. "Would that I might offer supplication and prayers to the goddess Aphrodite. Would that she might grant my wish as she granted his."

Chrys's chest tightened. "I think I'm missing something. Maybe you could express it in Turkish and I could—"

But Reyha stopped her with a finger to her lips. "What I am trying to communicate is best said not through words."

Chrys's heart raced, and she feared she might faint as she'd nearly done the day before. "Okay," she said, hearing her voice quake with anticipation. "Then how?"

"How indeed." Reyha let her finger linger on Chrys's lips, began to trace the outline of her mouth as she leaned toward her.

Panic hit Chrys in the stomach, and she gasped with short panting breaths while pushing away. "Please, I can't. I'm not…my leg, my scars…I can't."

Reyha stopped her forward momentum. "But the way you have…I do not understand."

Chrys held up her hands and moved away.

Reyha's face changed, her voice, too. "I am sorry. I have been too forward, too presumptuous. I did not mean to put you in this awkward position."

"No! I mean, no," Chrys added more calmly. "I want…" She hung her head. Here it was, what she wanted, but the imagined revulsion in Reyha's eyes if she were to see her mangled body was enough to cool the heat building inside her.

"I do not understand what you want," Reyha said. "Tell me."

"The tie. Just do the tie."

"The tie. Of course." Reyha stepped toward her and loosened the tie. But she didn't step away when she finished. Instead, she put both hands on Chrys's shoulders, and leaned in and whispered along her neck, into her ear. "Sleep well. Dream of daisies and yellow roses, of rain showers in the desert, of another world and another time where you are not injured and I am free to give you all you desire."

Chrys wavered, closed her eyes. "Dear God, Reyha, stop, you'll break my heart." Before she lost her mind completely, she tore herself away.

Then Reyha said, "Broken hearts are inevitable, my friend." And, without turning to face Chrys, added, "The dung heap is all around us."

Chrys moaned and hurried to her bedroom, where she tore off her waistcoat and fell down onto the bed and cursed into her pillow. It was one thing to have a secret infatuation, to fantasize all the what-ifs. But it was another thing entirely to want someone and to know the feeling was mutual. Yet she would never be able to have her, not in this reality. Like a poor child window-shopping at Christmas, Chrys saw what she wanted, but had no means to acquire it.

Right then she heard pounding on the suite door. She bolted up and met Reyha in the living room.

"Mrs. Arslan, I'm sorry to disturb you," Banks's voice came through the door, "but I need to speak with you. It's important."

Chrys opened the door. "What's going on?"

Banks's face was pale, her mouth set in a hard line. "There's been another possible breach. I need Mrs. Arslan to come to the control room."

They huddled around the computer screens as they'd done before, and Christman brought up the feed.

"Did he return?" Chrys asked.

Banks shook her head and pointed. "Just watch."

Within seconds one screen showed the image of three men dressed in business suits pulling rolling luggage coming into view of the front doors. On the next screen, they could be seen entering the lobby. Carmichael was there suddenly, intercepting them. The oldest of the three, a man in his late seventies, spoke with Carmichael, who gestured with his hands and shook his head. On another screen, a different angle of the conversation displayed. It allowed a close-up of the men's faces.

"Freeze that," Banks said.

Christman pressed a button, and the faces froze on the screen, showing a clearer image of the older man and two younger men. The younger men had dark facial hair and clean-cut military style haircuts. The older man was nearly bald, and what hair he did have was streaked with gray. Still, none of them was the decapitated red horse man.

Reyha staggered, and Chrys caught her in her arms.

"What is it? Do you know those men?" Chrys asked.

Reyha stared at the monitor. "I know the older one. The others, I do not."

They all waited, but Reyha only continued to stare at the image.

"Who is he?" Banks pushed.

"His name is Tarkan Usak," Reyha said. "You will not find him on any of your watch lists. He is too clever for that."

Chrys gripped her tighter. "Who is he?"

Reyha turned to her. "Usak is a leader of an organized crime family known as the Red Bears. He himself is what you might call the alpha, and it is rumored he was the one to arrange for Emin's assassination."

The room exploded into a flurry of activity, computer screens lit up, and agents began to call in information. Banks shouted some orders, then motioned Reyha and Chrys out of the room.

In the hallway, Chrys rounded on her. “How the hell did he find her? And who are those two goons with him?”

Banks held up her hand. “First off, I’ve already had Agent Thomas verify all three have returned to the Turkish Embassy, and we’ve got surveillance on them now.”

Chrys stepped toward her. “That supposed to make her feel better?”

Reyha pulled her by the arm. “You are not helping.”

Banks nodded toward Reyha. “You were right, ma’am. None of them appear on any watch list. But we’ve learned Usak arrived three nights ago with the other two, who’ve been listed as his sons-in-law.”

Reyha covered her mouth and entered the suite.

Chrys followed after her and brought her into another hug. “It’s okay. They got them identified at least.” She glared at Banks. “I’ll bet you that Anderson jerk did their reconnaissance and notified Usak as soon as he found her.”

“Very likely,” Banks said.

“And have you found him yet?” Chrys asked. “Know who he is?”

Banks lowered her eyes.

Chrys fumed as her rage began to gain steam. “Seriously, Banks, what the fuck is wrong with you?”

Reyha shrieked, “Stop it. Stop it now.” She covered her face and wept. “Neither of you understands. Those two men are not his sons-in-law. They are his soldiers, his fellow Red Bears.” She walked backward toward her room, tearing at her scarf. “Usak does not have daughters. The one he had, he killed before she even turned eighteen. Brutally, inhumanly to save his honor.”

Chrys moved toward her. “Hey, it’s okay. I won’t let him hurt you. He’ll have to come through me first.”

“And me,” Banks said.

Reyha shook her head and continued to cry. “He has hated me my whole life.”

Chrys reached out her hand. “I don’t understand.”

“Mrs. Arslan,” Banks said coming closer, “if there’s something you can tell us that will help—”

Suddenly, Reyha was on her knees. “He took her from me.”

Chrys dropped down next to her. “He killed Ophelia?”

"It should have been me." Reyha rocked forward and fell face down onto the carpet and wailed as her shoulders shook.

Chrys glared back at Banks.

"I'll give you an update as soon as I hear anything," Banks said, and she left.

"Reyha, please, what's going on?" Chrys tried to lift her up, but Reyha resisted and continued to shriek in Turkish. Finally, Chrys hoisted her up with brute strength and held her against her chest. She dragged Reyha into her room, a room she'd not been in up until that moment. She laid Reyha on the bed and sat on the edge and tried to comfort her. But Reyha only wept harder, and by now her words were jumbled and slurred.

"Should I get you one of my tranquilizers?" Chrys asked.

Reyha moaned and shook her head.

Chrys glanced around the room, at the stacks of books clustered on the nightstand.

"You want me to read to you?"

Reyha held her arm across her face. "Leave me. Give me my dignity."

"But let me—"

"Leave me, I beg you."

Chrys backed out of the room and shut the door, pressed against it with her forehead while trying to figure out what to do next. In most cases, she'd want a beer right then, a double dose of tranquillizers, anything to calm herself down. But this time was different. Reyha was in real danger, and she needed all her wits if she was going to be ready to defend her.

CHAPTER FOURTEEN

Chrys jerked when she rolled off the sofa onto the carpet. One leg continued to hang on the cushions, the rest of her body wedged against the coffee table and sofa. She crawled up and hissed with pain, sat upright, held her head.

She glanced at Reyha's door and wondered if she was up yet, maybe in the shower. She checked the time. Breakfast would be delivered any moment. She stood and stretched and opened the suite door. Deleki had switched out with Thomas.

"Any news?" she asked him.

"The commander's been up all night, but so far nothing." He looked her up and down. "Weren't you able to sleep?"

"Some." She pointed toward the control room. "I just want to check in."

She found Banks on the phone. Some of her hair had escaped her ponytail, she'd removed her jacket, and she'd rolled up her sleeves. She was perspiring nearly as much as Chrys usually did, and the strap of her shoulder holster pressed against her back, making her shirt stick to her skin. The other agents looked similarly disheveled. When Banks saw her, she acknowledged her with an upward motion of her chin. In another moment she was off the phone and seemed to momentarily collapse around the shoulders. She stared, shook her head. "You look like hell."

"I could say the same about you," Chrys said.

"Sleep in your clothes?"

"On the sofa."

"Standing guard, weren't you?"

Chrys shrugged. "It's in my nature."

"Yeah, I know. Like I said, you'd make a good agent."

Christman appeared and put a paper cup in Banks's hand. "Extra sugar. I know you need the energy."

Chrys watched the subtle spark between them and felt a bit envious. She'd had her own spark last night, but she'd been forced to snuff it out. Still, it'd been the right thing to do, she was sure. She pointed toward the door. "I better go. I'm sure Reyha will be up any moment. I only wanted to know if you'd found anything else out."

Banks rubbed the back of her neck. "Actually, Usak and his friends haven't left the embassy since they went in last evening." She rolled her coffee cup between her palms. "But I do have something else. I'm not sure Mrs. Arslan needs to know, however."

Chrys waited, studied the expression on Banks's face.

Banks took a long breath. "Anderson's been identified. Ibrahim Jabali, Saudi national, no allegiance to any group in particular, but a known hit man for the right price." She blew air from her lungs and shook her head. "How he got in the country is beyond me. But I can tell you, it's got a lot of people shaken up and scrambling for an answer."

Chrys blinked, stunned by the revelation. "You think Usak hired him?"

"That's our best guess."

"He get picked up yet?"

Banks diverted her gaze.

Chrys took a step closer. "We know where he is?"

Banks shook her head.

Chrys cursed and threw her hands up. "Now what? She's got another month and a half before the UN. You expect her to just hide away inside this hotel?"

"As much as possible, but her treatment at the clinic starts tomorrow. She'll have to go out for that."

Christman returned and thrust a cup into Chrys's hand. "I don't know how you take it," she said, "but you look like you could use some. Hope cream and sugar are okay."

"That's fine. Thank you." Chrys took a sip. "I need to get back. She'll be looking for me."

"There's one more thing you should know," Banks said.

Chrys stopped and turned to face her. The expression on Banks's face made her sick with worry.

"Just now on the phone," Banks said, "we got confirmation from British intelligence. Looks like Jabali is linked to the bomb that killed Mrs. Arslan's assistant."

Chrys grunted and nearly threw the coffee in Banks's face. But instead she cursed in every language she knew and stomped out of the room. When she opened the door to the suite, the staff was busy setting out breakfast, and Reyha was pacing, wringing her hands together. When Reyha saw her, she rushed toward her.

"There you are. I knocked on your bedroom door and called for you. But when you did not answer, I thought you had…" Reyha lowered her gaze.

"Left? I never abandon my post," Chrys said.

Reyha brought her hands together, held them to her chest. "I worried after last night you might have reconsidered our arrangement."

They fell silent and waited until the hotel staff bowed out of the way.

Once the door had shut, Reyha asked, "Why are you still in your clothes?"

"I slept on the sofa. Like I said, I never abandon my post."

Reyha pointed to the paper cup in Chrys's hand. "You went out for coffee?"

"Christman did. She fixed me up."

"You have been talking with Commander Banks. And what news does she have?"

Chrys wiped her tired eyes. "Usak and his buddies are still at the embassy. For now."

Reyha nodded, turned toward the table.

Chrys watched her shoulders, saw the tension in them. "We need to talk about last night."

"I apologize for my reaction," Reyha said, her back still to Chrys. "However, I did not expect that monster to follow me all the way to the United States."

Chrys stepped behind her. "I'm talking about what happened between us."

Reyha pivoted. "I have made a mess of things, I know. You are being kind and accommodating, and I have allowed myself to…" She bowed her head. "I hope you will not think less of me for misunderstanding."

Chrys shook her head. "You didn't misunderstand. It's my fault. I realize now I've been giving you mixed signals."

"I do not know what that means."

Chrys pointed to the sofa. "Let's sit down."

"Do you not want breakfast first?"

"No. We talk first."

Chrys took up a spot opposite Reyha in one of the wide-backed chairs on the other side of the coffee table. Sitting next to Reyha would be a mistake. Her closeness, her scent, the way she'd no doubt touch her thigh; it would be too difficult to resist.

"I want you to know," Chrys began, "that I'm extremely flattered by your feelings for me."

"Misplaced apparently." Reyha seemed perplexed by Chrys's choice to put a barrier between them and sat upright, her ankles crossed with her hands folded in her lap.

Chrys sighed, wiped her hands down her face. "How could you possibly be interested in me like that? I'm a mess. Besides, you're so far out of my league, so much more sophisticated and worldly than I could ever be." She rubbed a scar along her temple. "Even if I felt worthy of you, I couldn't give you what you want."

"I want your friendship."

"And I *am* your friend. That I can do easily, but I can't be more than that. Not to you, not to anyone." She popped the plastic lid off her coffee cup and stared into the mocha liquid. She couldn't look into Reyha's eyes. She was afraid she'd lose her resolve.

"Do you feel this way because of your injuries?" Reyha asked.

Chrys bounced her head as she continued to watch her coffee.

"Is this what impacted your relationship with Mary?"

"Very much so." Chrys finally looked up.

"I am sorry for you," Reyha said, watching with eyes full of sympathy, "but you should know, I do understand how you feel. Still, you have been so affectionate to me that I interpreted your behavior as an indication of your intimate and romantic interest."

"I know. Like I said, I gave you mixed signals." Chrys took a sip of coffee. "The thing is ever since that morning in Syria, I haven't felt anything other than fear and anger. A lot of sadness, too. Remorse, regret. And the physical pain, sometimes it's overwhelming. Those are the only feelings I've had for months."

"And now?"

Chrys smiled. "Spending time with you has probably had the greatest impact on me, more than months of therapy and all the drugs and beer could have ever done. You make me laugh and think." She chuckled. "Sometimes you push me a little and make me grumpy, but I always come through it with a new perspective. And you're so easy to talk to. In any language." She looked down in her cup again, thought about her rage when she'd thrown her coffee against the wall in her apartment, how she'd just now wanted to chuck this one in Banks's face. "You call me out on my bad behavior, too. And since I've cut back on drinking and laid off the meds and been sleeping better, I haven't had any more hallucinations. You did that for me." She looked up and shrugged. "I wish things were different. I really do. If it were another time, under different circumstances, then maybe…"

Reyha looked down at her hands. "The difference in our ages, that I am a Turk and you a Greek, these are not the reasons?"

"I told you—I've never held resentment in my heart for the Turkish people. You said it. We're brothers and sisters." Chrys stood, held out her hand. "And you could be a hundred, two hundred, I don't care, I'd still be fascinated by you."

Reyha took Chrys's hand. "Ah, but it is you with the older soul, as I have said."

"And I'm feeling every single year right about now."

"You do look tired. You did not sleep well on the sofa, and all for my sake."

"I'd do anything for you."

"Yes, within reason."

Chrys winced, shrank back, but Reyha pulled her to the table.

"I am lucky to count you as my friend, and I will not put any other expectation on you. Now, let us eat and put this uncomfortableness behind us."

Chrys took her spot and began to fill her plate. But she could sense the tension building between them, could see Reyha wouldn't look at her directly. And there were unanswered questions, so many that she took a risk and finally broke open the silence.

"Was Ophelia your lover?"

Reyha's eyes grew wide. "What gave you that idea?"

"Last night you said Usak took her from you, that it should've been you."

Reyha's posture changed and her hands shook as she buttered her bread. "Ophelia was my friend, one of the few I could trust, but she was happily married. And yes, I am sure her death resulted from Usak ordering my assassination." She dropped her knife, and it clattered on her plate.

"Hey, it's okay." Chrys held her arm. "I didn't mean to upset you. I was only trying to understand."

"What do you wish to understand?"

"You, your relationships, your feelings."

Reyha held her head with one hand and closed her eyes. "If you are speaking about amorous relationships, I will tell you. I have had none since Emin's death nor while married to him." She indicated her chest. "As I said, I understand your unwillingness for an intimate relationship. You see, I had a mastectomy shortly after my diagnosis. Doctors offered to do reconstruction surgery, to give me an implant. I suppose it might have been a reasonable thing to do. But I chose not to." She looked up. "Yet I understand the loss of your leg and your other injuries are of much more significance. I do not wish to imply I have suffered as greatly as you."

Chrys's mouth fell open; she snapped it shut.

Reyha took a bite of food, and Chrys watched her as she chewed.

Finally Chrys said, "I'm sorry. I wasn't aware you'd had surgery." She waited, watched Reyha take a few more bites. "But I can't be the only woman you've ever been interested in. I mean, I used to be conceited about my looks, but I'm not so vain to think I've converted you in a few months."

Reyha frowned. "Converted me?"

"You've been in love before, right?"

"Of course, with one of my classmates in London. A most intelligent and charismatic woman."

"Did the two of you get together?"

Reyha smiled. "Yes, my friend, we *got together*, as you say." But then the mirth fell from her face, and she grew pensive as she stirred her coffee and gazed off. "She was a dear woman, a good friend to me. We had all of our literature classes together and shared a love of words, of poetry in particular. And we played with language often. I would teach her a good deal of Turkish proverbs, and she helped me untangle my English idioms. We laughed together, enjoyed those long moments of silence which indicate contentment with each other's company. I think I knew I was in love with her in a matter of months, but I feared to act on it, to disclose to her how I felt. She was wealthy, you see, her father a member of the House of Lords."

"What was her name?"

"Julia."

"What happened to her?"

"She married, had children, took up her proper place in society."

"Do you have any contact with her?"

Reyha shook her head and remained silent through a few bites. Then she said, "We made the agreement when we brought our relationship to an end that, for both our sakes, it would be best not to do so. I was going to marry Emin, she her new fiancé. And it was a tumultuous time in her country. There were no civil rights for women who loved other women. And considering the high profile status of her father, if she had rebelled and chosen me over her fiancé, she would have most likely been shunned by her parents, disinherited from her family's fortune. It was a no-win situation, as you Americans say. We might have loved each other, but the world would not have allowed us to be together."

"Do you miss her?"

"Every day."

"But you've been back in London for some time now. Why didn't you ever contact her?"

Reyha looked away. "Because some wounds should never be reopened. It was enough that she had been in my life, enough that I was allowed to love her for the short time we had."

Chrys nodded. "The impermanence."

Reyha smiled, but it was full of melancholy. "Yes, it made our love affair even more beautiful, despite the pain of ending it caused me. I would not have traded it for anything. And given the chance to repeat my choices, even knowing we were doomed to be apart, I would have committed myself to loving her all the same."

Chrys considered this. "I guess when you put it like that I feel the same about Mary. I think I'll always love her, always miss her, and even with the heartbreak we both experienced in the end, I wouldn't trade that experience away."

"As I said last night, heartbreak is inevitable."

Chrys stirred more cream into her coffee, frowning as she did. "Did Emin have any idea?"

"Yes."

"And he was okay with it?"

"He was an honorable man, and I respected him. He respected me as well."

"Yet you never acted on your feelings while you were with him."

Reyha scoffed. "We were married. That must count for something. Why would I dishonor a man who took me under his care? I would never have brought shame upon him. And for this reason, he never brought shame upon me or made me relive my horror."

Chrys stopped stirring and looked up. Her stomach knotted. "What does that mean, your horror, what horror?"

Reyha waved her off. "It is nothing for you to concern yourself with."

Chrys took the utensils from Reyha's hands. "No. Tell me what you meant."

"You have enough sad stories to tell. I will not burden you with more."

"Damn it, tell me." Chrys gripped Reyha's hands tighter.

Reyha sighed and pulled free. "Well then, I would ask you to join me on the balcony. It is too early in the day, I realize, but I will need to smoke a cigarette to get through this tale."

Chrys almost stopped her, but Reyha was up and out on the balcony before she could say anything more.

Now sitting together in the morning light, Reyha leaned back in her chair and lifted her chin to blow smoke rings in her usual manner. She smoked nearly one entire cigarette before speaking.

"I must first explain something of my childhood," Reyha said. "Perhaps then you will understand."

Chrys watched her, absorbed in her movements, in the grace of her arm as she lifted the cigarette to her lips.

"As a child," Reyha began, "I lived with my parents on a large estate in Konya. I grew up with servants all around me, you see. There was always a houseful of people." She lit another cigarette. "And when I was six, I fell in love with the gardener's daughter."

Chrys grinned. "Six? It wasn't until I was fifteen that I figured myself out."

"I am not certain I had *figured myself out*, as you say, but I have always been a romantic at heart even at such a young age." Reyha flipped the air with her cigarette. "Anyway, my mother discovered a love note I had written for this girl. She was not angry. Only worried for my safety. At that time, one was not a homosexual in Turkey. Even today, it is a risk for anyone to live his or her life openly."

"Yes, I'm aware how conservative your culture is."

Reyha drew another long drag from her cigarette. "My mother went to Leyla. She was in a panic and did not know who else to go to. She asked if perhaps she and Emin would agree to an arranged marriage between me and one of their sons. This way, my mother reasoned, I would be alleviated of any ill-placed desires."

"But you were only six."

Reyha wagged her head back and forth. "As I said, she was thinking of my safety." She put her cigarette out. "Before long, my father and Emin both were brought in on my secret. I am fortunate my father was not a man who felt he needed to protect the honor of his name and, therefore, to dispose of me in some horrifying manner. No, instead the agreement was reached that I would marry either Kerem or Cinar, whoever fancied me the most when we came of age."

Chrys frowned. "Then how—"

Reyha held up her hand. "Yes, I am afraid things became much more complicated. Not long after this incident of my love letter, the coup erupted, and shortly after that, my mother and Leyla were arrested and executed. Emin fled to Europe with his sons, and my father served a short prison term, returned to me and our household in Konya, and all was forgotten for many years."

Chrys leaned forward on her elbows. Something else lurked behind Reyha's eyes, some painful secret. "Someone hurt you. Who was it? Not your father. Was it a governess?"

A shadow passed over Reyha's face as she gazed toward the phallic shape of the Washington Monument. "After my father was released from prison, he spent a great deal of time away serving the state. And yes, I was left under the supervision of governesses, as I told you. Women too old to pay close attention to my activities, and who did not care what I did in my free time." She shook her head slowly. "I was seventeen, not a little girl, but a young woman, and before long I had found someone who transfixed my heart. And let me tell you this, she was no gardener's daughter."

"The two of you fell in love?"

"As much as seventeen-year-old girls can."

"Did your father find out? Did he punish you after all?"

Reyha watched her, hesitated. Finally, "I wish he had found out." She shook herself as if to rid herself of the awful memory as the shadow passed once more over her face. "However, it was her parents who discovered us." Her bottom lip quivered as she continued. "I would like to believe my Nalan was saved from a greater horror. Yet I would not have had her take my place."

Chrys heard the ominous tone in Reyha's voice and scooted to the edge of her chair. "Nalan? What happened to her?"

Reyha fiddled with her lighter. "I will spare you the details."

Chrys grunted. "Honor killing?"

Reyha bowed her head.

"God, Reyha, I'm so sorry."

"As I said, perhaps he saved her from a greater horror."

Chrys touched her arm. "Wait, what do you mean? What greater horror?"

Reyha flicked the lighter. When the flame went out, she said, "I was arrested one morning while my father was out, and I spent six months in a prison cell while"—she appeared to weigh her words—"while the guards cured me of my perversions."

The words punched Chrys in the chest, and she stifled a scream as she involuntarily dropped to her knees. She hung her head and steadied herself against the side of the table.

"I will not burden you with those terrible memories," Reyha continued, her voice quavering as she spoke. "But you must understand, my father wished to protect me from further abuse. So in his wisdom, he sent me to London for university. Once I was there, he and Emin began to exchange letters, and they agreed that it would be best for Emin to marry me and give me his protection so that once it was safe for us to return to Turkey, I would not fall under any further scrutiny."

Chrys couldn't look at her, could only stare with blurry eyes at the legs of the chair. "And why not one of his sons?"

"Because neither Kerem nor Cinar wished to take a wife who had been dishonored."

Chrys covered her face and rocked forward until her forehead rested against Reyha's leg. Her head pounded, and it felt as if something hot stabbed her eyes.

"And you see," Reyha went on, "out of respect for my father and in honor of the friendship between my mother and his dear Leyla, Emin agreed to take me as his wife. But he did not take me to his bed. He would not make me relive the trauma of my imprisonment. Instead, he gave me his name, his protection, his wealth, and his compassion. For this reason, I will always honor him and his memory."

Chrys looked up and wiped her hand across her eyes as she shook her head repeatedly.

"Why do you weep, my friend?" Reyha asked. "You should not spend your tears on me."

"I…I…" Chrys tried to speak, but she couldn't form words past the sobs stuck in her throat.

Reyha shifted, took Chrys's face in her hands, and gazed down on her. "Your heart is so tender, and I see now how much you do care for me. But do not be troubled that you cannot allow yourself more than a friendship. Believe me when I say I understand. For it is not only the scar I carry from my mastectomy, but also the many others my body bears."

Chrys squeezed her eyes tight in an attempt to deny the ugly truth Reyha was about to reveal.

"You see, even as much as I desired Julia, for all the passion I felt for her, it was difficult the first time. I was ashamed of what had happened to me in prison, of the marks those brutes had left on my body. Marks I must see every time I bathe and dress. So know, I do understand, and I can respect your boundaries."

Chrys sobbed harder as the images of Diren's scarred body, of the faces of the women they'd liberated flooded around her. She buried her face in Reyha's lap and half screamed, half cried out.

"Shh." Reyha stroked her head. "It is past. It cannot be undone, so we will not speak of it again."

But Chrys could not be consoled. All she could do was think of a seventeen-year-old Reyha being brutalized in prison, of the tragedy of her young lover Nalan's death at the hands of her own father, and of Julia, forced by social pressure to marry, ending their love affair. Yet here Reyha sat, regal and refined, always with so much enthusiasm for each day, joy at the most trivial of things, childlike in her wonder, adoring of her literature and art and music. How did someone do that after living through the things she had? This woman had to be made of steel. Steel sheathed in beauty and grace such as Chrys had only ever seen in Diren and her Kurdish sisters, those fierce mothers and daughters who'd taken a stand against slaughter and rape and enslavement, who'd taken up arms to defend themselves and their countrymen.

She looked up and locked eyes with Reyha, held her in a level gaze. She realized despite Reyha's upbringing in a family of wealth and privilege that she was not too dissimilar from those women she'd known in the Syrian desert. And she loved her as fiercely as she'd loved Diren, Asmin, and the others, and she would gladly die for her just as she would've done for them.

"Your courage is beyond amazing."

"As is yours," Reyha said.

Chrys shook her head. "I'm not sure I could've endured what you have."

"Each of us has our own burden, and each must face our own

nightmares. But we need not do so alone." Reyha kissed her forehead. "Not while we have the bonds of friendship such as ours."

Chrys pulled herself to a standing position, lifted Reyha to her feet, and brought her into a tight hug. She turned her face into Reyha's hair and said, "And I am honored to call you my friend. No matter what happens. I am always first and foremost your friend."

Reyha squeezed Chrys to her. "As you will always be mine."

❖

Chrys took her time in the shower, let the hot water spray into her face to keep the horror of what Reyha had just shared at bay. She couldn't let herself fall apart. She had to be strong, not just for herself, but for Reyha as well. The titillation and flirtation which had unraveled her the night before still prowled beneath her skin, but now she embraced the intense love and admiration that had blossomed in her heart and pledged herself with renewed commitment to seeing Reyha was safe and well cared for.

Back out in the living area, she found Reyha working at the corner desk.

Reyha looked up from her laptop. "You must call to have your tuxedo sent to the cleaners. You slept in it, and I noticed at breakfast you got a bit of yogurt on the shirtsleeve."

Chrys plopped on the sofa. "Good idea. I better make sure I take care of it in case I might have an occasion to wear it again." She grinned. "Of course, Carmichael's buddy Gustav hasn't sent me the bill yet. And who knows how much it's going to cost me."

Reyha chewed the end of her glasses, smiled. "Mr. Gustav's bill has already been paid. But yes, you should keep it well cared for."

"No, he hasn't sent me one, like I said."

Reyha got up and came toward her. "The bill was sent to me. As I requested." She sat down and crossed her ankles while her arm trailed along the back and her hand rested against Chrys's shoulder.

Chrys gaped at her. "Why did you do that? It had to be at least two or three hundred—"

"The cost is not important," Reyha interrupted, "only how you looked and felt while wearing it."

"But. Reyha, you can't—"

Reyha raised an eyebrow. "You presume to tell me what I can and cannot do? It was a gift, something I wished to do. Now accept it and say no more."

"Then thank you. That was very thoughtful of you." Chrys hugged her awkwardly and stood.

Reyha didn't meet her gaze. "You are welcome."

"So I guess we're housebound the rest of the day." Chrys tapped her fingers against her legs and looked around the suite.

Reyha nodded toward the laptop. "It will give us time to focus on this last bit of my statement. And of course, we must finish the adventures of Jim and Ántonia. Still…" She turned her head and gazed out the French doors. "Tomorrow I must begin my treatment. Yet look at the beautiful day, the sky. There are rain clouds on the horizon. It promises to be much cooler than yesterday and the day before."

Chrys shook her head. "Don't even think about it. There's no way with Usak and his minions two miles away in their embassy that Banks will let you out of here, not to mention they haven't found Jabali." She cringed as soon as she realized what she'd said.

"Jabali? Who is this Jabali you speak of?"

Chrys's shoulders sank. "This morning when I went to see Banks, she told me they'd been in touch with British officials. Apparently Anderson is one of the aliases for Ibrahim Jabali."

Reyha approached her. "And why was Commander Banks speaking with British officials about this Jabali?"

Chrys hesitated, sighed. "Because they're pretty sure he's the one who planted the bomb that killed Ophelia."

Reyha caught her hand on the back of the chair. "Has he been apprehended?"

"They don't know where he is."

Reyha took a wobbly step back.

Chrys reached out and steadied her and began leading her to the sofa. "So we're just going to lie low today. Okay?"

Reyha pushed away. "No, I will not let them intimidate me. I will not give them the satisfaction of seeing me cower with fear."

"But you have every reason to be afraid. I'm afraid. It's probably better if we—"

"The river cruise up the Potomac to Mount Vernon. I wish to do this," Reyha blurted out.

"What? No, let's just stay in. We need to work on that part of your statement like you said, and we can read, catch up on Jim and Ántonia."

"I will go on the river cruise to Mount Vernon." Reyha pointed to the floor as if to emphasize her point.

Chrys sighed. "Damn if you aren't as stubborn as me."

Reyha's stern expression melted. "That is quite the compliment, thank you."

Chrys shook her head and grumbled. "No, not a compliment. Not even close."

❖

Two hours later, they sat on the upper deck of a medium-sized riverboat. Large windows enclosed them, providing a panoramic view of the river and the lush landscape along the banks. As she'd done on the Ferris wheel, Chrys drew attention to the various points of interests for Reyha while she pressed against one of the windows watching with excitement as they passed landmarks, forts, and plantations.

Banks, Quinn, and Smith along with six more agents sat around them. Banks had managed to get a charter even with the short notice and had added to the team for additional protection. Even still, she seemed to be sulking, apparently perturbed with Chrys for not talking Reyha out of this last-minute expedition.

Once they arrived at Mount Vernon, Chrys was happy to discover there didn't seem to be the usual amount of tourist traffic. It might have been the lateness of the day or the threat of rain, for fat white clouds gathered in a thick blanket in the sky, cutting the intensity of the sun's rays. The storm would be on them by evening, and she welcomed the idea of cooler, although perhaps more humid, weather.

Together, with their entourage of black-suited security agents, they ambled about the expansive grounds of the historic estate. Like the museums and other monuments they'd visited, Reyha stopped and read each sign and plaque. The solemn mood that had borne down on them from that morning was long past, and the connection between them seemed to be stronger. For Chrys, the physical touch of Reyha's hand in hers, or her arm around her waist or linked to hers, was welcome. True, the penetrating tug of attraction was there, but the comfort of being close to Reyha was more important than anything. And she loved the way Reyha delved into some point, some abstract idea she'd pull up from some corner of her mind and relate to the things she read along the pathway. Reyha laughed, smiled, squealed at times even, and enjoyed herself as she always managed to do. Her spirit was infectious, Chrys realized, for not only was she having a good time, but she also caught some grins on the faces of the security team that hovered about them.

After viewing the main house and some of the smaller buildings, they entered the slave quarters. Reyha seemed to take extra time in reading the documents on the walls about how many slaves George Washington had owned, how many his wife Martha had brought with her to the marriage.

She shook her head slightly as she spoke. "These families were destroyed, torn from each other—husbands from wives, children from parents—sold to other plantations, moved to other parts of the country to be used up like raw material."

Chrys nodded and followed her into the next building, the women's residence.

Reyha studied the interior. "Even a country as great as the United States cannot escape the blemish of such sadism." She sighed and took Chrys's arm and led her out into the open, pulled her off to a path that wound around the gardens. "Yet no country, no people, no culture is blameless."

"I said it before," Chrys said. "It just never stops. We're the most brutal species ever."

"Hmm, indeed." Reyha strolled, taking deliberate steps along the dirt path, limping a little as she went. "But all animals are brutal to some degree. It only seems the human animal is so much more calculated in his brutality."

"But we're not animals."

Reyha pulled her to a stop. "Are we not?"

Chrys grinned. "No, we're little flowers, I thought. Growing out of a primordial pile of shit, am I right?"

Reyha scoffed and poked Chrys's ribs. "Listen to you being so big, wearing…Now let me see, I have forgotten your lesson. Are you wearing sassy pants or being too big for your britches?"

Chrys laughed. "A little of both, I think." She patted her own rear.

Reyha tilted her head and observed Chrys's hand on her bottom. "Yes, I see, and I must admit I like the way your britches fit your bottom. I have not been able to ignore that fact since the morning I walked into Secretary Collins's office and met you for the first time."

Chrys's eyes widened. "Reyha."

"What? You did not say I could not admire your bottom in your britches. Should I not speak of that admiration?"

"Technically, that's what we call flirting."

"I see." Reyha glanced back to the security detail, over to Banks, who followed closely. "I understand your bed is off-limits, but I did not know I am not allowed to be flirtatious as well. My apologies." She started walking again, leaving Chrys stunned where she stood.

"Wait a minute." Chrys caught up and gave her a sideways glance. "Have you been flirting with me this entire time? Since day one?"

Reyha shrugged. "You are not much of an interpreter if you need to ask." She winked and then let loose a peal of laughter.

"Now who's wearing sassy britches?" Chrys laughed along with her and caught Banks looking at them, her eyebrow raised.

CHAPTER FIFTEEN

They were given a private room at the clinic in Arlington with Banks in a chair by the door and the others outside. Reyha reclined in a bed, her hospital gown open partway, allowing the catheter from her chemo port to extend down her front. Chrys had held her hand and stroked her forehead as the doctor had numbed the area just below her left collarbone and sliced open the skin to insert the device, which would stay in for the full ten days and be used each time they came to the clinic for her sessions.

Now the medication was being infused into her body as Reyha relaxed back onto her pillow. But the ordeal of that morning wasn't quite over. Within twenty minutes of starting the procedure, a nurse came in with a large blue ice cap fitted with Velcro.

"We're going to use this to help prevent hair loss," the nurse said as she positioned a neck pillow behind Reyha. "It's super cold and will be uncomfortable for the first ten minutes or so, but soon you'll forget it's there." She slipped it into place and began to pull the Velcro secure.

"I feel like I am a cosmonaut," Reyha said.

"Astronaut," Chrys said. "We're in the US."

"Of course." Reyha moved her eyebrows up and down. "And so low onto my forehead?"

"You want to keep your eyebrows, don't you?" the nurse asked.

Reyha's teeth began to chatter. "Preferably, although I am not opposed to drawing them on as I did before."

The nurse grabbed an extra blanket from a cabinet. "Here you go, sweetie. You're going to get very cold, I'm afraid. It can't be helped." She smoothed the blanket over Reyha, and Chrys helped tuck it in.

"How long for today?" Chrys asked.

"Six hours, about," the nurse said. She touched Reyha's shoulder.

"That port area feeling okay? The local will wear off soon and you might feel bruised."

"I am fine, thank you," Reyha said.

"All right, sweetie, you have your friend"—she glanced at Chrys and over to Banks by the door—"or your bodyguard get me if you need something."

After the nurse was gone, Chrys adjusted the blankets for a snugger fit, saw Reyha was still shivering, and grabbed two more.

"Lucky you, getting to be cool in this heat," Chrys said, spreading the blankets out.

"Ah, but it is getting ready to storm, is it not?"

"Let's hope so. We sure could use some rain." Chrys pulled her chair closer to the bed. "Six hours. I didn't realize it took the whole day."

"You do not need to remain at my bedside for the entire time."

"I'm fine. Now, you relax and let me read to you. Is the book in your bag?"

Reyha pointed to her belongings.

Chrys retrieved the book and opened to the first chapter. "Why this book again?"

Reyha turned her head clumsily, the big blue ice cap making her head wobble on her graceful neck. "I told you, it is a story of unrequited love, one which I wish to have a happy ending."

"And you're sure you want me to read *this* story to you?"

Reyha tried to nod. "This is my first time to America, and I have never been to New York."

"I don't follow."

"The setting for the story, it is New York." Reyha moaned and chattered her teeth.

Chrys frowned, worried Reyha seemed to be having such a hard time already and they'd only been there for a few hours tops, the chemo going into her system for less than that.

"We will be going to the United Nations in a month," Reyha said with effort. "I hope after my statement that we can spend some time together seeing the sights. Will you be my tour guide there as well?"

"Of course I will."

Reyha smiled, her eyes still closed. "You are good to me."

"Okay, just relax as best you can, and I'll try to read as well as you read to me. But no promises. I'm not nearly as animated as you are. I hope I don't bore you."

"You could never bore me. Your voice is like music to me. Full of sweetness." Reyha shivered again.

Chrys made a face. "Hmm, you apparently need hearing aids to go along with your fancy space helmet there."

Reyha tried to grin. "Sassy britches."

Chrys swallowed. "That's right, your sassy britches." She cleared her throat and began to read, making the effort to keep her voice from going flat, and to pronounce the words clearly.

It was a grueling day, yet Wharton's novel, as dry as Chrys considered it, actually made those hours bearable. At one point when Reyha had begun to snore, Chrys had gotten up and used the restroom. When she'd returned, Banks had offered to take her watch by the bed.

"Go get something to eat, Ms. Safis. I'll keep my eye on her."

"I don't want her to wake up and me not be here."

"Then I'll send Quinn to get you something."

Chrys was grateful for the food and drink, but she found she didn't have much of an appetite. Instead she took a few bites and then went to the window and watched the clouds grow thicker. When Reyha moaned, Chrys returned to the bedside, picked up the book, and continued to read. If this gave Reyha any comfort, any at all, she would provide it as best she could. She looked up from the text, then turned to see Banks had just gotten up and left the room, leaving them alone for the first time all day. She looked back at Reyha, put down the book, and leaned over her. She didn't like the ashen color of Reyha's skin, the sallowness of her cheeks. She touched Reyha's face, felt how cold it was, then let her hand linger and follow the line of Reyha's jaw, down to her neck.

"Please be okay," she whispered. "Please fight this. Don't let me lose you, too."

"Is everything okay?" the nurse asked, coming into the room.

Chrys jumped back. "Should she look this wiped out from just the first treatment?"

"It's a very powerful combination of drugs," the nurse said, coming over to the bed. "A new protocol. I expect that she'll be quite ill from it. There's just no way to avoid it."

"Why are the doctors using such strong drugs? You say they're new? But are they safe?"

The nurse hesitated.

"What?" Chrys asked.

"Ma'am, are you family?"

"Yes, I'm her…" Chrys gazed down at Reyha's face. "Right, you can't disclose anything. I understand."

"I'm sorry. I wish I could."

"I know." Chrys flopped down in the chair. "She's my friend, and I'm worried about her, that's all."

"I can tell you this at least," the nurse said, "she's going to need a lot of help these next ten days. And even though doctors have prescribed her antinausea medicine, she'll most likely be sick to her stomach and feel like she has the worst case of flu ever. You'll need to do your best to keep her hydrated and eating whatever she can—broth, crackers, toast…anything. It'll be a struggle for her to keep it down, though."

"I understand."

"And be there for her, too. She's going to be scared. Keep reassuring her she can get through this."

"Don't worry. I'll be there for her. I won't leave her side."

The nurse adjusted the drip, checked something on the chart, and came over to Chrys. "I've been working here a long time. It's my experience it's the patients who have a good support system who do the best." She squeezed Chrys's shoulder. "She's lucky to have you."

Chrys shrugged. "Actually, it's me who's the lucky one."

❖

When it came time to leave, Reyha protested the need for the wheelchair, but the nurse wouldn't let her out of bed until she conceded. Chrys shook her head and chuckled. Reyha was stubborn, but from her experience with Mary, Chrys knew nurses were much more stubborn when it came to the care of their patients, so it was no surprise to her that the nurse won the battle.

Quinn pushed the wheelchair to the SUV, and Chrys and Banks helped Reyha into the back seat. Once they arrived at the Hay-Adams, she and Banks helped Reyha back into the wheelchair and into the hotel lobby, where Carmichael made such a fuss Chrys had to pull him aside.

"She's very weak, Mr. Carmichael," Chrys said. "Would you please have the kitchen prepare broth and crackers, some plain toast as well?"

"Of course, of course. Oh, my dear Ms. Safis, it breaks my heart to see her so ill. She will recover, yes?"

"She's strong. Don't worry."

Chrys joined Reyha and the others in the elevator.

"What did you say to him?" Reyha asked with effort.

"I told him to stop buzzing around you like a little gnat," Chrys said.

Banks snorted, as did Quinn.

"You did not," Reyha protested. "He is a gentleman and so gracious. You will damage his feelings."

"Don't worry. I only asked him to have the kitchen send up some broth and crackers."

Reyha moaned. "I doubt I will be able to swallow anything."

"But you'll try. You need to try," Chrys said, holding Reyha's shoulder.

Reyha reached up and patted her hand. "For you, I will try anything."

Chrys smiled and saw a look of approval in Banks's eyes just as the elevator doors opened.

Christman met them in the hall. "Ms. Safis?"

Chrys came over to her. "Did you take care of it?"

"Just as you asked, ma'am, but I had change left over." Christman held out some bills.

"You keep it for your trouble." Chrys pushed her hand away and noticed Banks studying them as Quinn opened the suite door and wheeled Reyha inside.

"I shouldn't, ma'am," Christman said.

"What are you two doing?" Banks asked, coming closer. She glanced at the money in Chrys's hands.

"I hope you won't mind," Chrys hurried to explain. "I had Deanna get some flowers for Reyha's room while we were at the clinic. I thought it would cheer her up."

"That was nice of you," Banks said.

"And I want her to keep the change for her trouble," Chrys said.

Banks took the money and folded it into Chrys's hand. "No, ma'am. We're all here to support Mrs. Arslan. It's our pleasure to do whatever we can."

Right then Reyha's strained voice reached them, and Chrys hurried to the suite where she found Reyha still in the chair and Quinn trying to help her up and into the bedroom.

"It would not be comely for you to do so, Agent Quinn," Reyha said. "You are very kind, but I will ask you to have your Commander Banks and Ms. Safis assist me."

"I'm here." Chrys turned to Quinn. "It's okay. I got her. Just set the chair outside the door."

"Ma'am, let me get the commander, she can—"

But Chrys moved too swiftly, and in one sweep she'd brought Reyha up and cradled her in her arms.

"You will injure your back," Reyha exclaimed.

"No, I won't. You're as light as a feather." Chrys smiled at Reyha's expression and turned just as Banks came inside. "Can you get the bedroom door?"

She carried Reyha across the threshold and helped her sit on the bed. The smell of the yellow roses Christman had placed there earlier filled the room. Reyha's eyes went to the large bouquet on the table by the window.

"Where did those come from?" Reyha looked at Chrys. "Yellow roses and daisies?"

"I thought they'd brighten up your room," Chrys said.

Reyha's tears couldn't be contained, and she grabbed one of Chrys's hands, kissed it, and held it to her heart. "Thank you for that kindness. Thank you so much, my friend."

Chrys and Banks left and shut the door to allow Reyha to change into the nightgown she'd left waiting for herself on the bed that morning.

"She likes flowers," Chrys said. "Yellow roses are her favorite." She grinned at the expression on Bank's face.

"And the daisies?"

"My favorite."

Bank's patted Chrys's shoulder. "Very classy, ma'am, and very sweet."

❖

Chrys stood, stretched, and switched off the television. It was after nine, and she'd zoned out sitting on the sofa. She glanced at Reyha's closed door and hoped she was sleeping soundly. She'd managed to coax her into having some broth and crackers, and now it looked like Reyha had been given a reprieve from being sick. Maybe the nurse had been wrong. Maybe it wouldn't be so hard on her after all.

She went out to the balcony and counted the extra agents on the sidewalks and the additional vehicles parked along the streets, then looked up at the night sky heavy with the low-hanging clouds. She was surprised it hadn't begun to rain yet. She glanced down at the sweatpants she'd put on once they'd returned to the hotel. She was sticky in the humidity and would've loved to put on some shorts right about then. As she came back inside wondering if she had the courage to change into shorts, she startled to attention. A noise had come from Reyha's room. Instincts took over, and she didn't bother knocking, but instead she opened the door, saw the bed was vacant and the bathroom light on. She heard retching and moved as swiftly as she could. She found Reyha on her knees hunched over the toilet.

"I'm here," Chrys said as she pulled the strands of Reyha's hair away and held them while she put a reassuring hand on her back. "It's okay. I'm here."

She cringed as Reyha's back muscles spasmed while her shoulders lurched, and the gagging sound tore from her throat. There didn't seem to be any more vomit coming up, but rather Reyha was caught in that gray area of needing to throw up and having nothing left in her stomach.

"Breathe through your nose if you can," Chrys said as she continued to stroke her back.

Reyha whimpered between heaves, her arms shaking even as her hands gripped the toilet seat for support. Then the dry heaves subsided for a moment, and her body went limp as she fell back against Chrys's chest.

Chrys held her steady. "Let me get you a washcloth." She got up awkwardly as her left leg refuse to move at first, but in moments she returned.

"You should not be doing this," Reyha said. "You are not my nurse." Her chest heaved as she panted for air with an open mouth.

"Nonsense, let me help." Chrys began to wipe her face with the washcloth.

Reyha's eyes focused on her. They were wet and red. "I will call Mr. Gordon and request a caregiver for the remainder of my treatment."

"There's no need. Besides, they'd have to wait for security clearance and a background check. By then you'll be through the worst of it." Chrys smoothed Reyha's hair. "And I learned plenty about caring for sick people from my yiayia. She was better than any doctor."

Reyha tried to shake her head in protest, but she seemed too weak to do more than lean against the toilet. "But you did not agree to this."

"It's okay. Really. Now come on, let's get you back in bed and get you some water."

Chrys stood Reyha up and put her arm around her waist while

Reyha leaned against her, almost her full weight. But after a few steps, she drew Reyha up in her arms again.

"Let me just carry you—you're too weak to walk."

Reyha whimpered. "How strong you are, my beautiful woman."

The words washed over Chrys, caused her face to burn and her limbs to tingle. "Why, yes, I am. And strong enough to get you through this."

She helped Reyha sit down on the side of the bed, and that was when she noticed the sheerness of the nightgown she wore and how it revealed a slender, almost too slender, body beneath it. But Chrys noticed, too, Reyha still wore a bra. She could see the outline of it beneath the nightgown.

"Would you like to remove your bra?" Chrys asked.

"I need the compression."

"Okay, I just want you comfortable." She lifted Reyha's feet, noticed the graceful sweep of her toes, the demure polish on her toenails. She pulled the sheet up along with the blankets as Reyha sank back on her pillows and closed her eyes. "Let me get you some water."

Chrys left for the kitchen and poured a bottle of water into a glass, turned to leave, then stopped to retrieve the plastic wastebasket from under the kitchen sink. Back in the room, she noticed Reyha was shivering and had pulled the blankets up under her chin. She set the wastebasket by the side of the bed and held out the water.

"You're still cold?"

"To the bone," Reyha said, her voice hoarse and her teeth chattering. "I cannot seem to get warm."

"I can adjust the room's temperature." But Chrys dreaded the thought of making the suite warmer.

"I believe the suite is on one unit. I do not wish to make you uncomfortable." Reyha took the water and tried lifting it to her mouth, but her hands continued to shake.

"Here, let me." Chrys steered the glass to Reyha's lips, her hand cupped around Reyha's. She watched Reyha swallow a few sips, noticed the beads of sweat forming on her forehead. She set the glass down and touched the back of her hand to Reyha's face. "You're burning up."

"This is not unusual."

"Maybe I should call your doctor."

Reyha shook her head. She'd closed her eyes again and seemed to be holding her breath.

"Are you going to be sick again?"

"I cannot tell." Reyha's teeth chattered almost violently, and she moaned as she grimaced.

"Hang on." Chrys got up and rushed to her room, rummaged in a drawer, and brought out a sweatshirt. Back in Reyha's room, she sat on the bed once again, pulled back the covers, and lifted Reyha to a sitting position. "Here, put this on. Your nightgown is awfully sheer. This will help warm you up."

Reyha focused on the sweatshirt Chrys held up, and a small grin grew on her lips. "The United States Air Force?"

"I have no idea why I packed it, but I'm glad I did. Now, here, lift your arms."

Reyha obeyed as Chrys maneuvered the sweatshirt over her head and pulled it down.

"There." Chrys tugged Reyha's hair from under the shirt and freed it. "You look like one of those wide-eyed recruits on her first day of basic training."

Reyha tried to chuckle as she folded her arms around herself. "I feel warmer already. Thank you."

Chrys brought the blankets up. "I put the wastebasket here just in case you can't make it to the bathroom. And your water. Try to sip it all if you can. If you keep it down, we'll try some more crackers later."

Reyha watched her through slit eyes. "Thank you, my friend. I am indebted to you."

"There's no debt between us. And if there is one, it's I who owes you."

Reyha tilted her head. "How is that possible?"

Chrys looked down at her own hands, put one on her left knee. "Like I told you, you've managed to help me in ways I can't even explain." She glanced toward the window. The heavy curtain wasn't drawn, and past the roses and daisies, she could see it had started to rain. "Now, try to sleep if you can." She moved a damp strand of hair from Reyha's cheek. "I'll be right outside the door in the living room if you need me."

Reyha grabbed Chrys's hand before she could stand and brought it to her lips and kissed it. With that, Chrys had the sudden urge to pull her into her arms and cradle her, kiss her eyes, and rock her gently.

"Do you think you might read a bit more to me before you go?" Reyha asked. "The sound of your voice soothes me. I enjoy it so."

Chrys glanced at the stack of books on the night table and looked for Wharton's novel. "Is the book still in your bag?"

"Just some poetry, please." Reyha tossed her hand, indicating the stacks of books. "You choose."

"Poetry. Okay, but you should know I'm not very good at reading that either."

Chrys chose randomly and lifted a book to her lap. Inside the cover, she found a written note. *To my darling: Remember me and know I shall always love you.—J.* She winced with a momentary sting of jealousy and turned the book to read the spine.

"Sara Teasdale. I haven't heard of her."

"American writer. Passionate and romantic. Simple, clear," Reyha murmured. She roused herself a bit and added, "Sadly, she killed herself."

Chrys recoiled. "I'm sorry to hear that. Let's hope I do her justice at least." She turned arbitrarily to a poem, and as her eyes fell on the title, the little hairs on her arms stood at attention. "There Will Come Soft Rains." She read the title out loud.

"One of my favorites," Reyha said weakly. "Interesting that you should have chosen that one."

Chrys looked up, studied Reyha's face, her closed eyes and drawn mouth. "Yes, interesting." She read the poem aloud slowly and purposefully, letting the words weigh upon her.

There will come soft rains and the smell of the ground,
And swallows circling with their shimmering sound;
And frogs in the pools singing at night,
And wild plum-trees in tremulous white;
Robins will wear their feathery fire
Whistling their whims on a low fence-wire;
And not one will know of the war, not one
Will care at last when it is done.
Not one would mind, neither bird nor tree
If mankind perished utterly;
And Spring herself, when she woke at dawn,
Would scarcely know that we were gone.

She shut the book and watched Reyha's chest rise and fall. She set the book on the nightstand, stood, and started toward the door. But she heard Reyha moan and returned to her side in an instant.

"Shh, it's okay. I'm here." She placed a kiss on Reyha's damp forehead. "I won't leave you. Sleep now. I'll stay."

She pulled the large sitting chair in the corner of the room closer to the bed. Before she sat down, however, she went to the window and drew back the sheer curtain, then popped open the windows. The air hung with humidity, but it was cooler, so she threw the window wide and took a deep breath of the wet air. It wasn't the smell of desert rain, but it was rain, cleansing and fresh. She took another deep whiff, this time of the fat yellow roses arranged with white daisies. She touched their soft petals, then went back to Reyha's bedside where she relaxed into the chair and propped her chin in her hand. She would remain in that chair until morning, on her watch, doing her duty, guarding something so precious she could not put words to it, could not name it. It was something fragile, transient, yet she knew it was the impermanence that gave it its true value, a treasure she would fight to protect no matter the cost.

And outside, the rain began to fall harder.

Chapter Sixteen

The ten days of treatment were a living hell for Chrys, but they were merciless on Reyha. She watched helplessly as Reyha's strength drained from her body, as pain and discomfort tormented her day and night. By the third morning of treatment, Reyha was too weak even to stand in the shower, so Chrys ran a bubble bath, turned her back as Reyha sat on the bed and slipped out of her nightgown and sweatshirt and into her robe. Then she lifted Reyha into her arms and sat her on the edge of the tub, turned her back again and waited until Reyha safely slipped beneath the cover of the bubbles.

"Thank you for giving me my dignity," Reyha said.

"Call me when you're ready to get out." Chrys waited right outside the bathroom door and paced.

By the fifth morning, she not only had to help Reyha into a warm bubble bath, but also seat her at the vanity and comb her hair, for Reyha was too weak to lift her arms. As Chrys pulled the brush through her brown tangles, Reyha slumped in the chair and watched the reflection in the mirror.

"Is it falling out?" Reyha asked.

Chrys ran her hands through Reyha's wet hair and examined the brush. "Nothing in excess. I think your fancy astronaut helmet is doing the trick."

Reyha chuckled with effort. "I am glad for that. I am not an attractive bald woman."

Chrys knelt and smiled. "Oh, I don't know. I can't imagine you not being gorgeous even bald." Then she kissed the side of Reyha's head.

By the sixth morning, Chrys asked Banks why it wasn't possible for Reyha to remain at the clinic until the treatment was concluded.

"She's so weak, too weak," Chrys said, "and I'm worried for her and all this going back and forth, in and out of the SUV."

"I know," Banks said. "It's devastating to watch what she's going through, but we've already assessed that possibility. The clinic's location, plus all the traffic in and out, not to mention the number on staff, make it a security nightmare. It's better we bring her back to her room each afternoon."

Chrys grumbled, feeling nearly as haggard as Reyha. She'd not slept through one night since the start, had dozed only in the big chair by Reyha's bed. She'd gone every other day without a shower, taking only a quick one when either Banks or Christman agreed to sit in the living area and listen in case Reyha called out.

"Anything more on Usak or his hoods?" Chrys asked.

"We have another team keeping tabs on him. He and his two companions have been doing the regular touristy things just as you two did. Each night they return to the embassy."

"Anything on Jabali?"

Banks slumped. "I'm sorry, no."

As tired as she was, it took all Chrys's self-control not to throttle Banks. Instead she bit her tongue and forced herself to walk away.

Later in the afternoon of the seventh day, Chrys held Reyha in her arms in the back seat of the SUV as they traveled back to the Hay-Adams after treatment. She rubbed her left leg and winced with discomfort. She'd not been allowing the leg to breathe, and she'd been wearing a protective sock over the stump for two days at a time. The skin was beginning to chafe and her muscles to ache from having her prosthesis on twenty-four hours without a break.

"Are you in pain?" Reyha mumbled against Chrys's shoulder.

"My leg's acting up. It's nothing."

"You have not been taking care of yourself."

"Right now it's about you." Chrys hugged Reyha closer and kissed the crown of her head. "Just three more days. Three more days and it'll be over. Don't give up, okay?"

Banks turned in the front seat. "We're all pulling for you, Mrs. Arslan. We know you can do this."

Reyha whimpered as if to indicate she doubted her ability to make it through. But she responded, "Yes, Commander, I will make it through. Your confidence and the care here of my dear companion give me the courage I need."

As they'd been doing, Chrys and Banks got Reyha up to the suite. After Reyha changed into her nightgown and the Air Force sweatshirt she had become fond of, Chrys tucked her into bed and settled back to read more of Wharton's novel. She was nearly done, with only one chapter left.

"Will you save the last chapter until I feel better?" Reyha asked.

"Why's that?"

"Because I am going to have you change the ending and have Mr. Archer and Countess Olenska reunite. I want to be able to enjoy it when I feel myself again."

Chrys chuckled. "Are you sure Edith Wharton's ghost won't haunt me for taking liberties with her story?"

"She will understand, I am sure." Reyha moaned and rolled to her side.

Chrys shut the book and set it in her lap. She watched the back of Reyha's head, the mound of covers over her body. "What can I get you?"

There was no answer.

"You already asleep?"

Again no answer.

Chrys wiped her eyes with the back of her hand. She sure could use a soaking bath and a long nap herself. She debated whether she should go get Banks to sit by Reyha's bedside while she got cleaned up or if she could chance leaving Reyha to sleep unsupervised. She worried Reyha might need assistance and roll over to find her missing and no one there. Just as she stood up to go find Banks, she realized Reyha wasn't sleeping, but rather sobbing while trying to hide the fact.

"Hey, hey, it's okay. It's going to be okay." Chrys slid next to her on the bed and spooned her from behind.

"I am so tired. I hurt everywhere."

"I know. The nurse said it would be bad. The worst case of flu you've ever experienced."

Reyha rolled and buried her face against Chrys's chest. "I cannot do it. I have no will for this. There is nothing left in me."

"Don't say that." Chrys stroked her hair. "You're the strongest woman I know. You'll get through this. You will."

"But I feel so weak."

"We all feel weak at times. I understand."

Reyha sobbed. "I just want to die, to be rid of this pain."

Chrys hugged her tighter. "I know the feeling. Trust me, I do."

She laid her cheek against Reyha's head and let her own tears trickle down. She didn't bother to wipe them away, and they pooled against her chin and dripped into Reyha's hair. Feeling helpless, powerless to do anything more than hold her, Chrys began to sing a lullaby, and as soon as she began the second verse, Reyha seemed to relax, her sobs to slow, and in moments she was sleeping in her arms.

Finally, the tenth day of treatment arrived. When they wrapped up that afternoon, the doctor came in, removed the port, and stitched the wound.

"The worst is over, Mrs. Arslan," he said.

Then the nurse gave her a hug and told her that she was a brave woman. Some of the other clinic staff stood and clapped as Quinn wheeled Reyha down the hallway and into the lobby. The chief oncologist met them at the exit with a balloon bouquet and a card signed by everyone on the floor.

"We'll see you in four weeks for your scan, Mrs. Arslan. Let's keep confident," he said, grasping her hand. "Now take it easy for the next few days. In a week or so, you'll start to get your strength back and feel like your old self again." He glanced up at Chrys. "See if you can get her out into the sunshine. It'll do her good."

In the SUV, Chrys took a deep breath of relief. "So, what do you say in a couple of days we'll go out for Italian food and carb up, then walk some of it off around Lafayette Square with our Praetorian Guard in tow?"

"With a good red wine," Reyha added.

Chrys brushed a stray bit of hair from Reyha's eyes and tucked it back under the scarf. She couldn't believe this was the same woman from ten days ago. Reyha's cheeks were sunken, her color a pasty gray, her eyes dull. Chrys reached into the pocket of her trousers and brought out a lip balm.

"Here. Your poor lips are so chapped." Chrys applied the balm to Reyha's lips. "I don't think I'm keeping you hydrated enough."

"You have been more than diligent. I could not have asked for a more attentive companion to assist me through this. You will never know how much gratitude I have in my heart for you, my friend."

Back at the hotel, Chrys got Reyha comfortable and called for the kitchen to send up something to eat.

"Drink some water," she said, holding the cup to Reyha's lips.

Reyha did so and relaxed back on her pillows and studied Chrys with eyes strained with discomfort. "Are you eating well?"

"The kitchen has been sending meals up regularly. Don't worry about me."

Reyha closed her eyes. "I have lost track of time. What day is this?"

"Friday."

Reyha opened her eyes. "I do not recall you going to your support group on Wednesday or the Wednesday before that. Did you slip out of the clinic while I was sleeping during treatment?"

"No, I called in both times."

"And do you not have physical therapy as well? Have you also missed those appointments?"

"I called that in, too."

Reyha frowned. "I would not have you neglect your own needs."

"You needed me more."

Reyha scoffed.

"Now, don't scold me," Chrys said. "I'm an adult, and I made a choice."

"You are a stubborn woman," Reyha said scowling.

Chrys grinned. "Now, that's the pot calling the kettle black."

"You do know that is not uniquely an American idiom."

"I see, you're claiming it for the Turks just as you claim to have invented yogurt and coffee."

"You say that as if there is no factual evidence for those claims."

Chrys laughed. "Look here, not an hour after your last treatment and you're already full of piss and vinegar."

"And the origins of that idiom come from Steinbeck's *The Grapes of Wrath.*"

"Okay, now you're just showing off." Chrys nudged Reyha's leg. "And no, I haven't read that one either."

Reyha's eyes grew wide. "You have not read John Steinbeck's Pulitzer Prize novel? What is wrong with your American education system?"

Chrys groaned. "Tell me you're not going to make me read that one, too."

Reyha wagged a finger. "I will not make you suffer through another novel if you promise me you will return to your weekly schedule and attend your group sessions and physical therapy."

"Fair enough. Such a taskmaster. My goodness."

Reyha smiled and hugged her arms around herself. She wore the Air Force sweatshirt, and it appeared she'd claimed it for her own.

Just as the doctor had said, within a week Reyha's strength began to return. By now she was able to get herself in and out of the shower, able to keep down a good amount of solid food as well. The weather had turned cooler as autumn arrived at the start of October, and in the early mornings, Chrys would walk with her a bit in Lafayette Square with the security team in tow. She and Reyha would sit on one of the little benches for twenty minutes as Reyha lifted her face and smiled into the warmth of the morning rays.

But other than these short walks and Chrys keeping her group session and physical therapy appointments as she'd promised, they didn't leave the hotel for those first several days. Reyha continued to sleep for long periods, and Chrys was able to relax enough to remove her prosthetic leg in the evenings, soak in a hot bath, and on a few occasions, sleep almost twelve hours in her own bed. Although she was beginning to feel herself again, Chrys noticed she actually missed dozing in the big chair in Reyha's room. It was hard also for her to even leave the Hay-Adams and go about the business she needed to attend to, as she was anxious to get right back to the hotel and to Reyha's side.

As she sat in a session one afternoon listening to the others talk, she started convincing herself that she might as well cut ties altogether with the group. She didn't really need the weekly sessions any longer. Her nightmares were infrequent, the hallucinations were gone. She'd avoided both her tranquilizers and sleep aid while caring for Reyha and only took the pain medication as needed. And she couldn't even remember the last time she'd had a beer. She really had come out the other side of her long struggle and had completely lost her desire to be numb and drunk.

"You want to fill us in on your last weeks?" Woodley said, interrupting her deep thoughts.

Chrys glanced up at the faces watching her. She wanted to ask where Morrison was, but decided to wait until the end. "I had a friend who was getting a ten-day dose of really powerful chemo, and she needed me to take care of her."

"Through the VA?" Woodley asked.

"No, a clinic in Arlington."

"She military?" Dworsky asked.

"No, civilian."

"Not your fiancée?" Horrigan asked.

"What?" Chrys blinked. She couldn't remember talking about Mary much with any of them other than Morrison and mentioning her only once to Woodley.

"We were under the impression you were engaged," Woodley said.

Chrys shrugged. "That's been off for a while."

"How's your support system, then?" Torres asked.

Chrys turned her head and looked at each man with disbelief. They were all sincerely concerned for her. Having Ramos gone really did change the tenor of the group, and now she thought maybe staying with it a while longer might do her some good. At least these men understood some of what she'd lived through.

"My support system is good, actually." She nodded toward the empty chair Morrison usually occupied. "I know I've been gone two weeks, but how's Morrison?"

"She's still having a hard time finding work," Woodley said. "And since she told us last week, you might as well know, her son was having issues at school last year, and they finally got him diagnosed at the end of the summer. Autism spectrum disorder. He'll need some intervention, and she's worried about the cost."

"But he's under her benefits." Chrys fingered her phone and wondered if she had Morrison's number or if she'd only offered her own.

Horrigan moved his chair a smidge forward. "Everyone's struggling with the insurance companies playing politics, but none more so than the VA. The system's rigged against us."

Woodley turned the conversation away from criticism of the VA and brought the session to an end a bit early.

As everyone began to depart, Chrys went over to hold the door for Horrigan. "You got Morrison's number? For some reason I gave her mine, but never got hers."

He nodded down to the cell phone attached to a lanyard around his neck. "Go ahead and pull it up."

Chrys found the number and entered it into her own phone. After returning the phone, she asked, "How do you make calls?"

"I ask people to dial for me. My wife says she's researching this new voice-activated Bluetooth unit. But you know, other bills are more pressing at the moment."

"Yeah, I know."

"I gotta say, Safis, you're looking more together than I've ever seen you. This consulting job must've been what you needed."

"I think so." Chrys walked next to him toward the lobby.

"Give Morrison a call, won't you? She looks like hell, and I'm worried about her."

Chrys patted his shoulder. "Will do. And maybe I'll take her for lunch after group next week."

But the next week and the week after, Morrison didn't materialize. Chrys called three times and left messages, told Woodley one afternoon after session she was worried. He explained she'd called in, was busy following up on her son's care and fighting a bad cold. Still Chrys worried, a worry that nagged at her, yet one she was able to ignore once back at the Hay-Adams with Reyha. Now that Reyha was stronger and her color returning, they began to go out in the evenings for dinner instead of staying in, something that irked Banks. But as Reyha told her, they were refraining at least from any additional sightseeing.

And with Reyha feeling stronger, they were finally able to finish up Cather's novel.

Sitting together on the sofa, Reyha read the last bit. "*For Ántonia and for me, this had been the road of Destiny; had taken us to those early accidents of fortune which predetermined for us all that we can ever be. Now I understood that the same road was to bring us together again. Whatever we had missed, we possessed together the precious, the incommunicable past.*" She closed the book, looked up, and smiled. "And even to the end, the unspoken love between Jim and Ántonia remains."

Chrys scrunched her face with disappointment. "I guess I expected them to get together in the end. I wonder why Cather didn't write it that way."

"Because in Jim's memory, Ántonia had become a symbol," Reyha said. "She was not a real woman to him for most of his childhood and adult life. It is only when he returns twenty years later and sees her as fully human that he can love her completely."

"But they still don't end up together."

"No. She is married with many children."

Chrys frowned. "I feel sorry for Jim."

"For what reason? Does he not now understand what real love is?"

"But he can't act on it. As you say, she's married and has a family."

Reyha shrugged. "Is love only real if we can act on it? Are feelings only genuine when there are actions to back them up?"

Chrys scratched her head. "See, this is why I never liked reading literature. There's no black-and-white answer to anything."

Reyha chuckled. "You are looking for certainty again where life is ambiguous and transitory."

Chrys grumbled. "I know, I know. Impermanence is where the beauty lies."

"I will make a philosopher out of you yet." Reyha brushed Chrys's cheek and laughed at the expression on her face.

The next night, Reyha asked Chrys to read the last chapter of Wharton's novel to her.

"Would you like me to read to you in bed?" Chrys asked.

"Sitting here on the divan with you is fine," Reyha said. "You have spent too many nights at my bedside playing my nursemaid."

"Because I wanted to."

Reyha studied Chrys's face. "I am going in tomorrow morning for my scan. You will go to your physical therapy."

"I should go with you."

"No, Commander Banks and her team will accompany me. I want you to go to physical therapy."

"Did you schedule your scan on purpose to conflict with my PT?"

"Please." Reyha pointed to the book in Chrys's hand. "Read to me, and when you have finished, tell me your own version, this one with a happy ending."

Chrys wanted to argue with her, but Reyha had caught her in that gaze that meant she wasn't going to bend. So she sighed and opened the book to the final chapter and began reading. It took only twenty minutes to read the last chapter, and when she came to the final sentence, she turned to the next page, a blank one, and turned back to the final paragraph.

"Wait, I don't get it. Why doesn't he go up to Olenska's apartment and see her?" Chrys asked. "His wife is dead, she's still single, and he traveled all that way to Paris to see her. It makes no sense."

Reyha smiled. "I see you have become passionate about our two lovers."

Chrys tossed the book on the coffee table. "This is worse than Jim and Ántonia. I mean, at least there was a reason for those two not to be together. She was married with a family. But Archer and Olenska are single…old, but single." She shook her head and scowled. "I hate literature. How hard would it have been for Wharton to write a happy ending?"

"Now you know my predicament with the story," Reyha said. "So tell me, how would you have it end?"

Chrys tapped her chin and thought. "Well, he'd go up to her apartment and not watch from the street. He'd march right in and take her in his arms and tell her after twenty-five years he's loved no one other than her and that he'll commit every second of every day left to them on earth to be at her side."

"And why do you think he did not do so?"

"Because he's a coward. He wanted to keep the memory of a young countess and their love affair untarnished with age. At least I guess that's why." Chrys cocked her head. "Why do you think he didn't go up to see her?"

Reyha shrugged. "Social pressures and conventions. These things often stand in the way of love."

Chrys narrowed her eyes and replayed the afternoon Quinn had bought the books and handed them to Reyha in the SUV. Reyha had become emotional talking about the novel, had wept about some unrequited love. Then something else occurred to Chrys, the book of poetry with the handwritten inscription.

"This novel," Chrys said, "it means something to you because of Julia."

Reyha seemed to look through her as she spoke. "It was her favorite American novel." She closed her eyes as she recited a passage. "*I want somehow to get away with you into a world where words like that—categories like that—won't exist. Where we shall be simply two human beings who love each other, who are the whole of life to each other; and nothing else on earth will matter*."

Chrys fought off a stab of jealousy. "You saw yourselves in it."

"Yes. She was Archer, the proper and dignified gentleman of the wealthy and elite class bound to social conditioning, and I was—"

"The Countess Olenska."

Reyha inclined her head. "The *disgraced* Countess Olenska."

"No, not disgraced." Chrys took her hand. "There is nothing disgraced about you. Nothing. And you are worth every ounce of love and every bit of compassion any woman lucky enough to know you can give."

Reyha looked up. "Yet I do not want just any woman."

Chrys stuttered as the words jumbled inside her mouth. Before she could untangle her tongue, Reyha stood.

"Good night, my dear friend. Thank you for reading to me. Thank you for everything you do and are. I shall never know another woman as faithful and as kind as you. Sleep well." She bent and kissed Chrys's cheek, then turned and disappeared behind her bedroom door.

Chrys touched her cheek, stared at Reyha's door.

"You were a damn fool, Julia," she said to no one.

She glanced around, turned off the lights, paused by the coffee table, and lifted both books in her hands and considered the misplaced priorities of Jim and Archer. Then she tossed them back on the table and went to bed.

CHAPTER SEVENTEEN

The SUV pulled in front of a mammoth building, and Reyha leaned to look out the window.

"Is this the surprise you have for me?" she asked Chrys.

"Yes, and they're open until five, so we can spend the entire day here looking at the things you love best—art and books." Chrys smiled at the look of awe on Reyha's face.

Reyha hugged her neck. "Thank you for this."

"And there's even a coffee shop and café inside, so we won't need to leave to eat," Chrys added.

Banks and Quinn along with Smith and six others gathered about them as they walked up the steps of the Library of Congress into the lobby of the Thomas Jefferson Library. Inside, the massive gilded dome and the sunlight streaming in through the stained glass tiles gave the impression of a cathedral. For Chrys, it was fitting given that books were something holy for Reyha.

For the first two hours, they were given a private tour, which Banks had called ahead and arranged. There were enough visitors in the building that their group didn't garner any unusual attention, and they blended with the other small tours going on around them. After the tour, they took a short break in the coffee shop and refreshed themselves.

"Can we take some time going through the art again?" Reyha asked. "I want to study the prints and paintings as well as the sculptures. The tour was wonderful, but I want to go back and examine some items in more detail."

"Anything you want," Chrys said.

"And of course, I want to go to the rare books and special collections on the second floor. They have first editions of American classics."

"Sounds good." Chrys took Reyha's arm as they began moving again.

"You are humoring me."

"I'm having fun watching you."

"But you are enjoying yourself, yes?"

Chrys pulled her to a stop. "I'm with you. We could be picking up trash alongside the road, and I'd be enjoying myself."

"Do you mean that?"

"I do."

There was an awkward shift from the security team as they continued to stand close, gazing at each other intently. Then Reyha smiled, cast a glance at the agents who guarded them, and took Chrys's arm once more as they began their slow meandering exploration while she read each of the placards, studied the art, and taught Chrys some finer points of history. For Chrys, this tour was the more enjoyable one, better than anything the official tour guide had offered.

❖

It was a half hour before the Library of Congress was due to close, and they'd been in the rare books collection for the last two hours. They had eaten a light lunch midday, but Chrys's stomach was beginning to growl, and she started to think about where they might go for dinner later that evening. She glanced over at Reyha, who was engrossed in some rare text before her on a table. The collection's librarian, an aged man, was engaging Reyha in some esoteric conversation while both wore protective gloves and carefully turned the brittle pages of the book before them. Chrys sat off to the side and pretended to listen with interest, but she couldn't follow much of what they were saying and soon found her grumbling stomach becoming more uncomfortable. She glanced at the security detail and almost laughed at the bored expressions on Quinn's and the others' faces. Banks at least managed to look alert.

As the time ticked closer to closing, the other readers in the gallery began to return texts and gather their notes and leave. Reyha brought her conversation with the librarian to an end and thanked the man as she took his hand. He gave her a little bow and complimented her effusively, praising her for her immense knowledge.

Chrys shuffled up next to her as they left the gallery and headed toward the elevators. "You got yourself a new boyfriend there?"

"A remarkable man," Reyha said.

They waited by the elevators with a few others, but when the doors opened, Banks signaled for them to wait and motioned for the other readers to go on ahead.

"This has been a remarkable day," Reyha said as they waited for the next elevator. "Thank you so much."

"I'm glad you enjoyed it." Chrys noticed Reyha rubbing her hip. "You feel okay? Too much walking?"

"It is my hip again. As before, it has flared up."

"Yeah, my leg's aching, too. I think we could do with a hot bath."

Reyha smiled, raised an eyebrow.

"I mean, you know, in our own tubs," Chrys said, her face burning with both embarrassment and titillation.

"Ah. Of course." Reyha winked.

Chrys turned away, fanning herself. But in a matter of seconds, the playful flirtation was doused as Quinn and Smith moved in front of Reyha with hands on their weapons. Chrys swiveled around just as Banks took point and faced down an interloper while the other agents came up behind and flanked the group. Why the team had not seen this man coming was a mystery to Chrys. Maybe they'd gotten lazy, dulled by boredom after standing on guard in the rare books collection as Reyha and her librarian friend had gone on for two hours. But now here he stood with predatory eyes in a smug face.

"Stand down, sir," Banks said.

Usak held up his hands and smiled. In English he said, "My apologies. There must be some mistake. I only wish to greet my old friend. She and I are countrymen, you see."

Chrys had dropped into a protective stance, ready to neutralize the threat, her eyes glued to Usak's hands. If he moved one inch, just one, she'd rip his head from his body.

Reyha moved forward, put her hands on Quinn's and Smith's shoulders, and parted them. In her native language she said, "You have come a long way to greet me, Usak. I am sure a card or letter would have sufficed."

He sneered and replied in Turkish, "And I would have sent one had you not kept your location so secret."

"Not secret enough, apparently."

The elevator door opened.

"Mrs. Arslan, please get inside," Banks said as she kept her eyes on Usak and her hand on her weapon. Her other hand was on her radio, and she spoke code words into the receiver, alerting the other agents below.

However, Reyha ignored Banks's request. She slipped between Quinn and Smith and stepped next to Banks. "You do not frighten me, Usak. You did not intimidate Emin, and you will not succeed in doing so with me."

"Mrs. Arslan, please step back," Banks shouted as she motioned for her men to regroup.

Chrys cursed and almost tackled Reyha right then. She didn't see any weapon on Usak, but she also didn't know where his two goons were. And where was the library's security? The police? Why wasn't someone rushing him?

Reyha held up her hand to address Banks. "Let me say my piece." She turned once more to Usak and said in Turkish, "If you have tracked me this far, you know what I intend to do when I go to New York and speak in front of the United Nations."

"I advise against it," Usak said. "You must know the consequences, just as Emin did. One does not betray his country or his race."

"I will not betray my humanity, Usak. Something I fear you lost long ago."

Usak snarled and spat on the floor.

Chrys had stealthily stepped away from the group by then. She trusted Quinn and Smith to cover Reyha while she advanced on Usak. Though she wished she was armed, she was willing to rely on her combat training to make an offensive move. She shot Quinn a look. He had his weapon leveled at Usak while Smith shielded Reyha and attempted to force her back, trying to make her step into the elevator. But Reyha still wasn't cooperating.

"Get in the goddamn elevator, Reyha," Chrys yelled. Then in Turkish she growled a warning at Usak. "Walk away, Usak, or I will end you right here."

It was then Usak seemed to notice Chrys. He turned his head, looked her up and down, and scoffed before calling her a camel's asshole.

"Safis, step away," Banks commanded.

Smith now took Reyha by the shoulders and pulled her into the elevator while Banks yanked Chrys by her arm into the compartment.

But before the door came to a close, Chrys pointed at Usak. "Fuck you, asshole."

She swung around on Banks as the elevator began its descent.

"What the hell is going on? How did he get this close?" She could feel her face blazing, her lips pulling taut as she formed her hands into tight fists.

Before Banks replied, Reyha rounded on Chrys. "You will stop this at once. You should not have attempted to intercept him. You are not part of the security detail."

The elevator opened and the agents herded them out of the building and into the waiting SUV, which peeled out even before the doors had shut. Banks had slipped into the back seat with them and was busy shouting orders into her radio. Chrys watched out the back windows as the second SUV brought up their rear. She also scanned out the front and passenger windows, looking for any vehicle, any bystander out of place.

"How the fuck did he get that close?" Chrys asked again. She saw Reyha staring at her with something that looked like anger.

Banks shook her head. Her face flushed and her chest heaved. "It's unacceptable, I know." She turned to Reyha. "My apologies, Mrs. Arslan. I don't know where the breakdown happened, but I'll get to the bottom of this, I promise you."

Reyha seemed to be the only one remaining calm, although she was clearly irate. "I doubt he planned on shooting me right there in the Library of Congress, Commander Banks."

"He could've had a bomb," Chrys interjected. "And what the hell were you thinking by confronting him? That was fucking stupid of you."

Reyha tilted her head and said in Turkish, "I would ask you not to speak to me in that manner. You are being disrespectful, and I will not tolerate it."

Chrys raised a finger and opened her mouth to protest, but stopped when she saw the fury flowing from Reyha's eyes. She turned away and cursed under her breath while she wiped sweat from her face. She sulked against the window and listened to Quinn's and Smith's one-sided conversations as they spoke on their phones. She also listened as Banks continued to give orders over her radio. The hotel was being searched. Security footage was being brought up. The additional team who'd been watching Usak and his men were being instructed to prepare an explanation for the breakdown, their commander ordered to meet Banks in an hour. Chrys listened and fumed, aware the entire car ride back Reyha watched her, apparently waiting for an apology.

❖

Close to midnight, Banks knocked on the suite door and came into the living area, sat down with Reyha and Chrys, and debriefed them on the breach. A young agent had been tricked into thinking Usak and his two men were secure inside the embassy, when in fact a decoy had been used to allow Usak to slip by undetected. How he'd known Reyha would be at the Library of Congress was still unknown, but Banks reported they were currently trying to determine if their communications were being intercepted or if the hotel was being watched by another party. Before she left, Banks assured Reyha that Secretary Collins had already been informed and was calling in another team as backup.

Once Banks had gone, Reyha took her cigarettes and a glass of wine and went out on the balcony. She'd not given much more than one- or two-word responses to Chrys since they'd been back, and now Chrys followed her out, knowing she needed to apologize and make things better.

"I'm sorry I yelled at you," Chrys said, looking down at the traffic in the street. She could spot most of the additional agents, noticed a few looking up at the balcony.

Reyha didn't respond.

Chrys turned, watched the smoke rings floating above her head. "Please accept my apology."

Reyha only glared at her.

Chrys pulled up a chair. "Are you going to stay angry at me because I lost my temper out of worry?"

"You should not have confronted Usak. You should not have spoken to him, particularly not in my language. He now knows you. You are in his sights."

"So?"

Reyha sat up so quickly, that Chrys sat back, startled.

"Do you have any idea the kind of man he is?" Reyha asked. "What he could do to you? He took her from me, made her suffer because of me, and I will not have you meet the same fate."

"Ophelia?"

Reyha's face contorted, her mouth twisted. "His daughter, Nalan, my first love." She covered her face with one hand as the cigarette drooped in the other.

Chrys blinked rapidly as Reyha's words sank in. "Usak's the father of your first…Oh, shit, that's what you meant about him hating you your whole life." Right then she wanted to scream, to shake Reyha and make her see some sense. But she controlled herself and said, "Now I understand, but that's even more reason for you not to confront him yourself."

Reyha pounded the table, the cigarette in her hand showering little flares of ash. "The consequences of my actions are for me to face alone, not for you. Your life and safety are not to be threatened because of my decisions. I have already cost the lives of those I love. I will not lose you as well."

"You don't get to face this alone."

Reyha shot up on her feet. "Again, you are not a part of the security detail. You are not to put your life in danger for me."

"Well, guess what?" Chrys stood and put her hands on her hips. "You don't get to tell me what to do."

"I can have you dismissed."

"Go right ahead. But Banks said she'd hire me on even with my bum leg, so I'll just go to work for her and continue to be a pain in your ass whether you like it or not."

Reyha seemed to grow ten feet as she stepped right up into Chrys's face, dominating her space. "I will call Secretary Collins and demand you be removed from Commander Banks's detail if you do such a thing."

"I'll just get hired on here at the Hay-Adams, then. Maybe as a housekeeper or in the kitchen, anyplace where I can keep an eye on you. You can't get rid of me that easily." Chrys held her breath but could not keep herself from shivering. The adrenaline released from their earlier confrontation along with the intensity of Reyha's angry stare ignited something inside her.

Reyha leaned closer, narrowing her eyes. "Your defiance is unacceptable."

Chrys continued to stand her ground as the silence between them filled with the sound of traffic below. Still, she could hear Reyha's breath, feel it on her face as the air came more forcefully from her flared nostrils and parted lips. She dropped her voice to a whisper, but kept her eyes on Reyha's. "Don't you realize how scared I am?"

Reyha fumed, her chest heaving.

"I won't stop trying to protect you. I can't because…"

Reyha scoffed.

"Because I'm in love with you."

Reyha blinked, stepped back.

This allowed Chrys the opening she needed. She put her hand behind Reyha's neck and pulled her into a kiss.

A muted yip rose from Reyha's throat as she pressed her mouth to Chrys's. At first, Reyha stood rigid. Then, without breaking the kiss or taking a breath, she turned her head and opened her mouth and took control, delivering a long, sensuous move, her tongue finding Chrys's. When the kiss came to its natural end, she stood back and regarded Chrys with wide eyes before she snatched up her cigarettes and wine and went inside.

Chrys watched the doorway and listened for returning footsteps. Finally, she allowed herself to breathe, gasps that came in shallow gulps while her hands began to shake and her teeth to chatter. She hugged herself as she shivered harder. Her body was shutting down, going into shock. She waited a few seconds more, not sure what she should do next, then opened the French doors and looked inside. The kitchen light was on, but no others. Reyha's door was shut, light seeping out from under it. She stared at that door, willing it to open and Reyha to appear, but she didn't, so she walked numbly into the kitchen, drew a beer from the refrigerator, and went into her own room.

She sat on the end of the bed with her door open so she could see across the living area to Reyha's door. She popped open the beer and took a swig but made a face of disgust and set it aside. She turned again and watched Reyha's door as she debated what she should do now while the gnawing inside her grew unbearable.

She went into the bathroom, turned toward the mirror, and leaned forward on the sink while she glared at her own reflection. The weakness in her knees gushed up her spine into her heart while her core throbbed, burned almost, as the excitement of the kiss still pulsed inside her. She turned on the faucet and splashed cold water over her head. She grabbed a towel and held it to her face as she tried to concentrate on her breathing, the shallow gulps still tugging at her and making her hyperventilate. She moaned with frustration at not being able to bring her body's reaction to the kiss under control. She could still feel Reyha's tongue against hers, the taste of the wine and clove tobacco in her mouth. She tossed the towel into the sink and stomped back into her bedroom, where she paced and watched out her door toward Reyha's bedroom.

Desperate to get relief, she growled and flopped on the bed. Her left leg ached and her body still trembled as if she was cold, in shock, falling apart, having a meltdown, losing it. She covered her face and wiped her hands upward, slicking back her damp hair. Sweat stung her eyes, and she held fists to her temples while stifling a scream. What she wanted, what she needed, was in the other room, and she cursed herself for allowing the kiss, for admitting the truth of her feelings, for being too weak to resist her desire. Finally, she couldn't stand the agony in her body any longer. She marched with a military stride to Reyha's door, started to knock, but instead pushed the door open to find Reyha sitting on her bed with something like relief passing over her face when she saw Chrys standing there.

Chrys swallowed back another curse and took methodical steps toward her. She came right up to her, so close that Reyha's knees brushed against her pant legs.

Reyha looked up, keeping her eyes fixed on her, and Chrys gazed down as her chest rose and fell unevenly. Timidly, she touched Reyha's hair, let her hand brush against her cheek, her fingers caress her mouth.

Reyha put her hands on Chrys's hips and held her, tugging on her belt.

Chrys resisted, but then gave in to Reyha's pull and pushed her back onto the bed in one motion as she allowed her own body to fall forward. Her left leg gave at the joint and she scooted so it lay on the outside of Reyha's leg while she pushed against her and drove upward into her. She began to kiss Reyha on her lips, her neck, below her ear. She could feel Reyha's hands on her sides and back, pulling her closer. She slid down and angled onto the floor and ran her hand along Reyha's inner thigh. The folds of her tunic and pants seemed impenetrable, but somehow Chrys found an opening and her hand found flesh.

By now, Reyha's eyes were closed, and she held Chrys's head against her chest as Chrys parted the tunic's collar with her chin and sought Reyha's lower neck with her mouth. All the while Chrys's hand circled Reyha's moist skin. Already she could smell the scent of Reyha's arousal, and it made her mouth water as she began to kiss along Reyha's collarbone just as Reyha pulled away a portion of her top and slipped it off one shoulder. Chrys momentarily brought her hand away and tugged at Reyha's bra to expose her erect nipple. She pulled it into her mouth and was rewarded with a groan of pleasure and a pulsing lift from Reyha's hips. Chrys answered that call by stroking Reyha lightly with her fingertips. When Chrys entered her, Reyha cried out and clutched her closer as Chrys began gliding in and out, drawing the pleasure from her gradually, not wanting it to end too quickly. But then Reyha took her wrist as if to direct her, and Chrys resisted the attempts at control and heard the frustrated moan from Reyha's lips. But her intention was not to tease. Reyha's pleasure was all she wanted. She bit down on her nipple before sliding down her body to the floor and resting on her knees. She brought her left leg under her and aligned it before parting the many folds of Reyha's tunic. Then she opened her mouth to receive her.

When she met Reyha's skin with her lips, she sighed with delight. Reyha had a glorious taste, musky and earthy. Chrys inhaled and began to devour her, taking her as fully as she could into her mouth, discovering every fold with her tongue, tunneling as deep as she might. At that moment, she could only taste her, smell her, feel her, and hear her as Reyha cried out over and over in Turkish. But when Reyha climaxed, no discernable words in any language Chrys knew could be comprehended. Instead something like a sob combined with a cry of shock tinged with joy leapt from Reyha's throat and rang out. Reyha was seized with a convulsion of pleasure as her legs closed around Chrys's head, and her back arched off the bed. She fell back and continued to twitch with each stroke Chrys's tongue delivered. Finally, she pressed down on Chrys's head and whimpered.

Chrys rested her forehead against Reyha's stomach and panted for air. Her own body no longer shook, her head no longer pounded, but she continued to throb with need. She lifted her head and found Reyha watching her. She was crying, but smiling all the same. Chrys smiled back as Reyha reached and stroked her face. They gazed at each other, the smiles never leaving until Reyha sat up and hugged Chrys's head, kissing the top of it. Chrys could hear the rapid beat of Reyha's heart and nestled against her, closing her eyes. Then Reyha pulled her away and stood up, bringing her up as well before she sat again and rested her hands on Chrys's belt while looking up at her.

Chrys tilted her head, frowned. Right then panic gripped her. It was clear from the look in Reyha's eyes what she wanted. She shook her head as she said, "I can't."

Reyha unbuckled Chrys's belt, her eyes still on her face.

"No." Chrys covered Reyha's hands.

Reyha stopped, but kept her hands in place.

"I can't let you." Chrys's face burned with shame. "I can't let you see me."

Reyha nodded, and with one hand, she slipped off the other

shoulder of her tunic and dropped her bra to reveal not only the freshly healed wound where the port had been weeks ago, but also the diagonal scar where her left breast had once been. The long-healed scar, slightly pink, curved down under her armpit to her side.

Chrys sucked in her breath when she saw it and pulled her gaze away. But Reyha took her hand and guided it to her chest and pressed her palm against the scar. Chrys closed her eyes and shivered. The scar was warm, soft even.

"I'm sorry," Chrys said opening her eyes again.

But sorry for what, she wasn't sure. Sorry for Reyha's illness? For the loss of her breast? Sorry she was too ashamed of her own disfigurement to allow Reyha to touch her even though her body screamed out for that touch?

Reyha then lifted her arms to reveal small raised bumps along the tender inner skin.

Tears flooded Chrys's eyes. She recognized those marks, evidence of old cigarette burns. She'd seen them on Diren and the others.

"We are not our scars," Reyha said, "but they are a part of us. There is no shame to carry them on our bodies. They do not make us ugly. They make us real."

Chrys spread her fingers against Reyha's mastectomy scar. No, it was not ugly. In some ways it was beautiful.

Reyha pulled Chrys's hand to her mouth and kissed her fingertips. "You do not owe me the honor of touching you. I would never force or coerce you." She kissed the back of Chrys's hand and held it to her heart. "But I would show you the beauty of your scars, the strength you carry because of them, not despite them. I would touch my scars to yours and share your pain. For that is all any of us can give. That is the only gift we truly have, to share each other's pain."

Chrys opened her mouth to speak, but no words came. Instead, her face contorted as tears surged down her face, releasing the last of her resistance.

Reyha stood and switched positions with her, pivoting Chrys and sitting her on the bed. Her hands went to Chrys's belt once more.

Chrys could only cry harder but did not protest. And with each movement Reyha's hands made—first undoing her belt completely, then unzipping her fly, and then pulling her pants from her hips—Chrys wept harder. She fell back on the bed and covered her face as Reyha pulled her pants to her knees. But suddenly she shot up.

"Wait, please. It's ugly. Not like your mastectomy. Not that clean. And my side, it's shredded."

Reyha leaned forward and kissed her. "You are beautiful to me. And not only your body, but more importantly your heart and mind. These are beautiful beyond description." She pulled Chrys's pants all the way to her ankles and rested her hand across her prosthetic leg.

Chrys fell against Reyha's shoulder and sobbed.

Reyha kissed her hair and cooed terms of affection. Then she lifted Chrys's face. "Help me remove it. Let your body move freely with mine. Let me show you what joy you bring me."

Chrys's hands shook as she released her leg. When she'd done so, she leaned back and watched Reyha lovingly remove the sheath and sock. She whimpered when the mangled and knotted flesh became visible and gasped as Reyha leaned forward and pulled her leg against her chest to touch one scar to the other.

Reyha looked up as her own tears fell and said in her native tongue, "Beauty passes, my friend, but love and wisdom remain."

Chrys reached for her, pulled her by the shoulders, and kissed her. In a flurry of movement, she pulled off the rest of Reyha's clothes and soon found herself free of her own. What followed next was so fluid that Chrys couldn't tell where her body ended and Reyha's began. Reyha rolled her and moved about her as she seemed devoted to concentrating kisses over every inch of her body as well as stroking the visible skin, paying particular attention to the scars along Chrys's left side. When Reyha parted her, Chrys buried her face against Reyha's neck and allowed her to thrust within her. She began to shake again, but this time it was out of anticipation, not fear or need. She knew Reyha would bring her to the edge and drop her over in a free fall. There was no escaping it. So when she climaxed the first time, lying beneath her, Chrys gave in to the loss of control and let her body quiver with unrestrained pleasure. And when Reyha transitioned quickly to move down her body and between her legs, Chrys could only moan as Reyha took her into her mouth. As Reyha drew the pleasure from her, Chrys cried out and knew she was probably making too much noise, and the thought crossed her mind the security detail might come crashing through the door, but she didn't care.

Reyha finally relinquished control of her body, and she rolled against Chrys as she joined her on the bed.

"You're not angry at me anymore?" Chrys asked.

"No," Reyha said into her ear. "I was only afraid."

Chrys rose up. "You said you didn't fear him."

"Not for myself, but for you." And then in Turkish, Reyha asked, "Do you not see I am in love with you as well and that your life means more to me than my own?"

Chrys touched Reyha's lips, kissed her, and snuggled down against her. And in that position, they lay through the night, sleeping soundly against each other. It didn't matter Reyha's legs were touching her old injury, that her hands rested on her damaged side. It didn't matter that she was vulnerable and weak with her entire body exposed; for Chrys knew beyond doubt Reyha truly loved her, scars and all.

CHAPTER EIGHTEEN

The curtains were drawn against the morning light, leaving the room cooler than usual. It was cool enough that Chrys had burrowed under the covers and buried her head under the pillows. She was waxing and waning between wakefulness and a dream state with images of the Syrian desert morphing into the plains of Nebraska with the aroma of her grandmother's dolmadakia mixing with the scents of ripe cucumbers and stewing lamb. She began to stir, first stretching, then pulling the pillows from her head and peering about the room. She could smell the aromas of coffee and fresh baked goods wafting through the open bedroom door, and she heard someone humming.

"Reyha?"

Reyha peeked inside. "Good morning. I hope my moving about did not wake you."

Chrys sat up in bed but let the covers rest along her hips to allow her bare chest to enjoy the cool air of the room. "It's sort of chilly in here. Did you turn down the temperature?"

Reyha was at the window where she drew back the heavy curtains, causing sunlight to blast into the room.

Chrys squinted and raised a hand to shield her eyes.

"I did," Reyha said coming over to the bed. "You were perspiring all night. When I woke, I decided to cool the room for your sake so that you might sleep as long as possible."

Chrys's eyes adjusted to the bright room, and she saw Reyha fully now. Her hair was down, wild and messy, and she wore the Air Force sweatshirt, but no bottoms.

"Oh, my," Chrys said grinning.

"Yes?"

"Do I smell coffee?" Chrys continued to grin.

"The staff delivered breakfast a moment ago."

"And did you answer the door wearing that sweatshirt?"

Reyha looked down her body. "You know I chill easily, so yes, I put on this sweatshirt."

"But your backside's hanging out. Tell me you at least had on some bottoms."

Reyha frowned. "My backside?" She turned her head and looked over her shoulder. "I see. Why, yes, it is." She climbed into bed, straddled Chrys's hips, and leaned down for a kiss. When she pulled back, she added, "I did not answer the door. I had called down and told them to deliver breakfast, then listened for them to leave."

Chrys squirmed and stroked Reyha's bare bottom. "So breakfast in bed?"

Reyha raised an eyebrow. "We can have our first course at the table, but I plan on taking my second"—she kissed Chrys's mouth—"and third"—she kissed her neck—"and fourth in bed."

Chrys pulled Reyha down on top of her and rolled her over, wrapping them up in the sheets and tangling their bodies together. "How about we just take all our meals in bed today?"

Reyha smiled up at her. "I see we are of the same mind. I have already called Commander Banks and told her we will not be going out today, but rather spending it together in bed."

Chrys's mouth dropped open. "You what?"

"You surely know she is keenly aware of our relationship."

Chrys groaned and rolled to her side. "I have no doubt her powers of observation have led her to suspect, but now you've confirmed her suspicions." She bit Reyha's shoulder. "Let's hope this doesn't get into the papers or we'll have an international incident on our hands."

"I somehow think she will keep this knowledge to herself."

"I suppose she will." Chrys propped up on one of her elbows and traced along the bottom hem of the sweatshirt, letting her fingers feather the soft skin of Reyha's lower abdomen. "You know, she and Christman are engaged to be married, thinking about starting a family even."

"This does not surprise me. I detected an energy between them the first time I was introduced." Reyha appeared to ponder something. "Yes, they make an excellent pair. I shall have to send them a wedding present once I return to London."

Chrys turned Reyha's face to her. "I want to go with you when you go home."

"Do you?"

"Don't you want me to?"

"You indicated you wished to return to Syria as a mercenary. Is that not true?"

"That was before." Chrys studied Reyha's face, noticed she was smiling her secretive smile. She shifted as she cleared her throat. "Well, this is awkward. I just U-Hauled you, didn't I?"

Reyha's brow knitted. "What is this? I do not understand where have you hauled me."

Chrys fell back and laughed. "Wow, I don't think I've ever done that with any other woman before."

Reyha rose up. "How many women would that be? And please, explain this hauling business."

"Not that many, really. And you've eclipsed every one of them, you should know." Chrys twirled a finger in Reyha's hair. "And U-Hauling is a phrase that is sort of a joke about the stereotypical way women react after sleeping together for the first time."

"It is a sexual technique?"

Chrys chuckled. "No, not like that. It means that women often jump right into a committed relationship after one sexual encounter with each other before taking the time to know one another better."

Reyha frowned even more.

"So one woman packs up all her belongings," Chrys explained, "and moves in with the other. The U-Haul is a type of moving truck."

Reyha shrugged.

"It's a joke. An American thing. Not so funny, I guess. Anyway." Chrys cleared her throat again. "Let's go have some breakfast. I'm starved." She sat up in bed and pointed toward her clothes and prosthesis piled on the floor. "I need to use the restroom first. Can you hand me my leg?"

Reyha scooted off the bed and brought the items over and set them before her. "I am interested to see how this works. Will you show me?"

Chrys hesitated at first, but then began putting her leg in place, explaining the process while being aware of her own ease and peace of mind while doing so. Once her prosthesis was secure, she pulled on her pants. "And that's how it works."

"And the special prosthesis you desire, the one which allows you to run?"

"Right, the blade. It works in a similar way as this prosthetic leg, but the shaft is a carbon fiber in a J shape that stores energy. Also, I'd put on a socket here where the shaft snaps in instead of it being attached directly like my standard prosthesis. I'm lucky in a way because my knee joint wasn't damaged."

"Yes, quite fortunate." Reyha touched Chrys's leg where it met the socket.

"Each one has to be custom built to fit the weight of the individual and the type of running they do, along with their stride. It's pretty high-tech stuff. That's why they're so expensive."

"I can see that." Reyha put on her robe over her sweatshirt. "We have a little less than four weeks left here in DC before we go to New York, correct?"

"Yes. Why?"

"Come, let us eat breakfast." Reyha pointed to the bathroom. "I brought your robe in this morning. I'll wait for you at the table."

❖

Reyha had already poured them coffee and was preparing a plate when Chrys joined her.

"I have been watching carefully these last months," Reyha said, "and I believe I have prepared your coffee just as you like it."

Chrys took a sip. "It's perfect." She took one of Reyha's hands and kissed the back of it. "Just like you."

"You are full of flattery, but there is no need. You have already captured my heart."

"Have I?" Chrys grinned. "So that means I can come with you to London when you're done at the UN?"

Reyha chewed a bite before answering. "And what would you do in London?"

"So you don't want me to come with you."

"I did not say that. But I understood you had a passion for the Kurds, to help them rid their lands of the Islamic State."

"That was before I met you."

"I see." Reyha fell silent and continued eating.

Chrys shifted in her chair. "I meant what I said last night. I love you."

"And I believe you."

"I could help you, you know, with your foundation. I could serve as an interpreter, write emails, make phone calls. I don't care what it is, anything so I can be close to you."

Reyha put her fork down and wiped her mouth. "Ophelia did many of those tasks for me. She along with my accountant, Margaret Bradley, did much of the clerical work for the foundation."

Chrys narrowed her eyes. "Does this Bradley live in London?"

"Her residence is in Florida. But she will be coming to DC in two days to visit and discuss an ongoing project."

"That's nice." Chrys concentrated on buttering her muffin and tried to ignore her irrational jealousy of this Bradley woman.

"I would like you to meet her."

"Sure." Chrys could feel Reyha watching her. "So basically you'll have no use for me when this is all over, will you?"

Reyha's face melted. "My love, never say that."

"But you don't need me in London, or want me."

Reyha repositioned her chair so she faced Chrys head-on. "Do you remember the first evening together and you told me you hoped you could help me fulfill my goals, and I said, perhaps beyond my stay?"

Chrys dropped her muffin on her plate. "Yes."

"I had to wait, you see, to know you better, to see if you had the right temperament." Reyha stood and began pacing, talking with her hands. "You know of my foundation's mission. We've opened two encampments in northern Syria, both for women. A third is being built outside of Kasan as we speak. It will be more elaborate, a true settlement with a school and a hospital. There are plans as well for a family settlement and one for men and boys. I do not know how much longer the civil war will rage, but even now, neighboring countries, including my own, cannot handle more refugees. We need these settlements." She stopped and held her hands out in supplication. "And without my Ophelia and with Margaret getting older and expecting her first grandchild, I am without a coordinator, someone who can oversee the operation, someone who understands the languages, the people, the cultures." She knelt and took Chrys's hands. "Someone I can trust to do the right thing no matter how difficult."

"Are you offering me a job?"

"I am asking you to consider it. And in two days, I would like you to sit with Margaret and me and listen to the details. After which I would ask you to search your heart and to weigh your options."

Chrys nodded, gazed out the French doors. "I looked into NGOs when I learned the Air Force wouldn't take me back. But being a mercenary seemed a better bet." She shrugged. "You know, those women aren't just auxiliary units. They're their own independent fighting force, fully autonomous. While fighting alongside them, I realized that the YPJ have the potential to do what no others have done before, particularly in that area of the world."

"I understand that."

"I mean, this fight could really transform the lives of all women in that region."

Reyha sighed. "And you wish to return and fight alongside them. I understand."

Chrys leaned her elbow on the table. "I figured I didn't have anything else to live for, but now…" She focused on Reyha, touched her hair. "Do you really think I'm the right person for the job? You have that sort of faith in me?"

"I do."

"And how many months out of the year would I be able to live with you and still help with the establishment of these settlements?"

Reyha faltered, swayed on her knees. "As many as we might manage. That is all I can promise you."

"And does this Bradley woman have to approve of me or is it your decision?"

"No, the foundation has a board of directors, one of whom is your Senator Granger, but ultimately it is my decision. However, Margaret will be one of your main contacts, and I would like her to meet you."

"Okay, well, I look forward to meeting her, then." Chrys smiled down at her. "Now up off your knees. You don't have to beg me. I'd do anything for you. You know that." She stood and helped Reyha to her feet.

"Yes, anything within reason." Reyha winced and held her hip.

"I think you know by now there's no limit to anything you ask me." Chrys watched her sit. "Is your hip hurting again?"

Reyha waved her off. "It is nothing."

"I can have Quinn or Smith run me down to a pharmacy and get you something." She nodded toward her bedroom. "Of course I have an entire pharmacy myself almost."

Reyha patted her hand. "I am fine, my love. As I told you, I wish to stay in and keep you to myself the entire day." She popped a piece of fruit in her mouth and winked.

Chrys's entire body warmed. "You'll spoil me if you're not careful."

"My exact intention. How did you know?"

❖

They might have spent another whole day after that first glorious one secluded in their hotel suite making love and ordering food from the kitchen if Chrys hadn't had a med-check appointment to keep the next morning. But it was a late morning appointment, so they took their time waking up, eating breakfast, and then soaking together in a bubble bath in Reyha's large sunken tub.

"Your hair is getting so long," Reyha said as she massaged the shampoo into Chrys's scalp.

"I used to wear it cut really short," Chrys said, "but after coming home this last time, I've let it grow. Covers the scars on my face some."

"As I have told you, there is no need to feel shame for your scars." Reyha used a cup to pour water through Chrys's hair and rinse the suds.

Chrys leaned back against Reyha's chest. "When I was a kid, Yiayia used to brush my hair every night. For church, she'd pull it back into this really cool braid and tie it off with ribbons. I hated the dresses she'd make me wear, but I always liked the braid." She chuckled and splashed a bubble. "I cut my hair short my senior year in high school, and you would've thought I'd murdered someone the way that old woman carried on. God, I miss her." She swiveled on her bottom. "But you know, I found a lot of women really liked me with shorter hair. I could never tell her that, but it's true."

"I suspect your grandmother understood you better than you knew."

Chrys moved her legs around Reyha's lap. The tip of her partial leg bobbed a little above the bubbles.

"I never told her about me, but you're right. I think she knew."

"Of course she did."

Chrys smiled, chuckled. "She got to meet Mary once. I was on leave and we'd only been dating a year and we flew in to Omaha for a few days. And even though Yiayia was ill, she pulled herself out of bed and invited all the family over to meet her. Then she stood on her feet and cooked all day." She sank down into the water. "When we got ready to leave, she gave Mary a big hug, told her to come back anytime. But that time never came. She died a month later in her bed with my uncles and her other grandchildren around her while I was off in Iraq."

Reyha wiped Chrys's cheek, dabbing her tears with bathwater.

"Yet you were her firstborn grandchild from her own firstborn. Nothing can endanger that bond."

"I know. She never leaves me." Chrys pointed to her head. "She's always here, always watching." She snickered and waved around the room. "And sometimes really watching." She sighed. "I'm glad those hallucinations stopped. But I have to tell you, I sort of miss seeing her. Diren, too."

Reyha leaned forward and placed her hand over Chrys's heart. "They are always here." She stroked Chrys's skin. "I hope you will find room here for me as well next to your grandmother and your friend Diren." She paused. "And Mary as well."

Chrys rose up out of the water and started to speak.

"No, no," Reyha said pushing her back down. "I am not a fool. I can see and hear how you still love her, and I am happy to share your heart with her."

Chrys tried to protest, but Reyha shushed her.

"Love has no limits. For this reason, you should not put limits on yourself as to whom you love. Will you promise me this?"

"I'll try, I guess."

Reyha scooped some suds into her hand and blew them in the air and giggled as they floated down, successfully washing away Chrys's passing sadness.

Reyha and Banks were talking on the sofa when Chrys returned from her med check. From their body posture and the expressions on their faces, she could see it was nothing serious, and in fact, she was relieved to learn they weren't discussing any impending danger to Reyha's life. Instead, they were discussing New York and the various points of interest Reyha might want to check out for her upcoming visit.

"And here you are," Reyha said, standing and greeting her with a quick kiss on both cheeks. "Look here, Commander Banks has brought a certified letter addressed to you."

"Really?" Chrys took the envelope from Banks and saw it was addressed to her in care of Sean Gordon at the Secretary of State's office. She turned the envelope over and noticed the return address indicated an out-of-state sender. "That's strange."

Banks touched her arm. "I'll see myself out. Have a good rest of your day."

"Commander Banks?" Reyha said. "You will remember to arrange the reservation for us tonight at Marcel's? Seven will be fine."

"Yes, ma'am, I'll take care of it."

Chrys looked from one woman to the other, wondering what the heck they were up to.

"Open it." Reyha pointed to the letter once Banks had shut the door behind her. "Do you not want to see what it is?"

"What's going on? Is this related to Bradley coming to interview me?"

"Of course not. And I told you—I have the final say. Now please." Reyha pointed to the envelope in Chrys's hand.

"Uh-huh. Something's up." Chrys gave her a playful stink eye and kissed her quickly on the lips. "Marcel's an awfully pricey joint. Most people only ever go there for an anniversary or a promotion or"—she smiled—"a wedding dinner. Are Banks and Christman having a rehearsal dinner or something?"

"No, this is a celebration dinner for you. Now would you please open your letter?"

"Celebrating what?"

"Chrysanthi, open your letter."

"Okay, okay, sheesh, you're impatient." Chrys chuckled at the glare Reyha gave her and opened the letter on one end. She slid out the rich parchment paper, unfolded it, and recognized a familiar logo. She read the first sentence twice, looked up. "My God."

"What is it?"

"I got funded." Chrys read the first line once more to make sure she'd not been mistaken. Then she began to read the rest, to scan over the letter again. One phrase kept popping out at her, waving at her—*fully funded by an anonymous donor*. She looked up again, holding back the tears. "My blade. Someone funded my running blade. The composite parts will be delivered next week to the VA, and they're sending a technician to work with Kayla to get me fitted."

Reyha pulled her into a hug. "I am so happy for you."

"I'm going to run again," Chrys said, weeping against Reyha's shoulder. "I'm really going to run again."

"Yes, my love, you will run again."

Chrys pulled back, her mouth open. "It was you. It had to be you. First my tux, now this."

Reyha wiped away a few tears of her own. "It was I who made the request, yes. Months ago when you first told me about your desire to have one, I contacted Sean Gordon and told him to make a personal request on the part of the Secretary of State's office. Then I had the money wired for payment."

"But you'd only just met me. Why would you do that for someone you didn't even know?"

"Why does anyone do anything for anybody? Because it is the right thing to do. When you have the means to help, you help. But I have to tell you, I was growing impatient that it would not come through before I had to leave for London. I so want to see you run again with your new device."

Chrys's breath caught in her throat. "You do?"

"Your joy is my joy. To see you run again, to watch the pleasure and elation on your face would be a gift a hundred times more valuable than the cost of funding it."

Chrys shook her head, stuttered out her words. "What you've done, no one has ever…I can never…For as long as I live, I'll never be able to repay you."

"You will let me watch you run for the first time, yes?"

"Of course I will."

"Then that is all the payment I ask for."

They stayed out late at Marcel's and stayed up even later after returning to the suite where they fell into each other's arms and made love until the early hours. They slept in the next morning, took their time eating breakfast and bathing together before Chrys forced herself to get dressed so Quinn and Smith could drive her to her afternoon group session.

"I won't be gone long," Chrys said as she kissed Reyha good-bye.

"Margaret will be here at six," Reyha said, "and Mr. Carmichael is having the kitchen prepare an elegant meal. So please, be sure to be back in time to clean up."

"Don't worry. I'll be back by four at the latest. That's plenty of time." Chrys patted Reyha's bottom as she hugged her once more. "And I'll be on my best behavior so she likes me."

"I know she will like you. That is not the point. But she will be a guest in our house, and I want things to be respectful and appropriate."

"Our house?" Chrys grinned.

"Yes, our house." Reyha patted Chrys's bottom in turn. "Now go and make good use of your time with your group."

❖

Chrys arrived five minutes late and slunk in and took her seat. The others turned and looked at her strangely, and she noticed with some disappointment Morrison was absent again.

"Sorry, I had a late night and a hard time getting myself going."

Woodley turned to her. "I was just telling the group some sad news. I wanted to let you all know before you saw it in the news. These sorts of things can be upsetting, set off a whole slew of turmoil."

Chrys glanced at Horrigan. She thought she could see tears in his eyes. "What's going on? What sad news?"

Woodley leaned on his elbows. "I'm afraid Cherae Morrison was killed last night at one of the Metro stations."

Chrys's lower body went numb while her stomach cramped and her guts twisted.

"Witnesses told police they saw her lose her balance before she fell into an oncoming train."

"Ah, shit," Dworsky said as Chrys's vomit splattered onto the floor and sprayed his dead legs.

Woodley dropped to his knees and steadied her shoulders. He looked up at one of the other men and shouted at him to get some help.

Chrys spent herself and left all of her breakfast and lunch and her fancy dinner from the night before on the floor before sitting back on her butt. She lifted her head and let loose a series of curses, screaming them almost.

Horrigan moved his chair closer. "Pull yourself together, Safis. Get off your ass."

"You're not helping," Woodley said to him. He pulled her to her feet and sat her in a chair, being careful not to step in her vomit. "I know this is hard. I understand the two of you had become friends. It's never easy to lose our friends or our fellow servicemen. But it was an accident. As terrible as it is, we can be comforted in knowing it was an accident."

Chrys's face contorted as her tears burned hot down her face. "An accident? Are you fucking kidding me? You think that was a goddamn accident?"

"Shut up," Horrigan yelled. "Shut the fuck up."

Chrys glared at him, saw he was in fact crying. She looked at Woodley. He knew. He had to know. Then she looked at the other men, at the one who'd returned with a custodian who came rolling a mop bucket. They all knew. Of course they did. But no one would admit it. The VA wasn't about to admit to the truth when there was an opportunity to label it as an accident. But that was what Morrison had wanted.

She shivered and held herself as she rocked back and forth. She tried to take deep breaths to calm herself while the custodian made quick work of her mess and excused himself.

Then Woodley righted his chair and smoothed back his hair. "I know all your feelings are raw right now, but we need to talk through this. I want each of you to feel free to say whatever you need." He looked at Chrys. "Even if it's over the top and outrageous. Get those thoughts out. Let's hear them."

Chrys continued to rock herself in the chair, paying no attention to the others, yet she could hear in her daze that the men spoke of Morrison with respect. That was at least something. A few like Horrigan cried as they spoke about their feelings. She wondered if Morrison knew how much she'd been respected and cared for.

"You have anything you want to add, Safis?" Woodley asked near the end.

Chrys shook her head and her teeth chattered. "No, sir, and I'm sorry for my outburst." She nodded to the still damp place on the floor. "And sorry I caused a mess."

"I know it's a shock. It is for all of us."

When the session was done, Chrys waited for the others to leave, glanced at the empty chair where Morrison had sat for all those months, then staggered out the door and bumped into Horrigan.

"I'm sorry I yelled at you," Horrigan said. "But her mom and son need her benefits. You can't blow that for her."

"Then you know."

"I know. She called me a few days ago, but I got busy and didn't return her call." He grimaced as a sob fought its way up. "Anyway, I gotta catch my ride. I'm sorry. I know she was your friend."

"Yeah, my friend."

He looked up at her. "She call you, too? Did she tell you she had it planned?"

"She never called me back. I left messages and…" Chrys diverted her gaze. "No, she never told me her plan."

She watched Horrigan leave, then pulled her phone from her pocket. She'd not even bothered to look at it since yesterday. As she stared at her screen, her fears materialized. A text message, last night, around seven, just when she and Reyha were at dinner celebrating.

Hey Safis it's Morrison. sorry I haven't called back. wondering if u had a sec to talk. got to hear a voice of reason. call me pls.

Chrys took a few steps, fell against the wall. Someone passing by asked if she was okay, but she ignored him and held the wall for support. She tried to focus on the floor tiles, on something to give her perspective, to lead her out of the building. When she looked up, Diren stood in front of her with a colorful scarf tied over her head.

"It should have been me, not you," Chrys said. "They needed you to lead them."

"There was no other way," Diren said.

"But I could've saved you." Chrys pointed back to the group meeting room. "I could've saved her."

Diren shook her head as she began to fade. "Sometimes you must first save yourself, heval, and at other times, you must save others."

CHAPTER NINETEEN

Quinn checked the time on his phone. "Ms. Safis, it's after four. Wouldn't you like to head back to the hotel now?"

Chrys glared at him over the rim of her shot glass. "I want a few more." She tapped the bar. "Another round?"

The barkeep poured the whiskey and spoke to Quinn. "You sure you don't want nothing but coffee, buddy? You gonna let your woman do all your drinking for you?"

Chrys snickered. "He's not my damn boyfriend. He's my bodyguard."

The barkeep studied her. "You some sort of celebrity? Politician's wife or something?"

"Or something," she said, slurring her words. She shot back the whiskey and waved. "I gotta have a beer chaser on that."

Once the barkeep set her beer in front of her, she turned to Quinn. "Really? You can't have one damn drink with me? We've been practically living together these past months and you won't share one goddamn drink with me?"

"Ms. Safis, I think you've had enough. Why don't you let me and Smith get you back to the hotel? I understand Mrs. Arslan is having a guest for dinner. Don't you want to be cleaned up and presentable?"

Chrys gave him a drunken snort. "Hmm, yeah, maybe we should get going." She drained the beer and teetered off the bar stool. "Give me a sec, I gotta pee."

She staggered toward the back of the bar. Quinn followed.

She stopped at the restroom door. "Shit, Quinn, you can't follow me in the bathroom again. It's the ladies' room. See?" She pointed to the sign. Then she felt her pockets. "Damn, I left my phone on the bar. Could you grab it for me?"

Quinn glanced back to where they'd been sitting. "Okay, but wait right here for me."

As soon as he turned, she scanned the adjoining hallway and noticed a door that led to the back alley. She managed to get to it and found herself outside in the late afternoon.

"Fuck him, I'll drink as much as I want."

She glanced around the corner, spotted the sign for another bar across the street, and stumbled toward it.

She had trouble recalling how long she'd stayed at the second bar or how many drinks she'd had, but she had some vague recollection of a bouncer escorting her out after a disagreement with another patron about some trivial political issue. She never argued politics with anyone, at least not when she was sober.

After being booted from that bar, she roamed the streets for a while. She stopped in two more establishments, which by that time of night were crowded and loud, with music and laughter pouring out into the streets and into their open courtyards. But the crowds became too much for her, and after two drinks, she left and wandered the streets for a while longer until she finally found a small dive off a side street in an industrial neighborhood, which was quieter than the more frequented touristy places. At a corner table, she downed a number of shots followed by beer chasers before she realized she had no idea where she was. She teetered over to the bar and asked the bartender for the cross streets.

"How about I call you a taxi," he offered.

She wiped her face, wobbled in place. "Naw, I'm good. I'll just call Quinn to…" She felt in her pockets for her phone, began to panic as she realized she didn't have it.

Right then a patron who'd been watching her sidled up close and leered into her face. "Lose something?"

She continued to feel her pockets. "My phone. I had it with me earlier, but now…"

"Let me help," he said as he slid his hand behind her and down her ass.

She recoiled and shoved him backward, cussing at him.

He jeered at her. "Fuck off."

She swung blindly at his face, felt a shearing pain in her fist, then struggled to free herself as someone lifted her from behind and dragged her outside and tossed her to the curb. She continued to hurl obscenities at the entryway while other patrons coming and going snickered and stared at her. She turned and nearly fell over but managed to catch herself. Her fist throbbed, and when she looked at it, she saw blood, some swelling. She couldn't remember making contact with the guy's teeth, but she must've landed a good one. She glanced up and down the street and tried to remember what the bartender had told her about the cross streets. But her mind was soaked, so she started toward a lighted corner and was relieved to discover a bus stop. She tried to focus on reading the information for the route, to determine where she was, but she couldn't make her eyes focus. She dropped onto the bench. She had no idea when the next bus would be along, but she figured when one did come by she could ask the driver where she was.

As she sat there, her thoughts circled back to Morrison. She began to weep as she pictured her face the day they'd gone to lunch. She remembered Morrison's desperation, and that spilled over into another terrible memory of the morning of the attack. A rapid succession of images ranging from Syria to her return to DC shot across her blurred memory. She thought of Diren and her self-sacrifice, of Mary and all she'd given up because of her, and then she thought of Reyha and how upset she was going to be that she'd missed the dinner with Bradley.

"You are stronger than this," her grandmother said.

Chrys tossed her head to the side and observed her grandmother rolling out dough and pinching it together on a nonexistent countertop.

"I let her down, Yiayia. I'm a terrible friend."

Her grandmother morphed into Diren. "No friends but the mountains."

"You were my friend," Chrys said. "I wish you hadn't done that. We could've all gotten out."

"It was my choice." Diren smiled, and her face transformed into Morrison.

"My choice, Safis, not yours," Morrison said, the creases in her forehead growing deeper.

Chrys reached out. "I'm sorry I wasn't there for you." Her hand stopped against the bus stop's enclosure. She shook herself and rubbed her eyes. "Shit, I'm fucking losing my mind."

She staggered up and headed toward the far corner. If she was lucky, she might spot a cab. As she walked, she felt her body veering, and without warning, she toppled off the curb into the street where she skidded on her knees and rolled over on her ass. She lumbered to her feet and cursed when her left knee buckled. Finally, she made it to the curb and sat while she closed her eyes and raised her face skyward. Pulsing lights cut through her shut lids, and a sharp chirp of police sirens brought her out of her stupor. She pulled herself up to her feet as two uniformed officers approached her.

"Out for a walk?" one asked.

"Yes, sir, a long walk."

The second officer hung back, his flashlight pointed just below her chin. The other stepped closer.

"Your hand's bleeding. How'd you hurt yourself?"

She shrugged, pointed to the street. "I fell, I guess."

He nodded. "You been drinking tonight, ma'am?"

"Yes, sir, all damn night."

He looked over to his partner. "May I see some identification?"

Chrys pulled her wallet from her pocket, and after a few preliminaries, found herself in the back seat of the patrol car. An hour later, she was being booked for disorderly conduct and public drunkenness. She knew better than to argue with the police and silently took her orders to be fingerprinted and photographed. When she was led to a phone and told to make her call, she asked if she could have the number to the Hay-Adams, which drew some quizzical looks. Then she placed the call to Carmichael and asked him to connect her to Banks.

In another hour, she'd been released and was sitting in the back seat of the SUV with Banks next to her and Quinn and Smith in the front.

"We've been worried about you all evening," Banks said. "Quinn and Smith have spent the last seven hours looking for you."

"I'm sorry." Chrys glanced at both men, then at Banks. "Don't be mad at them. I gave them the slip. This was my fault."

Banks sighed. "Mrs. Arslan has been frantic. She and Mrs. Bradley had dinner, but then...Well, she's worried about you. You can understand."

"Worried and pissed, I'm sure." She leaned against the window and cradled her wounded hand. What would she say to Reyha, how would she ever be able to make up for this stunt? She glanced over at Banks, at the confident outline of her angled features. She cringed with embarrassment. But it wasn't only Reyha who would be disgusted with her. Once he knew of the charges, the Secretary of State would realize he'd picked the wrong person for this mission. She grunted with disappointment. "I'm sure Secretary Collins won't be looking to me for any future assignments after this. Not that I'd take another."

Banks shrugged. "Actually, I called Gordon. He'll take care of the charges and expunge the event from your record. Secretary Collins won't have to know anything about it."

"Why would Gordon do that for me?"

Quinn looked at her in the review mirror. "Because we got to stick together, that's why."

Smith turned in his seat. "Gordon's a good man. He looks out for a lot of us."

Banks smiled. "I told you, he and I are old friends. In fact, he's going to be best man at my wedding."

"Ah, okay, I get it." At least she'd be able to keep face with the Secretary of State. All that remained was the uphill battle explaining herself to Reyha. And as they drove the rest of the way to the hotel, she wondered what in the hell she'd been thinking by getting that drunk.

It was coming up on eleven thirty by the time she stumbled toward the suite door and tried to pull her room key from her wallet, but her throbbing hand made her clumsy.

"I got it, ma'am," Quinn said, waving his passkey over the sensor. He held the door for her.

She turned to face the three agents, but she was unable to look them in the eyes. "I'm sorry I was so much trouble tonight. Thanks for coming and bailing me out." She glanced up. "Thank Gordon for me, too."

Banks motioned Quinn and Smith away. Chrys looked into her hawklike eyes and looked away again.

"I don't know what happened to you tonight," Banks said, "but if you'd allow me to make an observation."

"That I'm a fuckup?"

"Yes."

Chrys scoffed. "Tell me something I don't know." She turned to enter, then Banks gripped her by the shoulder.

"You're your own worst enemy, Safis, but I think you already know that." She released Chrys's shoulder. "But you don't have to accept it. You can fight it, rise above it."

Chrys shrugged. "I'm not so sure I can anymore."

"That's too bad. Then I guess you're not the woman I thought you were." She marched away, shaking her head.

Chrys recoiled from the rebuff, stepped inside and pulled off her boots, and paused to listen. The suite was quiet. When she reached the living area, only one table lamp was on, and in its light, she could see Reyha waiting on the sofa with her arms and legs crossed. Chrys walked over and stood before her. She wasn't sure how much Reyha knew, but by the expression on her face, she had to know something.

Reyha looked her up and down. Finally, she stood and took a step toward her. "Explain."

Chrys couldn't meet her eyes. "I'm sorry, Reyha, I didn't—"

"I do not want an apology. I want an explanation."

Chrys shifted on her feet; her left knee joint was beginning to ache.

Reyha took another step toward her. "Answer me now."

Chrys took a step backward and held up her hands. "I'm trying. Just let me…" She wobbled and covered her face.

"How much have you had to drink?"

"I don't remember."

Reyha grabbed her arm. "Enough to have you arrested, apparently."

Chrys attempted to pull away. "You don't understand. I let a friend down. I promised to be there for her, and I let her down."

Reyha wrinkled her brow. "Mary?"

"I let her down, too." Chrys stumbled backward and plopped into one of the wide-backed chairs and held her head in her hands. "In group, the woman I told you about, the petty officer—Morrison—she needed me, and I didn't come through." As she spoke, her voice broke on her sobs.

Reyha sat on the corner of the coffee table and brushed Chrys's sweat soaked hair "You saw her today in your group session?"

"She's dead. Woodley said it was an accident, but everyone knows it wasn't." She looked up. "I know it wasn't."

"What do you mean?"

Chrys tried to explain, tried to make coherent words come out of her mouth, but she couldn't. She dissolved into a blubbering mess as she attempted to explain Morrison's confession months ago about wanting to be dead, wanting it to look like an accident.

"All right, all right," Reyha said as she brought Chrys to her shoulder. "Let me get you out of these clothes. You smell of alcohol."

Chrys allowed Reyha to lead her into the bathroom, to unbutton and remove her shirt. Reyha scowled when she saw Chrys's swollen knuckles.

"What have you done to your hand?"

Chrys shrugged. "I think I punched a guy."

Reyha's eyes grew large.

"He grabbed my ass or something…I don't know." Chrys wavered against the counter.

Reyha shook her head and ran a sink full of warm, sudsy water and had Chrys sit on the counter.

"You can get a serious infection with that. Let me look." Reyha examined the swollen knuckles and the deep puncture wounds. "Soak your hand in the warm water. I am going to speak to Commander Banks."

Chrys did as she was told and waited miserably there on the counter. Reyha was taking so long to return, and she wondered what they were talking about, what Banks was telling her.

"She will see about getting you some antibiotics to begin tonight," Reyha said when she returned. "In the morning, I want you to see a doctor."

"But there's a waiting list at the VA. It'll take weeks to get in."

"Then you will go to an urgent care clinic."

"I can't afford out of pocket."

"I will pay for your care." Reyha massaged Chrys's hand and worked the soapy water into the cuts.

Chrys winced. "I'm embarrassed to have you pay. I'm sure with some antibiotics I'll be fine."

"You should not be embarrassed by my generosity." Reyha looked up. "But for losing your temper and acting like a fool and for allowing yourself to become so intoxicated that you became lost on the streets of DC. These are the things for which you should be embarrassed." She patted Chrys's hand dry, then put her hands on either side of Chrys's hips and leaned close. "You have a problem with alcohol, my friend, and anger as well. Problems you must address. Until you do so, I cannot agree to have you work for my foundation."

Chrys scoffed. "You're firing me? I haven't even been officially hired yet."

Reyha continued to trap her there on the counter.

"I'm not an alcoholic," Chrys said.

"Are you sure?"

"I was upset about Morrison. I intentionally set out to get drunk. I had no idea I'd lose my phone and my bearings. And like I told you, some asshole grabbed my ass. What was I supposed to do?"

Reyha didn't move.

"Besides, you drink wine every night."

"Not in excess."

Chrys scoffed again. "Fine, then I won't work for your foundation. I'll find some other type of work in London."

Reyha backed away and folded her arms across her chest. "You will not come with me to London unless you promise you will no longer drink, that you will seek help for your rage."

Chrys slid off the counter. "Are you kidding?"

"I am quite serious."

"Are you saying we're done if I don't stop drinking?"

"Exactly."

Chrys ground her teeth, and like Reyha, folded her arms across her chest. "I'll admit I probably drink to excess at times, maybe fly off the handle when I get pissed off, but fuck it if I don't deserve it. I've been through hell and back, and I have every right to cope the best way I know how."

"You are making excuses."

"Excuses?" Chrys tossed the hand towel into the sink. "And how do you suggest I deal with everything? Read a book? Listen to classical music?" She took a lurching step. "Oh, I know, I'll bore myself silly in some stupid fucking museum. That'll do it! Right." She clapped her hands together and flitted her fingers in a mock wave. "PTSD, bye-bye."

Reyha's eyes turned fiery, and her voice was blistering when she said, "You are being insolent, and I will not tolerate this disrespect from you any longer."

Chrys sputtered and contorted her face. A sudden shock of fury traveled through her, and she lunged forward with fists at her side. "And you're being a holier-than-thou fucking bitch."

Reyha did not give ground, but her eyes grew wider. "Would you strike me as well, now that I have angered you?"

Chrys stumbled backward against the bathroom counter and glanced down at her clenched hands.

"Go on," Reyha yelled, now issuing a challenge. "Hit me if you must."

"Stop it!" Chrys sank to the floor and covered her face. "Just stop." As she hunkered on the floor and sobbed, she could hear Reyha's rapid breathing, feel her shadow on her.

"Is this who you have become?" Reyha's voice was distant and defeated. "A cruel and callous woman who has let the ugliness of the world into her heart to twist her soul?"

Chrys lifted her eyes. "I'm not like that, I didn't mean—"

Reyha held up her hand. "Tell me, what hope do I have that my legacy will continue if I cannot find even one person in this entire world who has not surrendered to her most selfish urges only to wallow in self-pity? All the work I have done, Emin has done, will be for naught." She waved her hand as if to dismiss her and walked out of the bathroom.

Chrys leaned against the cabinet door. She was unable to move, paralyzed by the shock of what she'd done, the brutal language, the aggressive move directed at the woman she admired, worshipped, and most certainly loved. What was she doing to herself and Reyha? Where was her honor, her dignity? Banks was right—she was her own worst enemy.

She hung her head in shame, but something brushed against her skin and the smell of fresh bread swirled around her. She raised her gaze and found her grandmother sitting on the side of the tub.

"There is no dishonor in grief," her grandmother said. "But you cannot let it consume your love of life, to make you into someone cruel."

"Are you real?" Chrys crawled toward her, reached out her hand. To her shock, her grandmother's image was solid. She wrapped her arms around the old woman's frail shoulders and wept. "Give me strength, Yiayia, help me do the right thing."

Her grandmother kissed her head. "You have my strength, Chrysanthi, for you are of my blood." She lifted Chrys's face. "Now hold your head up, reclaim your honor, and bloom."

As her grandmother began to fade, Chrys clutched at the air. "Don't leave me."

"But I am always with you," her grandmother said as she vanished. "Always."

Chrys fell against the side of the tub and reeled with anguish. Eventually, she found the strength to pull herself up and splash her face with water. She glared at her own image in the mirror as she replayed Reyha's condemnation. *A cruel and callous woman.* No, that was not who she was, not who she would become. She would not dishonor herself, her family, or her people. With a renewed sense of determination, she wiped her face with a towel and went to the bedroom where she found Reyha sitting on the end of her bed with her face in her hands, her shoulders shaking.

"I'm sorry," Chrys said as she knelt with difficulty before her. "I've been disrespectful, but worse, my behavior just now was completely unacceptable. I have no excuse for what I've done. None. But I'm begging you to forgive me. Please. Let me show you I'm not that woman."

Reyha lowered her hands and revealed her troubled face.

Chrys went on, "And you're right, I lost control of my drinking and my anger. I let myself get caught up in my grief, my guilt, my self-pity, everything."

Reyha nodded. "I see I have put expectations on you that you have not asked for. It is my fault for putting all my hope in one solution. Perhaps there are others I might turn to. Perhaps I will have time to arrange for other means."

"I don't understand."

Reyha cupped Chrys's chin. "My dear friend, I love you, and I want you to find as much happiness in this world as you may."

"My happiness is to be with you."

Reyha shook her head. "There is little time for us. I think you know this."

"What are you…" Chrys focused intently. "Reyha?"

Reyha leaned forward and rested her forehead against Chrys's. "Weeks ago when I returned for my scan results, they discovered the cancer has moved to my bones."

Chrys's shoulders fell. "No, I won't accept that. You're healthy. Look at you. You're—"

"It is no use to deny the truth."

"How long?" Chrys asked, her voice childlike.

"Six, perhaps as long as eight months."

Chrys seized the side of the bed as the room began to spin. Her renewed determination, her grandmother's infusion of strength vanished. "But the treatment, the new drug, no, you have to be better, you have to keep fighting." She fell prone on the floor and pounded her fist against the carpet, cursed in every language she knew, and howled at the injustice of it all.

Reyha dropped down from the bed and pulled her into her lap where she stroked her back. But Chrys could not be consoled, and she continued to rage.

"You can't stop fighting this," Chrys cried. "You can't give up. I need you, and you need me, your foundation needs me."

"I have made my peace. You must respect that."

Chrys sat up and gripped Reyha's hands. "But you have to keep fighting. There're other treatments, other medicines." She released Reyha's hands and tore at her own hair. "There has to be a way," she cried in a panic, "a way for all of us to get out. No one gets left behind. I won't leave you behind."

"All of us?" Reyha frowned, reached out to steady her. "I am not your friend Diren. That is in the past. You must let go of her. Let her memory be of happier times, not of her death."

Hysterical now, Chrys held her hands together and pleaded, "I can't lose you, too. Don't you see? I can't lose you. I can't do this without you."

Reyha stroked her cheek. "You are strong, Chrysanthi, stronger than any woman I have known."

"No, I'm not, I can't, there's nothing left."

Reyha held her by the shoulders. "Remember your grandmother. Remember all she endured and how she rose above the tragedy and horror she experienced. This is the time to claim your birthright, my love. You have her resilience, her perseverance. Call upon them now."

Chrys crumpled into a heap and buried her face in Reyha's lap and wept. After twenty minutes, she was drained from her ordeal. She pulled herself up and leaned against the bed. Her eyes were swollen from her intense weeping, and her voice was hoarse with wailing. But she was calmer, at least, with a sense of resignation that pressed down on her shoulders.

"You won't pursue any more treatments, not even for me?" she asked with just a hint of hope.

"As I told you, I have made my peace."

Chrys exhaled and acquiesced with a nod. "Then I'll respect that, as hard as it is."

"Thank you."

Chrys looked around the dim room, at the pile of books on the nightstand, the silver cigarette case next to them. "Tell me the truth—you knew you weren't getting better, didn't you? You've known all along."

Reyha nodded.

"But you put yourself through that awful treatment. Why?"

Reyha lifted a shoulder and let it fall. "Even though I did not have much faith in your American doctors and their claims of this new drug halting my cancer, I was willing to try once more, to put myself through the trauma of poisoning my body to save it." She chuckled bitterly. "I had not expected the ordeal to be so brutal, however." She moved some of Chrys's hair from her eyes. "Yet, I had you here with me to care for me. I do not think I have ever felt so loved in all my life." She smiled tenderly and nodded. "I knew I was dying when I came to your country. Yet I needed to find someone to whom I might pass my legacy. I wanted it to be you, Chrysanthi, my beautiful flower."

Chrys wiped her nose. "It can still be me, if you'll let me."

Reyha shook her head. "You have so much pain to work through, and the timing is unfortunate. I cannot ask you to commit to this position when you have not yet dealt with your own issues. I cannot risk the organization's integrity or the success of its mission."

Chrys clasped Reyha's hand. "I'll quit drinking completely. I'll never touch another drop, I promise. I'll go to Alcoholics Anonymous or whatever you want. I'll find someone to talk to about my anger issues. Just let me be with you, work with you, please. I'll do anything you ask. Anything."

"Yes, I know, anything within reason."

"No, I mean *anything*." Chrys released her hand and swallowed a few times. "Please don't push me away."

Reyha hesitated.

"Please," Chrys said again.

"Only if you promise to address your drinking and anger sincerely."

"I give you my word." Chrys took her hand again, held it to her heart.

Reyha studied her face, nodded. "And you also promise you will commit yourself to the success of my foundation, to the women and girls of Syria?"

"I promise."

Reyha bent forward and kissed her cheek. "Then I will put my faith in you to honor your promises to me."

Chrys caught Reyha's face, brought her close. "But you have to promise me something," she said, lips trembling. "I want only one thing in return."

"I will not seek more treatment, I have said."

"No, that's not it."

"Then what is the one thing you wish?" Reyha asked as she gazed into Chrys's eyes.

"That I come back with you to London, but postpone my return to Syria until"—she choked on a sob—"until the end."

Reyha shook her head, tried to pull away. "I would not have you see me in the state I will be in for my last days."

Chrys held her firm. "I won't let you die alone, Reyha. I love you, and I'm going to take advantage of every minute, every second left to us. Please don't deny me this. Please, I'm begging you."

Reyha's eyes went wide with disbelief. "You would hold me as I die?"

"Give me that honor."

Reyha covered her mouth as she sobbed. "But it is you who honor me, my love."

CHAPTER TWENTY

Kayla finished the adjustments on the socket attached to Chrys's leg and said, "Now remember, it's a lot of stored energy. Don't go crazy until you have a feel for it."

Chrys perched on a bench while Kayla adjusted the fitting. "I know. I've read up on it." She was dressed in a T-shirt and running shorts with one running shoe on her right foot. On her left, her running blade swept in a J-shaped curve from the socket. She had her hair pulled back into a braid and a huge smile on her face.

Reyha sat next to her and watched while she rubbed one of Chrys's shoulders. The security detail looked on as well. Christman had joined them, too, and she and Banks stood right behind the bench while Quinn and Smith took up a post by the double doors to the indoor running track Banks had requisitioned for Chrys's first run on her new blade.

Kayla was still kneeling when she finished the last adjustment to the socket. She looked up. "You ready?"

"Yep," Chrys said.

"All right, Safis, show me what you got." Kayla stood and held out her hand.

Chrys smiled at Reyha and gave her a quick kiss on the cheek. "Here goes."

She took Kayla's hand and stood. She bounced a little while standing in place, then she looked down the track. Suddenly, she was self-conscious and felt her cheeks burning. She glanced back at Quinn and Smith, at Banks and Christman, at Kayla, and at Reyha, who seemed to be holding her breath. This was it. She was going to run again. Or trip and fall on her ass, but either way, her dream of having a running blade had come true thanks to Reyha's generosity.

She took a few tentative steps toward the outside lane of the track. She glanced down at her legs, at the blade, closed her eyes a moment, and imagined herself running as she used to do along those back highways, the long stretches of gravel road with the wind in her hair cooling her moist skin, the smell of damp grass and wet ground rising up to greet her. All of it came back to her in an instant; she glanced once more at the others.

Reyha watched with her soft smile, her eyes glinting, her thick hair flowing beneath a cinnamon-red scarf. Chrys could've kissed her right then, the way she looked. But instead she gave a little wave and turned toward the track where she started off at a slow pace, then a few quick steps, and then, once she had her balance, she picked up the pace and began to jog.

She gasped with surprise at the way the blade propelled her forward, and she lengthened her stride. In moments she picked up speed and rounded the first corner, leaning into the curve while her arms pumped and her right leg kicked up behind her and the blade sliced through the air with such grace it felt as if she was floating as she came down the far stretch. She couldn't contain herself any longer and shouted as she broke into a full run.

"I'm running, I'm running," she repeated over and over.

Reyha stood. Quinn and Smith walked over to the others. Banks and Christman both cheered while Kayla nodded.

She rounded the next corner, her eyes fixed directly on the path in front of her while her face twisted into a mixture of laughter and weeping. As she passed her audience, she waved and then picked up even more speed as she made her second lap. The large indoor facility echoed with the rhythmic tapping of her foot and blade. As she slowed on the second curve, angling this time toward the group, the clapping started. First it was Banks, but soon she was joined by the others, even Kayla. They all applauded as she jogged over and bent forward to hold herself by the knees where she wept and panted for air.

"I ran, I really ran." She wheezed on the words.

The clapping came to an end, and Reyha went to her, lifted her by the shoulder.

"You are my champion, and for your bravery, you shall have my favor." Reyha slid her scarf from her head and looped it around Chrys's neck.

Chrys brought one end of the scarf to her face and kissed it. As she did, she caught Reyha's scent, the sweetness of cloves mixed with her distinctive perfume. She pulled Reyha into a hug and clung to her, kissing her hair.

Kayla patted Chrys's shoulder. "Good job, Safis. Damn good job."

Afterward, as they gathered their belongings and Chrys packed her blade into the customized case, she observed the way Banks and the others studied Reyha, particularly Quinn and Smith, who'd never seen her without her head covering. Chrys kissed the end of the scarf once more and fashioned it as a kaffiyeh around her neck, just as she'd worn the colorful scarf Diren had given her, the one that'd been cut from her bleeding body nearly a year ago, abandoned somewhere in the desert.

In the two weeks they had left to them in DC, they continued to do little but spend alone time together. Chrys adjusted her workout schedule so that each morning after breakfast, she would go to the fitness center and train with Quinn and Smith, then come back up to the room and shower with Reyha. On some evenings, they'd go down to a local high school in the area, and Chrys would run the track while Reyha and the security team watched from the sidelines. But most often in the afternoons and evenings, they'd sit together in the living area as Reyha continued to put the finishing touches on her UN statement. She had a great deal of material prepared, and she read and reread sections to Chrys, asking for her input.

One afternoon after they'd eaten lunch, Chrys sat on the sofa and read through a section Reyha had been troubling over.

"You're planning on pissing everyone off, I see," Chrys said chuckling. "You know, I'm not sure it's necessary to mention every single human rights violation of the last four centuries to make your point."

"No? I thought contrasting all the rhetoric about our modern and industrialized societies reaching their peak of humanity to our ongoing brutality would add weight to my argument."

Chrys peeked over the edge of the papers. "No nation wants its sins thrown back into its face. Besides, you're bringing up events that've already been apologized for."

Reyha sipped hot tea as she held Chrys's foot in her lap, rubbing the toes and arch and massaging the calf.

Seeing Reyha wasn't going to give her a response, Chrys asked,

"This speech, tell me, what's its true purpose? Why did the State Department bend over backward to accommodate you?"

Reyha looked affronted. "You do not believe in my statement?"

"Of course I do. The Armenian Genocide was despicable and your government should acknowledge it. But I still don't see what it'll accomplish to have a Turkish woman, without any political power and who lives in exile, provide that confession."

"Emin had political power, my father as well."

"Yes, before the coup."

Reyha bobbed her head back and forth. "But you see, in my country political alliances ebb and flow quite frequently. The members of parliament move toward theocracy and our military leaders pull them back toward the center. Left leaning groups come to power and conservative forces denounce them and regain control. And so forth."

"I'm familiar with your country's political culture." Chrys sighed, pulled her foot away, and sat up, crossing her good leg under her so she could face Reyha directly. "But again I ask you, what is it you want to accomplish with this statement? Only a third of it is a plea for more funding for refugee encampments and aid to women and girls. The rest is just one big reprimand for all the terrible things each member nation has done to its people."

"In particular to women and girls." Reyha pointed to the papers.

"Yes, I know, but see, that's getting lost in your history lesson. I don't know why going all the way back to the fifteenth century is necessary. Staying focused on the events leading up to World War I and those that occurred after are really where you need to put your emphasis."

Reyha tilted her head. "You do not see the thread, do you?"

"What thread?"

Reyha sipped the last of her tea, set the cup aside, and stood. She began to pace as she talked, gesturing with her hands as she always did. But there was a slight limp to her step.

"Even prior to the spread of Christianity," Reyha began, "women and girls were persecuted for being female. There is no doubt of this. Our potential to produce offspring became a coveted power to men who saw offspring as property, just as they did their wives. More sons, more hands to work the land, more wealth. And of course, our unpaid labor factored into it and made our oppression necessary for men to accumulate even more wealth. But it was not always so."

"Really? Don't tell me you believe in some golden age of equality between the sexes." Chrys smiled as she watched Reyha, always fascinated by the depth of her knowledge.

"I do, in fact. Do you know, as little as five thousand years ago, there is evidence that before societies became largely agricultural, there was a balance within communities where a woman's reproductive powers were worshipped, and her wisdom after her child-birthing years was honored."

"And where was this? Some fantasyland in one of your novels?"

Reyha stopped her pacing. "As I told you, I was born and lived my childhood in Konya."

"I've passed through there. It's a beautiful city."

"And are you familiar with the Neolithic site called Çatalhöyük, which overlooks the plains of Konya and where archeologists have been investigating for decades?"

Chrys shook her head. "Never heard of it, but I know the Konya plains. They're beautiful as well."

"Ah, then let me tell you." Reyha's eyes flashed with enthusiasm. "You see, experts claim this site is one of the world's earliest settlements, and there is evidence of men and women living more or less in an egalitarian society. In fact, one of the most ancient artifacts found there depicts a goddess upon a throne with two great cats around her. And along with a number of other female images, it is suggested early people aligned themselves within matriarchal societies."

Chrys tapped the papers. "You're not going back that far, are you? You've already brought up the slaughter of women in the fifteenth century. I think you're going to lose the audience at this point."

"I do not need to bring up the seated goddess. What I need to do is to establish that once man's false religions, which promoted a warlike God to power, became the dominant political structure of the modern state, women and girls have been systematically brutalized."

Chrys narrowed her eyes. "So now you're planning on attacking religion?"

"In a manner of speaking."

"All of them or Islam in particular?"

"All of them. They are all oppressive."

Chrys whistled through her teeth. "Like I said, you're going to piss everyone off."

Reyha put her hand on Chrys's knee. "There are only three articles in the Declaration of Human Rights which mention religion. They indicate one should have the right to practice or change one's religion as well as the right to not be persecuted for one's beliefs. However, religion itself is not a right. There is nothing natural in its essence. It is merely another man-made system of oppression."

"And how is attacking the world's religions going to promote the welfare of women and girls in Syria?"

"Because at the root of our oppression is man's religion. It is used to justify our subordination and persecution." Reyha tapped the papers once more. "Beginning in the fifteenth century, it is estimated sixty thousand people, perhaps as many as one hundred thousand, were tortured and killed, most of whom were women and girls. They were not killed because of their race or class. They were killed because they were female, and they dared to refuse the false gods of war and greed, to be viewed as less than human, to be the property of men. It was the first true genocide carried out by state governments." She tapped the papers again with an accusatory finger. "Every single modern state has its origins in the Burning Times. Rulers and government officials broke our great-grandmothers, and the persecution continues even today under sharia law, tribal custom, and even your own country's obsession with a woman's reproductive rights."

Chrys held Reyha's hand and kissed the back of it. "Like I said, you're going to piss off a whole lot of people." When she saw Reyha glower at her, she added, "And did I mention you're beautiful when you get fired up like this?"

"I somehow doubt my beauty will do much to alleviate the irrational anger those present at the UN will feel, particularly the men." Reyha made a mock face of anger and added, "How dare that woman speak up on behalf of the pitiful female sex." She shook her fist in faux rage before falling forward and pushing Chrys back on the sofa, where she climbed on top of her and began to kiss her, effectively ending any further discussion on the matter for the rest of the day.

❖

The morning they packed and departed from the Hay-Adams was emotional for Chrys. She could tell it was for Reyha, too. After Quinn and Smith had taken their bags down to the SUV, she and Reyha stood in the living area together and took in the room.

"I'm going to miss our little home," Chrys said. "I'll miss sitting out on the balcony with you while you smoke and sitting here on the sofa while you read to me."

Reyha hugged her around the middle. "And I will miss sleeping with you in the king-sized bed and bathing together in the sunken tub."

"Banks told me last night that Gordon has reserved rooms at the Baccarat Hotel. We should have big beds and tubs there, too." Chrys raised her eyebrows. "You know that's one of the more expensive hotels in New York City?"

"I am aware," Reyha said. She put her forehead against Chrys's. "Only the best for you, my love. But I did request for Commander Banks to call and arrange a suite with a king- sized bed."

"You're not even trying to keep us a secret any longer, are you."

Reyha shrugged. "I have no need to. There are no consequences for my honesty." She kissed Chrys's nose and turned away, picking up her purse and draping her headscarf about her. "Shall we? I wish to give my thanks to the staff before we depart."

As they left, Chrys glanced back once more at the interior of the suite and remembered how months ago she'd left her apartment in Huntington in much the same way, knowing she'd never return.

Downstairs, the staff who'd served for the duration of Reyha's stay were lined up waiting to say good-bye. She went down the line like a queen inspecting her servants while taking each person's hand and thanking him or her. Chrys trailed along thanking the staff as well. She was impressed to witness Reyha had learned each individual's name, even down to the dishwasher's. When she came to Carmichael, Reyha took him by the shoulders and planted a kiss on each cheek.

"Mr. Carmichael, you have been a gracious and kind host. I will forever be in your debt for making me feel welcome in your country."

"Mrs. Arslan, dear lady," he said, clearly emotional. "You are a bright star in the heavens. It has been my honor to be your servant." He bowed his head and clicked his heels.

He turned to Chrys. "Ms. Safis, it has been my pleasure providing for you. Please, anytime you wish to retreat from the troubles of life, return here to the Hay-Adams. I will always have a room for you."

Chrys thanked him, but knew she could never do so. Without Reyha, the place would no longer have any meaning for her.

Once they were secured inside the vehicle, they were driven in a caravan to the airport, where a private jet waited to take them to

New York. Chrys was impressed that the size of the security detail had grown, just as Banks had promised after the confrontation with Usak over a month ago. Once at the airport, she saw agent after agent pile out of the other SUVs. Then the troop made way their way to a private security checkpoint, through a private gate, and finally onto the waiting jet. Chrys could tell from Banks's expression that she was being hypervigilant as she barked orders often into her radio.

Once they were on their way for the short flight, Chrys cuddled next to Reyha and rested her head on her shoulder. "I'll miss DC. I thought I'd never say that, but I'm going to miss it, especially being there with you."

"You will have the memories," Reyha said.

"I know." Chrys swallowed. After a long pause, she said, "Gordon got us some tickets for the musical *Wicked* just like you wanted. It should be a lot of fun."

"With you it will be quite enjoyable." Reyha kissed the top of Chrys's head.

"He also got us reservations at Aureole for dinner. He even managed to get the private dining room. Pretty fancy stuff, I'd say."

Reyha lifted Chrys's chin and looked into her eyes. "He feels the need to give me the best your cities have to offer, yet he does not know I already have all I need and desire." She ran her thumb along Chrys's bottom lip. "I would be more than happy to have only bread and water as long as I had them with you."

A swell of tears pressed against Chrys's eyes, and she blinked them back and glanced past Reyha to where some of the security detail sat. None were watching, but she was sure by now they were all aware of what was going on between them. So without embarrassment, she lifted her mouth to Reyha's and kissed her.

"I want to make sure you get to see what you want while in the city," Chrys said, "but I also want to be alone with you as much as possible."

Reyha nodded. "I want that as well. We have only one business matter to attend to."

"Your UN statement, I know."

"No, previous to that," Reyha said. "Last week while you were doing your morning exercises, I called my solicitor in London. She will be flying in tomorrow night, and we will be meeting with her so that she may arrange my assets to be transferred into your name. She will also establish a trust from which you will draw your salary. It is important I make sure all my property and financial holdings are under your name."

Chrys pulled away and looked out the small window at the thin clouds whizzing by.

"What's wrong?" Reyha asked.

Chrys turned to Reyha. "Can't that wait until we return to London? Is there a reason we need to do that this week?"

Reyha looked past her and watched out the window. Finally, she smiled and patted Chrys's thigh. "Do you believe in a sixth sense? Premonitions?"

"What do you mean?"

Reyha smiled again, and this time it was laced with sadness. "I am not afraid of dying. You need to know this. But with Usak and the other individual, that Jabali, I feel an impending doom about me, one I cannot shake."

Chrys glanced over to Banks who was reading something off her tablet. Then she looked back at Reyha. "I won't let anyone harm you."

Reyha touched her cheek. "And neither would I let anyone harm you."

❖

In the grand Baccarat Suite, they stood together and gazed out the floor-to-ceiling windows down on the massive city below.

"It is wonderful," Reyha said. "Simply wonderful." She turned from the window and tried the bed, sat down and bounced a little. "Very nice."

Chrys joined her and fell back to look up at the rich wooden ceiling. "This is something. Who knew a girl from Nebraska could ever end up in a place like this?"

Reyha lay back as well and turned her face to look at her. "I know you prefer the countryside, the open sky of the desert, the mountains and grasslands. But you must confess—this is an elegant accommodation."

"I do like the outdoors, particularly the desert."

Reyha stroked Chrys's chin. "Why do you suddenly look so sad?"

"Because I want to be in the desert with you."

"I must return to London and get my other affairs in order." Reyha rolled closer. "If there is time and I am able, however, perhaps I will return with you to Syria for a short while, to the encampment outside of Kasan."

"That's where I'll begin?"

"Yes. It has not been named yet, but there is a group of Kurdish women along with some Yazidi currently living there. They have elected a commander, a woman named Nasiba who I have only written to. She is looking forward to having someone help her coordinate with other NGOs. You will need to procure civil engineers first off, women if you can. Margaret will provide you with the roster of contacts." Reyha brushed Chrys's face with her fingertips. "You will have many tasks to accomplish. So much to keep you busy. It will help you work through your grief."

Overcome, Chrys moved closer to Reyha's shoulder. "I don't want to talk about it. I can't even think about it."

Reyha ruffled her hair. "I do not have words that will soothe you, my love. There are no words which might ease the grief in your heart. I am sorry." She began to sing the Turkish lullaby she'd once offered, and while she did, she rocked Chrys in her arms and continued to stroke her hair and shoulders. Once Chrys had stopped crying, Reyha rose up on her elbow. "I want you to do something for me."

Chrys wiped her nose. "Okay."

"After I have gone and before you leave for Syria, I want you to go see Mary."

Chrys shook her head. "She doesn't want to see me."

"You love her, and I cannot imagine she does not love you."

Chrys shook her head again. "She's not going to want to see me—I'm telling you. And she's probably already dating again and moved on. I'm not going to be an ass and disrupt her life all over again."

"No, you misunderstand me." Reyha shifted to a sitting position. "I do not expect that the two of you will resume your romantic relationship, but I do think you will need a friend, someone who knows you, someone you can trust." She took Chrys's hand. "You cannot return to the past and reclaim what the two of you were before, but you can salvage your friendship, find support and love all the same."

"I don't know. I'm not sure she'd even agree to see me. She wouldn't even let me know when she reached her mom's place, told me I didn't get that privilege any longer."

Reyha squeezed her hand. "Please, will you at least try? I want to know you will have someone there for you."

Chrys looked upward and stared once more at the paneled ceiling. "How about I promise to write her a letter at least, to give her the opportunity to make the decision how much she wants me back in her life." She turned her head. "Will you be okay with that?"

Reyha bent and kissed her. "That is a start, yes."

CHAPTER TWENTY-ONE

The next evening over dinner in their suite, Reyha introduced Chrys to Patricia, her lawyer from London. Chrys could tell by the way the two interacted they were close. At one point, Patricia fought back tears as she and Reyha discussed the details of the cremation. Reyha wanted to have her ashes scattered over the plains of Konya near the archeological site of Çatalhöyük.

"Chrysanthi will see to it," Reyha said, putting her hand on Chrys's leg as they all three sat together in the living area. "She will be returning to the Middle East shortly after my death."

Chrys sat through the entire interaction feeling numb all over. Her gaze kept falling on Patricia's gentle eyes. The way Patricia looked back at her indicated a silent understanding of how difficult this all was. It was then it occurred to Chrys there were other people who knew Reyha, who loved her, and who would miss her as well. She wondered just how many there were. This lawyer, Margaret Bradley, her friends in London, her students back in Istanbul, her neighbors, the postman? Who else had been touched by Reyha and would feel the stab of sadness at the empty space her death would leave in their lives?

At the door, the two old friends said their good-byes.

"I will have these arrangements in place quite soon," Patricia said. "With your signatures this evening, I will process it all and have it filed and stamped by the time you return."

"And if by chance I do not see you again, know that I have cherished your friendship and good counsel," Reyha said.

"But I shall see you in London once you return next week," Patricia said. "We must have our afternoon cuppa together. I have missed that so."

"Of course. Next week."

Chrys watched this exchange, watched them hug once more. It seemed Reyha was truly saying good-bye to her friend for the last time.

When she'd shut the door, Reyha faced Chrys. "I know that was a difficult discussion, but one we had to have."

"I don't want to spread your ashes. I want to keep them."

Reyha pulled Chrys into her arms. "No, take them to Çatalhöyük. Let my remains be among my ancestors and the great seated goddess."

"But I could keep them in a—"

"You will not build a shrine to me." Reyha touched Chrys's chest. "I am enshrined here, in your heart. That is all I wish."

Chrys began to protest once more, but Reyha put her finger to her lips and stopped her.

"No more. If you need a tangible reminder of me, then plant flowers, lots of beautiful flowers wherever you go. Brighten the world around you and think of me."

"Yellow roses?" Chrys asked, trying not to cry.

"And daisies, my love. Let the two always grow together."

The next few days could have been filled with touristy activities. Gordon had arranged private tours of the Statue of Liberty and the Empire State Building, but Reyha told Chrys she was tired and her hip hurt too much for so much walking. She asked instead that they take tours about the city in the SUV. There was a lot of traffic, and often it was difficult to see much, but Reyha sat contented in the back seat while Chrys narrated various points of interest.

They did have their night out on the town, however. They first took an early dinner at the famous Aureole restaurant in the private Halo dining room. The food was some of the best they'd had together, and Reyha seemed to have quite the appetite, even enjoying a dessert at the end. Afterward, they were escorted to a performance of *Wicked*. Reyha appeared thoroughly delighted with the musical and afterward discussed the significance of Baum's *Wizard of Oz* allegory.

"Dorothy is the first example of a female protagonist in American literature," Reyha said as they were driven back to the Baccarat. "Do you know, many tried to ban the book for that very reason?"

"That hardly seems like a good reason," Chrys said.

Reyha shrugged. "Well, there were other reasons, of course. Baum had been critical of the bankers and of the gold standard. He had seen the devastation to the common worker when the silver exchange rate was decimated. But alas, as it was then, so it is now, bankers are the true power in the world. They fund nations and armies, play the world as if it was a giant chessboard, and all of the people their pawns. If you look carefully and follow the money, as you Americans say, you will find a cabal of bankers behind every single war in human history."

"I thought you believed religion was the great evil."

"It is."

"So what's with the banker conspiracy theory?" Chrys grinned at Reyha's expression.

"It is no theory. It is reality."

Chrys laughed. "Please tell me you aren't planning on also attacking international bankers in your speech. I think you're going to make enough heads explode as it is."

Reyha wasn't laughing. "I know my statement will not be well accepted. I expect to be ridiculed in every nation's press."

Chrys took Reyha's hand. "But I'll be there. Right there, standing shoulder to shoulder with you."

"And when I am gone, will you continue to stand for me?"

"Always," Chrys said, swallowing back her tears.

Right then Banks yanked up her phone. Her tone brought Chrys out of her sadness and put her on alert. Once Banks disconnected, Chrys leaned forward.

"What now?"

Banks looked like she was about to explode. Her usual stoic expression was replaced with obvious alarm. In a surprisingly calm voice she said, "I've just been informed a large group of protestors has gathered across the street from the hotel," Banks said.

"Protestors?" Reyha asked. "For me?"

"I'm afraid so. From what our men on the ground can tell, it's an amalgamation of Turkish Americans along with some recent immigrants. There's a counterprotest under way as well. Armenian Americans and a few leftist groups with antiwar types mixed in. Police have set up barricades to keep them separated and prevent confrontations."

Chrys glanced at her phone. "It's after midnight. Do they plan on staying out there until morning?"

"That would be my guess," Banks said. She shook her head while she and Quinn exchanged worried looks. "There's something more."

Chrys grew rigid. "More?" She felt Reyha stiffen, and she pulled her close. "What more?"

"Our patrols, our dogs. They went on point this evening while we were at the theater. They've picked up on something, some scent in the parking garage, but so far nothing conclusive has been found."

"Explosives?" Reyha asked.

Chrys gripped her tighter.

"Like I said, nothing conclusive. But…" Banks cleared her throat. "We'll disembark outside the hotel on the street for now until we can determine what's setting the dogs off."

"On the street? Where the protestors are? Really?" Chrys tried to suppress her growl.

Banks held her gaze. "In my judgment, it's the best action."

"You got surveillance on the area? People watching the tops of buildings and parked cars?"

"Yes, and the State Department is on alert. So far the protestors are mostly civil and peaceful, and officers are on the ground monitoring the situation closely."

Chrys kicked at the floorboard. "Fuck."

"Shh." Reyha soothed Chrys along her shoulders even though her own hands had begun to quiver.

The SUV slowed as uniformed officers directed traffic and others worked to maintain order among the protestors. Chrys could see a swell of people, mostly men, massed along the sidewalk across the street from the entrance to the Baccarat. They held up banners and signs and shouted as they pumped their fists in the air. A smaller group of mostly women, some young college students, and a mix of older people, was being corralled on the sidewalk between the hotel and the Brazilian steakhouse next door. Chrys peered through the window and watched the more aggressive protestors across the street.

"Death to apostates," she read. She sat back. "Fucking assholes."

"But look here." Reyha directed Chrys's attention to the peaceful group. "Never forget. We deserve recognition. Honor our people."

"Yeah, well, I'm not worried about that group." Chrys pointed to another sign, this one in Turkish. "Traitors must die." She growled. "Idiots."

Officers directed the caravan of SUVs to the front of the hotel. The chanting picked up volume, and Chrys cringed with the insults being hurled at them, some in English, others in Turkish. She held Reyha's hand tighter and tighter. Once the SUVs came to a stop, Banks radioed to have the security team assemble. Once they were in place, she opened the door.

Reyha stepped out and was hurried through the glass entry doors, cocooned among Banks, Quinn, and Smith. Two other agents flanked Chrys. But she panicked that she'd been momentarily separated from Reyha. Once inside the hotel, the team hurried them toward the elevators. That's where Chrys pushed herself closer to Reyha, took her hand again, and gave her a reassuring smile.

"You good?" Chrys asked.

"I am well," Reyha said, but her flushed face and wide eyes betrayed her distress.

❖

That night Chrys couldn't sleep. She tossed around and stared up at the ceiling while Reyha slept against her. Finally, after two hours of this, she got out of bed and reattached her leg, pulled on sweats and a T-shirt, and tiptoed out of the room. When she exited to the hallway, one of the two agents on guard greeted her.

"Can I do something for you, ma'am?" he asked.

"I need to speak with Banks."

He spoke into his radio, then pointed the way. Down the hallway and into a smaller two-bedroom suite, she found agents monitoring computers, talking on their phones.

Banks looked up from her laptop. "What is it, Ms. Safis?"

"Can we talk?"

Banks motioned her outside the room, and they took the elevator to another floor. Once they stepped off, Banks pulled her into a conference room and shut the door.

"What is it?"

Chrys looked her over, noticed her taut mouth, pale skin. She was haggard, sweaty, and for a moment, she pitied her. "Any leads on how those protestors discovered she's here?"

"We're still working on it."

"And the dogs? They find anything in the parking garage?"

"No."

Chrys exhaled. "There's something you're keeping from me."

Banks looked away.

"Is it Usak? Tell me you at least have eyes on him."

Banks rubbed her face. "Our intelligence indicates he's still in DC."

"And nothing more on Jabali?"

"No, I'm sorry. We haven't picked up his trail. No one has."

Chrys moved closer and lowered her voice. "You have any idea where these breaches are coming from?"

Banks shook her head.

"Could it be"—Chrys stopped, considered her words carefully—"someone in our own agencies? CIA, NSA?"

Banks's face hardened. "What are you suggesting?"

"Come on, you're not an idiot and neither am I. Turkey's our biggest ally in that region, and no matter all the hand-wringing the international community does about their past atrocities, there are people in our own government invested both politically and financially in keeping that government appeased. Tell me I'm wrong."

Banks turned away. "If you have any reason to suspect collusion between the State Department and one of our security agencies, I'm afraid I'm not the person to speak to."

"I'm not suggesting Collins himself intentionally put Reyha in danger," Chrys said. "I'm not accusing him of anything. All I'm asking you is if you think it's possible the breach came from there. Think about it. It makes sense. Jabali was on her within a week taking her picture and later trying to get a room at the hotel. Usak and his goons show up not long after. And the Library of Congress, how'd he know she'd be there? You didn't even book that tour until that morning. And now"—she pointed randomly toward one of the walls—"those protestors out there?"

Banks turned. "Are you suggesting it came from someone on my team?"

"Or the hotel staff at the Hay-Adams, maybe here."

"The staff has been vetted, the guests, too."

"Then who?" Chrys took a step closer. "Barbara, listen, you and I have butted heads practically from the first day. Most of that's on me, and I'm sorry. I've questioned your competence, and that was wrong of me. I can tell you care about her. I can tell you're a decent person. But please, if you suspect anyone, have any suspicions at all, you need to tell me."

Banks flexed her jaw. "I trust my people. Every one of them." She shook her head and fumed. "And I trust Collins and Gordon. But I can tell you, it isn't just people in our government who'll side with Turkey no matter what. The Russians are pretty damn friendly with them, too."

Chrys scoffed. "The Russians? What kind of red herring shit is that?"

Without warning, Banks grabbed Chrys by the collar of her T-shirt. "Listen to me. I was in the room, remember? Back by the door. I was there. I know who Collins brought in on this. I got briefed on every detail."

Chrys wrenched out of Banks's hold. "What the hell is wrong with you?"

But Banks ignored her questions and continued, "And I told him he needed to reconsider which senators to trust. I warned him. And let me tell you, since all this shit has come down, he's gotten his eyes opened."

Chrys ran that morning through her head, but the memory was jumbled. She'd been on edge, free-falling from drugs and alcohol, and hallucinating. But then…

"Zobava?" she asked.

Banks glared at her.

"Are you kidding me? He's head of the Senate Committee on Foreign Relations, he got the votes to help supply the Kurds. Why would he…" She slumped against the wall. "Oh, shit, it's just like Reyha said. They play the world like a giant chessboard."

"That's right, and there are bigger players in all this than you and I, hidden agendas and conspiracies we can't even fathom." Banks brought her face close and whispered, "My advice? Get her through this and then the two of you disappear somewhere until it all blows over. Collins will help. I will, too. But don't keep digging. If you try to connect the dots, you'll see too much." She stepped back. "And trust me, for all the horrible things you witnessed in Iraq and Syria, once you realize who's supporting it all, you'll just want to give up and throw in the towel because there's no way to defeat them." She shook her head. "And I'll tell you, giving up isn't an option because living without hope is not living at all. I think you know what I mean."

Chrys nodded. "The world's a shit hole."

"It is."

"But you keep fighting and planting your flowers, right?"

"Flowers?" Banks cocked her head.

"Sorry I came by so late," Chrys said. "More sorry you confirmed my fears. But like you said, I'll get her through this and we'll disappear for a while." She looked down at her hands. "For as long as we have, anyway."

❖

The next day they spent in the suite and ordered room service for breakfast and lunch. In the late afternoon, Banks brought up one of Chrys's suits from the laundry where it'd been cleaned and pressed. Reyha set out one of her finest gowns along with expensive pieces of jewelry and a silken headscarf.

"I still have the scarf you gave me," Chrys said, watching from the bed as Reyha laid out her outfit.

"And you shall keep it. It is yours."

"It has your scent. The clove cigarettes."

Reyha turned from the closet. "Then you shall wear it and remember me always."

"I'll remember you always no matter what."

Reyha walked to the bed and sat down. She put her arm around Chrys and kissed her cheek. "Let us run through my speech together, then order a fine dinner, have a soothing bath, and then retire to bed."

"I hope I don't mess up and embarrass you tomorrow."

"I do not believe that possible."

"What happens if people start shouting? I've seen videos of that. Someone starts saying something objectionable and the delegates start shouting and throwing off their headsets and storming out of the hall."

"Let them. The important thing is we say all we need to say."

"Should be interesting." She debated whether to tell Reyha about Banks's suspicions concerning Zobava, but figured it wouldn't stop her from her commitment to give the speech anyway. "Well, come on, let's give it a run-through."

Reyha held her back. "Promise me that no matter what happens, this statement will be given. You must promise."

"Of course it will. We're on the docket for ten o'clock in the morning." Chrys pulled Reyha along. "Now come on. I'm hungry for dinner, so let's get this done so I can eat and have my dessert."

Reyha giggled. "I believe I indicated a bath in there somewhere."

"You're my dessert either way," Chrys said, forcing a chuckle to mask her sadness.

And just as Reyha had asked, they ran through the entire statement in an hour, had a wonderful dinner served in their room, then played together in the large tub where they washed each other's hair and teased one another endlessly. By the time they fell into bed, they were both so aroused that their lovemaking took on a feverish pace, almost aggressive in nature. After two hours of taking each other from every angle and position they could manage, they slowed their pace and lay together with their damp skin sticking to each other and their limbs intertwined. Reyha lay on top, angled to her side, and stroked Chrys's body as she gazed into her eyes.

"You know I love you deeply."

"And I love you," Chrys said.

"You have given me a gift like no other, the gift of your heart and soul."

Chrys grinned. "You mean my old soul?"

Reyha smiled as well. "You know, I cannot help but feel you and I have been together in the past, and may find ourselves together in some distant future."

Chrys touched Reyha's lips. "If we do get recycled, promise me you'll find me again."

"I will find you again." Reyha kissed her eyes. "Or you shall find me."

Overcome with grief, Chrys cried out and wrapped her arms around Reyha's neck. "I don't know how to do this. I'm trying to be strong, but my heart is breaking into pieces."

Reyha held her, rocked her gently. "But as I told you, heartbreak is inevitable. Yet I know you will find the strength. You have the soul of your people, of your grandmother. You will be strong for me, for the women and girls who will depend upon you."

Chrys shook her head as tears flooded down her cheeks. "I don't know if I can."

Reyha took Chrys's face in her hands. "Now listen to me," she began, her voice firm, yet tender all the same. "You will find the strength to live. You will find joy and love where you can."

Chrys shook her head again.

Still, Reyha continued, "Do not despair, my love, when life is cruel. And when your heart is breaking, look for me in the flowers that grow in the darkest of places. Feel me with you when rain thunders across the horizon, and lift your eyes to the heavy clouds to let that rain fall upon your beautiful face. You will know then I am with you. I will always be with you, for in every drop that touches your skin, you will feel my tears mingle with yours."

She pressed her forehead to Chrys's, and her tears fell.

❖

Chrys tried to eat breakfast, but she was too nervous to get more than a piece of toast down along with a few cups of coffee. Reyha, however, ate heartily and chatted on about what they might do together once their appearance at the UN was completed.

"But I think we should lie low for a while," Chrys said.

"Nonsense, I wish to see more of New York. Perhaps even take a plane to your home state of Nebraska. I would very much like to see your family's bakery, meet your brother, and see your childhood home."

"Sure, we could do that. But just so you know, Giorgos is super opinionated, very conservative. He and I don't really talk much anymore."

"I see. Well then, perhaps the two of you will be able to reconnect."

"Or have a big fight like usual." Chrys rubbed her temple, remembering their past arguments. "But sure, I guess I could see him. It's been a long time. Maybe he's mellowed out." She wondered then if Banks had meant what she'd said, if she'd help her and Reyha, maybe even provide ongoing security in some remote part of Nebraska until the impact of Reyha's statement had subsided.

After breakfast, they showered together and dressed for the day's occasion. Chrys stood for a long time in front of a full-length mirror, trying to decide if she should wear a white or beige shirt with her suit. Reyha was already dressed in a yellow tunic, undergirded with dark brown layers. Her headscarf matched the russet colors of the bottom layers, and it brought out the warmth of her hair and eyes.

"Wear the scarf I gave you," Reyha said, coming up to the mirror, "and the beige shirt."

Chrys pulled on the shirt and tucked it into her trousers. After pulling on her jacket, she put the scarf around her neck and threaded it under the lapel. The coarse linen material added depth to the dark suit. She looked at Reyha's reflection, pulled her over, and linked her arm through hers.

"We make a fine pair, don't you think?"

"Yes, a very fine couple," Reyha said.

They shared a kiss just inside the entry door then exited to be greeted by the team.

Banks held a protective vest in her hands and looked more rattled than ever. "Ma'am, will you please secure this on your body?"

Reyha stepped back. "I will do no such thing."

"Please, ma'am, it's for your own protection. You can remove it once we're safely inside the vehicle."

Chrys tugged on her arm. "Maybe it's a good idea."

"I will go with my head held high," Reyha said. "I will not cower. Now come." She took Chrys's arm. "Let us do what we came to accomplish."

When they reached the ground floor, a wall of dark-suited agents waited. Chrys held Reyha's arm and watched out the glass doors as some of the banners wavered with a pulsing wind that managed to eddy up from the East River through the barricade of skyscrapers.

Banks paused, turned, and considered both Reyha and Chrys. "Stay close to me, ma'am. And please, no loitering. Right into the vehicle."

They approached the glass entry. Reyha craned her neck. "There are good people out there. You saw them."

"No time for autographs," Chrys said.

Reyha smiled. "It is such a sunny day, so pleasant. I would like to greet them."

Banks reached out her hand. "Please, ma'am, right to the vehicle."

Reyha adjusted her scarf. "My hip is giving me so much trouble. I will need your arm, Commander." She disengaged from Chrys and took Banks's arm.

"Reyha?" Chrys reached for her.

Reyha turned. "I love you, Chrysanthi."

Chrys tried to protest, to take hold of her, but she was blocked by two agents. "And I love you," she said through the wall of black suits.

The doors opened, and Reyha held her scarf with one hand as the wind kept catching it while her other hand remained hooked through Banks's arm.

The roar of the mob assaulted them just as they stepped on the sidewalk. Right then a commotion rose up as the men across the street broke through the barriers and stampeded toward them. Car horns and police sirens shrieked and a woman's voice, carried on the wind, called out in Armenian.

"Ma'am, please," Banks said with urgency, pulling her along roughly.

But Reyha halted, disconnected from Banks, and turned to wave back at the supportive group which had by now inched its way along the sidewalk closer to the hotel entrance despite the police attempting to push them back. Suddenly, the discordant sounds exploded into rapid gunfire. Reyha turned and lowered her arms, allowing her headscarf to float up and away. Chrys dove to block her as blood sprayed her face from the shot Quinn took to his arm. Glass from the SUV's windows showered down on them. Banks leapt to protect Reyha, but collapsed as her leg exploded with a hit. Chrys pushed Reyha back while glancing over her shoulder to the woman who'd called out, only to see her on the ground taking cover while Jabali stood over her aiming a short scoped rifle right at her. His beard had been shaved, but there was no mistaking his evil grin. Chrys opened her body, spread her arms to make the biggest target she could and flung herself in front of Reyha just as Banks threw herself in the fray once more.

In a sickening dance, Reyha ducked Banks's outstretched arms and bear-hugged her at the same time while turning her own body and exposing her back to Jabali's aim. Blood sprayed outward and jerked Reyha's shoulders backward. Chrys screamed as she was shoved from behind by Quinn who dove against them, pushing all three into the back seat. In moments, the SUV jerked and jolted about as Smith yanked at the wheel. Banks, collapsed on the floorboard, screamed commands into her radio and held her bleeding leg with one hand while she clung to the seat with the other. Quinn doubled over in the front seat, yelling into his phone as blood oozed over the sleeve of his jacket.

Chrys pulled Reyha up into her arms, cradled her as her legs draped across the seat. "I'm here," she said, heaving for air. "I'm here. You're in my arms. I'm here."

Reyha looked up and a soft smile spread across her face just as the black stain of blood grew beneath her yellow tunic. She lifted her hand, touched Chrys's face, then dropped it. Her eyes stayed fixed as she whispered, "My love."

Chrys gazed down into Reyha's eyes as they went still. She cupped her face, shut her eyes, and kissed her forehead.

"What the fuck," Banks screamed. "Why did she do that? I should've taken that bullet. What the goddamn!"

Chrys looked up into Banks's terrified face. She felt no anger, no need to blame, for she understood what Reyha had done. "She was dying. She couldn't let you give your life for hers. She just couldn't."

Banks shook her head. "No, goddamn it, no." She clasped Chrys's hand, one of Reyha's and buried her face in the yellow tunic and sobbed. "I'm sorry, Chrys. I'm so sorry. I fucked up. Goddamn it, I fucked up."

Smith watched in the rearview mirror, his eyes damp.

Quinn glanced back, his face drawn with pain. "Subject has been eliminated," he said, panting each word. "NYPD took the shot. We have three agents injured, including myself and you, Commander." His gaze fell on Reyha, and his face dissolved into sorrow.

Chrys looked down at Reyha's serene face, pulled her head to her chest, and gave herself over to weeping, cries that came from her depths.

CHAPTER TWENTY-TWO

Outside Kasan, Syria

Along the horizon, fat rain clouds gathered in the late afternoon sky. The air held the promise of a downpour. Chrys bolted up a low hill and shifted the weight of her rifle. She stopped at the top and caught her breath as she looked out across the desert mountains and down onto the activity in the camp below. The children would be done with their lessons soon, and before long, their laughter and chiming voices would swell around her as they played outside before the dinner hour. She checked her watch and looked northward. The airplane bringing the new medical team was due anytime. She bent down and adjusted a setting on the socket of her blade. Her daily jog around the outskirts of camp each afternoon often caused minor alignment issues, but that was to be expected running in the country and along rocky paths.

She turned to make her descent, but stopped when she heard the far distant hum of an aircraft approaching. She shaded her eyes with her hands and saw the plane approaching the airstrip, which was situated on the other side of camp. As she began down the hill and toward the access road, she pulled the end of the cinnamon-red scarf she wore to her face and wiped away sweat. She continued to jog along, keeping her eyes on the plane as it moved lower in the sky. Soon the southern gate came within view, where four women held guard with their weapons about them and their dark hair pulled back into long braids. They greeted her with smiles and comments about her crazy need to go out running each day in full gear.

Behar, one of the guards, said in Kurdish, "It will rain before nightfall."

"Let's hope so," Chrys replied in the same language.

She continued past the gate. By now she couldn't see the plane in the sky and knew it had probably landed and was taxiing to a stop. But she couldn't run any quicker, for the children had been released from the one-room schoolhouse that had been completed just a month ago. And as they always did when they saw her, they came running, swarming her with outreached arms. She had no choice but to stop and greet them in return. She picked up the little ones and swung them in the air, hugged and kissed the foreheads of the others. Their bright faces gleamed up at her, and they all talked at once, telling her about their lessons that day. She laughed with them and praised them for their hard work. Finally, she managed to untangle herself and continue on.

As she did, others greeted her as they looked up from their work. She stepped around two women hauling planks of wood. In the last eighteen months since she'd arrived, a lot of progress had been made, yet there was always construction going on for new buildings. She called out to others who worked the garden area where ripe cucumbers lay swollen on the vine and tomatoes hung heavy. She stopped off at the open-ended building that was used as a garage. There the women repaired and maintained the camp's vehicles as well as taught each other how to work on engines.

She waved down Nasiba, the delegated commander of the camp, who loved tinkering with engines.

"Medical team just landed," Chrys said. "You ready to meet them?"

"Yes, I received the radio call," Nasiba said, "and have prepared the trucks and a van to bring our guests and their belongings. I am waiting on Suzan and Vejan to return. I sent them to change into clean clothes." She pointed to the refurbished US Army Jeep they'd obtained a few weeks ago. "Let us take this. Alal can drive."

Chrys smiled. "Yeah, I can't work a clutch with this," she said, indicating her blade.

Nasiba motioned for Alal, who jumped in behind the wheel while she climbed in the passenger side and Chrys took the back. Soon they were weaving among the buildings toward the northern gate. Chrys waved at more of the camp's inhabitants and took in all the progress that had been made, including how beautiful each mud brick building looked, the gardens planted with yellow roses and daisies and other vibrant flowers.

Within minutes of leaving the outer defense wall, Alal pulled to a stop just off the airstrip. The large military transport hissed as its engines ground to a stop and a staircase was rolled into position. Chrys climbed out of the Jeep and waited for Nasiba to join her. Soon a few people appeared at the top of the stairs and waved just as a soft sprinkling of rain began.

"Welcome," Nasiba called out. "Sorry we are late meeting you."

Chrys echoed her words in English.

Alal joined them as two covered trucks and a panel van pulled up close to the aircraft. Suzan and Vejan along with a half dozen other women got out and came over to stand with the others as the passengers came down the stairs and across the tarmac. As members of the new medical team came forward, Nasiba shook their hands and welcomed them again. Chrys translated her welcome in English and introduced Nasiba as the camp's commander. The women escorted some of the doctors over to the van while the rest of the medical personnel came forward. Among them, a woman with red hair hung back and watched.

Chrys's heart thudded against her chest and tears gathered in her eyes when she made eye contact.

But Mary waited at the end of the line until the others had been greeted and escorted over to the vehicles. Finally, she was before Nasiba and Chrys with a huge grin on her face and tears already falling down her cheeks.

"Welcome, friend Mary," Nasiba said and brought her into a hug.

Chrys translated, but before she could say another word, Nasiba said, "Take your time with your friend. I will see you at the Jeep."

When Nasiba was out of earshot, Mary said, "You look amazing."

Chrys grinned. "And so do you." She opened her arms, and Mary stepped into her embrace. "Thank you for coming. I didn't think you would."

Mary stood back and held Chrys at arm's length. "I didn't think I would either, but Barbara and Deanna were very convincing." She glanced over at one of the trucks which bore a hand-painted image of the camp's logo, a circle of flowers and children intertwined. "And here I am at…" She wrinkled her nose. "I'm still not sure how you say it."

Chrys pronounced the Kurdish words clearly. "It means yellow rose. Camp Yellow Rose. Nasiba liked my suggestion for the name, so it stuck."

"Do they grow roses in Syria?"

Chrys looked Mary up and down, enjoying the familiarity of her. "Not sure, but I've had them planted all around."

Mary shook her head. "I never thought I'd see that smile on your face again." She touched the fringe of Chrys's scarf. "This is beautiful."

"A gift."

Mary looked over at the others still making their way into the van. It wasn't big enough to hold them all, so one of the new doctors was preparing to climb into the Jeep but was having some difficulty with his duffel bag.

"I almost didn't come, you know," Mary said. "My mom was completely against it, too, but Barbara said you'd protect me. That was enough to convince her." She looked back at Chrys. "And I read your letter a hundred times I think." She giggled. "I never knew you could wax so poetic. I'm impressed."

"Yeah, I got a little artsy-fartsy thing going on now." Chrys gazed into Mary's eyes. "I can't tell you how much this means to me, to have you join me out here. We're doing great things."

Mary squeezed Chrys's hand. "I know you are, and it isn't like I've ever been good at telling you no."

Vejan called over that the van was ready. Chrys responded in Kurdish for them to go on before the rain picked up. When she turned back, she saw the look of admiration Mary always had for her language skills.

"Do you think I'll be able to pick any of that up?" Mary asked.

"I'll give you private lessons each night after dinner. And besides, they're learning English, so no worries."

"Private lessons?" Mary's fair cheeks glowed.

"Just for you." Chrys led her by the waist toward the vehicles. "But for tonight, after Nasiba gives her welcome and we have dinner, it's off to bed for you and the others. You'll need to work through your jet lag."

Alal had returned to the wheel, Nasiba was waiting for the stray doctor to climb into the back of the Jeep, and Mary had slowed the pace as she and Chrys walked toward them.

"So, I had a phone call from Sean Gordon."

"Yeah? What'd he want?" Chrys asked.

"He wanted to tell me about the impression you left on the UN General Assembly when you gave that statement. I wish I could've been there to see you."

Chrys shrugged. "I'm not sure what kind of impression I made, but I needed to read it. It needed to be said." She took Mary's backpack. "I owed her that."

Mary hesitated to climb into the Jeep, glanced at Alal and Nasiba, who were busy chatting away. She took a step closer to Chrys and lowered her voice. "I wanted to say I'm sorry you lost your friend. Barbara and Deanna said she was quite the woman."

"She was."

"Also, Barbara told me to remind you that she could always use you as part of her team if you ever want to come back stateside."

Chrys laughed. "I'm not so sure what I could do with a cyber security firm, but I'm glad she and Deanna got out of protective services."

Mary nodded. "Especially now. Oh, and they told me to tell you, thanks for the gift."

Chrys grinned. "One of the women, Ezma, made it. She makes a lot of the blankets for the kids here." She cocked her head. "It should be anytime now, am I right?"

"Any day, I think."

"I'm happy for them."

"Yeah." Mary continued to linger.

"It's really good to see you," Chrys said after a long pause of them grinning at each other. "Did I already say that?"

"Yes, but I like hearing it." Then Mary stepped even closer. "Also, they wanted me to tell you one more thing."

"What's that?"

"The baby, it's going to be a girl, and they're naming her Chrysanthi Reyha."

Chrys's mouth dropped open. "Poor kid, no one's ever going to be able to pronounce that name."

"Well, they're calling her Chrissy Rey for short. You know, Barbara's Southern roots and all."

Chrys smiled. "It's perfect."

"Yep, they said they wanted their daughter to be named in honor of the two bravest women they knew." Mary leaned forward and kissed her cheek. "I'm sorry I didn't get a chance to meet her."

Chrys lowered her head, swallowed. "You would've liked her."

The stray doctor finally climbed into the Jeep and settled in. Nasiba patted Chrys's shoulder and held the seat for Mary to take her spot in the back.

"You coming with the trucks?" Mary asked as she glanced at the ones still being loaded with luggage and medical equipment.

"I'll jog back."

Mary looked down at Chrys's legs. "I'm happy for you, Chrys. I know how much you love to run. Maybe you'll let me go out with you sometime?"

"I'd like that."

Alal started the Jeep and put it in gear.

Chrys tapped on the door. "I'll see you back at camp. Again, you don't know how happy I am you're here, how grateful I am you agreed to come."

"Thank you for wanting me to come."

Chrys stood back and waved as the Jeep, followed by one of the trucks, turned and headed toward camp. She began helping to load supplies onto the remaining vehicle, but when a large bolt of lightning cut across the sky followed by a boom of thunder, she directed the crew and the remaining women to shut the plane's cargo bay and keep the rest for the morning. Suzan offered a ride in the truck, but Chrys declined and watched as the last vehicle headed down the road.

She was alone now in the rain, which fell in large drops streaming down from above. She pulled her scarf to her face and took in a deep breath. It still held the faint scent of cloves after all this time. She tossed the ends behind her and began a comfortable jog along the roadway, lifting her face upward. And as she ran, she laughed with joy, wept with sorrow. But she would not despair, for there were women, children, and a little baby girl soon to be born back in the States named for her, her and Reyha. She would not stop working for them, for all of them, nor would she stop believing in the love that could transform the heart. Her own heart, though broken, continued to beat strong, filled now with gratitude for the sacred scents all around her, the smell of rain and the promise of new flowers, the sweet impermanence of life.

About the Author

Born in Arizona, Cameron prefers the heat and open skies of the desert over any other locale. She earned her PhD from the University of Arizona and has been teaching for three decades. Her debut novel, *By the Dark of Her Eyes*, won the 2017 Golden Crown Literary Society award for Paranormal/Horror. Currently she lives in the Phoenix area with her partner and their daughter and teaches writing and literature at Scottsdale Community College. She can be contacted at cameronmacelvee@gmail.com.

Books Available From Bold Strokes Books

Breakthrough by Kris Bryant. Falling for a sexy ranger is one thing, but is the possibility of love worth giving up the career Kennedy Wells has always dreamed of? (978-1-63555-179-2)

Certain Requirements by Elinor Zimmerman. Phoenix has always kept her love of kinky submission strictly behind the bedroom door and inside the bounds of romantic relationships, until she meets Kris Andersen. (978-1-63555-195-2)

Dark Euphoria by Ronica Black. When a high-profile case drops in Detective Maria Diaz's lap, she forges ahead only to discover this case, and her main suspect, aren't like any other. (978-1-63555-141-9)

Fore Play by Julie Cannon. Executive Leigh Marshall falls hard for Peyton Broader, her golf pro…and an ex-con. Will she risk sabotaging her career for love? (978-1-63555-102-0)

Love Came Calling by C. A. Popovich. Can a romantic looking for a long-term, committed relationship and a jaded cynic too busy for love conquer life's struggles and find their way to what matters most? (978-1-63555-205-8)

Outside the Law by Carsen Taite. Former sweethearts Tanner Cohen and Sydney Braswell must work together on a federal task force to see justice served, but will they choose to embrace their second chance at love? (978-1-63555-039-9)

The Princess Deception by Nell Stark. When journalist Missy Duke realizes Prince Sebastian is really his twin sister Viola in disguise, she plays along, but when sparks flare between them, will the double deception doom their fairy-tale romance? (978-1-62639-979-2)

The Smell of Rain by Cameron MacElvee. Reyha Arslan, a wise and elegant woman with a tragic past, shows Chrys that there's still beauty to embrace and reason to hope despite the world's cruelty. (978-1-63555-166-2)

The Talebearer by Sheri Lewis Wohl. Liz's visions show her the faces of the lost and the killers who took their lives. As one by one, the murdered are found, a stranger works to stop Liz before the serial killer is brought to justice. (978-1-635550-126-6)

White Wings Weeping by Lesley Davis. The world is full of discord and hatred, but how much of it is just human nature when an evil with sinister intent is invading people's hearts? (978-1-63555-191-4)

A Call Away by KC Richardson. Can a businesswoman from a big city find the answers she's looking for, and possibly love, on a small-town farm? (978-1-63555-025-2)

Berlin Hungers by Justine Saracen. Can the love between an RAF woman and the wife of a Luftwaffe pilot, former enemies, survive in besieged Berlin during the aftermath of World War II? (978-1-63555-116-7)

Blend by Georgia Beers. Lindsay and Piper are like night and day. Working together won't be easy, but not falling in love might prove the hardest job of all. (978-1-63555-189-1)

Hunger for You by Jenny Frame. Principe of an ancient vampire clan Byron Debrek must save her one true love from falling into the hands of her enemies and into the middle of a vampire war. (978-1-63555-168-6)

Mercy by Michelle Larkin. FBI Special Agent Mercy Parker and psychic ex-profiler Piper Vasey learn to love again as they race to stop a man with supernatural gifts who's bent on annihilating humankind. (978-1-63555-202-7)

Pride and Porters by Charlotte Greene. Will pride and prejudice prevent these modern-day lovers from living happily ever after? (978-1-63555-158-7)

Rocks and Stars by Sam Ledel. Kyle's struggle to own who she is and what she really wants may end up landing her on the bench and without the woman of her dreams. (978-1-63555-156-3)

The Boss of Her: Office Romance Novellas by Julie Cannon, Aurora Rey, and M. Ullrich. Going to work never felt so good. Three office romance novellas from talented writers Julie Cannon, Aurora Rey, and M. Ullrich. (978-1-63555-145-7)

Bold Strokes Books
Quality and Diversity in LGBTQ Literature